Dave Saunders's spirited introduction to documentary covers its history, cultural context and development, and the approaches, controversies and functions pertaining to non-fiction filmmaking. Saunders examines the many methods by which documentary conveys meaning, whilst exploring its differing societal purposes. From early, one-reel 'actualities' to the box-office successes of recent years, artistic complexities have been inherent in non-fiction cinema, and this *Guidebook* aims to make such issues clearer.

After a historical consideration of international documentary production, the author examines the impact of recent technological developments on the production, distribution and viewing of non-fiction. In addition, he explores the increasingly hazy distinctions between factual and dramatic formats, discussing 'reality television', the 'docudrama', and less orthodox approaches including animated and fantastical representations of reality.

*Documentary* encompasses a broad range of academic discourse around non-fiction filmmaking, introducing readers to the key filmmakers, major scholars, central debates and critical ideas relating to the form. This wide-ranging *Guidebook* features global releases from the 1920s through to 2009, including:

| | |
|---|---|
| Nanook of the North (1922) | My Winnipeg (2007) |
| The Man with the Movie Camera (1929) | Sicko (2007) |
| Night Mail (1936) | Waltz with Bashir (2008) |
| Night and Fog (1955) | Say My Name (2009) |
| Roger and Me (1989) | Anvil: The Story of Anvil (2009) |
| Tarnation (2003) | |

**Dave Saunders** is working on a number of research projects, the latest of which is a history of rock musicians acting in the cinema. His previous publications include *Direct Cinema: Observational Documentary and the Politics of the Sixties* (2007) and *Arnold: Schwarzenegger and the Movies* (2009)

# Routledge Film Guidebooks

The Routledge Film Guidebooks offer a clear introduction to and overview of the work of key filmmakers, movements or genres. Each guidebook contains an introduction, including a brief history; defining characteristics and major films; a chronology; key debates surrounding the filmmaker, movement or genre; and pivotal scenes, focusing on narrative structure, camera work and production quality.

Bollywood: a Guidebook to
Popular Hindi Cinema
*Tejaswini Ganti*

James Cameron
*Alexandra Keller*

Jane Campion
*Deb Verhoeven*

Horror
*Brigid Cherry*

Film Noir
*Justus Nieland and Jennifer Fay*

Documentary
*Dave Saunders*

Romantic Comedy
*Claire Mortimer*

# DOCUMENTARY

*DAVE SAUNDERS*

Routledge
Taylor & Francis Group

LONDON AND NEW YORK

First published 2010
by Routledge
2 Park Square, Milton Park, Abingdon, Oxon OX14 4RN

Simultaneously published in the USA and Canada
by Routledge
270 Madison Ave, New York, NY 10016

Reprinted 2010

Routledge is an imprint of the Taylor & Francis Group, an informa business

Typeset in Joanna by
Taylor & Francis Books
Printed and bound in Great Britain by
TJ International Ltd, Padstow, Cornwall

British Library Cataloguing in Publication Data
A catalogue record for this book is available from the British Library

Library of Congress Cataloging in Publication Data
Saunders, Dave.
    Documentary / by Dave Saunders.
      p. cm. – (Routledge film guidebooks)
    Includes bibliographical references.
    1. Documentary films–History and criticism. I. Title.
    PN1995.9.D6S28 2010
    070.1'8–dc22
                    2009043661

ISBN10: 0-415-47309-8 (hbk)
ISBN10: 0-415-47310-1 (pbk)
ISBN10: 0-203-85268-0 (ebk)

ISBN13: 978-0-415-47309-5 (hbk)
ISBN13: 978-0-415-47310-1 (pbk)
ISBN13: 978-0-203-85268-2 (ebk)

# CONTENTS

# LIST OF ILLUSTRATIONS

# ACKNOWLEDGEMENTS

Thanks, for all the usual reasons, go out wholeheartedly to my family and friends (as the cliché says, they know who they are). For getting this book into the public domain, the ever-helpful Aileen Storry and Emily Laughton at Routledge should be held accountable. Thanks also to Women Make Movies, for quickly supplying an all-important screener, and to Hajnalka Elek, whose love and support are invaluable.

# INTRODUCTION

> Documentary has a power, if not directly to reveal the invisible, none-
> theless to speak of things that orthodoxy and conservatism, power and
> authority, would rather we didn't know and didn't think about. And this is
> exactly why we need it.
>
> Michael Chanan (2008: 132)

In the decade or so prior to the writing of this book, filmic documentary (and, slowly but surely, attached discourses of criticism, historical analysis and praxis) has undergone something of a boom. The
litany of box-office successes in recent years that can reasonably be
categorised under a general – but not, as we shall see, always comfortably exclusive – rubric of 'non-fiction' extends ever onward towards
some presumed future drop-off back to the dark days of the 'cine-tech
and cine-club' (Goldsmith 2003: 6). According to a few watchers, this
renaissance has peaked, yet the evidence would suggest that much life
remains in a multitude of subjects before the public loses its appetite
for 'true stories' writ large.[1] As I write, Larry Charles's *Religulous* (2008)
and Nathan Frankowski's *Expelled* (2008) are doing brisk trade, taking
roughly opposing sides in a cultural struggle for minds; numerous other
films, including *March of the Penguins* (Luc Jacquet, 2005), the polemicist
Michael Moore's tremendously popular *Fahrenheit 9/11* (2004) and *Sicko*

(2007), and Martin Scorsese's Rolling Stones 'rockumentary' *Shine a Light* (2008), will likewise not fade to obscurity soon. Relative to the still prevalent cinema of outright dramaturgy, such productions' budgets have often (though not always) been small, yet modest initial outlays seem encouragingly and regularly to yield results beyond festival acclaim. Often documentaries are 'hits' in the sense that they recoup vastly more than was spent on their making, as was the case with Jonathan Caouette's autobiographical *Tarnation* (2003), discussed in Chapter Five; sometimes they are hits outright, competing even in the biggest industrial context of international cinema-ticket and video format sales. (Steve James's *Hoop Dreams* (1994), 'one of the great moviegoing experiences of my lifetime', according to Roger Ebert (Ellis and McLane 2007: 318), may be seen as having partly catalysed the new boom. The eleventh-highest-earning documentary of all time, 'it easily made its money back', wrote the *Telegraph*'s David Gritten, 'a signal to investors that documentaries were worth a punt' (Gritten 2003: 1).) Notwithstanding the difficulties faced by certain national cinemas in achieving global distribution despite creatively very fecund non-fiction outputs (Spain's *cine social* is a particular case here),[2] the new wave of big-screen non-fiction, whilst perhaps not constituting the tsunami for which some filmmakers may hope, still has not hit the shore. Although it should be borne in mind that, broadly speaking, non-fiction is overall not as profitable an enterprise as its counterpart, it nonetheless seems absurd that, as recently as 1996, Britain's *New Statesman* magazine was plausibly able to denigrate documentary as a 'fringe pursuit for a few consenting adults' (quoted by Chanan 2007: 3). A word at one time cursed by marketers, documentary – for reasons only partially understood, and to which we shall return – is currently seen as having the potential to do big business, across manifold platforms from the multiplex to mobile phones, and to fulfil an audience's needs in respect of not only intellectual edification, political motivation and social engagement, but also spectacle and entertainment: the bangs for our bucks, so to speak, have more than ever been found to issue from sources located in unscripted, 'non-acted', 'real' life.

My inverted commas here raise several theoretical and philosophical issues, and deliberately so: they are my rhetorical set-up – the opening of a narrative, of a kind, by which to explain how non-fiction film works. A word of caveat: this book is not a practical 'how to' guide for aspiring filmmakers seeking to get to grips with technical matters (many such guides exist online and in rapidly obsolete hard copy: Andy Glynn's *Documentaries … and How to Make Them* (2008, Kamera) being a fine exemplar); it is not, overall, a survey-type work covering as much as possible in as complete a manner as an editorially imposed page limit will allow (that book has already been written numerous times in recent years – admirably by Patricia Aufderheide (2007) and Bill Nichols (2001a)); nor does it attempt to trace a comprehensive, globally encyclopedic history of the documentary form in all its manifestations on television and in the cinema – a virtually Sisyphean job far beyond a book such as this. Following Chapter Two's delineation of a timeline of sorts, continuous chronology largely gives way to widely thematic grouping: a temporal rehearsal of received documentary history is given to impart background, but should not be taken in and of itself as a categorically evolutionary model whereby great works beget all else like starter dominoes.

It should be noted that documentary, in the intellectually contested 'canon' and at the less-discussed margins, comprises a vast, diverse and non-linear matrix of films not easily given to precise genealogical or evolutionary explication. The adoption and abandonment of certain traits and styles is in a manner analogous to linguistic selection processes and natural communicative strategies – doubtless, filmmakers and films do directly cross-pollinate – but the geopolitically dispersed, globally fragmented character of human knowledge and learning means that this can take place across continents and decades. Consequently, the discretely compartmentalised 'family tree' is viewed by many scholars (see esp. Bruzzi 2005: 3–5) as a reductive prescription liable to encourage the imagining of a 'trajectory' of gradual supersession, where in fact the situation is ever more nebulous. 'Old-fashioned', traditionalist documentaries are still produced, after all, frequently to effective ends: compare Robert Flaherty's early films with 2003's *The Story of the Weeping Camel* (Byambasuren Davaa). Will the 'neo-Rousseauism' of Flaherty *et al.*, or the video blog, be around longer? Need these approaches be exclusive? And how do these non-fiction productions connect over time, vibrating over a web of multi-point influence? 'Documentary filmmakers working today', avers Marsha McCreadie in her exuberant book *Documentary Superstars* (2008: 183), 'seem to approach their craft like cafeteria Catholicism. They take what they consider the best of the recent splashy innovations in the doc form, picking and choosing at will, while never giving up some traditional labels.' Given the abundance of conventionally identifiable documentaries currently attaining commercial and critical prominence, John Corner's divination that we are entering a 'post-documentary age' is most likely not correct – though certainly digression from formal archetypes (and the limitations many would see these as imposing), in combination with mushrooming new-media outlets and their effects on technique, form and distribution, will continue to give rise to fresh voices (and, naturally, fresh problems for those attempting to make sense of non-fiction film's place in a broader knowledge scheme).

What this *Routledge Film Guidebook* does attempt, within its compact form, is selective coverage of: the differing methods by which non-fiction film through history has conveyed, and in the present conveys, meaning; extant academic discourse around non-fiction, including all the major scholars, debates and critical ideas; global documentary's changing societal purposes and contexts; and the impact of recent technological developments affecting production, distribution and viewing. After an introductory part undertakes concisely to examine definitions and major trends, the book moves on to its central section: a series of essays each examining the textual (and contextual) import of one film with a thoroughness often lacking in broad-spectrum works. Some of the chosen texts – and we shall be considering the documentary as a text, to be 'read' or studied as one would any other linguistic or artistic statement – will be familiar even to casually interested readers; others far less so. To those coming anew to *Nanook of the North*, or *Night Mail*, or *Night and Fog* (and there will be many), I offer these acknowledged classics as formally vital, theoretical schemas from which much subsequent contemporary art has unarguably sprung. Including these 'great works' of course risks appearing deferential towards ostensibly staid 'oldies', and betrays something of the didactic John Grierson in this author; nevertheless, to omit them from the *Guidebook*, and to let them drift further from sight in the eyes of younger potential audiences, would be a mistake. Even if we are moving towards the moment when documentary's drift from meaningful distinction becomes inexorable, as some have averred (see Austin and de Jong 2008: 2), nonfiction in its notionally classical, modernist–realist and post-classical forms ought still, I contend, to be assimilated – albeit with an eye to its flaws as well as its virtues.

Conversely, the thematic assemblage of newer films might at times seem arbitrary, as maybe it has to be, given the necessarily cherry-picked nature of any short monograph and my elucidatory purpose here, which is to explore documentary film as artistic practice. A greater weight given herein to polyglot or non-Western productions – though desirable in many ways – would be both tokenistic skewing and perhaps overly egalitarian, given that this English-language *Guidebook* is designed to make a little sharper what has typically been called a 'fuzzy concept' (Nichols 2001a: 21), occupying 'blurred boundaries' (Nichols 1994). Rather than trying to be all things to all people, I have endeavoured to select films that, individually, do something unique, are influential in terms of filmic innovation, speak saliently to our times, or offer especial potency in their arguments or effects, be they emotional or material. Again, I have tried to strike a fair and useful balance, appropriate to this primer, between the old and the new, the mainstream and the leftfield, the hallowed and the underappreciated, and the populist and the radical. It is not my intention, for example, to belittle or downplay Asian, Latin American or Eastern European contributions by what might look like an unfair proportional dearth; certainly, these deserve greater coverage in a separate, dedicated volume less concerned with consolidation. (In the meantime, I point the reader to the current, vital work of Michael Chanan, Julianne Burton, Paola Voci, Nada Hishashi and Markus Nornes; Chanan and Burton's scholarship takes in Latin American non-fiction, Voci's Chinese, Hishashi's and Nornes's Japanese.) The overall global cinematic dominance of the Occident, for better or worse, is reflected here not in deference to a hegemonic scheme, but in acknowledgement of the west's formative cinematic primacy regarding technological invention, commercial might and the nurturing of film culture. (And the sad fact that certain theocracies, especially, have historically placed – and continue to place – 'extreme restrictions' (Anon. 2009: 1) on the types of film that can legally be made: something that limits somewhat the documentary's dissenting potential and curtails, generally though not without creative exceptions, a country's artistic voice while forcing many into Western exile.)

Making the 'final cut', when it came to choosing which films would be the focus of my case studies, was nonetheless troubling – as was the realisation that this selection would naturally be interpreted as reflecting qualitatively personal preference: however, any student should remember that not a handful, nor a hundred examples, as with a taught film course, can ever properly stand for 'documentary' as a 'whole' (even if such a semantically bedevilled, theoretically slippery and ever-growing corpus in all likelihood eludes conclusive definition, almost by definition). I wish neither to reinforce a canon, nor to redress an imbalance, but simply to guide the reader, via some hopefully interesting – and unabashedly contentious – pointers, to a vantage of self-motivated criticism. My critical focus is chiefly on theatrical releases, with the understanding that the bulk of formal conventions and aesthetics can be comfortably transposed, extrapolated and understood in relation to televisual programming where space does not permit expansion. In addition, all the films covered in Part II are readily available on DVD – another criterion for inclusion by which an understanding and enjoyment of these works might easily be attained without recourse to the archives.

*The Routledge Film Guidebook: Documentary* will, I hope, clarify. But it will also, inevitably, complicate as it does so. As media proliferate, diverge, conflate and overlap in an ongoing process arguably best logged by those media themselves, the non-fiction film, in all its shifting shapes, finds its voice afresh via the assimilation, processing and evaluation of art that has gone before. Documentary is not, and has never been, about finding an absolute 'truth' – a futile quest that commissioning editor Ralph Lee describes as 'like chasing the end of a rainbow' (de Jong 2008: 169). It has never been apt, either, to occupy a magically objective or authoritative zone outside the realms of human partiality. The legendary American broadcaster Edward R. Murrow spoke his own germane truth when he declared that 'Anyone who believes that every individual film must represent a "balanced" picture knows nothing about either balance or pictures' (quoted by Aufderheide 2007: 2). Aspiring to journalistic notions of 'fairness' has never been documentary's forte, and the ideological 'health' of a democratic public sphere might, in any case, depend not on such ideals, but on personal expression inclusive of subjectivity, authorial voice and reflexive practice, all operating inextricably within Nichols's 'fuzz'. Rather, as Lee continues, documentary is best thought about in terms of the distinction between 'a true story and the true story' (de Jong 2008: 169). '"Documentary" in the twenty-first century', writes Paul Ward, 'is a complex set of overlapping discourses and practices, and we need our theories, critical approaches and – perhaps most of all – our documentarists to be equipped to recognize and deal with this fact' (Ward 2005: 3). In the pages that follow, we shall thus begin to explore how, and why, humankind chooses to enter into an ongoing audio-visual dialogue with and about itself: in other words, to tell itself 'true stories'.

## NOTES

1 For a detailed investigation into this phenomenon, see Austin (2007).
2 Since 1975, Spanish documentary has flourished – in part a bouncing back due to its stifling under Franco. See, especially, *Work in Progress* (2001, José Luis Guerin) and *Memory Train* (Marta Arribas and Ana Pérez, 2005).

# Part I

## 'A troubled and difficult art'

A brief introduction to non-fiction film

# 1

## THE 'D' WORD

### Definitions, 'obligations' and functions

Appearance is knowledge, of a kind. Showing becomes a way of saying the unsayable. Visual knowledge … provides one of our primary means of comprehending the experience of other people.

David MacDougall (2006: 5–6)

Life being all inclusion and confusion, and art being all discrimination and selection.

Henry James (quoted by Amigoni 2000: 102)

## DEFINITIONS

What, then, is documentary? We can be fairly sure, to begin, that something like the Wachowski brothers' *The Matrix* (1999) is not – at least, the only thing it would seem to have in common with works marketed as 'non-fiction' is an indexical link to heavily contrived actions and scripted exchanges that once took place in front of the camera: it is a documentary solely in the sense that it is a record of a fiction dreamed up by a *real* person, living in *actual* times, and bound up, like you and me, in a socio-political context. Works of obvious fantasy and imagination, from Peter Jackson's *Lord of the Rings* (2001) to the James Bond movie *Quantum of Solace* (Marc Forster, 2008), represent varying degrees of fidelity to our own experiences (none of us has seen a hobbit; a very few of us will have seen gun fights), but both are products of the human psyche and its real-life sources. As Bill Nichols, probably the foremost academic theorist of non-fiction, would say, George Lucas's *Star Wars* (1977), despite its documentary-like claim to have taken place in a real time and location ('a long time ago, in a galaxy far, far away') is a 'documentary of wish-fulfillment', as distinct from a 'documentary of social representation' (Nichols 2001a: 1).

The latter, in their differing forms, are what concern us here. Documentaries of social representation stake a claim on a certain kind of truth: a 'relationship to history which exceeds the analogical status of its fictional counterpart' (Renov 1986: 71). If the world in front of George Lucas's lens was, evidently, not evidential in any proper respect, then by contrast, other types of film have long proffered an alternative take based on the representation of reality, however this reality might have been manipulated, and a notional 'agreement' between filmmaker and audience that what is on screen is fundamentally conveying accurate information not liable seriously to mislead. This 'agreement', naturally, is not set in stone; it is rather a difficult moral question of how much distortion or creativity is permissible in order to tell a story or make a case (for documentary is frequently a rhetorical form: a form based, however loosely, on the construction of an argument for or against something); indeed, the balance between historical record and art – between index and artifice – is the most central debate in nonfiction cinema studies. The very term 'documentary', first applied to film by a young Scot abroad in America, John Grierson, implies worth as historical *record*. British 'Documentary Film Movement' founder Grierson, of whom we shall hear much more, was describing an ethnographic film by Robert Flaherty (*Moana*, 1926), in a review in the *New York Sun* dated February 8, 1926: 'Of course, *Moana* being a visual account of events in the daily life of a Polynesian youth and his family, has documentary value' (quoted by Ellis and McLane 2007: 3). Later, Grierson – who famously went on to define his life's work as 'the creative treatment of actuality', still perhaps the best condensation of non-fiction's essence – would concede that, 'Documentary is a clumsy description, but let it stand' (see Beattie 2008: 1).[1]

Grierson's admission that the term might in some way be inadequate is important. He knew that the word itself already imposed artificial limits on the theoretical potential of films dealing with or representing actuality. In 1973, film scholar Richard Barsam proposed the more encompassing appellation 'non-fiction' – 'not to replace documentary film as a label, but to include it in a larger, more flexible concept, one that recognizes the many different approaches to this exciting form of film making' (Barsam 1973: 2). Barsam's greater point was that not all non-fiction films are, *per se*, documentaries in the strictest sense. Many filmmakers, over the entire history of cinema, have worked using methods other than the most 'conventional' documentary tactics of filmic mimesis (recording 'real life' as it is lived in front of the 'candid' camera or recalled by testimony) – observational, 'on-the-fly' camerawork, studio- or location-based 'talking heads', etc. – but still adhere to a key tenet: to express basic truths. Certainly, contemporary readers will feel able to talk of both *United 93* (Paul Greengrass, 2006) and Davis Guggenheim's *An Inconvenient Truth* (2006) as non-fiction. The former is entirely reconstructed, that is to say, recreated from research into actual events on September 11, 2001, as accurately as possible given the need for dramatic coherence; the latter strives to build a case for climate-change control and communicate a number of statistics propitious for its argument. Both these disparate films have non-fiction credentials; both are engaged in a 'truth-telling discourse' (Austin and de Jong 2008: 2); yet arguably only Guggenheim's film, a piece anchored in the passionate and real belief of rhetorician Al Gore (and a work beset by accusations of 'propagandising' apropos its 'nine certifiable errors, most of them of overstatement' (Cathcart 2007: 33)), is a documentary in form.

*United 93*, although it convincingly mimics the characteristics of non-fiction – in this case a hand-held, 1960s '*cinéma-vérité*' style of filmmaking (see Chapter Two) – is more usefully thought of as a hybrid: a 'documentary drama', or a 'docudrama', built up from historical

FIGURE 1.1 Al Gore makes a point (*An Inconvenient Truth*, 2006)

documents, but not constituting an empirically valid document in and of itself.[2] (The terms 'docudrama', 'documentary drama', 'drama documentary' and 'dramatised documentary' are, somewhat confusingly, employed by filmmakers and critics to denote differing proportions of dramatisation and verifiable documentary. Commonly these terms are interchangeable, with semantic weight on the second word: by this logic, *United 93* is a drama documentary, whereas Jeremy Sandford and Ken Loach's well known realist melodrama *Cathy Come Home* (1966), or Gabriel Range's *Death of a President* (2006), are documentary dramas. See Kilborn and Izod 1997: 135–59; Paget 1998: 90–3; Biressi and Nunn 2005: 160.)

It could be argued that, for instance, James Cameron's *Titanic* (1997) exhibits recognisable features of the docudrama within its final, crowded act: the real-life factuality of the ship's sinking, coupled with a general concern for humanity. Partly what makes a film a documentary, it must be said, is the way a viewer (or spectator) watches it. The way we look at, react to, and anticipate a film, crucially, has a bearing on how 'real' we perceive it to be. The marketing of a film must send a message, coded in its stylistic and generic symbols, telling us how to interpret it. Nobody, it is safe to say, really viewed *Titanic* as a documentary; Cameron's IMAX-specific follow-up, *Ghosts of the Abyss* (2003), a film thoroughly concerned with reconstituted technological spectacle and billed as 'The greatest 3D adventure ever filmed', all the same sold itself mainly as a factual, didactic production, with elements of poetic licence (a documentary staple) and period reconstruction (plus its star and narrator, Bill Paxton) harking back to the commercially huge parent film. Filmed biographies, or so-called biopics, normally are distinguishable from docudrama, as are period dramas (which utilise specific epochs or historical events as a narrative backcloth). In these cases, very sizeable liberties are taken, and very large speculations made, for the sake of dramatic emphasis around classical story arcs: something that sets films like *Nixon* (Oliver Stone, 1995), concerning the titular president, or *Control* (Anton Corbijn, 2007), a 'kitchen sink' portrait of Joy Division singer Ian Curtis, clearly apart from *United 93*. 'Should scriptwriters tamper with detail of the lives of real people?' asks *The Guardian*'s Nick Fraser: 'they must do if they are to keep us entertained', he concludes (2009: 27).

Paul Arthur (2005: 20) suggests documentary is a 'mode of production, a network of funding, filming, postproduction and exhibition tendencies common to work normally indexed as documentary'. For the purposes of this book, we should perhaps take documentary to mean a 'mode' of filmmaking, as opposed to a style or genre: 'a mode of response founded upon the acknowledgement that every photograph is a portrait signed by its sitter. Stated at its simplest: the documentary response is one in which the image is perceived as signifying what it appears to record; a documentary film is one which seeks, by whatever means, to elicit this response; and the documentary movement is the history of the strategies which have been adopted to this end' (Vaughan 1999: 58). Styles (film *noir*, expressionism, realism) and genres (the western, the musical, horror) are more easily construed and definite concepts than Dai Vaughan's 'mode', in this case a particular approach to putting a story or argument together based on an unfixed but strong assertion of truth by attachment. Although 'most documentary filmmakers consider themselves storytellers, not journalists' (Aufder-heide 2007: 1), the means of a documentary story's telling will usually have a link to the story's source, whether via the direct witness testimony of those involved (either the filmmaker, the subjects, or both), or by direct capturing through the lens – and in addition be able to be taken in good faith as *bona fide* for the purposes of authentic record. Despite *United 93*'s appeal to the emotions *and* the intellect, and its telling of a story *based on actual events*, the film's connection to the events themselves is one step removed by total reconstruction. Its use of 'non-actors' (many of the air-traffic controllers on duty the day of the hijacks) gives it an air of authenticity, yet more than anything else, the lack of their spoken testimonies denies *United 93* absolute documentary status. They are complicit in the retelling of their story, but not the authors of it. Greengrass ultimately presents *only* reconstruction, not evidence. By way of an illustrative contrast, *Touching the Void* (Kevin Macdonald, 2003), about the life-threatening and life-changing challenges overcome by a pair of mountain-climbers, similarly offers reconstructed material where nothing directly evidential exists (this material is highly aestheticised, too). What this documentary also offers, however, is the guiding, original narration of the two men involved. It is their words, spoken from remembrance, that drive the conventional, three-act narrative: to evoke Grierson, the 'creativity' of the story as it is constructed from the 'actuality' of the mountaineers' minds.

Narrative, or the way a story of any kind is told – including its ordering, embellishing and hence its plotting – is structurally important to many documentaries, as it is important in our everyday lives. Narrative is what distinguishes a story from a mere list of events, and sets a documentary apart from raw footage. The famous 'Zapruder film' of US president John Kennedy's 1963 killing in Dallas is without doubt a striking example of evidence in as unaltered and isolated a form as it usually comes. (Of course Zapruder filmed subjectively, with a single camera, from a single viewpoint. A hundred Zapruders would not have given an unconditional, omniscient truth.) Alone it is not a documentary, but the basis for numerous, probably entirely spurious conspiracy films. Stella Bruzzi (2005: 20) muses over its undeniably 'momentous significance', while lamenting a lack of 'imposed narrative, authorial intervention, editing and discernible bias', standard devices available to the non-fiction filmmaker that might paradoxically help educe a truth about, and not simply dispassionately show, JFK's murder. Rodney King's beating by Los Angeles policemen in 1991 was caught on tape by an amateur video-cameraman (who then promptly sold the recording to a local TV station for $500); the assailants' acquittals, in the face of this 'inverse surveillance' of police by the public, led to riots in the city the next year. The 'Rodney King incident' tape, as with the Zapruder film, is an example of ostensibly very reliable and unimpeachable evidence gathered with no prejudice. Neither has it been edited, narrativised or recontextualised: its rawness proved a critical flaw that served only to harm King's case while police defence lawyers skilfully picked the untreated footage to pieces, angle by angle, in a process film professor Michael Renov likened to 'dehumanising the victim' (Chanan 2007: 54). As Carl Plantinga argued, 'though the video clearly showed a man's beating, it remained mute about his or the policemen's intentions and motivations' (ibid.: 55).

But documentary can, should and does do more than just bear detached witness or produce evidence for our perusal. Its core appeal is rooted less in the pleasure of looking, than in 'epistephilia', a 'pleasure in knowing that marks out a distinctive form of social engagement' (Nichols 1991: 178). Documentary at its most socially potent can compile, argue, scrutinise and appeal for reform in a way that untouched footage cannot. Moreover, it has in certain circumstances definitely effected change, as was the case with former lawyer Frederick Wiseman's 'muck-raking' tract *Titicut Follies* (1967), set in a modern-day 'snake pit' of a mental asylum, and Errol Morris's noirish *The Thin Blue Line* (1988), which helped overturn Randall Adams's death sentence for a murder he did not commit. News reporting, another media outlet for actuality-as-information that has, over the years, inspired political change in complex ways, permissibly can structure its presentation too, but its ideals are different. The news – influenced though its slant has often been by network ratings chasing, ideological concerns and corporate pressure – should *ideally* maintain an aloof position outside the sphere of partial political or social activism. Documentary acceptably may walk a fine line between polemic and propaganda, machinate to make the everyday dramatic, accentuate, amplify, distil, and render poetic the unspeakable.

## 'OBLIGATIONS'

Documentary, then, unlike news programming and, to a lesser extent, current-affairs broadcasting, does not have an absolute ethical and moral obligation to strive, where reasonably possible, for complete fairness and objectivity. 'There are no rules in this young art form,' wrote Michael Rabinger, 'only decisions about where to draw the line and how to remain consistent to the contract you will set up with your audience' (in Aufderheide 2007: 3). Grierson opined that a 'sense of social responsibility makes our realist documentary a troubled and difficult art' (Hardy 1979: 25), though he was at heart an educator – and what of documentaries other than the 'realist'? 'The documentary', according to Marsha McCreadie, 'is turning out to be a kind of pluripotent stem cell that can develop into many new forms; like stem cell research, it has a lot of controversy surrounding it' (2008: ix). Leaving aside codes of ethics set down by broadcasters and regulators (a fine-point legal topic best left to practitioners and relevant guides), what obligations, if any, does the responsible documentarist face? Do documentarists even need to be 'responsible' with their material? What are the terms of the non-binding moral 'agreement', or 'contract', tacitly made between a filmmaker of non-fiction and a viewer?

A useful case study here is the (in)famous Michael Moore: Flint, Michigan's most famous citizen, and a crusading, 'pot-bellied slob from the American heartland in a baseball cap who looks like he buys his clothes from Kmart and sleeps in them' (Sharrett and Luhr 2005: 253). Moore, whose masterful *Sicko* is discussed in detail in Chapter Five, has attracted probably a greater level of published criticism than any other living filmmaker for his supposed distortions (and affectations). *Roger and Me* (1989), Moore's often-brilliant debut feature, catalogues the devastating effects of General Motors' withdrawal from Flint. Whilst few could plausibly argue that the manufacturer's shutting down its plant did not have negative consequences for redundant employees and their families, *Roger and Me* nonetheless came under heavy critical fire for its rhetorical altering of chronologies and its politically charged selectivity. Events, complained some, did not happen in the order Moore depicts them. Harlan Jacobson, in *Film Comment* (of November/December 1989), discovered some, for him, 'disquieting discrepancies':

1: Ronald Reagan, depicted visiting laid-off auto workers, was a presidential candidate, not the President, when he made his visit ...

2: The evangelist who is depicted visiting the city after the Great Gatsby society party in 1987 actually visited in 1982, several years before the crucial 1986 lay-offs ...

3: The three big civic development projects which are seen in the film as more or less concurrent attempts to counter the effects of the 1986–87 lay-offs ... had all closed before these lay-offs ...

4: The number of jobs lost during the 1986–87 closures seem to be far less than indicated in the film ...

(in Corner 1996: 165–6)

Moore, when quizzed by Jacobson, proved to be more than aware of the actual dates of these occurrences, and hit back by saying: 'It's a *movie*, you know; you can't do everything. I was true to what happened. Everything that happened in the movie happened ... If you want to nit-pick on some of those specific things, fine, but ... ' (*ibid.*: 167). Obtaining an interview with Roger Smith, CEO of General Motors, whom Moore sees as personally culpable, is never an earnest goal; on the contrary, it is Moore's personal journey up the river to find his own Colonel Kurtz that provides the film's genuinely affecting moments of (frequently manufactured) irony, pathos and black comedy. Despite the situation in Flint – and the town's somewhat tragicomic response to its own folk's destitution – being undeniably heartrending, Pauline Kael called Moore a 'gonzo demagogue', and the film an 'aw-shucks, cracker barrel pastiche. In Moore's own jocular pursuit of Roger, he chases gags and improvises his own version of history' (ibid.).

Since *Roger and Me*, whose mix of journalism, observation and provocation, according to Emily Schultz, constituted 'an incredible shift in the documentary form' (2006: 62), an anti-Moore industry has grown up around pointing out the filmmaker's numerous temporal infidelities and his apparent lack of regard for sticking to the absolute facts of a situation in favour of hard-hitting polemical tracts. *Bowling for Columbine* (2002) and *Fahrenheit 9/11* (2004) have faced comparable attacks (and generated even more impressive revenue). Moreover, because Moore's campaigns are usually of a left-liberal bent, he has been accused on many occasions of hypocrisy and pretension: he cynically presents himself as an everyman, complain his enemies, but has made millions of dollars from a high-profile media career and now lives not in Flint, but in a costly apartment in New York. (Moore is admittedly vociferous, and has not always demonstrated restraint when challenged: 'I'm filthy rich,' he is quoted as saying on *Fox News*. 'You know why I'm a multi-millionaire? 'Cause millions of people like what I do ... Pretty cool, huh?' (Hardy and Clarke 2004: 88)). Should he now *seriously* consider moving back to show solidarity with his impoverished old friends?

Brian Winston, however, staunchly defends Moore's methods, 'monumental chutzpah' and motives as perspicacious and necessary:

> To see Moore as a 'gonzo demagogue' ... was to fail to see Roger Smith, GM's chief executive, as a corporate barbarian with no civic sensibilities at all. Anyway, the criticisms were actually without foundation since Moore does not say that the film chronicles only the events of 1986/87 and its aftermath or that Reagan was a candidate [sic] and so on. In fact he doesn't date anything particularly. The attacks were therefore doubly picayune since not only was *Roger and Me* making no claims to offer a day-by-day account of the events it

portrayed, but whether the film was chronologically accurate or not was utterly beside the point … The people of Flint were devastated however long it took.

(Winston 2000: 38)

Whether Moore is morally 'right' to manipulate his material to argue a case in which he believes, and therefore also to manipulate the viewer's emotional response, is thus continually open to debate. One's opinion apropos Moore is likely to hinge, for better or worse, on one's personal opinion of Moore himself: a divisive character, as he well knows, with a larger-than-life *modus operandi* in every respect.

Controversy around documentary techniques of representation is nothing new. Robert Flaherty's *Nanook* (see Chapter Three), and *Moana* (1926), anthropologically aspirant films by an explorer-cameraman, significantly modified the behaviours and customs of those they depicted in order to create greater levels of 'exotic' interest for their intended audiences. Upon arriving in Samoa for *Moana*, Flaherty was dismayed to find little there that Hollywood would expect of him: instead of a great and noble struggle for survival – one of the central themes of *Nanook* – he found natural abundance, happiness and the consequent problem of how to structure a film about Samoans. The answer, decided Flaherty, lay in reviving a long-dead initiation rite whereby young men would subject themselves to painful, all-over body tattooing. This gave Flaherty's production a climax, of sorts, as the young man Moana underwent his ordeal for the camera; it was not enough, though, to save the film from commercial death due to an inherent lack of excitement. For *Man of Aran* (1934), Flaherty asked the Aran islanders to relearn the dangerous art of basking shark hunting (which, remarkably, they did); considering the facts about contemporary interpersonal relations on Aran disagreeable, he simply ignored the location's sectarian conflicts. 'Direct cinema' practitioner Frederick Wiseman catalogued the appalling conditions at the Bridgewater hospital for the criminally insane in *Titicut Follies* (1967), leading to a number of protracted court cases brought against the film to seek injunctions against its screening. It was alleged that Wiseman misrepresented the inmates (who were seen in the nude, in 'humiliating' mental states, or being interviewed about highly sensitive matters), and that he was dishonest and editorially manipulative in his portrayal of the apparently brutal warders and the institution in general.

Reviewing the film, Arthur Knight asked: 'Where does the truth stop and common decency begin?' (in Barsam 1973: 275). Wiseman, notes Richard Barsam, 'reveals to us the ugly truth that institutions such as Bridgewater were built to hide' (ibid.) – a fair assessment, given that quite unquestionably various aspects of the secure hospital were repulsive. The film's lengthy prohibition by the state of Massachusetts, however, demonstrates that people may feel differently about vehemently constructed reformist positions if they are either personally involved, or of a conservative persuasion. Suppression of any sort, for Wiseman, was

FIGURE 1.2 A scene from Frederick Wiseman's *Titicut Follies* (1967)

not an option: 'The censoring of *Titicut Follies* or any other film prevents people in a democracy from access to information which they might like to have in order to make up their minds about what kind of society they'd like to live in – it's as simple as that' (Grant 1998: 250). Wiseman dismisses the 'objective–subjective' argument as 'a lot of horseshit' (Winston 1993: 49). 'Fairness', for Wiseman as for Moore, matters little in comparison with the power and the supposed righteousness of the message.

Subjectivity is one thing, but what of complete invention? Aside from obvious 'mockumentaries' – *David Holzman's Diary* (1967, Jim McBride), Rob Reiner's *This is Spinal Tap* (1982), *Borat* (Larry Charles, 2006), Matt Reeves's 'queasy-cam' Godzilla update *Cloverfield* (2008), or Neil Blomkamp's *District 9* (2009), for example – which do not usually attempt seriously to pass themselves off as anything other than pastiche, there exist certifiable shams. From the very beginnings of cinema, the 'enterprising' faked and embellished – 'if only', notes Michael Chanan (2007: 62), 'for lack of any standard of comparison.' Albert Smith, to back up a boast, mocked up footage of the 'Battle of Santiago Bay' in 1898, using miniatures and wafted cigarette smoke (it proved a hit); in 1907, William Selig came up with *Hunting Big Game in Africa*, supposedly a film of Roosevelt doing just that (Selig hired a double). The list of the exposed goes on into our own times. Preceded by German producer Michael Born's prosecution for selling more than 20 bogus documentaries, the 'Great British Documentary Scandal', as Brian Winston calls it, saw Carlton TV fined £2 million in 1998 by regulator ITC for mocking up 1996's *The Connection*: a film supposedly about drug-running from Colombia, which in fact involved 'a wholesale breach of trust between programme makers and the viewers' (ITC Chair Sir Robin Biggam, quoted by Winston 2000: 15). Headlines such as 'CAN WE BELIEVE ANYTHING WE SEE ON TV?', and 'CHANNEL 4 IN NEW DOCUMENTARY FAKE ROW', brought into question the trustworthiness of television 'reality' footage, in addition shining an interrogative lamp on other shows of doubtful authenticity, including Channel 4's *Rogue Males*, about cowboy builders (see Winston 2000: 10–17), the 'docu-soap' *Driving School* (of which it was discovered scenes were staged) and *Much Too*

*Young: Chickens* (about rent boys and their clients – the latter actually members of the production crew). 'Factual television and documentary practice', notes Jon Dovey (2008: 255), 'was under severe epistemological pressure.' More recently, and much more seriously, the Rubicon has (allegedly) been crossed in the pursuit of exclusive sensation: as of August 2009, disgraced Brazilian lawmaker-cum-presenter Wallace Souza stands accused of ordering as many as five grisly killings to boost his television crime show *Canal Livre*'s ratings. By commissioning ostensibly drug-related murders, the reasoning goes, Souza and his strong-stomached crews – posses whose almost instant arrival at the scenes of such carnage eventually prompted suspicion – were able to obtain uncommonly graphic footage that may well point to the first alarming incidences of premeditated death by reality TV. An ultra-cynical implementation of Lord Northcliffe's fabled editorial edict to 'Get me a murder a day!', Souza's invention of news, if proven, constitutes a possibly inevitable, particularly twenty-first-century realisation of long-expressed satirical condemnations apropos mass-media iniquity. (Currently, Souza remains free due to legislative immunity, and insists that it is *he* who has been set up.)

'Directors', states the British Guild Code of Practice on documentary, 'have a responsibility to keep faith with their contributors ... In a documentary or factual programme, it is the director's responsibility to ensure fairness and accuracy ... The director must not deliberately mislead the viewers' (Winston 2000: 116). 'Mendacious documentarists', concurs Winston (*ibid.*: 157), 'should be vigorously exposed and denounced in the marketplace of ideas.' There is a distinction here, a moral line, drawn between the acceptable rhetorical and interventionist practices of Michael Moore, and the 'artless' construction of sensationalist artifice (as exemplified, albeit with extraordinary legal implications, in the currently unfolding Souza case): the creation of false history by passing off dramaturgy as actuality. Appealing to a 'common sense of injustice, inhumanity or barbarism' (Nichols 1991: 135), the rhetorician or social commentator may thus more-or-less freely assemble a case and then answer countering views, should they arise; the out-and-out fabricator, assuming a breach of regulations or libel has been committed, is liable to prosecution. But these are finely drawn lines, and our appetite for ultimately undisprovable 'counterknowledge' ('the easiest way for the demagogue to exploit gullibility and ignorance'; see Beevor 2009: 11) shows no sign of abating: witness, for instance, the abiding popularity of Dan Avery's Internet-based *Loose Change* series (2005–7), a specious litany of seditions pertaining to 9/11 that nonetheless attracts large audiences.[3] An epoch of mutable mass information and beliefs disseminated as fact, the 'Wikipedia age' will, in addition to providing generally easy access to an ever-growing plethora of resource materials desperately in need of some kind of regulatory parsing, see a deluge of bunkum pollute the work of less sagacious documentarists. Despite the imperfect nature of moral or academic censure where no actionable illegality exists – and its potential implications for free speech – such a force is perhaps all a democracy can offer as a safeguard from outright lies. Moreover, digital imaging software will one day soon be able to mimic undetectably the actions and faces of humans: 'The camera's capability to capture the real will not be erased by this,' opines Winston (2008: 9), 'but a far greater sophistication on the part of the viewer will be needed to determine documentary's authenticity.' The success of 'LonelyGirl15''s teen-confession video blog on YouTube – which attained a large cult following prior to its artist creators owning up – gives some idea of the informational minefield into which more seriously intended digital documentary is running. Most likely only those keenly attuned to developments, trends, styles, Internet demography and new-media jargon will be able quickly to sort the 'authentic' from the bogus: '[T]here already is a momentous assault on our sense of reality', declared Werner Herzog in 2007. 'We must be like medieval knights doing combat' (in McCreadie 2008: 8).

## TYPES AND FUNCTIONS

David Bordwell and Kristin Thompson, in the sixth edition of their popular textbook *Film Art: An Introduction*, bifurcate non-fiction into *rhetorical* and *categorical* camps: simply, films that aim respectively to persuade or inform. A few scholars, most notably Bill Nichols and John Corner, have gone further and attempted to formulate a taxonomy, or a nomenclature, of documentary, whereby to explain and delineate its various means of operation by grouping together traits. Corner writes of a 'documentary tradition': 'specific production practices, forms and functions all work to "hold together" (or not) the documentary identity at different times and places' (in Beattie 2008: 2). Function number one is 'democratic civics': providing a model for good citizenry in the mould John Grierson, in 1930s Britain, posited as a noble ideal. Function number two is 'journalistic enquiry': film as reporting. The third function is 'radical interrogation and alternative perspective': independent, personal and experimental. Function number four is 'documentary as diversion': popular entertainment, 'voyeuristic' reality shows, or fast-moving coverage of incidents or situations (see *ibid*.: 2–3). Nichols identifies 'six modes of representation that function something like sub-genres of the documentary film genre itself: poetic, expository, participatory, observational, reflexive, performative' (2001a: 99). (Nichols calls documentary a 'genre', though the term, as we have seen, is problematic.) It is important to remember, prior to any explanation, that these 'modes' are hardly ever completely exclusive – many films exhibit a tendency towards a dominant mode, but most mix these approaches in order to find a means of expression that works best for a particular filmmaker and/or subject matter. Also, as we will recall from Stella Bruzzi's (2005) critique, these classificatory categories are not meant to imply a definite evolution, even though they may correspond roughly to certain eras, movements and impulses (an impulse being more general and geographically/politically dispersed than a movement).

The poetic mode includes films such as Joris Ivens's impressionistic *Rain* (1929); Flaherty's *Man of Aran* (1934); Basil Wright's *Song of Ceylon* (1934); *Olympia*, by Leni Riefenstahl (1938), which celebrates its own subjective 'truth' – the Nazis' physical ideal; *Powaqqatsi* (Godfrey Reggio, 1988); and *Baraka* (Ron Fricke, 1992). The expository mode addresses the spectator directly, maintains an impression of objectivity, assumes logical and fixed notions of 'right' and 'wrong', and imparts a didactic lesson on a particular subject. Usually adopting a 'voice of God' commentary, edificatory subtitles, or the presence of an authoritative presenter, expository films include much of the work of those under John Grierson's aegis, most wildlife documentaries and films on historical events. The observational mode is found at its purest in the works of the direct cinema movement, which came to flower in 1960s America. This approach, pioneered by those such as Michel Brault (in Canada), Richard Leacock, D. A. Pennebaker and Frederick Wiseman (in the USA), finds its artistic locus in 'candid' filming – unobtrusive recording, as if a 'fly on the wall', using hand-held, mostly sync-sound camera units. There is, in the observational mode, minimal obvious interference by filmmakers with the subject, usually minimal accompanying narration or titling, predominantly 'classical' continuity (cuts are effected to give the illusion of special and temporal logic, as in classic–realist fiction), and often no extra-diegetic (i.e. not emanating from the 'diegesis', or the world created by the film) sound or effects. It is, however, very common for stories and dramatic thrust to emerge during the fastidiously selective editing process, as many hours are whittled down: thus, in no way should observational films be mistaken for more 'objective' or 'truthful' records than other types of documentary. (Theoretical issues relating to observational cinema and its legacy are taken up in Chapter Five of this book.)

The participatory mode is characterised by an affinity with 'participatory anthropology', or participant-observation: a means to lend a film a 'sense of what it is like for the filmmaker to be in a given situation and how that situation alters as a result' (Nichols 2001a: 116). As opposed to strictly observational documentary, the participant-observer does not simply watch; he or she becomes visibly or audibly involved in some way, and acknowledges that involvement's impact on the subject in front of the often 'first-person' (or, seen to be *affected by* and *part of* events) camera. The 'pro-filmic' world – the world as recorded and in the presence of a camera crew – such films attest, is, irrespective of the level of subjects' awareness, quite distinct from the cinematically elusive

'putative' world: life as it unfolds away from the documentarist's gaze
and presence, like the proverbial tree falling in a forest making no
sound unless it is heard – the implication being that everything, unless
consciously observed, is meaningless. (See also the mysterious 'observer
effect' (often confused with the less bizarre Heisenberg principle),
whereby particles, on the level of quantum physics, behave differently if
they are being watched. Those who wish to delve deeply should beware
that this is one of the universe's more mind-blowing secrets.) Jean
Rouch and Edgar Morin's *Chronicle of a Summer* (1960) is a good example
of participatory (or interactive) filmmaking. The respective filmmaker–
anthropologist and sociologist from the outset interrogate the nature of
their encounters with the lives of Parisians, beginning the film with a
discussion of whether or not one can act with sincerity in the presence
of a camera, and ending by screening the film to their subjects, who are
then quizzed on the level of truth educed. As direct cinema filmmaker
Richard Leacock opined, 'it seems to me that, although his [Rouch's]
films are so interesting, the most important thing that has ever happened to the people he chooses to film is the fact that he has filmed
them' (in Marcorelles 1973: 89). Rouch and Morin called their
experiment '*cinéma-vérité*' – cinema truth – after Soviet Dziga Vertov's
earlier '*Kino-Pravda*'. Chris Marker's *Le Joli Mai* (1963), *Sherman's March* (Ross
McElwee, 1985), and to varying degrees the films of Michael Moore
and of Britons Louis Theroux, Nick Broomfield (*Kurt and Courtney*, 1998;
*Biggie and Tupac*, 2002) and Molly Dineen (*Geri*, 1999; *The Lie of the Land*,
2007), are further instances in which the participatory mode dom-
inates (although the intentions of Moore and Broomfield *et al.* are more
openly and playfully provocative, and rather less anthropologically
inclined, than their briefly fashionable antecedents in 1960s France).

Reflexive documentaries acknowledge and call attention to the processes at work – chiefly the shooting, editing and compilation, but also
possibly issues such as funding (see Broomfield's *Driving Me Crazy*,
1988) – behind a film's construction. They bring to the forefront the
mechanics and/or intellectual methods of production and flaunt these
as integral to a film's epistemic honesty and hence effectiveness,

entering into a dialogue about film, and film's workings. *The Man with the Movie Camera* (Vertov, 1929; discussed in Chapter Three) represents the most obvious early model, but works as diverse as Isaac Julien's *Territories* (1984), an experimental documentary about race relations in the UK following the Brixton riots, and the Maysles brothers and Charlotte Zwerin's *Gimme Shelter* (1970), about the Rolling Stones' ill-omened concert at the Altamont Speedway, contain large portions of self-reflexivity: the former shows the film's editors at work, manipulating the sound and image; the latter uses the edit suite as a means of forcing the Stones to confront their own image (and egos) in relation to a fatal stabbing captured on film at Altamont (we see Jagger and cohorts scrutinise a rough cut, and a replay of the murder). An essentially postmodern conceit also found in works of high modernism (see Vertov), differing strategies of self-reflexivity abound in *Chronicle of a Summer, The Thin Blue Line* (Errol Morris, 1988); Wim Wenders's *Lightning Over Water* (1979); Chris Waitt's *A Complete History of My Sexual Failures* (2008), in which the filmmaker calls his former girlfriends so they might catalogue his deficiencies as a lover ('I'm making a film … '); and Morgan Spurlock's 'stunt-doc' (cf. the series and spin-off movies of *Jackass*) hit *Super Size Me* (2004), a film in large part concerned with its own motivation – Spurlock's 30-day McDonald's diet, and its chances of killing both him and the film. Arising mostly from documentary's classical maturity and a related desire to deconstruct the form's intricately coded systems of knowledge communication, reflexive films analyse *themselves* as much as a nominal subject, setting out to 'puncture the epistemological and ontological promises that underlie the spectatorial expectations of the documentary form' (Scheibler 1993: 135).

Nichols's performative mode is the most problematic and contentious of the six postulated. This mode, says Nichols, 'underscores the complexity of our knowledge of the world by emphasising its subjective and affective dimensions' – a definition that would place a good number of 'performative' films also well within the bounds of the reflexive (see Ward 2005: 21). Films as diverse as Marlon Riggs's *Tongues Untied* (1989), a quest seemingly to 'perform' the experience of being part of a black and gay subculture, Alan Resnais's *Night and Fog* (1955), a poetic, subjective 'performance' of memory dealing with the Holocaust, and Caouette's *Tarnation* (2003) fall comfortably into this grouping in accordance with its originator's ideas. Stella Bruzzi, however, takes issue with this classification, dedicating the majority of *New Documentary: A Critical Introduction*'s two editions (2000 and 2005) to a thesis around performance and documentary, a relationship she sees as an inseparable 'negotiation between filmmaker and reality' (2000: 154). Bruzzi outlines her notion of the performative, drawing on the work of J. L. Austin, as more inclusive: 'namely, that they function as utterances that simultaneously both describe and perform an action':

> Examples of words that Austin identifies as being 'performative utterances' are 'I do', said within the context of the marriage ceremony, or 'I name this ship the Queen Elizabeth', said whilst smashing a bottle of champagne against the ship's side … a parallel is to be found between these linguistic examples and the performative documentary which – whether built around the intrusive presence of the filmmaker or self-conscious performances by its subjects – is the enactment of the notion that a documentary only comes into being as it is performed, that although its factual basis (or document) can pre-date any recording or representation of it, the film itself is necessarily performative because it is given meaning by the interaction between performance and reality.
>
> (Bruzzi 2000: 154)

Bruzzi goes on to evaluate Jennie Livingston's *Paris is Burning* (1990), and the interventionist films of directors-as-stars Molly Dineen and Nick Broomfield, as examples of films that accentuate all aspects of documentary performance, and that – in opposition to the direct cinema school, which mostly used media-literate social actors (politicians, singers, sports stars) whilst downplaying their 'natural' ability to act for the camera – highlight the artifice of the filmic self. This, according to Caryl Flinn, is appropriate, because 'documentary films, in many ways more so than other cinematic forms, reveal the constructed – indeed, performative – nature of the world around us' (Flinn 1998: 429): life, as it were, as a stage. Performative documentary, then, should be taken, with caution, to encompass films explicitly *about* traditional performance or performers, films '*performing' some aspect of experiential subjectivity*, and films wherein the filmmaker positions *his or herself* centrally to the narrative or argument (see Moore, Dineen, Broomfield, Theroux, or Werner Herzog in *Grizzly Man* (2005), who comes across as 'author' of both the film and video-diarist/performer Timothy Treadwell's legacy).

In this chapter we have seen how documentary has posed problems for those trying to delineate its functions and traits; indeed, by dint of its claims on the always slippery concept of truth, it defies neat taxonomy in a way that differing types of film do not. Documentary's methods interact with those of fiction in numerous and not always schematic ways; it persuades, expresses or elucidates by presenting us with formally organised indexes to actuality, yet at the same time frequently employs the grammar of dramaturgy. Whilst non-fiction film unquestionably ought not to be entirely incorporated with fiction in a discursive, evidential, generic or philosophical sense, documentarists of all stripes perhaps hold a licence, as Linda Williams stresses, to 'use all the strategies of fictional construction to get at truths' (Williams 1993: 20), whatever they may be. We have also seen how non-fiction enters into a negotiation around factuality, and into a 'contract' of sorts with its spectators, whose subjective, culturally dependent expectations and receptive preconceptions shape these discourses according to particularities of time and place. In Chapter Two, we shall trace a timeline of better-known non-fiction film over the decades, with the aim of positing such issues within a clearer contextual frame of comparative reference.

## NOTES

1 This is still the received story regarding the word's first widely appreciated use in this context. Edward Curtis in fact employed the term much earlier,

in 1914, in his film company's prospectus. See Macdonald and Cousins 1998: 21.

2 Brian Winston (2000: 24) traces the tradition of drama's stylistic aping of factual coverage back to Orson Welles's 1938 radio production of *War of the Worlds*.

3 The film forwards a number of discredited theories. See http://en.wikipedia. org/wiki/Loose_Change_(film), accessed on 12/12/08.

# 2

## MAJOR TRENDS, MOVEMENTS AND VOICES

All art is a kind of exploring. To discover and reveal is the way every artist sets about his [sic] business.

Robert Flaherty (in Flaherty 1972: 10–11)

### BEGINNINGS

Emerging as it did from a number of artistic, commercial and scientific endeavours, non-fiction (and in fact all) cinema lacks a birthday. Chief amongst its pioneers, however, were perhaps Thomas Edison and Auguste and Louis Lumière. Edison, whose Kinetoscope enjoyed short-lived success in 1894, employed bulky camera and processing equipment to the end of making studio-originated films – usually of professional performers – for this peep-show-type device. More crucially for documentary, the Lumières, in 1895, developed a five-kilogram, hand-cranked (and thus portable) camera capable of capturing life 'on the run', outdoors in daylight and with minimal preparation. The same year, in Paris, they publicly unveiled their invention: a machine, the *cinématographe*, that heralded the arrival not only of the famous train (in *L'Arrivée d'un Train en Gare*, 1895), generating the legendarily (and maybe apocryphally) unsettling illusion of motion towards an audience, but also cinema as a *projected, enlarged* and *shared* phenomenological experience. Making short films on a variety of usually unscripted subjects (the majority of these were termed 'actualities'), the Frenchmen took their shows to every continent bar Antarctica. As Erik Barnouw notes, 'Edison began the process; Lumière and others carried it forward ... In the end it was Louis Lumière who made the *documentary* film a reality – on a worldwide basis, and with sensational suddenness' (1993: 5). '[S]o far as the genesis of film art is concerned,' concurs Dai Vaughan, 'those early shows mounted by the Lumière brothers represent the nearest we will find to a singularity' (1999: 1). Cinema proper was thus instigated – as was a fascination with its mimetic ability to capture the incidental details of quotidian life and play them back as in a dream. The titular subjects were often not as captivating as airborne brick dust, leaves or the undulations of the sea: the random playing of time and nature on the Earth and on humankind – a simple poetry to be found in the new magic of the moving image.

Narrative, of course, was not yet present at this time. The Lumière films and their immediate successors are schematically framed, picture-postcard views through a fixed window onto a simple event never lent any context or purpose beyond the most basic 'cinema of attractions'. In the 1910s, despite the ubiquity of the weekly 'newsreel', 'an extension into motion pictures of equivalents to the rotogravure (photographic) sections of the tabloids' developed by Pathé (Ellis and McLane 2007: 5), the novelty of non-fiction productions wore thin. Mostly unimaginative compilers sought attention-grabbing footage of extreme situations, intemperate or far-off lands, and eventually war (much of which was faked), in attempts to wrest public interest away from the increasingly popular fiction cinema's nascent continuity system. Usually, the newsreels constituted not high art, but bill-filling fluff shown between main attractions: '[S]omething which delights the eye and soothes the mind without touching any emotional chords ... dainty bits of animal life, scenes from the beautiful countries of the world, monuments of architecture, glimpses of foreign lands' (Samuel L. Rothapfel, manager of New York's Strand Theatre, quoted by Bottomore 2001: 172).

'Ironically,' state Kevin Macdonald and Mark Cousins, 'in order to find its first really successful model, the documentary had to move further away from reality and adopt the dramatic and technical features of the fiction film' (1998: 19). A few pictures comprising scripted romances set against exotic locales, including the ethnocentrically titled *In the Land of the Head Hunters* (1914), foreshadowed Flaherty somewhat (and it seems that Flaherty did, in 1915, see Edward S. Curtis's melodramatically embellished tale of 'the Indian and Indian life'; Curtis in Winston 2008: 11); but it would not be until Flaherty's 1922 *Nanook of the North*, which absorbed with elegance the recently conventionalised methods of Hollywood screen grammar, that the now-familiar synthesis of filmic storytelling (via narrative construction, titling, musical accompaniment and continuity principles) and the representation of reality came into being. In essence, Flaherty brilliantly combined the principles of drama with the principles of salvage anthropology: the result is a series of ethnographically infused films that clearly evince characteristics still fundamental to virtually all narrative documentaries. Like D. W. Griffith, Flaherty was perhaps less of an inventor than a synthesist, but he brought together, effectively for the first time, the means of making a cogent, cohesive, financially winning drama out of the daily tribulations of those with whom he spent time; *Nanook* might best be described as doing for non-fiction cinema what Griffith's *Birth of a Nation* (1915) had done for its counterpart. A school did not coalesce around Flaherty; nevertheless, others made analogous works that would appear very much to draw on his techniques, including Americans Merian C. Cooper and Ernest B. Schoedsack (*Grass*, 1925; *Chang*, 1927), Martin and Osa Johnson (*Wonders of the Congo*, 1931), and Frenchmen Marc Allegret and André Gide (*Voyage to the Congo*, 1927).

### Soviets

At the same time as Flaherty was spending years with the Inuit or in Samoa, the Soviets were conducting experiments in film and its potential to serve an ideological purpose for the good of the

Communist cause. Following the 1917 Revolution, the new government quickly set up a film subsection of the Department of Education, headed by Lenin's wife Nadezhda. The State Institute of Cinematography was instituted to produce filmmakers whose job was to convey messages from the state to citizens; the Soviets were taking film, its modernity and its illustrative possibilities very seriously as a re-educative tool capable of instilling the illiterate, 'lumpen' masses with Bolshevik fervour: 'Of all the arts,' declared Lenin, 'the cinema is the most important to us' (Ellis and McLane 2007: 27). Amongst many others, Sergei Eisenstein, Dziga Vertov and Alexander Dovzhenko left the traditional arts and embraced the cinema – which became, essentially, a government-funded cinema of propaganda, carried out in part via the 'Leninist Film Proportion', a decree stating that a large percentage of film output should be of a 'factual' nature. Chief amongst the architects of this new Soviet cinema of politically motivated (semi-)veracity was Dziga Vertov (whose real name was the rather more prosaic Denis Kaufman). Having begun work in a Moscow basement making films for the 'agit-trains' to take to the rural populace, Vertov, in 1922, began to produce a series of films under the banner *Kino-Pravda* ('film truth'); railing against the sins of fiction film, appropriating Marx, he believed that: 'Kinodrama is an opium for the people. Kinodrama and religion are deadly weapons in the hands of the capitalists ... Down with the bourgeois tale scenario! Hurrah for life as it is!' (Barsam 1973: 24). Further expanding his theoretical ideas into what he called the *kino-eye*, and working with his mysterious 'Council of Three' (Vertov, his wife Elizaveta and his brother Mikhail), Vertov, a dazzling editor taking the notion of 'life caught unawares' and reassembling it in a highly cinematic fashion appropriate to the premise of dialectical materialism, arrived at his most famous work: *The Man with the Movie Camera* (1929), an ambitious, coruscating work of reflexive and joyous absorption in post-revolutionary city life (see Chapter Three). Although Eisenstein (a proto-docudrama filmmaker of sorts) is arguably more important in the scheme of so-called Soviet montage, and his films are certainly better known, 'Vertov's films', writes Jay Leyda, 'dared to treat the present and, through the present, the future with an approach as revolutionary as the material he treated (*ibid.*: 24). Vertov idolised the camera, considering it more perfect than the human eye: an instrument for 'the sensory exploration of the world through film ... I am kino-eye, I am mechanical eye. I, a machine, show you the world as only I can see it' (Vertov in Macdonald and Cousins 1998: 55).

Fellow Russian Esfir (Esther) Shub, who had influenced Vertov and Eisenstein (though she disagreed with them on many points, contrapuntally arguing for the 'greatest austerity of execution'; Stollery 2002: 93), introduced the 'compilation' film. A master of archival research, her first three films (*The Fall of the Romanov Dynasty* (1927), *The Great Road* (1927) and *The Russia of Nicholas II and Leo Tolstoy* (1928)) form a historical trilogy drawing on material accumulated from months of searching in such locations as the Museum of the Revolution (in which she found, remarkably, the mislabelled home movies of the last Tsar, later to be juxtaposed rhetorically with images of put-upon workers). Shub advanced the artistic development of the newsreel tradition, especially when considered in relation to the 'March of Time' (1935–51) series in the United States, and was one of the first documentary proponents of heavily ironic concatenation (the rich are seen to make play, then the poor are seen to make sweat) – something now familiar to modern audiences from the work of Michael Moore, via Emile de Antonio (*In the Year of the Pig*, 1968) and many others. Turning counter-revolutionary material against its originators, Shub was under no illusion about her (to modern viewers) unsubtle films' dearth of objective 'authenticity':

> The intention was not so much to provide the facts but to evaluate them from the vantage point of the revolutionary class. This is what made my films revolutionary and agitational – although they were composed of counter-revolutionary material ... Each of my compilation films was also a form of agitation for the new concept of documentary cinema, a statement about unstaged film as the most important cinematic form of the present day.
>
> (Shub in Petric 1984: 24, 37)

Perhaps underappreciated alongside evaluations of Vertov *et al.*, Shub remains important for her appropriation of found footage: a conversion and reversal of ideological intention in the service of the people. 'What Shub achieves', comments Michael Chanan, 'is not just the reconstruction of history through documentary footage, but the creation of a film-historical discourse which transcends the simple present tense of the camera which took the original footage' (2007: 91). Making copious documentaries now less well known than the above-mentioned, including *Spain* (1939) on the Spanish Civil War (and the sadly uncompleted *Women*, a mooted history of modern Russian womanhood), Shub's writings to this day are mostly untranslated into English.

Victor Turin was another Soviet film pioneer, whose *Turksib* (1929) eulogised the construction of the Turkestan–Siberia railway and depicted indigenous folk along the route – much to the fascination of Western audiences. Structured in five acts, the epic undertaking extols, with Walt Whitman-like titles and vastly expansive visuals, the future role of wheat transportation in raising 'cotton for all Russia' in Turkestan. Turin, like Vertov and in disagreement with Flaherty, looked upon the machine as humankind's friend: a sympathetic ally in the struggle for utopian levels of socialist productivity. (Grierson was impressed – he edited the English version – though perhaps *Turksib*'s influence was felt more in the United States, a little later, by the meliorative chroniclers of the Great Depression.) After a brief golden age of documentary film-making in the USSR, when doctrine and dogma shaped, but did not crush, the work of Vertov, Shub, Eisenstein, Turin, Mikhail Kalatazov, Yakov Blyokh, Lev Kuleshov and others, Stalin's regime, growing insecure under increasing international pressure, applied duress on filmmakers to adhere to and promote its economic tenets at the cost of creative freedom. Newness hence gave way to the schematic, and the challenging to the anodyne. The early years of post-revolutionary enthusiasm, however, would ensure that the Soviet Union's experimental contributions to non-fiction filmmaking methods would never go forgotten – not least due to the huge volume of theoretical writings by its practitioners. And, certainly, ideological filmmaking did not die with the end of Bolshevik cinema's great flush and the onset of the Five-Year Plans; Nazi Germany's dubious filmed works carried the flame of fervency on into the 1940s, while the Soviets' methods of persuasion have been absorbed by numerous artists, in all subsequent decades, concerned with putting aesthetic or juxtapositional flair to use by advocating political viewpoints, whether seeking progress, change, reform or stasis.

## THE EUROPEAN AVANT-GARDE

In the late teens and twenties, the modernist impulse sweeping Europe began to manifest itself across all the visual arts, which progressed beyond verisimilitude and into an interrogation of reality, motion and perception. Dadaism, surrealism, cubism and futurism (amongst multifarious other 'isms') burgeoned at around the same time; all were cross-fertilising attempts to reorder or reconstitute reality, and all rejected art as simple mimetic record. This impulse was greatly accelerated by the ubiquity (and imminent classical–realist maturity) of narrative cinema, whose global pervasiveness provided those so inclined, as we have seen in relation to Vertov and Shub, with a springboard into more experimental waters. Painters explored the relationship of space to time; writers played with temporality and narrative non-linearity; and a general sense of the importance of urban life to modernity begat numerous responses to humanity's changing condition. Film – the most mechanical and obviously representative of the new emergence of machines and technocratic authority – was thus a medium especially suited to experimental reactions against the fiction form's diverting illusions: one avant-gardist likened Hollywood's prevalent modes of storytelling to 'someone playing a grand piano with one finger' – a limiting and old-fashioned waste of art's potential (see Ellis and McLane 2007: 44). Writers, painters, architects and photographers eagerly studied film and turned their talents to producing works for the screen: the cinema, in an age of ambivalence about mechanised living *and* killing, offered more to the attuned than mere plot, escape and catharsis. The avant-garde's 'emphasis on seeing things anew through the eyes of the artist or filmmaker,' notes Bill Nichols, 'had tremendous liberating potential. It freed cinema from replicating what came before the camera to celebrate how this "stuff" could become the raw material not only of narrative filmmaking but of a poet cinema as well' (2001a: 90).

*Ballet Méchanique* (1925), a Cubist effort by the French painterly artist Fernand Léger, constitutes a sort of abstract documentary. It shows images, cut in rhythmic sequence and in close-up, of cogs, eyes, kitchen utensils, bottles, levers and sundry other objects denied any context other than the frame of the film's *gestalt*. Prior to this, German Hans Richter and Swede Viking Eggeling had made experiments with abstract film, photographing natural or familiar objects and rendering them 'fragments of reality': a 'creative synthesis' of discovery and manipulation (Barnouw 1993: 72).

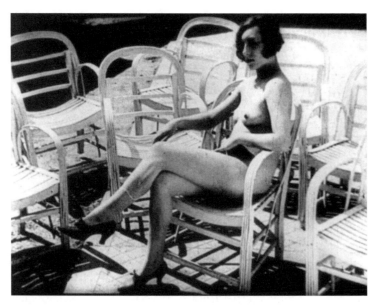

FIGURE 2.1 Decadence on the French Riviera in *Apropos de Nice* (1930)

Dadaist Marcel Duchamp made *Anemic Cinema* (1926), a similarly intended piece; *Apropos de Nice/On the Subject of Nice*, by Jean Vigo (1930), is an experimental short documentary about the French Riviera ('a whole town begging from sheer laziness'; Macdonald and Cousins 1998: 83), strongly utilising Vertov's kino-eye tactics (hidden cameras, tilts, slow-motion, and associative cutting whereby meaning, *à la* Lev Kuleshov's discoveries, is dependent on the apposition of shots); Luis Buñuel's *Tierra Sin Pan/Land Without Bread* (1932), a dream-like and reflexively sardonic look at intense poverty in the Las Hurdes region of Spain, absorbs the influence of surrealism; and Dutchman Jores Ivens's *The Bridge* (1928), *Breakers* (1929) and the Amsterdam-located *Rain* (1929, looking at the city during a downpour) likewise toyed with montage techniques, with the interplay of shadows and light, and with reality as re-formed experience. Ivens, as did his modernist analogues, largely disregarded 'content', which he saw as a formally constraining imposition, in favour of other elements judiciously combined to give an overall cinematic impression: in the case of *Rain*, of the tender loveliness in rainclouds, ripples and light on wet cobblestones.

Maybe the most ambitious non-fiction productions spawned by the European avant-garde, however, are the so-called 'city symphonies': notably Paul Strand and Charles Sheeler's *Manhatta* (1921), an early prototype, *The Man with the Movie Camera*, *Rain*, Alberto Cavalcanti's (later the Brazilian would become a leader of the British documentary movement) episodic *Rien que les Heures/Only the Hours* (1926), combining staged scenes and surreptitiously filmed material in a meditation on Paris, and Walter Ruttman's 70-minute *Berlin: die Sinfonie der Grosstadt/Berlin: Symphony of a Great City* (1927), which gave a name to this sub-type. What concerns all these films alike is the encroachment, for both good and bad, of the city on humanity, and the oddly elegant workings of the metropolis: 'it is cramped, dirty, brutalizing, and almost unbelievable', writes Richard Barsam (1973: 28), 'but, at the same time, it has eccentricities, its charms, its beauties. Where others [namely Flaherty] saw man in a romantic conflict with nature, these filmmakers saw man in a realistic conflict with the city streets.' Ruttman's *Berlin* is a majestic, diurnal examination of the city, its movement and its people. Replete with optical effects, the film depicts a day in the 'life' of Berlin, from morning until night, imposing a chronological structure to give form and solve a dilemma inherent in avant-garde films: how to begin and end something not concerned with the conventions of story-based drama. Ruttman's viewpoint absolutely prioritises aesthetic poesis over ideological or social instruction − a functional relegation for the most part avoided by the Soviets and, later, the British. But it is arguably an approach, as Jack Ellis and Betsy McLane point out, that means *Berlin* 'may have more value as a document than do those documentary films made with more explicit social biases and programs … From this film we can learn a great deal about the appearance of life in Berlin in 1927' (2007: 53). *Berlin* attained wide circulation in commercial cinemas, in time proving one of the most successful and influential documentaries to come out of the pre-sound era.

## PRE-WAR

A number of factors conspired in putting an end to the avant-garde's prevalence, if not its influence. Spoken words, with the coming of synchronised-sound facilities, suddenly saw the film image relegated; studios, with the financial power to build soundstages, now enjoyed commercial dominance. For the visually preoccupied avant-garde in Europe, this meant either working in the greater industrial context or for the new governmental agendas, with any compromises this might entail, or falling into obscurity. The 1920s were for many a time of excess and frivolity, but they also gave rise to tremendous artistic and aesthetic innovation; by contrast, the following decade (though it should be remembered that history does not divide *itself* into separate slices) brought depression and growing political turmoil as continents drifted towards total war. If the avant-garde largely thus came to a halt, giving way to a more civically focused documentary of social concern, its poetic reso-nance was nonetheless felt heavily on both sides of the Atlantic. As Bill

Nichols argues, perhaps 'documentary' in the strictest sense – usually a permutation of the 'primitive' 'actuality', the newsreel, the experimental film, the narrative film and the socio-political tract – could not and did not take shape until the avant-garde had paved the way:

> Without the capacity to disrupt and make new, documentary film would not have been possible as a discrete rhetorical practice. It is the modernist avant-garde that fulfils Grierson's own call for the 'creative treatment of actuality' most relentlessly. The explosive power of avant-garde practices subverts and shatters the coherence, stability, and naturalness of the dominant world of realist representation … The 'creative treatment of actuality' is authored, not recorded or registered.
>
> (Nichols 2001b: 592)

Documentarists, newly so named, began incorporating voiceovers and audio effects, putting sound and image to synergistic, educational use in shaping their nations' hearts and minds.

With the 1929 creation, in England, of the archaically named Empire Marketing Board (EMB) Film Unit, the non-fiction film found new thrust under the auspices of John Grierson. Dedicated to public information and notions of responsible service (akin to the declared aims of the nascent BBC), Grierson saw in film 'a means of bridging the enormous gaps of comprehension and sympathy in the complex society of our times' (see Levin 1971: 12). Drawing on the above-mentioned works of the European and Russian avant-garde, and the writings of the political science school of Chicago University, Grierson believed in a duty to shepherd the masses towards enlightened democracy: 'I look on cinema as a pulpit', he remarked, unfrightened by the word 'propaganda'. By implication hoisting himself to a tenuously held vantage supposedly aloof from his life's central dilemmas (of placatory content versus political purpose, and of socialist principles versus deep-rooted capitalist demands), Grierson, engaged on a personal level in another 'creative treatment', deplored the commercial film profession as 'notably a world of fly men, fast men, noisy men, and thoroughly vulgar men. You might say that, if it is publicly responsible, it is only for a buck. You might also say that if it ever does anything good, this is only because the innate goodness of mankind occasionally creeps up on it through a producer' (Grierson 1954: 48). The EMB Film Unit, later to become the General Post Office (GPO) Film Unit and then, during the Second World War, the Crown Film Unit, for many years played host to a number of luminaries working together with, in effect, a single purpose, including Basil Wright, Paul Rotha, Arthur Elton, Edgar Anstey, Humphrey Jennings, Alberto Cavalcanti and Stuart Legg. Freed from the commercial pressures of the box office, these 60-odd film-makers were often funded by government; often they sought financing from industry; and always they were working on relatively low budgets and for low pay. Somewhat patrician in attitude, well meaning but starchy, and infused with a scrupulously romanticised, unquestioning respect for the noble endeavours of the working classes (who are nevertheless rarely given much identity beyond functional typicality or victim status), the Grierson school set about its selective depiction of Great British industry and empire with focus and determination, guided by 'the chief''s vision of a propaganda mostly aiming not to inspire transformation, but to uphold the ceilings of the class system – a stasis required by Grierson's backers. Professing to find virtue in stories 'taken from the raw', and the realness of 'spontaneous gesture' (in Macdonald and Cousins 1998: 97), Grierson and cohorts in fact continually fell short of conveying these, and into a tendency towards worthy tediousness. Though placing scant importance on Vertov's 'life caught unawares', and evincing heavy dependence on scripts, sets and reconstruction, the British movement's influence has, for better or worse, been pervasive.

Drifters, which was produced in 1929, directed by Grierson (it was the only film he ever directed), and photographed by Basil Emmott, represents the Unit's simple beginnings. Concerning the work of her-ring fishermen in the North Sea, the film combines elements of Flah-erty (the brave struggle for survival against the weather) with traits more usually found in the films of Sergei Eisenstein (the dynamically composed engine sequence reminiscent of *Battleship Potemkin*, 1925), to provide a drama of the everyday. In contrast with Flaherty, the struggle takes place in a thundering, heavy-industrial world of 'steam and steel', not around the quaintness of a croft. There is no radical agenda in effect – all Grierson is attempting is to afford the men a kind of muscular dignity as buttresses of Britain. We see their faces, we see their labour and we hear snatches of their speech, yet they speak only as *pars pro toto* representatives of a broader class: Grierson, notes Graham Roberts, 'seems happier with inanimate objects or fish than people' (2007: 93). Maybe reluctantly, but in structural terms unavoidably, he ends the film by lending the workers' lives an economic context, showing the herring – products of all this magnificent adventure – gone to market for money: the hard currency of modern exchange systems is now in plain sight, although this section of *Drifters* feels tagged on, suggesting directorial ambivalence. Basil Wright's *Song of Ceylon* (1934) is regarded as a classic of its kind: a sponsored (by a tea company) but remarkably non-commercial-feeling film replete with artistically and poetically personal images and sounds, *Song of Ceylon* even incorporates, via a montage entitled 'The Voices of Commerce', a gentle critique of industry's encroachment on paradise. It does, however, 'totally [avoid] the question of colonial labour and the economic exploitation of the colonies' (Hood 1983: 102).

*Granton Trawler* (Edgar Anstey, 1934) and Cavalcanti's *Coal Face* (1935), respectively, revisit the world of *Drifters* and audio-visually augment the dreary, vital toil of the coalminer with experimental music and poetry ('O lurcher-loving collier, black as night'), whilst Harry Watt and Basil Wright's *Night Mail* (discussed in Chapter Three), mixing ethics and aesthetics in an exposition following the postal train from London to Glasgow, has become the movement's most iconic work. (Watt would develop further the narrative approach in *The Saving of Bill Blewitt*, a 1937 puff-piece for national savings plans; and *North Sea*, 1938, much along the lines of *Drifters*.) *Housing Problems* (Arthur Elton and Edgar Anstey, 1935) begins a cycle of socially remedial films including *Enough to Eat?* (1936), *The Smoke Menace* (1937) and *Children at School* (1937). *Housing*

*Problems*, itself drawing on the recently launched 'March of Time' newsreel series, was pioneering in a critical respect: the crew took their huge sound equipment to record subjects' testimonies *in situ*, a naturalistic approach positing context as crucial to an audience's understanding of a particular predicament – in this case, that engendered by the slums of London. As in all such films, the commentary nowadays sounds comically stiff, its middle-class concern commendable but politically non-committal: the filmmakers are inevitably divorced from the titular problems and prompted, rehearsed pleas by an ideological pusillanimity stemming from the twin strictures of institutional or sponsored funding and obligation to government. 'The British documentarists', writes William Glynn, 'identified themselves as socialists with a "progressive outlook" [but] they worked within a conservative state bureaucracy that demanded restraint and self-censorship' (in Chanan 2007: 143). (A left-wing British documentary culture – the Workers' Film and Photo League – did come into existence at the same time, but never troubled the mainstream.)

Planned housing, as per the (never completed) Leeds Quarry Road Estate, is forwarded as the natural solution irrespective of any deeper malaise: relocated, so the film suggests, the erstwhile slum-dwellers will thence learn proper hygiene in accordance with their new surroundings, from which *Housing Problems'* financier, the Gas Light and Coke Company, stood to benefit. It is hard, though, not to empathise with the folk on camera, their voices visually emanating from the depths of an undeniably disgusting condition. Several of the slum-dwellers had never seen a film, but sensed they were being given a platform through which they might at least inform the wider world of their rat-infested, decaying houses, if not of their individual personalities. 'The camera is yours, the microphone is yours, now tell the bastards what it's like to live here', said the film's assistant director, John Grierson's sister Ruby (quoted by Rothwell 2008: 153). (The direct-interview techniques at work in *Housing Problems*, of course, have since become staples of the television documentary.) The British movement generated much writing on the non-fiction form, notably by Grierson and Paul Rotha: the former's faintly bigoted theorising on his long, evangelical 'adventure in public observation' (Grierson in Barsam 1973: 38) is still popularly anthologised, and the latter's *Documentary Film* (1935) remains an early classic devoted to explicating its author's creative context. Eloquently summing up the Griersonian tradition's flaws, Mike Wayne writes that 'its vision of the world was one of controlled, well-ordered industrial and social processes and the conflict-free operations of Empire' (2008: 82). Cavalcanti, one of the more inventive of the Griersonians, perhaps was insightful in his dismissal of the 'D' word, the most abiding of the 1930s British EMB and GPO films arguably depending far more on the *art* of creativity than the sometimes staid or condescending 'cinema of the actual' favoured by Grierson: 'I hate the word "documentary". I think it smells of dust and boredom' (in Winston 2008: 15).

In 1939, with war looming, Grierson was dispatched to Canada, there to set up the National Film Board (NFB) and continue his methods' propagation by establishing an organisation active in documentary filmmaking throughout and beyond the war years (and that would become the model for national film boards the world over). 'In a few years', notes Erik Barnouw, Grierson and his colleagues had 'changed the expectations aroused by the word "documentary". A Flaherty documentary had been a feature-length, close-up portrait of a group of people, remotely located but familiar in their humanity. The characteristic Griersonian documentary dealt with impersonal social processes; it was usually a short film fused by a "commentary" that articulated a point of view – an intrusion that was anathema to Flaherty. The Griersonian pattern was spreading' (Barnouw 1993: 99).

Depression-era North America, riven by the Dust Bowl tragedy, was a fertile seedbed of expressive non-fiction, much of it made in response to national crises and possessed by the spirit of Franklin Roosevelt's New Deal. 'Like its European counterparts,' notes Paul Arthur, 'American social documentaries conspired in a public belief that it was advantageous to address pressing needs through a discourse purporting to offer the highest quotient of immediacy, responsiveness, clarity, and verisimilitude … Similar virtues were located in the popular reception of radio, weekly news magazines, political theatre as "living newspaper", and the first versions of public opinion polls' (Arthur 1993: 110). Finding its roots in agrarian populism (the belief in limited state control – of capitalism's monopolistic and exploitative tendencies), unlike the socialism of Grierson in Britain, American non-fiction film of the 1930s, already popularly under way with 'The March of Time' and imitators, developed a tradition of understandably subtle though genuinely leftish critique exemplified by the many assignments in film and photography undertaken for the government's New Deal Resettlement Administration (later to become the Farm Security Administration, FSA). Virginian (via New York) liberal Pare Lorenz's elegiac *The Plow That Broke the Plains* (1936) criticised the Dust Bowl's origins in careless handling of natural resources whilst lending the consequent human displacement and misery a socio-political context. Similar in spirit to the President's famous 'fireside chats' over the airwaves, *The Plow* was 'a dramatic account of the tragic misuse of our Great Plains … a report to the nation on its government's efforts to meet the emergency' (Arthur Knight quoted by Levin 1971: 14). Lorenz was a filmmaking tyro, yet his at-times John Steinbeck-esque 'melodrama of nature' (Lorenz in Barsam 1973: 102) exhibits finely wrought argument (always expressed in terms avoiding the language of outright activism; the inevitable efficacy of federal compassion is instead gently asserted), accomplished marriage of image to music and narration, and beautiful, often starkly arresting compositions framed by hired-hand cinematographers Paul Strand, Ralph Steiner and Leo Hurwitz, all formerly of the (US) Film and Photo League.

*The Plow That Broke the Plains* was not shown as widely as it might have been (Lorenz, in naivety, failed to made adequate provision for the film's distribution), but it received positive reviews, encouraging Lorenz to propose another film to the FSA, this time dealing with soil conservation and flood prevention. *The River* (1937) is Lorenz's poetic rendering of the Mississippi River, its past, its present and its future under the benevolent care of the Tennessee Valley Authority (TVA): 'From as far West as Idaho', reads the film's prologue, 'carrying every brook and rill, rivulet and creek.' Simply, *The River* avers that bad planting and har-vesting denude the land, leading to devastating floods; the TVA, given a mandate, can thence restore a balance to the lives of those on the river's tributaries. The problem, suggests Lorenz, is an *American* concern trans-cending social boundaries, and one best viewed as the responsibility of every citizen. Ralph Steiner and Willard Van Dyke's *The City* (1939), made especially for the 1939 New York World's Fair and sponsored by the American Institute of Planners, is a plea for urban rectification in order that the great mess of American city life might be cleaned up and reorganised into greenbelt communities. Scored by Aaron Copland, scripted by Lewis Mumford, edited with brio and lacking in neither humour nor vitality, *The City*, though it argues for a utopian future based on sadly impossible interpersonal harmony, comprises an episodic, optimistic city symphony asking of its audience a certain hope in human endeavour (the possibility of upcoming war is ignored) and the insubstantial nourishments of the American Dream: 'There must be something better. Why can't we have it?' intones the film, assured in its 'trope of individual freedom embedded within a unifying consensus of social directives' (Arthur 1993: 113). *Power and the Land* (1940, Joris Ivens), a government film entrusted to a Communist director, centres on the arrival of electricity to rural districts and goes as far as making a case for the setting up of farming cooperatives; in essence, despite Ivens's initial wish to turn the film into an anti-corporate tract, it is ultimately an emotional eulogy to family life in Ohio.

Away from institutional obligation, the Frontier Film Group, born of the liberal–progressive cinema outfit Nykino, produced many works made outside the 'system' that took a more militant stance aimed at 'exposing the brutalities of capitalist society' (Campbell 1978: 118). They made only a small number of what Nykino had fervently called 'flaming film-slogans', usually designed to address societal ills domes-tically and on foreign soil. *Heart of Spain* and *Return to Life* (both Herbert Kline, 1937) deal with the situation in Spain, and show sympathy for the Loyalist cause; made for the purposes of fund raising, *Return to Life* boasts photography by Henri Cartier-Bresson. *Crisis* (1938), not a

Frontier production but also by Kline, is an account of the Czech people's fight for freedom from the Nazis' oppression; *China Strikes Back* (Harry Dunham, 1937) is a pro-China piece about the Chinese–Japanese war, showing the young Mao; *People of the Cumberland* (Elia Kazan and Ralph Steiner, 1938) looks at the economic prospects of Appalachian miners in a manner redolent of *Housing Problems*; and *United Action* (1939) covers a General Motors automobile-workers' strike in Detroit. But perhaps the group's most illustrious achievement is 1942's *Native Land*, by Paul Strand and Leo Hurwitz, featuring narration by Paul Robeson. It is largely a re-enactment, using actors, of workers' legal struggles for unionisation and civil rights, taking as its central theme the 'irony of injustice in a land of independence and freedom, the irony of tyranny and conspiracy in the land of the Bill of Rights' (Barsam 1973: 112). Other films of the period include *The Wave* (Strand and Fred Zimmerman, 1935); *The Spanish Earth* (Ivens, 1937), a pro-Republican film about the Spanish Civil War; *The Four Hundred Million* (Ivens, 1938); *Lights Out in Europe* (1939, Kline, 1939); *Valley Town* (Van Dyke, 1940); and Robert Flaherty's *The Land* (1941), an atypically discontinuous film (given its maker's past tendencies) whose dismalness, as America entered the war, was deemed unsuitable by its sponsors at the Agriculture Department. Flaherty's heartfelt effort at socially minded documentary was an interesting failure; for all its fragmented poetry of lamentation, *The Land*, as incoherent as it was lovely, was never officially released for fear that it might serve enemy purposes better than domestic ones. The end of the Depression, coupled with the Second World War and its pulling together of disparate factions against a common external enemy, signalled the demise of the first wave of leftist documentary activism in the States.

In Nazi Germany, propaganda drives under Goebbels resulted in much now patently repulsive cinema produced before and during the war – see, for instance, Fritz Hippler's *Der Ewige Jude/The Eternal Jew* (1940), a 'spectacularly odious' (Barnouw 1993; 141) anti-semitic invective. Of all the documentaries to come out of the Third Reich, two astounding films by Hitler's favourite filmmaker, Leni Riefenstahl – *Triumph des Willens/Triumph of the Will* (1934) and *Olympia* (1938) – deserve mention. *Triumph of the Will*, shot at the Nuremberg Party rallies of 1933, contrived to show Hitler and his deputies as avatars descended to bestow inspiration and nationalist spirit upon their subjects, amassed in multitudinous ranks and in thrall to what Susan Sontag called 'orgiastic transactions between mighty forces and their puppets, uniformly garbed and shown in ever swelling numbers' (Sontag 1975: 91). Heavily manipulated and orchestrated for the camera crew's best advantage, the film, potently constructed by 172 operatives working under the director's authority, is undeniably a cinematic masterpiece marking the zenith of history as theatre; that its specific politics are repugnant is maybe secondary to Riefenstahl's aesthetic and formal attainments. Though working from within the regime, she nevertheless accurately *records* a historical moment (the genuine ascent and mass adoration of Hitler-as-saviour, 'sixteen years after Germany's crucifixion'), rather than perpetrating something as simple as comprehensive invention. *Olympia*, opening with a misty-mountaintop sequence of which Nietzsche would have approved, covers the notorious 1936 Olympic games held in Berlin. The athletic, and above all *Aryan* physique, is shown as a natural descendant of the classical Greek ideal, as the torch of health and 'purity' through sporting endeavour is literally and figuratively handed down from the ancient world to the Reich. Standing as valuable documents of a pivotal epoch, and as spectacular films even when regarded outside the darkened vaults of historical reflection, Riefenstahl's fascistic odes to Nazi gods represent the propaganda-documentary (which, as the war took hold, became a globally represented form not unique to Germany) at its ideologically excruciating peak.

## WAR AND POST-WAR

At the outset of the Second World War, the nature of documentary altered to reflect the interests at work in that conflict. Filmmakers on the left, who were usually critical of capitalist regimes, moved to uphold positions against fascism, whilst well-known directors of fiction began to turn their services to documentary in the cause of an all-consuming war; concomitantly, the non-fiction film – a medium by which events abroad and in the field could be witnessed by those at home – enjoyed a surge in popularity. Following the December 1941 attack on Pearl Harbor and this provocation's drawing of America into war, the US government prevailed upon Hollywood to produce films in support of the war effort. Frank Capra, joining the military in the rank of major, made a number of propaganda films whose aim was to arouse soldiers' patriotism by elucidating both the general *casus belli* and America's duty to the world. The 'Why We Fight' series, featuring footage captured from enemy sources, didactic animations and fervent voiceovers leaving no doubt as to the films' stance, comprised, among others, *Prelude to War* (1942), *The Nazis Strike* (1942) and *War Comes to America* (1945). Stars such as Walter Huston and the composer Alfred Newman, though they worked anonymously, lent their talents to these films, which not only were mandatory viewing for recruits, but also received a good deal of public screening. Manipulative, full of 'blatant chauvinism' (Levin 1971: 19) and indoctrinatory shallowness, 'Why We Fight' is often rightly chided, but still important at least from a historical standpoint, providing an example of wartime American 'orientation' techniques alongside its bravely assembled, multipart chronicle. John Ford, then America's foremost director of westerns, entered the Navy heading up the Field Photographic Branch; he and his crew, putting themselves in no small amount of personal danger, were on Midway Island xxxx with 16 mm cameras when the critical battle took place. The resulting film, *The Battle of Midway* (1942), earned an Oscar. William Wyler, in the Air Force, made *Memphis Belle* (1944) about bombing sorties over Germany; John Huston, encountering difficulties with censorship, made *The Battle of San Pietro* (1944), a humanistic, movingly anti-war piece that upset the military hierarchy, and 1946's *Let There Be Light*, an apparently non-rhetorical film whose frank depiction of shell-shock victims nonetheless led to its banning until three decades later. Additional films of this era include Samuel Spewack's *World at War* (1943), *The Town* (Josef von Sternberg, 1944) and, amongst many more from Canada, Stuart Legg's

Food – *Weapon of Conquest* (1942) and *Zero Hour – The Story of the Invasion* (1944).

In Britain, Roy Boulting's *Desert Victory* (1943) covered the North African campaign with aplomb, garnering a best documentary Oscar. The Crown Film Unit produced the well liked *Target for Tonight* (Harry Watt, 1941), showing a raid on the enemy that, although composed mainly of reconstructions, is acted out by genuine American and British service personnel – 'from Commander-in-Chief to Aircrafthand' – in the style of a fictional combat film 'perfectly [embodying] the Government's message of a "British way" to win the war' (Stewart 2008: 1). Humphrey Jennings, a founding Mass Observationist, poet and artist, had worked for the GPO Unit, previously making 1939's *Spare Time* (a work that angered Griersonian traditionalists for its refusal to ennoble the working classes, seen here at leisure). With collaborating editor Stewart McAllister, Jennings shaped a technique whereby dialogue from

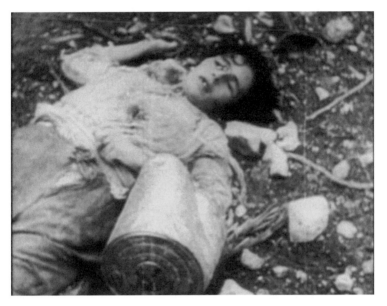

FIGURE 2.2  Huston's *The Battle of San Pietro* (1944)

one location would continue over visuals from another, thereby offering the viewer associative comparisons between unfolding events. Focusing on public stoicism, as opposed to the spectacle and drama of fighting, Jennings, alongside Watt and Pat Jackson, made *The First Days* (1939), around evacuation procedures and the capital's defences for bombardment, and *Britain Can Take It!* (1940, co-directed with Watt), on the Blitz spirit. Firmly in the poetic mode, the American-funded, 18-minute *Listen to Britain* (1942, with McAllister) utilises sound effects and music to accompany images of a country in the grip of war and austerity, but still immersed in the everyday: concerts are attended, books are read, tea is brewed, and journeys are made, all the while under the shadow of barrage balloons and thrumming Merlin engines. (Its value as propaganda was doubtful. Edgar Anstey lamented Jennings's apparent view of his homeland as a 'curious kind of museum exhibit' (Sussex 1975: 144).) *Fires Were Started* (Jennings, 1943), also made with American money, is a feature-length look at the National Fire Service's role in dealing with blazes caused by incendiary bombs. Entirely staged and replete with what are rather unnaturally assured performances of characters under duress, the film is a lyrically composed, morale-boosting period piece that includes many memorable moments; *Fires Were Started* entertainingly mixes jollity and sobriety, contemplation and ribaldry, in a heroising paean to selfless duty. Jennings did not film any actual fires, instead he ignited bombed-out buildings; his methods were apparently convincing enough to impress real firefighters, although as Michael Rabiger opines, the film, and in particular the dialogue, seems 'self-consciously arranged' (1998: 22). Jennings's *A Diary for Timothy* (1945) apposes scenes of the eponymous young boy with images from the recently ended war, telling the story, for a post-war generation whose lives and responsibilities are indelibly coloured by its effects, of a just crusade. The Crown Unit, having served its purpose and in addition created some of 'the few war films that can be seen decades later without embarrassment' (Barnouw 1993: 147), was disbanded after the war, but its members continued to work making sponsored films (Jennings himself, whom Lindsay Anderson called 'the only real poet the British cinema has yet produced' (Leach 1998: 154), died in 1950, while undertaking pre-production). Other films of the period include *They Also Serve* (Ruby Grierson, 1940), *Merchant Seamen* (J. B. Holmes, 1941), the compilation film *World of Plenty* (Paul Rotha, 1943) and *Burma Victory* (Boulting, 1945).

German non-fiction during the Nazi era was composed mainly of shorts and newsreels, inevitably promoting the National Socialist agenda, but not always explicitly. Walter Ruttman was engaged in making the series *Deutsche Wochenschau*, or 'German Weekly', for the government; the suffering of troops was not dealt with, instead the films portrayed practical difficulties encountered and surmounted in the field. Post-Stalingrad, the enemy's aggression was emphasised with greater fervency. Contrapuntally, in Soviet Russia, films outlined the hardship and pain of the soldiers; as the war dragged on, the USSR claimed more victories, and celebrated these in works such as *Defeat of the German Armies Near Moscow* (Leonid Varlamov and Ilya Kopalin, 1942), *Stalingrad* (Varlamov, 1943), and *Fight for Our Soviet Ukraine* (Yual Solnetseva and Y. Avdeyenko, 1943). When the war ended, theatrical documentary diminished in presence, but the technological advances made by the military – especially in the way of camera and sound equipment – would influence the future direction of both fiction and non-fiction filmmaking, as would newly acute audience expectations apropos the presentation of the everyday. Almost immediately, the short-lived Italian neorealism movement, which emerged from the changed political climate, after Mussolini's stifling of creativity, assimilated documentary's use of non-actors, location filming, fast film stock and an interest in socially relevant themes: 'The raw life of a tragic era', as Arthur Knight described it (Levin 1971: 22).

Three feature-length, narrative documentaries, standing above a glut of relatively insipid educational output, define post-war non-fiction in the States: Robert Flaherty's final film, *Louisiana Story* (1948), about a Cajun family whose life is changed by the arrival of drillers from Standard Oil (an arrival about which Flaherty was ambivalent); Sidney Meyers's *The Quiet One* (1949), about a school for disturbed adolescents;

and *All My Babies* (1952), by George Stoney, which amounts to a medical film with sincere emotional depth lending it extra resonance amongst others of its class. In France, Alain Resnais's *Night and Fog* (1955; see Chapter Four), 'possibly the single most powerful documentary ever made about the human capacity for destroying our own kin' (Rabiger 1998: 23), represents a watermark, turning the Nazis' own footage of Auschwitz, liberated a decade earlier, against them. Fellow Frenchman Georges Franju's best known non-fiction works, *La Sang des bêtes/Blood of the Beasts* (1948) and *Hôtel des invalides* (1951), are mischievous, surrealistically infused documentaries about an abattoir and a war memorial, respectively, undertaken at around the same time that countrymen Chris Marker and Jean Rouch were making their first forays into filmic travelogues (in the case of the former) and ethnography (the latter). The Canadian NFB produced films including *City of Gold* (Wolf Koenig and Colin Low, 1957) and Terence Macartney-Filgate's 1958 *Blood and Fire*, which at this time appeared alongside much European and Asian material usually of didactic essence. But, by and large, as Jack C. Ellis and Betsy McLane concisely note:

> Efforts to hang on to the occasion provided by World War II to have documentary-like films playing in the theatres petered out by the early fifties. The war years had marked a high point of documentary achievement. More filmmakers had made more nonfiction films for larger audiences than ever before. Given this vastly increased activity, with films being used in all sorts of new ways, it was assumed by most that the trend would continue onward and upward in the post-war years. Instead, what happened following wartime expansion was a severe cutback in the amount of money available for production, in the number of filmmakers employed, and in the quantity of films produced.
>
> (Ellis and McLane 2007: 152)

'Both in spirit and quality,' opined Richard Barsam, 'the nonfiction film hit its low point in the late 1940s and early 1950s' (Barsam 1973: 225). The coming of television, however, would, in addition to killing off the cinema newsreels, see a boom in other kinds of non-fiction, brought newly into people's homes.

*See It Now*, a 1950s US news magazine show aired on CBS and fronted by Edward R. Murrow, constituted the first series of its kind. In some ways analogous to *60 Minutes*, on air still, the sometimes staid, mostly studio-anchored programmes nonetheless were frequently memorable and politically charged – especially those dealing with Senator Joseph McCarthy's anti-Communist 'witch hunts' and their pernicious implications for democracy. Criticised heavily by subsequent filmmakers for its 'yak, yak, yak, one cigarette after another' approach (Richard Leacock in Saunders 2007: 10), *See It Now*, at its best, indubitably offered a vital critique of American society during a complacent time. At its worst, it engaged, like its lesser equivalents, in 'hopscotching the world for headlines' (Barnouw 1990: 169). Eventually killed by the quiz shows' superior ratings and dominion over schedules, *See It Now* gave way to *CBS Reports*, whose meliorative episodes included Thanksgiving Day 1960's 'Harvest of Shame', regarding migrant workers' struggles against institutionally ingrained hardships, and 1968's 'Hunger in America', which takes credit for prompting the introduction of food stamps. Other significant and influential series of this era include NBC's *Project XX*, harking back to 'Why We Fight'; CBS's current affairs-based and very topical *White Paper*; *The Twentieth Century*, a look at past events often compiled from archive footage; *Close-Up!*, from ABC-TV, which tentatively aired the aesthetically (though not politically) revolutionary first productions from observational pioneer Robert Drew and his Associates, in financial connection with Time-Life's broadcast division; and *The Race for Space* (1958), produced by David Wolper. Stymied in some respects by the demands of the 'Fairness Doctrine', a passive–aggressive means of imposing censorship on films deemed not in the 'public interest' or unduly critical of American government, many of these programmes succeeded in presenting reasonably biting critiques, analyses that culminated in 1971's controversial 'The Selling of the Pentagon' (a CBS Special by Peter Davis), exposing the huge diversion of public funds into militaristic endeavours. The big-name presenters born of the post-war TV documentary boom – trusted, avuncular figures such as Walter Cronkite, Charles Kuralt and Dan Rather – became household names and familiar faces, but perhaps the chief legacy of the first wave of television documentary is the extensive (and some would argue over-) use of 'talking-head' interviews to put across information where no other footage exists; made with television's then low-resolution and small size (theorist Marshall McLuhan would call television, in distinction from cinema, a 'cool medium') in mind, such techniques are excusable, but have led to an overwhelming lack of visual, rhetorical and narrative imagination on the part of journeyman non-fiction filmmakers that pervades to this day.

## OBSERVERS: THE RISE OF THE 'FLIES'

Providing a challenging and dynamic (though not always in every way successful) counterpoint to such programmes were those filmmakers caught up in the observational impulse intensifying in Britain, France, Canada and the USA from the late 1950s. Predicated in no small part on technological innovations, yet not entirely brought into being by any flashpoint of technological determinism *per se*, an urge to get 'out there' on the streets, or intimately with the action, was manifest. Lightweight cameras and, a little later, portable, synchronised sound units gave documentarists (and others, including the playful cineastes of the French New Wave, who followed in many respects the ethos of the Italian neorealists) the opportunity to realise a method of filmmaking freed from the shackles of the tripod and dolly.

The ephemeral Free Cinema movement in Britain sprang from a group of filmmakers broadly on the left, and broadly in favour of a new, poetic representation of the working classes not solely concerned – in contrast to Grierson – with reductive extolments of their value as labour. Against a backdrop of empire in decline, the new 'welfare state' and a minor revolution in the arts that saw the birth of the literary 'angry young man', documentary kicked against the class system's imposition by the 'Establishment', and espoused a revitalisation of proletarian identity. The group's *de facto* leader was Lindsay Anderson; he and others who were eventually associated with Free Cinema (an appellation that Anderson conceded was 'nothing more than a label of convenience' (in Chanan 2007: 154)) – including Karel Reisz, Lorenza Mazzetti and Tony Richardson – had written for *Sequence* magazine, a periodical that criticised American domination of the film industry and called for a cinematic reassessment of the British national character away from the didactic, industrially fixated, sponsor-beholden films of the GPO alumni. Screened at the National Film Theatre in the mid- to late 1950s, *bona fide* Free Cinema pieces are scant (most of the group rapidly moved on to what would become well known fictional works under the rubric of 'kitchen-sink' drama), but lively and noteworthy examples of filmic non-fiction's attitudinal and technological upthrust at this time. Anderson *et al.*'s manifesto stated their aims clearly: 'No film can be too personal. The image speaks. Sound amplifies and comments. Size is irrelevant. Perfection is not an aim. An attitude means a style. A style means an attitude.' Writing in *Sight and Sound* (in 1956), critic Gavin Lambert declared that the newly born Free Cinema 'sprang from non-conformism, from impatience with convention, sadness about urban life', whilst comparing the filmmakers to author D. H. Lawrence (in Ellis and McLane 2007: 198). Understandable technical difficulties meant that, most usually, sound and picture did not tally. Instead sourced from snatches of conversation or music gleaned by the crew where possible, the audio track's disembodied separateness, though at times serving well to 'amplify and comment', means that a good deal of observational verisimilitude is lost to what is now an archaic characteristic born of an inability to match up a so-called 'wild track' with accompanying film footage.

*Thursday's Children* (Anderson and Guy Brenton, 1954) visited the Royal School for Deaf and Dumb Children. An intimate, optimistic portrayal with narration by Richard Burton, the film, as might be expected of a public-relations exercise, paints a favourable picture. More representative is Anderson's ironic *O Dreamland* (1953), which goes to an amusement park in fruitful search of the tawdry and tasteless (and stops cautiously short of lambasting the park's owners and clientele for vulgarity), but it is the triumvirate of Momma Don't Allow (Riesz and Richardson, 1955), Every Day Except Christmas (1957) and Reisz's We Are the Lambeth Boys (1958) that has fairly come to stand for the movement. Shot in a Wood Green jazz club, most memorably whilst the music is in full swing and the young dancers are in enthusiastic motion, Momma Don't Allow is a vibrant, rhythmically composed study, frequently cut to give the illusion of synchronous sound. The favourably received film features a plot, of sorts, involving a debunking of middle-class myths about the supposedly violent behaviour of 'teddy boys' and 'toffs', and was funded by the BFI's Experimental Film Fund to the sum of £425. Every Day Except Christmas concerns the goings-on at Covent Garden Market, and in so doing demonstrates a level of Jennings-like affection for its working-class subjects, as opposed to the cynicism of O Dreamland: 'I want to make people – ordinary people, not just Top People – feel their dignity and their importance,' said Anderson (in Barsam 1973: 235), and he succeeds here in composing a warm tribute to the virtues of ceaseless labour and a whistle-while-you-work devotion to productivity. (That the chain-smoking, jauntily hatted subjects of Every Day Except Christmas today seem anachronistic goes without saying; they indeed seem as if beamed in from an age fondly remembered in anecdotage but difficult, for post-industrial citizens of only a half-century later, to imagine as reality.) Amongst the happily industrious, however, are seen the weary and seemingly aimless; Anderson depicts the nature of Covent Garden as liable to inspire only monotonous resignation, at least for those who do not show the requisite temperament to make the best of the situation. We Are the Lambeth Boys, using unobtrusive, close-up filming techniques, follows some youngsters around their south London haunts. The film discovers, in addition to a predictable quantity of sexual stirrings and shouted expression, an un-stereotypical keenness to fellow humanity and the value of emotional experiences – particularly such as are shared with an inspirational mentor at the Alford House youth club. An at-times charming 'film essay', blighted, like Every Day

*Except Christmas*, by the use of a paternalistically intoned voiceover, *We Are the Lambeth Boys* does its utmost to promote the young men's cheeky congeniality, a commendably liberal view that, spectators of all epochs will suspect, is generous if not rose-tinted.

These films, though owing much to Jennings in their poesis, and to Grierson in their 'valorisation of the lives of ordinary people' (Biressi and Nunn 2005: 43), constitute a significant progression in terms of the working classes' filmic presentation. The slightly anarchic-feeling wryness in evidence throughout Free Cinema, an approach that stemmed from a sympathetic desire to communicate post-war Britain's shifting character and the role of a burgeoning 'youth culture' in drawing the nation away from the years of conflict into an age of new growth (and new uncertainties), allows for and mostly promotes individuality; its general trope is one of tribal belonging, to be sure, but the person is seldom entirely subsumed into a drone-like collective functionality, as was the case in antecedent productions. The lifeblood of the nation, according to Free Cinema, remains its vital base of (mostly older) workers, yet the voice of a new generation – one sees its future not as pre-ordained but as potentially socially mobile – is discernible. Financial opportunities afforded by work performed not solely for industrial or imperial growth, but also for the sake of *personal* reward, brought the chance for typical 'teenagers' to pursue dance, music, rumination on civics and more prolonged courtship: this was, in many respects, a Britain in transition. Of Free Cinema, John Berger wrote: 'It reveals a new kind of vision. Every time an art needs to revitalise itself after a period of formalism ... artists will turn back to reality: but their attitude to reality, and the way they interpret it, will depend on the particular needs of their time. That is why realism can never be defined as a style, and can never mean an acquiescent return to a previous tradition' (in Biressi and Nunn 2005: 44). Sometimes ambivalent about the way its subjects chose to spend their time and money, Free Cinema's attitude reflected a sense of cautious distancing from old certainties; its somewhat Orwellian methods of non-pedagogic, naturalistic study often strove, as much as was possible due to disembodied sound, to give an earthy voice to the people it surveyed (words like 'bloody' found their way into the cinema for the first time, prompting audience gasps and Louis Marcorelles's slightly exaggerated description of Free Cinema films as 'weapons against attitudes of Victorian puritanism'; Marcorelles 1973: 42); and its style partly begat the subsequent epithet 'gritty', a cliché as meaningless and unhelpful as it is overused.

While the French proponents of *cinéma-vérité* were carrying out their exercises in assaying film's anthropological potential – and these exercises were, in the end, few in number – the Canadians of the NFB's 'B unit' were working at their own, parochially fixated variation of observational cinema made without recourse to reflexive strategy. The television series *Candid Eye*, which ran in 1958 and 1959, produced amongst others the Free Cinema-influenced films *Blood and Fire* (1958), *The Days Before Christmas* (1958) and *The Back-Breaking Leaf* (1959), all by Terence Macartney-Filgate. Using (mostly) non-synchronised sound – captured on what would become a standard for location sound recording in documentary, the lightweight, shoulder-strapped Nagra tape recorder – small, 16mm cameras and telephoto lenses, the filmmakers let the story, such as it was, emerge in the editing. These works, which are often peculiar to Canada in their focus, are not concerned with narrative thrust or any obvious agenda; hence they are at times aimless-seeming studies of the quotidian, lacking somewhat in any especial element of interest outside the historical. French-Canadian identity and culture were explored via *Pour la suite du monde* (Michel Brault and Pierre Perrault, 1963) and a number of other projects, though these remain virtually forgotten. *Lonely Boy* (Wolf Koenig and Roman Kroitor, 1962), following the young pop singer Paul Anka, and *Les Raquetteurs* (Michel Brault and Gilles Groulx, 1958), about a convention of snowshoe enthusiasts, however, are minor classics whose intimate following of their subjects and on-the-fly methods foreshadowed the greater technological and dramatic achievements of the 'direct cinema' (confusingly, *cinéma-vérité* is frequently used interchangeably with this term) practitioners to the south. Importantly, direct cinema – which in its strictest sense means *observational*, *sync-sound* filmmaking – was born equally from new technology, and the initial employment of this technology in subtle service of its originator's political masters.

'More than anything else', asserted media magnate Henry Luce in 1960, 'the people of America are asking for a clear sense of National Purpose … What is the National Purpose of the USA?' (in Jeffries 1978: 451). Looking to exploit the growing television market in a way that would reflect Luce's ethos by lending the news schedules some of his publications' well known mixture of social melioration and aspirational leadership, Time, Inc. sought the contribution of an ambitious picture editor at *Life*, Robert Drew, who outlined, in an essay titled 'See It Then' (with reference to *See it Now*), a new form of programme that would improve on the earlier methods of Flaherty and Grierson:

> Grierson's documentaries were instructional in nature. That is, he, as a teacher, which he viewed himself [*sic*], would come up with a thesis for information people ought to have … And Grierson's school of documentary filmmaking on reality, I thought, was propaganda … And propaganda doesn't work, for real people … If Grierson was at heart a sociologist and a propagandist, then Flaherty was at heart a naturalist … and his aim was to discover. [*Nanook of the North*, 1922] was a strange cross of realism and naturalism, of form from the novel, but more than that, from real life. Grierson remained cut off from real life on one hand and the great currents of story-telling on the other … I know that Flaherty set up and posed … but as a theoretician it was to me a compatible, better way of viewing the potential of film for enlightening people … drama would be the spine and strength and power of this particular reporting medium.
>
> (Drew quoted by O'Connell 1992: 35)

Drew wanted to combine Flaherty's commercially potent style – a melding of narrative conventions with footage based on 'discovery' – with the self-effacing recording methods of which his charges (and especially the still-photography veteran Alfred Eisenstaedt) had availed themselves at *Life* magazine. Whilst the *cinéma-vérité* exponents in France were paying tribute to Vertov's *Kino-Pravda*, Drew did not follow this self-reflexive tradition, but focused instead on the potential of discreetly obtained footage. Aware that subjects may, as *Life*'s Wilson Hicks wrote, be 'inclined to think of the photographer as a gross fellow ... who drives nice folks to distraction by his bedeviling insistence on "just one more"' (in Evans 1997: 19), Drew proposed instead to lessen the television cameraman's intrusion. He imagined an ostensibly more perceptive type of broadcast journalism with a 'capacity for mobile reporting on real life in the un-public situations that make up most of what is important about the news' (Drew quoted by O'Connell 1992: 41). As Drew recollected in 1962, 'It would be a theatre without actors' (Drew speaking in the 1994 British television film *Arena: Theatre Without Actors*).

'Voice of God' narration, a patronising (in Drew's opinion) staple of established American current affairs shows, was to be downplayed in favour of 'picture-logic'; there would, ideally, be no directorial interference, prompting of, or interaction with subjects; and available light, natural sound and locations were to be used whenever possible. The major obstacle to bringing about this 'theatre without actors', however, would be the cumbersome film technology of the day. If the will was in place, then the technical means were not. Drew, providentially, would thus assemble a team of talented cameramen and engineers with a common interest in freeing the camera of its restraints: lightweight, *synchronous* recording facilities would prove vital in realising Drew's ambitions.

Donn Alan Pennebaker was a young, technologically skilled filmmaker who had previously made non-synchronous, short observational films such as *Daybreak Express* (1953), a sequence of New York locations set to Duke Ellington's eponymous tune, and *Baby* (1954), a superior home movie following his daughter around a zoo. While editing *Baby*, Pennebaker experienced an epiphany: he became aware that he should not impose a story upon his material at the production stage, but rather let the story and rhythm emerge later, in the film's assembly. Richard Leacock, a friend of Pennebaker and Drew who had worked with Robert

Flaherty on *Louisiana Story* (1948), would also join the group. Leacock, in a similar vein to Pennebaker, was at this time experimenting with hand-held cameras in unplanned situations; 1954's *Jazz Dance*, made with Robert Campbell for Roger Tilton, is Leacock's frenzied portrayal of a dancehall session (the film in many ways pre-empts Riesz and Richardson's *Momma Don't Allow*). Although lacking synchronised location sound, the film gives an impression of synchronal audio and visual events due to its carefully timed, musical sequencing. The filmmaker revelled in mobility, but saw room for improvement: 'I was all over the place having the time of my life, jumping, dancing, shooting right in the midst of everything ... But you couldn't film a conversation this way. It gave us a taste, a goal' (Leacock in Tobias 1998: 47). All the Associates were in agreement that they must depart from the approach of Murrow and others, and strive to bring forth in their viewers a feeling of 'being there' with the action (Leacock in O'Connell 1992: 67). Brothers David and Albert Maysles (Albert would later coin the term 'direct cinema') were recruited, as was, for a short time, Terence Macartney-Filgate; typically, all the so-called Drew Associates would participate in different capacities, depending on what was required, in these early films.

Personally dynamic human subjects, Drew realised, were critical in generating commercial curiosity within a broadcast industry unused to 'picture-logic'. Equally important were the inherently dramatic situations – crises or competitions – he and his filmmakers chose to film. Direct cinema, in its first phase, depended very much on these to give it story arcs and a convincing element of unscripted performance: an apparent, if illusory, unawareness of the camera at which only the media-savvy excel. The Drew Associates' landmark first film, *Primary* (1960), follows John F. Kennedy, then a young senator, in his Wisconsin election contest of 1960 with fellow Democrat Hubert Humphrey, a contrastingly down-home figure. Only partly successful – mostly because the crew's equipment was constantly breaking down, with the result that sound merely intermittently ties up with picture – the film nonetheless does convey a sense of 'national purpose', in this case the

benefits of American democracy and inspirational leadership as perso-
nified by *Life* magazine stalwart John Kennedy, an urbane figure (with an
obvious if basically insubstantial air of political zest) whom the film
subtly but continually endorses. Moreover, as Stella Bruzzi (2000: 131)
writes, Kennedy's 'responsive and engaged style mirrors that of observational documentary itself', a mode that sits 'at the confluence of
contradictory philosophical streams' (Wayne 2008: 83): that of 'scientific' observation, and that of 'sympathetic' response to life's
rhythms.

Direct cinema's obsession with celebrities continued with Drew's
*Crisis* (1963), a more adeptly constructed (by this point the crystal-
synchronised sound equipment was fully functional) promotional piece
for JFK's 'New Frontier' liberalism, centring on the desegregation of an
Alabaman school and the repugnance of Governor George Wallace in
comparison with the good-looking, cinegenic Kennedy brothers. ('I
know what they'll do', remarked Wallace: 'They'll have Bobby Kennedy
looking like an eloquent statesman, and they'll have me picking my
nose' (in Carter 1995: 144). Wallace, seen in *Crisis* slurping his food
and brooding around his mansion, was not far wrong.)

Drew made one more film about his favourite subject. JFK: *Faces of
November* (1963), about Kennedy's funeral, gave Drew personal licence,
albeit too late, to be more poetic and less strait-lacedly journalistic;
broadcasters, faced with a glut of elegies to the curtailed 'Camelot', sadly
rejected what was Drew's most heartfelt work. Other Drew-orchestrated
films of this period include *On the Pole* (1960), a crisis-based film about
racing driver Eddie Sachs; *The Children Were Watching* (1961), a look at
desegregation in New Orleans schools that was for many a first experience of racism addressed in the media; and *The Chair* (1962), featuring
another high-profile crisis, in this case black convict Paul Crump's fight
to have his death sentence commuted.

After the Drew Associates' 1963 break-up, partly due to a lack of
interest from the networks, and partly due to Leacock, Pennebaker and
the Maysles' disgruntlement with Robert Drew's conservatively journalistic need to prioritise story over comment (and by dint of his

FIGURE 2.3 A pensive-looking JFK in *Crisis* (1963)

adherence to the Fairness Doctrine 'disinterestedly' to serve the interests of government), direct cinema found a new voice in rough sympathy with the emerging 'counter-culture'. Leacock's *Happy Mother's Day* (1963) sarcastically critiques the old-school reporting of a quintuple birth, as the bewildered parents find themselves in the eye of a media storm with seemingly only Leacock, his cynical attitude elevating him from the other reporters, for comfort; Pennebaker's *You're Nobody 'Til Somebody Loves You* (1964) is a short about the wedding of LSD guru Timothy Leary (the wedding is never shown – but Pennebaker's filming methods are certainly getting 'hip' to the joss-stick-scented cultural underground); and the Maysles brothers' lively *What's Happening!: The Beatles in the USA* (1964) follows with affection the phenomenon of 'Beatlemania', as the energetic but already worn-out group tours the States enacting an increasingly grating routine in an eternal series of corridors, trains and hotel rooms. *What's Happening!*, its place in film history somewhat unfairly relegated, has the eminent distinction of being the first observational documentary to do entirely without voice-over or narration: an eschewal easily made possible by audiences' total familiarity with the 'Fab Four', and their film-friendly skills as 'natural' performers. The band's facade never slips, but the film is too enjoyably caught up in the act to be spoilt by a shortcoming it shares with the majority of analogous films: a failure to see behind the mask of prac-tised celebrity. Musical stars form the basis of an unofficial quartet of very popular, theatrically distributed documentaries – if you will, 'rock-umentaries' – that trace the rise-and-fall trajectory of the youth culture through its chief means of expression: Pennebaker's epochal *Dont Look Back* (1967), about Bob Dylan on tour, the exuberant, 'flower-power' hymn *Monterey Pop* (Pennebaker, 1967), the sympathetically epic film of *Woodstock* (Michael Wadleigh, 1970) and the baleful *Gimme Shelter* (Mayl-ses and Charlotte Zwerin, 1970).

FIGURE 2.4  Bob Dylan warns of the impending counter-culture in *Dont Look Back*

Frederick Wiseman, though he never worked with the originators, remains the world's pre-eminent direct-cinema purist, still finding an outlet on American station PBS. Nearly always relying solely on diegetic sound, and never using subtitles, story-type narratives or voiceover, Wiseman's slide-puzzle-like films are frustratingly nebulous and grimly austere, yet at times devastatingly acute to American social malaises in their depictions of ordinary Americans trapped in an unfair system and let down by federal democracy. Rapidly moving on from *Titicut Follies'* (1967) unsubtle muck-raking to more considered portraits of public institutions (locations that serve both as microcosms and as arguably too-convenient, ready-made framing devices), Wiseman's early, New Left-influenced satires remain his most intellectually engaging: *High School* (1968), *Law and Order* (1969), *Hospital* (1970) and *Basic Training* (1971) deserve attentive consideration as civically minded, *gestalt* political statements in operation far beyond the initially apparent jumble of vignettes; these are works of protest and reform deeply embedded, for all Wiseman's quasi-anarchic disavowals, in sixties politics and an essential humanity. Direct cinema's influence has of course been massive, long-lasting and pervasive, but few other than Wiseman today stick closely to its strictest tenets. Its initial and extremely naive claims of a new level of objectivity (claims that were almost instantly regretted by those who made them) gave way quickly to a realisation that direct cinema could and should be as subjective and personal as other kinds of non-fiction filmmaking: hence, the observational pioneers have authored a legacy that is undeniably important – and important in a pan-generic sense – but perhaps more about surface aesthetics than ontology or knowledge-gathering. As Peter Graham perspicaciously observed, back in 1964 and only a short time after Drew's Associates had disbanded: '[The observational school] present not *the* truth but *their* truth. The term *cinéma-vérité*, by postulating some kind of absolute truth, is only a monumental red herring. The sooner it is buried and forgotten, the better' (Graham 1964: 36). 'Flies on the wall' (a term the filmmakers hated), one ought to remember, were and are never wholly invisible, nor omniscient. '[T]he documentary as prescribed by advocates of observational realism', stresses Stella Bruzzi, 'is an unrealisable fantasy ... documentary will forever be circumscribed by the fact that it is a mode of representation and thus can never elide the distance between image and event' (Bruzzi 2005: 217).

## HYBRIDS, DIVERSITY, PERSONALITIES: THE 'NEW DOCUMENTARY'

Filmmaker Errol Morris, in a well used but illustrative quote, sums up his and his ilk's feelings about observational cinema:

> I believe *cinéma-vérité* set back documentary filmmaking twenty or thirty years. It sees documentary as a sub-species of journalism ... There's no reason why documentaries can't be as personal as fiction filmmaking and bear the imprint of those who made them. Truth isn't guaranteed by style or expression. It isn't guaranteed by anything.
>
> (In Arthur 1993: 127)

Much of the stylistic history of documentary film, after the heyday of *cinéma-vérité* and direct cinema (both of which were memorably scorned by Werner Herzog for purveying 'the accountant's truth'; McCreadie 2008: 8) can broadly be understood as a reaction against these movements' apparent transparency and lack of bias. Michael Chanan outlines a 'crucial shift in the documentary idiom, almost an epistemological break, in which the old idea of objectivity is seen as naïve and outmoded, and is revoked by asserting the subjective identity of the filmmaker within the [text] of the film' (Chanan 2007: 241). Non-fiction cinema, in film's post-classical and 'post-modern' age, is thus increasingly cross-pollinated, reflexive, idiomatic, reconstructive (sometimes of past events via the archives or re-enactment), autobiographical, personal, polemical, authorial and performative. In keeping with social and political gains apropos civil rights, 'bound up with the moment and ethos of identity politics' (Biressi and Nunn 2005: 74) and aided by the proliferation of smaller video cameras, 16 mm film-funding opportunities and cable television, non-fiction, its technical processes newly (semi-)democratised, also begins commonly to express the concerns and identities of various minorities. In the early 1970s, as Ellis and McLane note, 'a new generation of documentary filmmakers, those who had not lived through the experiences of world depression and WWII, began to come into their own' (2007: 228). Intellectually buoyed by cultural radicalism on the left and the expansion of film studies degree programmes, the ethos behind the 'Hollywood Renaissance' – a philosophy based on assertions of authorship, independence of expression, general counter-cultural sympathy and an informedly mischievous attitude to film conventions – would likewise be manifest in documentary.

Emile de Antonio, though he was already middle-aged in the mid-Cold War period, is notable in this context for, amongst others, the highly politicised films *Point of Order!* (1963); *Rush to Judgment* (1966), an early film about JFK's assassination; *In the Year of the Pig* (1968); and *Millhouse: A White Comedy* (1971). *Point of Order!* was put together from CBS's kinescope recordings of the Army–McCarthy senate hearings of 1954; *Millhouse* brilliantly satirises, through the apposition of archive footage (especially the notorious 'Checkers speech', previously thought lost), Richard (Milhous) Nixon for virtually every personal shortcoming exhibited during the sixties phase of his political career. Most influential, though, is *In the Year of the Pig*, a work that seeks to redress public perceptions largely shaped by television's reflection of the political establishment's interests. The film, more than two years in the making, reconstitutes historical and archival material, juxtaposed with interviews, to comprise an ironic, agit-prop polemic against US involvement in Vietnam – a country in which around half a million young American troops, many of them drafted, would soon be literally and figuratively swamped. Somewhat similar in purpose to the accessibly liberal (and camera-friendly) Michael Moore, de Antonio ridicules authority with ironic montage, but, in distinction, comes from a rather more rigorous and steadfastly Marxist standpoint than the new documentary's doyen.

(De Antonio's committed stance extends to an often-expressed loathing of direct cinema: 'Bland, floury stuff offensive to no one, only the art of films' (in Zheutlin 1981: 158).) From Argentina, the similarly charged 'Third Cinema'[1] broadside, *La hora de los hornos/The Hour of the Furnaces* (Octavio Getino and Fernando E. Solanos, 1968), is both a stylistically diverse, portentously militant attack on Western culture and colonialism (fittingly, the 'retrograde nostalgia' (Shohat and Stam 1994: 264) of the ruling classes is attacked), and a conga-accompanied call for violent action in the revolutionary service of freedom: 'Are there other alternatives for liberation?' ask Getino and Solanos, whose avant-gardism is suggestive, in its multifarious borrowing, of Vertov, Eisenstein and French New Wave luminary Jean-Luc Godard. In totalitarian Cuba, the revolution fostered a paradoxical situation under which filmmakers such as Pastor Vega, Sergio Giral and Santiago Alvarez (a major figure in the Cuban Institute of Film Art and Industry and a collaborator on *The Hour of the Furnaces*) were not hampered by the commercial pressures exerted in democracies. Indeed, as Michael Chanan has described, cinema in Communist Cuba 'became a unique cultural space as a major site of public discourse ... a kind of surrogate public sphere, in which documentary occupied a key position' (2007: 199). Alvarez's striking works include *LBJ* (1968), on President Lyndon Johnson, and *79 Primaveras/ 79 Springs* (1969), an experimental tribute to Vietnamese leader Ho Chi Minh.

*David Holzman's Diary* (Jim McBride and Kit Carson, 1968), a spoof of contemporary non-fiction methods and an early (if fake) example of the filmed diary, skewers the processes and ethos of direct cinema via its protagonist: a filmmaker (played by Carson), defiantly first-person camera permanently in hand, who becomes obsessed with truth and self-discovery. A 'slap against [observational documentary's] truth-telling pretensions' (Winston 2008: 202), the film angered D. A. Pennebaker, who walked out of a screening, saying to Carson, 'You killed *cinéma-vérité*.' Carson, later, perhaps correctly declared that Pennebaker was wrong in his assessment: 'Truthmovies are just beginning' (*ibid.*). '*David Holzman's Diary*', notes James Latham, 'is both an example of and a critical statement about filmmaking theories and practices that would become integral to contemporary documentary expression' (2007: 1). Miles Orvell outlines the influence of this playful, hybridised film on subsequent productions, claiming that Michael Moore's combining of Nichols's interactive and reflexive modes, which jointly interrogate the relationship between subject, audience and filmmaker, 'has its precedents in several other projects dating at least from Kit Carson and Jim McBride's quasi-documentary' (ibid.).

Canadian Michael Rubbo's *Sad Song of Yellow Skin* (1970), an NFB film not about the war itself, but about lives on the periphery, vividly examines the people of Saigon through the personal experiences of young journalists – among them John Steinbeck Jr – on a voyage of discovery, meeting and forming bonds with street children, pimps, dealers and refugees, all dispossessed by the conflict. Rubbo's *Waiting for Fidel* (1974) is a more abiding film (and one that has proved an undoubted and obvious narrative influence on the 'unfulfilled' quests of Moore and Nick Broomfield). Shot inside Cuba with the aim of including the eponymous leader (who had apparently invited the crew over), the feature-length *Waiting for Fidel* instead reveals much about the filmmakers themselves: Rubbo and company never do secure Castro's 'rich and rare' time, but while waiting in their requisitioned mansion and walking amongst the people, engage in a tortuous dialogue on socialism, Cuba, capitalism and other pertinent issues. At the end of this protracted, reflexive dissection of filmic endeavour, the men are seen deliberating over what to do with their footage: 'That's our film: *Waiting for Fidel!*'

*Grey Gardens* (1975), by the Maysles brothers, is a post-*vérité* masterpiece of benign voyeurism – and maybe the pioneering siblings' last work to achieve any significant presence. Concerning the eccentric housemates Edith 'Big Edie' Beale and her middle-aged but still glamorous daughter, Edith ('Little Edie') (who are, improbably, the aunt and first cousin of Jacqueline Bouvier Kennedy Onassis), *Grey Gardens*, a camp curio which has attracted sufficient devotion to qualify as a minor cult, peers into a world of happy isolation as the women's crumbling,

28-room mansion falls victim to structural delapidation and the attention of raccoons. Clearly enamoured of the filmmakers, also familially related characters who likewise are seen and heard (if seldom) in the film, Big Edie and Little Edie seem willing to open their unusual lives to a surprising degree, although in truth many things about the situation remain mysterious – not least the handsome teenage handyman, Jerry, who may or may not be moving in. Distancing themselves further from their roots in strictly observational cinema than they had done with *Gimme Shelter* or the mordant Arthur Miller homage *Salesman* (1968, with Charlotte Zwerin), the Maysles have here discovered a beauty in untypical friendship, and the joy of giving a symbiotically composed filmic voice to the Beales: ever outsiders (and thus a gift to documentarists), but also truly human in their endearing renunciation of all conventional American high society has to offer.

Facing a much darker aspect of American poverty, the Oscar-winning *Harlan County, USA* (Barbara Kopple, 1975) charts the unfolding drama of a miners' strike. Mixing direct cinema with interviews and television news-style vox pops, all to an emotive soundtrack of local workingman ballads, Kopple paints a slightly muddled but rousing, unromanticised picture of indignant passion in the face of biting industrial oppression. Peter Biskind, in *Jump Cut*, noted that, 'Unlike the Pare Lorentz documentaries of the 1930s or the work of photographers like Dorothea Lange and Walker Evans, the film rarely aestheticises the miners … There are no artfully composed shots in *Harlan County, USA* … The film's poetry is not one of the image but of action, clarity, strength' (Biskind 1977: 3). Kopple's political grasp is sometimes tenuous and her sympathies unclear; she offers no alternatives and is maybe simplistic in her treatment of the struggle's moral intricacies – especially concessions given by Miners for Democracy man Arnold Miller. Despite this, it is an affecting portrayal of the honourable, ongoing plight of a proletarian sector blighted by lung disease, murderous thuggery and class war. 1980's *The Life and Times of Rosie the Riveter*, by Connie Field, adapted Emile de Antonio's techniques (of archival salvage augmented with interviews) in order to tell a nostalgic but sour story of women who had gone to work for war – an empowering development iconically (and perhaps unrealistically) represented by the titular Rosie – only to find their new-found status revoked as America's men returned. One of the best known works of 'second-wave' feminist non-fiction from this time, *Rosie the Riveter* looks afresh at women's mid-century struggle for equality, a social issue once more very pertinent by the century's last quarter; in hindsight, the contradictory absurdities inherent in the archival propaganda border on ludicrous: 'They are taking to welding as though the welding rod were a needle and the metal a length of cloth to be sewn', narrates a male voice, clearly aiming at a male audience. *The Wobblies* (Deborah Shaffer and Stewart Bird, 1978) takes a stylistically similar approach in its examination of the Industrial Workers of the World; *Babies and Banners* (Lorraine Gray, 1978) tells, with interview and archive, of the women involved in a motor-industry strike in 1930s Michigan; and Julia Reichart and Jim Klein's *Union Maids*, of 1977, does likewise with the 1930s-based tales of three Chicago women. *Atomic Café* (Jane Loader, Kevin Rafferty and Pierce Rafferty, 1982) uses a wide range of found footage, compiled without recourse to voiceover narration, to make an ironic, blackly humorous statement about the early years of nuclear weaponry. Much of what is used now looks archaic and bizarre, lending it a new contextual potency – released as it was in the midst of international campaigns to ban the bomb – through its displaced, juxtaposed and absurd-seeming anachronisms. (Rafferty would go on to work with Michael Moore, who had sought his advice while making *Roger and Me*.) Other anti-nuclear films from this era – and there are many – include Jon Else's *The Day After Trinity* (1980) and Dennis O'Rourke's *Radio Bikini* (1987). Adopting a different methodology for reconstructing and evaluating historical events, Claude Lanzmann, in his epic Holocaust documentary *Shoah* (1985), relied totally on interviews and witness testimony to put together what remains one of the most captivating studies of the past and its long shadow over the present.

Representing homosexual culture, The Mariposo Film Group's *Word is Out* (1977) and Robert Rosenberg, John Scagliotti and Greta Schiller's *Before Stonewall* (1984) are formative examples of 'queer cinema' – a movement born of mounting calls for gay liberation and equality in America. *The Times of Harvey Milk* (1984), by Rob Epstein and Richard Schmiechen, concerns the life and tragic death of the United States' first openly gay man elected to the position of district supervisor (the accomplished and thoughtful film won an Oscar), whilst in Britain, the work of Isaac Julien, and of the Black Audio Collective, represented a different, usually video-based take on inner-city minority issues: largely those of homosexuality and second-generation ethnicity as experienced under the rule of Britain's long-serving, right-wing Prime Minister Margaret Thatcher (see, for instance, *Handsworth Songs* (John Akomfrah, 1986), and Julien's extraordinary *Territories*, of 1984). Complex, fragmented, challenging and many-layered, these films constitute a vivid expression of sexuality and racial politics possibly unique to their era and geographical origin – although some similarities can be seen in the forthrightly sexual films of controversial American gay rights radical Marlon Riggs, notably *Tongues Untied* (1989), which outraged conservatives (who branded it indecent, naturally for the most part unseen), and *Color Adjustment* (1992). *Paris is Burning* (Jennie Livingston, 1990) is an academically much-dissected film about the subculture, in the Harlem African and Latino communities, of transvestite 'balls': extravagant events in which dragged-up contestants compete for titles, curiously emulative of white aspiration, including 'schoolgirl', and 'executive realness'. Raising questions around gender as performance (see also Judith Butler's groundbreaking book *Gender Trouble*, also of 1990), filmic subjectivity, subject and authorial positions (just what is the white, educated, middle-class Livingston's attitude and ethos?), *Paris is Burning* was successful financially and critically, bringing to wide public attention a social group, existing within a bigger urban community, with its own tribal values formed both as a celebratory reaction to this state of being and as a means to escape it. Terrence Rafferty praised 'a sympathetic observation of a specialised, private world' (in Flinn 1998: 434), but Livingston's socially detached ethnography, as Peggy Phelan opines, might still be considered to constitute the retelling of an all-too-familiar story from a vantage of privilege and ideological domination: 'What could be more reassuring to a white public … than a documentary affirming that colonised, victimised, exploited, black folks are all too willing to be complicit in perpetuating the fantasy that ruling-class white culture is the quintessential site of unrestricted joy, freedom, power and pleasure' (in ibid.: 435).

Pioneer of the 'personal essay' film, Ross McElwee's Sherman's March (1986) marks the beginning of a tendency towards director-as-subject and first-person filmmaking. Using funds he was given to make a film about General William Sherman's 'March to the Sea', McElwee, recently and painfully broken up from his partner, instead used the money to examine his relationships with women and the lives of the women he encounters on his journey. Educated at film school, as were his analogues Alan Berliner (see, especially, Nobody's Business, 1996), Nick Broomfield and Molly Dineen, McElwee's works, also including Something to do With the Wall (1991) and 2004's Bright Leaves, evince a dryly comic and very entertaining perceptiveness that has proved influential on and emblematic of an officially unaffiliated group that British television filmmaker–journalist Jon Ronson, in a tracing of his own methodological forebears, has impishly called Les Nouvelles Égotistes:

Then I came along and nicked it from Nick Broomfield (whom I still consider the master of the art) for television series from The Ronson Mission (1993) to The Secret Rulers of the World (2001), and then Louis Theroux came along and nicked it from me for his 1998 programme Louis Theroux's Weird Weekends. Over in the US Michael Moore's rendition of the style just evolved, I think, in the way African and Indian elephants just evolved. I was surprised by the accusation made [that] the implication that what we do is utterly divergent from what the Maysles brothers did. The Maysles brothers also distrusted the fly-on-the-wall convention of pretending real reality was unfolding while a camera and sound team were frantically composing shots in the corner. This is why they would include glimpses of themselves in the mirror, for instance. And surely that's all we do – only on a slightly more epic scale?

(Ronson 2002: 1)

FIGURE 2.5 Nick Broomfield, trademark boom in hand, is berated by white supremacist leader Eugène Terre'Blanche in *The Leader, his Driver, and the Driver's Wife* (1990)

Ronson, though, was already sensing a backlash against 'faux naïfery' – the delicate and potentially grating art of pretending to be a little dim in order to ingratiate oneself and lower the defences of otherwise unco-operative subjects (an art learned perhaps in part from Peter Falk's fictional Lieutenant Columbo, and to this day practised wholeheartedly by Sacha Baron Cohen's Ali G, Borat and Brüno incarnations). Moreover, at a 2002 conference at London's ICA, Ronson was charged, alongside his fellow *Égotistes in absentia*, with driving the final nail into *vérité*'s coffin. According to his accuser, a passionate advocate of Drew-era direct cinema-type filmic invisibility, Ronson and his like had 'cruelly trampled the purveyors of documentary truth, elegance and aesthetic *vérité* in our stampede to the top' (ibid.). An understandable preference for visual elegance is one thing, but the argument cracks when one considers that, ostensibly, the most ubiquitous contemporary upholders of direct cinema traditions are 'reality television' staples – chiefly the class-warfare rabble-rousers *Wife Swap* and *Big Brother* (both programmes have eclipsed, for instance, the subtler efforts of Frederick Wiseman, whose 'reality fictions' are not condensed into a litany of ratings-chasing outrages, or 'the televisual equivalent of bear-baiting'; Roberts 2007: 92); whilst their aesthetic is indeed fly-on-the-wall austere, their premises are cynically contrived under the disavowing fig leaf of 'social experiment', and their tabloidish, demagogic pillorying-by-media of the fame-hungry and interpersonally unpleasant represents *anything but* a reflection of found reality (although it speaks volumes about the timeless public appetite for scapegoating, hypocritical censoriousness and sexual gossip).[2] Should not the participants, in a genuine microcosm, be allowed to show their true colours, even if they are revealed as unabashed bullies, racists and schemers? Ronson is far from an observational purist, but nonetheless educes a level of what at least appears like authentically personal revelation, via his peripatetic interactions, not often attained by the machinations of reality TV and arguably never attained by its revered ancestors, most centrally Franc Roddam and Paul Watson's 'warts-and-all' 1974 British series *The Family* and its 1972 American prototype: neither convincingly reconciled an ethos of detachment with the inevitability of editorial shaping and their subjects' behavioural adaptation; in fairness, as Wiseman has repeatedly stated, the likelihood is that nothing ever will.

Going from 'glimpses in the mirror' to fully appreciable film personalities in their own right, the new documentary's most high-profile practitioners have unremittingly redrawn direct cinema's boundaries, and unflinchingly questioned its essential values, while clearing their own paths to an enlightenment informed by, but not ruled by, the observational commandments of Robert Drew or the anthropological pretensions of Rouch and Morin. That non-fiction's household names are almost all those of men, however, is mysterious. By contrast to the almost exclusively male-run world of fiction film production, women make up around 30 per cent of documentary filmmakers active today; as yet, though, we have not seen a single distaff version of Moore or

Spurlock: a woman filmmaker, in other words, forwarding themselves on a global basis as either populist rabble-rouser, political spokesperson, unabashed star/entertainer, or all of those. (Somewhat similar in her interactive/observational modus operandi to Nick Broomfield, Molly Dineen, who is her own camerawoman, remains a peripheral, heard-but-not-seen presence, both in her films and in culture at large.) Is this because our culture is somehow suppressing female filmmakers, or is it because women documentarists simply prefer a lower-key approach? Marsha McCreadie's research, somewhat inconclusively, indicates that the comparative dearth of big names within non-fiction might have something to do with 'the male ego', or that 'possibly women are not that terrific in the salesmanship aspect … women [filmmakers] don't present themselves as representative of society in any way, nor apparently do they feel compelled to star in their own docs' (see McCreadie 2008: 18–19). *Say My Name* (2009), by Nirit Peled (discussed in Chapter Five), attempts to wrest the rockumentary form away from its masculine base – it is, however, undeniably culturally obscure by comparison, say, with Sacha Gervasi's vacuously funny but rampantly masculinist *Anvil: The Story of Anvil*, of the same year. Some innovative exceptions, often made for television and in multi-part formats, exist that 'star' female presenters-cum-auteurs: for example, Jennifer Fox's six-episode, nearly six-hour exploration of global womanhood *Flying: Confessions of a Free Woman* (released in 2007 but shot over four years) which, in addition to conventional direct-cinema and film-diary/essay methods, employs a 'pass-the-camera' technique to give voice to numerous women across divides of class, race and geography. The organisation *Women Make Movies*, dedicated to independent films by and about women, continues to back similar, marginally distributed projects, including many festival-acclaimed documentaries; *Searching for Sandeep* (Poppy Stockwell, 2007) features its maker, on camera, taking a light-hearted look at lesbian Internet dating – but again, these films, by women, tend towards intimate coverage of minority issues as opposed to headline-seizing, big-tent matters. Of the ten top-grossing box-office documentaries of all time, according to boxofficemojo.com, none is by a woman (though the arguably co-authored – with its star – *Madonna: Truth or Dare* (Alex Keshishian, 1991) makes number 7). Best Documentary Oscars show a little more diversity, but not much. It is food for thought, and perplexing, that the best known female documentarist is still Leni Riefenstahl.

## BOOM

The most recent pivotal moment in non-fiction film history is the mushrooming of documentary at the box office, a phenomenon beginning in and around the early 1990s. Films as diverse as *The Thin Blue Line* (1988) and the almost universally praised (yet creatively uninteresting) *Hoop Dreams* (1994) opened up non-fiction markets and paved the way for what Bill Nichols has described as a commercially efficacious but discursively problematic return to classically dramaturgical emphases:

> The willingness to revert to the fictional filmmaking techniques that Dziga Vertov railed against and that John Grierson regarded with disdain also marks a dramatic renaissance of the documentary form … Theatrical documentaries attach considerable importance to emotional effect. They acknowledge their subjectivity and the clash of perspectives that constitutes the arena of public debate … To what extent is staging acceptable? Can interviews be fully scripted? Can past events be recreated and different versions of an event be presented to convey different conceptions of what happened? … Every documentary seeks to win the viewer's trust, which it then violates at its own peril.
>
> (Nichols 2007: 82–3)

Just as there is no guarantee of absolute truth, there are no easy solutions, but it remains incontrovertible that, as Macdonald and Cousins note, 'At their best, today's documentarists pick and choose from the forms of the past – the observational, poetic, essayistic, investigative or explorational – and produce films which are more varied, imaginative and challenging than anything we've seen before. At their worst they churn out thousands of hours of virtually indistinguishable "reality TV"' (Macdonald and Cousins 1998: 311).

Some critics have taken such issue with non-fiction's profitable turn away from an earnestly conveyed cinema of 'reality' to the 'varied, imaginative and challenging' that they have proposed a new nomenclature: 'mondo films', or 'docuganda' – though manipulation, obvious or otherwise, has of course been intrinsic to the form since at least the work of Robert Flaherty. As Michael Moore has said, unapologetically: 'I make movies. I write books. I don't write nonfiction books or fiction books. Same thing for movies.' Criticising President Bush, and by extension every officially sanctioned version of informational truth, Moore, during his Oscar-acceptance speech for Bowling for Columbine, declared that 'We like nonfiction because we live in fictitious times' (both quotes in McCreadie 2008: 71–2). Perhaps, then, in 'fictitious times', the documentary has a responsive duty to explore and partake in the cultures of celebrity, subjectivity and political manipulation: certainly, such immersive, Wiki-age talking points have proven popular means of attracting audience sympathy, along with consequent commercial benefits; though as often, non-fiction has turned back to conventional, timeless storytelling. A short list of recently successful (and stylistically disparate) productions of critical note, only very partially representative of the bigger picture, might include To Be and to Have/Être at avoir (Nicolas Philibert, 2002), Spellbound (Jeffrey Blitz, 2002), Capturing the Friedmans (Andrew Jarecki, 2003), The Fog of War (Errol Morris, 2003), Bowling for Columbine (Michael Moore, 2003), Fahrenheit 9/11 (Michael Moore, 2004), Super Size Me (Morgan Spurlock, 2004), Metallica: Some Kind of Monster (Joe Berlinger and Bruce Sinofsky, 2004), March of the Penguins (Luc Jacquet, 2005), Wal-Mart: The High Cost of Low Price (Robert Greenwald, 2005), An Inconvenient Truth (Davis Guggenheim, 2006), The 11th Hour (Leila Conners Petersen and Nadia Conners, 2007), Taxi to the Dark Side (Alex Gibney and Eva Orner, 2007), Man on Wire (Simon Chinn and James Marsh, 2007), Nanette Burstein's American Teen (2008) and

Werner Herzog's *Encounters at the End of the World* (2008). To account for the differing means by which non-fiction filmmakers have used the properties of cinema to create a filmic *art* of truth, and so that we might understand the distantly wrought origins of – if not attain answers to – Nichols's eternally pointed questions, the second part of this book initially returns to the early years of the theatrical documentary, and to a box-office hit from the Canadian Arctic.

## NOTES

1 Octavio Getino and Fernando Solanos would go on to coin this influential term, in *Afterimage* 3: Summer 1971.

2 2009 is turning out to be a vintage year for documentary-related crime. On September 10, just as I was about to submit this manuscript, the bizarre news broke from Istanbul of nine women who had been duped into starring in Internet pornography. The victims, eager for another kind of exposure, had answered an advert, signed a contract and entered a *Big Brother*-style house. The 'show' – which the respondents thought was to be called *Somebody's Watching You* – was non-existent; the cameras were, however, very real.

Part II

# **Reading non-fiction**

Case studies, concepts and criticism

# 3

## PIONEERS

### *NANOOK OF THE NORTH* (ROBERT FLAHERTY, 1922): NARRATIVISING THE REAL

Robert Flaherty, a man born into indubitably patriarchal times, and history's most legitimate claimant to the nowadays rather odious but unavoidable designation 'Father of Documentary', grew up on the Canadian border, becoming both a successful mineral prospector and a keen explorer of foreign lands – especially the vast, barren plains lying due north. In his late 30s, he took to combining his interest in travel with a burgeoning desire to record these lengthy expeditions and communicate a mutual affection for the indigenous people he had met and befriended. On the suggestion of Sir William Mackenzie, Flaherty took a motion-picture camera to the Arctic, thereupon enthusiastically shooting 70,000 feet of film; however, these efforts would go up in flames in the relative safety of a Toronto editing facility, as the result of a dropped cigarette. 'I wasn't sorry', he recalled: 'It was a bad film; it was dull – it was little more than a travelogue. I had learned to explore, I had not learned to reveal' (in Flaherty 1972: 13). Flaherty's carelessness was propitious; the cigarette sparked not only the destruction of mediocre footage, but also by extension a determination that would see

Flaherty, this time amply funded by French fur company Revillon Frères, return to the Inuit of Hudson Bay and bring back a work of engaging dramatic impetus – a contrived, composed and compromised tale of a family's struggle against the elements – whose arrangement borrowed ingeniously from contemporaneous fiction cinema.

Arguably the most significant documentary ever made, the resulting story of 'life and love in the actual Arctic', despite – and in part because of – its faults, brings a degree of theoretical force to bear on discussion of all narrative documentaries to follow. In addition, it invokes numerous (and timeless) ghosts: the problematic ethical and moral phantoms, already touched upon in Part I, whose continued presence at non-fiction filmmaking's discursive feast should be addressed by all students of the form, in the twenty-first century and beyond. *Nanook of the North*, foundationally useful due to its textual richness, formal legacy and (mostly) justifiable status amongst scholars as a beautiful but deeply flawed touchstone of occidental endeavour, is an imperfect kernel containing much of the DNA from which every 'creative treatment' of actuality (or at least those treatments that seek a classically dramatic resonance) has since – however indirectly – sprung. It is nowadays, without doubt, an old-seeming film; its purposes are not always noble, nor its 'savages' all they seem; it is sometimes quite apparently the doubly archaic product of Flaherty, a 'child of the last age of imperial expansion', hauling another's history from the grave in order to stage an ethnographic song and dance while he himself supposedly 'lived like a king' (see Winston 2008: 24–5); but it is critical to this study: if one understands *Nanook*, a film 'turbulent with self-contradiction and with all the doctrinal issues that still confront documentarists' (Thomson 2002: 293), one begins to understand non-fiction cinema's perpetually inherent tensions.

Opening with a series of establishing vistas and intertitles that set out the film's stall while giving some context (much as had Flaherty's counterparts in the world of fiction cinema, especially the influential D. W. Griffith, with whom Flaherty had met), *Nanook* immediately emplaces its subjects within the discourse of ethnographic study, albeit from a populist and distilled perspective. Affectionately, but somewhat patronisingly, the titles tell of 'The fearless, loveable, happy-go-lucky Eskimo', set upon by the 'sterility of the soil and the rigor of the climate', or by the ravaging inexorability of a natural world gloriously unbound by technology. And it is this 'natural' drama of 'simple' humanity ('fearless' and 'cheerful') versus the elements, a humanity paradoxically made viewable (and at the same time significantly altered) by the corporate presence that was encroaching on the already dying romantic ideal Flaherty wanted to convey, that will herein be both 'revealed' and constructed. 'The mysterious Barren Lands – desolate, boulder-strewn, wind-swept', aesthetically captured and providing a sort of condensed, romantically emotive poetry of desolation, form the backdrop against which Flaherty casts for an improbably nuclear family of good-looking protagonists whose countenances echo soothingly the silent era's facial ideals; in so doing, the filmmaker transposes his potential audiences' own narrative expectations onto the northern lands, in the process gaining identificatory purchase by rendering some aspects of the 'mysterious' quite the opposite. Time and again unable properly to reconcile urges both to mount an honest exhibition and 'distort a thing to catch its true spirit' (Flaherty in Barsam 1973: 133), Flaherty, an empathetic but nonetheless implicated agent of that which he despises, simultaneously disavows the impact of the modern world, especially if that impact does not tally with his romanticism, whilst imposing its devices as he sees fit: as William Rothman has noted (1997: 9), and as we shall see, Flaherty is capable of quite progressively self-reflexive expression, yet this is continually counteracted by a dissonant compulsion to render everything satisfyingly familiar, or retroactively in keeping with his idea of what might or should comprise a palatable (for a mass audience) storybook depiction of a less-than-unspoiled way of life. 'The urge I had to make Nanook came from the way I felt about these people, my admiration for them', said Flaherty (in Barnouw 1993: 45). For Flaherty the showman-cum-'salvage ethnographer', this was crucial; he would, as much as possible with respect to his sponsors, sanctify a time 'before the white man', and in addition, with little apparent sense of irony, make over the Inuit as cinematic darlings playing out ethnographically acceptable versions of themselves and their lives.

A trope crucial to Hollywood-style dramaturgy, and therefore a trope crucial to Flaherty's reinvigorated commercial purposes, is the hero, most often uncomplicated and easily construed, as hard-toiling product of the wilderness. Consequently, we first see 'Nanook' in close-up and (nearly) meeting the lens with his gaze. Looking modest yet staunch, his furred hood pulled up against the cold, he has in probability been told to present himself for the camera, and for the film's (the 'big aggie''s) eventual viewers. This more-or-less introductory shot, an implied condensation of Nanook's nature, says much, though the character says nothing: here is a man whose face, Flaherty seems to say, deserves attention and scrutiny as an individual, as the paternal face of human nobility pitted in opposition to a treacherous world still in

FIGURE 3.1 Nanook regards the camera (*Nanook of the North*, 1922)

existence long after the closing of the frontier – an expansive territorial drive that had proved pervasive in its shaping of American notions of masculine identity, curiously here projected upon one whose traditions are threatened by the economic results of that drive. Moreover, Flaherty, perhaps nostalgic for the days of masculine heroes like his own father, is allowing the titular patriarch, at once a lone cowboy *and* a family-centred Indian, a look of gravity and dignified *authority*, as befits his role as provider and hunter ('natural' roles to which industrialised man had grown comfortably unaccustomed), and as we must expect: even a 'happy-go-lucky' tribe, after all, needs a leader of conventional masculine resource if it is to be understood, within the scheme of modern, Western familial mythology, as sympathetically functional, or the basis of a 'story of life and love'.

'This first encounter with a "star" mentality', observes Richard Barsam (1973: 128), 'taught Flaherty much about the handling of "actors"'; though the stars of *Nanook* are, of course, not professional performers, they appear relaxed, unselfconscious and quite used to the camera: important traits for Flaherty in choosing who might best represent the Inuit. (Rothman conversely sees Nanook, during the introductory close-up, as 'enduring the camera's scrutiny' (1997: 7), a view that implies either Flaherty's ignorance of this possible spectatorial perception, or a certain honesty not typical of the rest of the film.) Nanook's soft-featured wife 'Nyla', 'The Smiling One', must inhabit her role also, offering a counterpoint and a customarily feminine balance to Nanook, the tough-but-kind hunter–father, the 'Bear'; we see Nyla making good on her name, and rocking playfully. There is without doubt a great mutuality in these frames – surely Nanook and his clan are communicating something approaching equality with Flaherty and a knowledge of cinema's power as imparted by the explorer (who processed on location and showed him the rushes in order to educe a cine-literate 'performance' of sorts, prompting David Thomson to venture that 'the most charming thing about [*Nanook*] is the sympathy between Nanook and Flaherty, the way in which the Eskimo smiles cheerfully at the Great White Father and draws the camera effortlessly into his life';

Thomson 2002: 294); but throughout the film's initial vignettes, and at the heart of Flaherty's whole venture, can be traced many liberties taken with the situation's truth – liberties that do not tally with Flaherty's supposed attitude of 'non-preconception', as his wife called it (Flaherty 1972: 10).

Some picture-postcard scenes of 'typical' Eskimo life – stylistically primitive and a hangover from the 'travelogue' film – work efficiently to set up Nanook's filmic household around an ethnocentric fantasy of monogamy. While the explorer certainly felt 'a powerful romantic belief in the purity of native cultures, and [that] his own culture was spiritually impoverished by comparison' (Aufderheide 2007: 28), ironically he was not accepting, in his capacity as a showman, of the Inuit's tendencies towards non-Western social arrangements. Flaherty's charming and quaintly comical depiction of Nanook, followed by an almost implausible number of ever-smaller others, emerging from within the protective husk of his kayak, tells us in no uncertain terms that we are witnessing the bringing forth into daylight, or into scrutiny, of a *family*, opened up like a Russian doll: this is a bronze-age family, which uses scant-growing moss for fuel and lives 'happily' at odds with its deadly surroundings, but one contemporarily recognisable and, to Flaherty's intended customers, morally acceptable. 'Nanook', moreover, in keeping with this spirit of manipulation and mythic condensation, was renamed (from the more unwieldy Allakariallak), and 'Nyla' (in fact only one of Allakariallak's wives) was in reality called Alice Nuvalinga. Downplaying or ignoring the other women's relationships to 'Nanook', the director sets up the Inuit, for entirely subjective reasons of narrative cogency, as 'low-temperature versions of bourgeois democracy' (Wollheim 1980: 14). 'These recastings', observes Brian Winston, 'as much as any direct faking or reconstruction, are what is ideologically significant in Flaherty's *oeuvre*. The major ideological thrust of his films lies in the universalisation of capitalist relations to other cultures' (Winston 2008: 25).

Early in the film, perhaps to decentralise such problematic issues, the clan makes its way to the 'Trade Post of the White Man', an obvious site of difficulty when addressing Winston's noted 'universalisation' apropos the pre-industrial culture Flaherty was trying to extol. Set up as 'authentic' hunters, especially Nanook, vanquisher of 'seven great polar bears, which in hand to hand encounters he killed with nothing more formidable than his harpoon', the Inuit, traders now to a fur company but supposedly not compromised or disgruntled by such a necessity, ply their wares in exchange for 'knives and beads and bright coloured candy of the trader's precious store'. Flaherty then presents a wide shot of a multitude of pelts, hung up for inspection and filling the frame. This is a spectacular sight, which articulates a number of unintentional dissonances. As William Rothman puts it, in his eloquent study of the film, 'This is at once an awesome display of the bounty of nature and an appalling testimonial to the magnitude of the slaughter sanctioned and exploited by the "white trader" (that is, by the fur trade that also sponsors Flaherty's film)' (Rothman 1997: 10). As the titles have attempted to illustrate via their reassurances of Nanook's tribal individualism, though, this should be taken less as evidence of a 'catastrophic intervention' (*ibid.*) into Nanook's way of life, and more a testimony to his tribally authentic, enduring abilities as a 'great hunter' – abilities that are now sold, quite beyond their natural means, at market. We see relatively little of the trader, whose presence is not, after all, ultimately desirable to Flaherty, but we do see more of Nanook's cute dogs, and his and Nyla's equally cute young child, 'one Rainbow, less than four months old', equated with the animal world in a verbal comparison with the dogs: 'Nyla, not to be outdone, displays her young husky, too.' Sitting with and petting the puppies, the baby nestles amongst the furs, absorbed into an anodyne world of commerce here seen to be harmonious in its co-relations with nature, for which read the Inuit, the dead polar bears, the dogs and all the land's resources upon which they depend. The taut, and in many ways threatening, facets of a natural sphere obviously exhausted in response to commercial exploitation are (tenuously) bound together by Flaherty's discourse as a simply construed, common-sense commodity offering mutual benefit: the new generation is thus, in *Nanook of the North*, quickly assimilated into the workings of a *caring* capitalism, coddled by its cinegenic mother, who still is sweetly smiling.

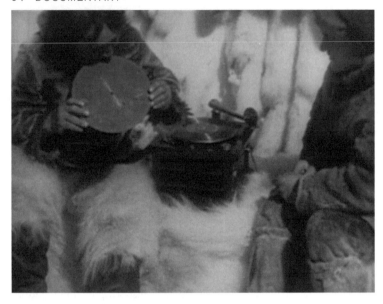

FIGURE 3.2 One of *Nanook of the North's* (1922) more implausible moments

This urge to render the Inuit as blissfully ignorant semi-animals (the ethnographic 'Other') extends to the next, extraordinary vignette. A title explains that 'In deference to Nanook, the great hunter, the trader entertains and attempts to explain the principle of the gramophone – how the white man "cans" his voice.' The trader cranks his record player, much to Nanook's apparent amusement, and lets the disc play; grinning widely, the 'Bear' then takes the record and *bites* it. We are, presumably, supposed to infer that he is trying to ascertain whether or not the disc contains a living entity – something that can, in Nanook's 'primitive', 'childlike' mind, be consumed, as all entities in his world – and, with deference to Western paediatric psychology, the world of an orally fixated baby – can. In other words, Flaherty is asking us to believe that Nanook is so unused to technological mimesis, or the process of recording life's sounds and pictures, that he must test and evaluate the record by mouth. Of course, this was not the case, merely a disingenuous attempt by the filmmaker to offer up an amusing tidbit to fans of condescending, Victorian-style cultural reduction. Flaherty had lived with the Inuit for years and indeed worked with them, and especially Nanook, on a technological basis. Far from being ignorant of such things, Flaherty's subjects eagerly learned modern skills, as Erik Barnouw explains: 'The full collaboration of Eskimos had already become key to his method. This seemed a philosophical necessity but also, in working alone, a practical necessity. Some of the Eskimos soon knew his camera [an Akeley] better than he did: they could take it apart and put it together – and did so' (Barnouw 1993: 36). But, aware of Flaherty's requirements, and that 'the big aggie' would have to come first, Nanook went along with direction: at moments like these, Flaherty becomes the very essence of the Victorian imperialist, unable to see fault or contradiction in his methods, which veer towards the regressive ethical bankruptcy of the carnival sideshow. The scene of one of Nanook's children, Allegoo, being offered castor oil by the trader for a stomach complaint caused by an overdose of 'sea biscuits and lard' is less patronising and provides an endearing moment (the bemused look of genuine disgust on the child's face, addressed to Flaherty and out yonder to some abstract future viewer); yet it is a metonymic and only superficially trivial betrayal of the relationship's corrupting essence, the trader attempting to redress a balance that has become upset due to his intrusion on the fundamentals of Inuit life. As a brief comic interlude whose function is both to counterbalance the dramatic concerns to follow and, more importantly, reassure of the benign intentions of Revillon Frères when dealing with the 'simple' Inuit, the gramophone and castor oil diversions speak volumes about Flaherty's conciliatory attitude to his backers, his basically imperialist heritage and his ultimate attitude to the importance of absolute truth.

Where Flaherty is undeniably ahead of his times, however, is in terms of narrative as applied to the documentary – his insightful ability to narrativise life, notwithstanding this imposition's ideological implications,[1] marks him out as one of cinema's true, if typically flawed, pacesetters. After a walrus hunt that Flaherty had asked the Inuit to perform 'done as in former days, before the explorers came' (Barnouw 1993: 36), during which the filmmaker ignored desperate pleas for help with his rifle, the film's second, and most imperative, act, begins: half an hour in, with the intertitle 'Winter'. The previous scenes all contain some inherent drama (will Nanook make the kill?), or didactic content (this is how the Eskimos build a boat), or comedy (the child has drunk the nasty, unfamiliar medicine of the trader); they are ripe with intentional and unintentional meaning; the basics of temporally and spatially logical continuity editing are in place (even if there are no analytical edits, such as inserts or action matches, and the camera never moves other than to tilt and pan); but they are all essentially random, unrelated and discrete. What the second section of the film offers is cause-and-effect narrative: the telling of a continuous story proper, with all the conventions of cinematic storytelling organisation in place. As Brian Winston notes:

> Flaherty's genius, and I do not use the word lightly, lay in building his story ... out of bits that by no means necessarily went together in this particular way. Understanding not just how to manipulate his 'everyday' material but also what dramatic necessity imposed on that manipulation is the essence of Flaherty's contribution. He was obeying the generally understood requirements of structuring a multi-reel fiction film at this time. As the subheadings for a chapter in an early screenwriting manual put it: 'Sequence and Consequence; Logical Cause and Complete solution; Sustained Climax; all Expectations Fulfilled.' That is exactly what happens in *Nanook* after 'Winter'.
>
> (Winston 2008: 111)

Flaherty, subsequent to what William Rothman (1997: 18) calls a 'Shakespearean transition' (specifically, how Nanook's killing of the walrus '"causes" nature to respond, "causes" the onset of winter'), arranges his material around the principles of dramatic composition. It matters not that events did not happen in the order he compiles them; what is important, as he had said all along, was the 'big aggie', and this extended, most importantly, to the methodology of compilation. This is *Nanook of the North*'s most innovative feature, and one it bequeaths in abundance to the general formal lexicon of screen documentary.

The first of the 'Winter' scenes (the intertitle here is possibly a little extraneous) features the family, due to what Flaherty tells us is extreme hunger – and Nanook indeed seems ravenous when taking his hard-won sustenance – embarking on an arduous journey to better-stocked hunting grounds. There is now a certain stateliness and gravity to the visual compositions, which paint a bleakly alien picture; the intertitles seem less whimsical and more directly concerned with imparting a genuinely oppressive sense of nature's barriers: they speak starkly of 'the fury of winter gales', 'gigantic blocks' of ice and 'chaotic wastes' that stand between Nanook's and his brood's destination. For the first time, there is a feeling that these people might not in fact always be so 'happy-go-lucky', and that their lives are not those of infantile primi-tives. After half an hour, Flaherty's film, having partly dispensed with the cheery patronising of its subjects, hits its stride and begins, spor-adically, to engage on a level much deeper than the travelogue. 'The Bear' traps a white fox, which, while it is a good plaything for his son, turns out to be no meal, so the group must press on and camp for the night.

In what is maybe *Nanook*'s most famous scene, the hunter, with a skill and speed accentuated by Flaherty's captivating treatment, builds an igloo. The scene is relatively adroitly edited, demonstrating an acuity to basic continuity principles, as Flaherty cuts between different vantages on the same action, different widths of shot and Nanook's son as he plays on his sledge. Rhythmically (in respect to the 'flow' of the cuts) and aesthetically, it is the film's most accomplished piece of montage, a technique to which the director obviously has grown used. Moreover, it is clear from this scene's construction, more so than in any previous section, that Flaherty is continually communicating his requirements to the Inuit, who repeat tasks and actions so the director can obtain an assortment of angles; the viewer will, after seeing this, likely have some appreciation of how such a home is built (or, at least, how it was done in the days prior to the white man), and this information has been put across, with some panache in respect of filmic précis, in a short period. Though Flaherty's intertitles sometimes are verbose and unneeded, at the conclusion of the igloo-building scene he dallies, quite effectively, with the device of intrigue apropos what will be made of a block of ice. 'Audiences', notes Erik Barnouw, 'do not know the purpose of the "one thing more". They soon discover: a square of snow is cut from the igloo, and the ice becomes a window ... The sequence has often brought applause. Part of the satisfaction lies in the fact that the audience has been permitted to be, like Flaherty himself, explorer and discoverer' (Barnouw 1993: 40). Finally, to top off the episode, Nanook emerges into the daylight from the door he has cut, smiling at the camera as if to say 'Done!' So that the audience might discover what the inside of the igloo looks like, Flaherty, famously, had Nanook build a special half-igloo (an 'aggie igloo') that would let in sufficient light for the camera. In the scheme of things an entirely permissible slight of filmic hand – and the only option in keeping with the film's didactic and observational mission – the false igloo stands as a convenient symbol for every technically crucial 'manipulation' ever faced by documentarists. If the option is not to show, not to 'reveal', an igloo's interior for fear of misleading one's audience or digressing from total fidelity to life-as-found, then by extension every supplemental light and boom microphone enters and changes the pro-filmic world to the point of what might be considered unethical distortion. (Flaherty's less allowable distortions, and there are many less obvious yet more pernicious than the bisected igloo, are of a different and usually more ideologically loaded variety.)

The rest of the film comprises a number of illustrative scenes (including Nanook teaching his young son to shoot a bow and arrow, in so doing giving the illusion of maintaining traditions largely eradicated by the arrival of the white man: this is the 'salvage' aspect of the film's 'salvage ethnography'), and sequentially concatenated – that is to say given temporal relationships, within the film's narrative, for the purposes of spectatorial appreciation – travails: the entourage catches a seal, but its meat sparks a savage fight between the dogs (that are not always containable as man's best friend, even by Nanook), leading to a delay in the search for refuge; there is then a blizzard, which prompts an urgent race to a 'deserted igloo' – actually the same igloo as before, the footage having been revisited to use shots of the family going to sleep and hence capping the film's chronology with an easily understandable reference to a (temporary) finality common to us all. 'Almost perishing from the icy blasts', inform the titles, 'and unable to reach their own snowhouse, the little family is driven to take refuge'; thus, at the climax of the film, we are not offered a conventionally satisfying resolution, instead Nanook in some respects bravely implying that life's hardships will endure, after this day and night's difficulties have been surmounted – and indeed endure, in distinction to the neatly tied-up strands of the Hollywood 'master narrative', despite 'The Bear''s noble struggle. As Richard Barsam, an enthusiastic endorser of Flaherty, describes, 'The film ends here, but it is not a happy ending; the family is lost, the dogs are shown sleeping under a heavy blanket of snow, and there is no suggestion that morning will come, or, when it does, that it will be good ... if the previous footage has not suggested that Nanook and his family have the strength to get through a fight, then no tacked-on ending would do it anyway' (Barsam 1973: 135). But then perhaps that is the point, and perhaps it is at this stage that Flaherty is most successful (if mostly accidentally so) in putting across a basic and difficult truth in which his project is implicated: no matter if his film shows a fallaciously nostalgic version of Inuit existence, there will in all probability be no generally pleasing conclusion to the story of Nanook, for as the twentieth century wore on, his people's age-old customs were gradually worn down by the encroaching march of civilisation, a danger as real, as difficult to adjust to, and as inexorable as the elements. 'Two years later', records Frances Flaherty, 'Nanook was dead – as so many of his people died – of starvation' (1972: 16). It now seems more likely that Nanook, already coughing up blood during filming, died of tuberculosis, a prehistoric disease but not, unlike the empty stomach and its usefulness as a motif suggestive of primal competition, one that held any romance for Flaherty, who surprisingly was little affected by his hero's death.

Contemporaneous critical response to Nanook was strong, Robert E. Sherwood remarking that 'It stands alone, literally in a class by itself. Indeed, no list of all the best pictures of the year or of all the years in the brief history of the movies could be considered complete without it' (in Barnouw 1993: 42). The legacy of the film, surprisingly to those involved, extended even to the most disposable levels of trash and kitsch culture. 'Ten years later in Berlin', Frances Flaherty wrote, 'I bought an Eskimo pie. It was called a "Nanuk", and Nanook's face smiled up at me from the wrapper' (1972: 17). A Broadway song of 1922 celebrated the film with the asinine lyrical declaration that, 'Polar bears are prowling, Wintry winds are howling, Where the snow is falling, There my heart is calling: Nanook! Nanook!' (see Barnouw 1993: 43). 'Such was the impact of this first film of its kind,' reminisced Frances, with not inconsiderable naivety, 'made without actors, without studio, story, or stars, just of everyday people doing everyday things, being themselves' (Flaherty 1972: 17). Of course, and as we have seen, Nanook of the North does, in its way, use actors; it does, in its way, use story; it does use its own cast-for and rehearsed stars; and these 'everyday people' are not, in every respect, either 'everyday' or 'being themselves'. The ever-outspoken documentarist Emile de Antonio offers a rejoinder typical of the anti-Flaherty school: 'I realise now, after years of work, how uncomfortable I am with the myth of Flaherty and why. The charm and power of his camera are marred by distortions, lies, and inaccuracies which pander to a fake romantic, fake nature-boy view of society … Nanook is a masterpiece of cinematography, and grossly wrong. The Eskimo did not live apart from Western influence. Nanook was not self-indulgent and romantic: he was an actor in a film by a self-indulgent romantic' (in Zheutlin 1981: 158).

It would be unfair, though, to let the naysayers have the last word. Nanook can teach us much, in its falsifications, of how documentary engages with the world, with actuality, and with the wider language of a culture-bound humanity forever given to palimpsestic reconsideration in a perpetual struggle for power and identity. 'Are we to condemn the whole work of the medieval painters because they showed the mother of Christ dressed like a medieval woman, or St. Jerome in what looks surprisingly like a Dominican habit?' asks Hugh Gray (1950: 47). Flaherty was categorically a man of his epoch, burdened by unresolved paradoxes related to a business model within which, to get his films made, he simply had to work. Wilfully caught up in an ethnographic paradigm of multiple falsehoods, Flaherty strove to communicate these to the masses via the popular cinema: a tool he did not entirely understand, but made widely respected use of nonetheless. Preconceptions he may have had, but when it came to the practical essentials, Flaherty learned his art almost totally on the job: 'We were going into interesting country, we'd see interesting people. I had not thought of making a film for the theatres. I knew nothing whatsoever about making films' (in Barsam 1973: 127). As a prototype – the first documentary to absorb the methods of fiction entertainingly and effectively – it occupies a hallowed and, in the end, untouchable place in film history, both regardless of and because of the fact that it is imperfect. Inevitably, it was compromised by commercial factors; inevitably, it reflected the bourgeois mindset of the 'Big White Chief'; but beyond its situation as a politically incorrect period piece hewn from materials that make up a fairly inaccurate portrait of a community under siege by progress, it is, in several equally appreciable ways, an invaluable voyage of *cinematic* discovery.

## *THE MAN WITH THE MOVIE CAMERA* (DZIGA VERTOV, 1929): MONTAGE AND IDEOLOGY

If *Nanook* can be seen to epitomise the realist/naturalist approach to non-fiction, or the construction of a story through tropes and conventions inherited from the cinema of narrative fiction, then *The Man with the Movie Camera* takes a mostly different tack. In fact, the two films represent opposing facets of the same coin: both reconstitute reality to portray versions of the world mediated via film form and art, yet Vertov's methods and ideas, though they too deal with and in basically didactic processes of illusion, are fiercely opposed to Flaherty's (not least because the patrician explorer sought to invoke a romanticised, imperialistically imagined past, whereas the Soviet attempted to galvanise and motivate for an exciting and productive future based on his and his political mindset's collectivist ambitions). *The Man with the Movie Camera* – in some ways a work more of the avant-garde than of the Bolsheviks – is not a politically committed film in the sense of constituting fervent or *explicit* partisan argument, but, like *Nanook*, it is replete with ideas and specifics born of its epoch and its creator's cultural heritage. It is an idealistically conceived, composite-city symphony (filmed in Moscow, Kiev and Odessa) of alternate shocks and mesmerism, coruscating visual effects and self-commentary, intended to work in diametric antagonism to the American 'Dream Factory' of Hollywood. 'Starting today', wrote Vertov in 1923, 'we are liberating the camera and making it work in the opposite direction' (in Roberts 2000: 19).

Born Denis Kaufman in 1896, Dziga Vertov (the name means, very roughly, 'spinning at speed') was the eldest of three brothers, all of whom had an impact on global cinema; the youngest, Boris, went on to shoot in France for Jean Vigo and in the States for Elia Kazan, while Mikhail, a filmmaker in his own right, collaborated with Vertov as his cameraman, most notably on *The Man with the Movie Camera*. Vertov learned the art of film by working (against a backdrop of emergent Constructivism and Futurism) on revolutionary newsreels, among them *Kino-Pravda* – a filmic equivalent of the Communist paper *Pravda* – which allowed him to experiment with techniques of *montage*, or methods of apposing and sequencing shots to create meaning, as per compatriots Lev Kuleshov (who claimed to have taught Vertov) and his famous experiments in contextualisation, and Sergei Eisenstein, who did much to develop the theory and practice of editing as applied to his celebrated early prototypes of the drama-documentary. (The dialectical, colliding systems at work in Soviet montage, fittingly, could be said to reflect

Marxist dialectical materialism: the interactive, history-shaping kinetics of the class struggle. '[M]y view [is] of montage as a collision', wrote Eisenstein: 'montage is conflict ... Conflict lies at the basis of every art' (1929: 21).) Producing material for the so-called agit trains, which brought State-endorsing films to the provinces and thus illiterate peasants, convinced Vertov of the primacy of the image over text: moreover, footage found in reality, and this footage's more mutually resonant nature, thought Vertov, would henceforth be dominant over filmic conventions learned from the theatre via Hollywood. *The Man with the Movie Camera* is one of a number of documentaries made by Vertov and his 'Kinoks' in the late 1920s and early 1930s, prior to Stalin's official sanctioning of 'socialist realism': the others are *The Eleventh Year* (1928), *Enthusiasm* (1931) and *Three Songs of Lenin* (1934), but it is the film under current study that has proved the most vital and the least concerned with obvious adherence to the Party line.

Vertov, *de facto* head of the mysterious 'Council of Three' (actually consisting of Vertov, his wife Elizaveta and his brother Mikhail), expounded at great length on his theories and passions; most concretely, his beliefs regarding film can best be summarised by considering his ideas on the 'kino-eye': an idealised and worshipped vision of the film camera as a potentially omniscient, omnipotent recorder–shaper of reality, and a superior instrument to the human eye, something Vertov regarded – via his own, fallible eyes, of course – as a comparatively fallible organ. The kino-eye, during the course of its activity, could capture, rupture, apparently shift space and time, create dynamic effects of motion and temporal distortion, repeat, emphasise and catch 'life unawares' for later recontextualisation and exhibition. (Despite his works' foundations in reality, 'Vertov', notes Graham Roberts, 'is as much the child of [early cinematic illusionist Georges] Méliès as the Lumières, however much he might deny it'; Roberts 2000: 49.) The kino-eye would be the ideal tool, according to the Kinoks, to render the old bourgeois cinema forever obsolete, in its place instituting a new and aesthetically challenging 'cinema of facts' in sync with Russia's Stalin-led era of sweeping industrialisation. Vertov's

1923 manifesto, *The Council of Three*, puts it in fervently sweeping terms: 'Upon observing films that have arrived from America and the West and taking into account available information on work and artistic experimentation at home and abroad, I arrive at the following conclusion … The most scrupulous examination does not reveal a single film, a single artistic experiment, properly directed to the emancipation of the camera, which is reduced to a state of pitiable slavery … I am kino-eye, I am a mechanical eye. I, a machine, show you the world as only I see it' (in Macdonald and Cousins 1998: 53, 55). In the magazine *Kino-Fot*, in 1922, the filmmaker, a man not indisposed to verbiage in the name of promotion, effervesced with exhilaration at his own potential: 'We proclaim the old films, based on the romance, theatrical films and the like, to be leprous. Keep away from them! Keep your eyes off them!' (in Roberts 2000: 18). Although this view, *pace* Shub and Eisenstein's particular and often contrary ideas apropos film form, is as ironically hidebound – and in its own way quite blinkered – as many other proclamations stemming from the October Revolution, it nonetheless condenses the standpoint of a creative radical determined to bring cinema to the service of all people, not through blatant rhetorical propaganda or the vulgarities of Western dramaturgy, but through the persuasiveness of a freshly motivated medium positing Soviet humanity as symbiotic with its mechanical agents and beautifully functional, *productive* surroundings, in which the camera, and by extension film as a whole, is implicated anew.

*The Man with the Movie Camera*'s only titles come at the beginning, and read like another of Vertov's manifestos: 'This film presents an experiment in the cinematic communication of visible events: without the aid of intertitles, without the aid of a scenario, without the aid of theatre. This experimental work aims at creating a truly international absolute language.' Vertov's ambitions, then, are clearly grand in their scope: as the 'author–supervisor of the experiment', he will attempt to construct a film truly 'comprehensible to the millions' (Vertov in Roberts 2000: 30), a universally meaningful statement capable of leaping linguistic and artistic barriers, and a means of removing – and making plain by

FIGURE 3.3 The Man begins his work (*The Man with the Movie Camera*, 1929)

contrast – the burdens of narrative convention. After a brief special-effect sequence featuring Mikhail Kaufman (who appears in the film, continually, as the 'man with the movie camera', though this designation more properly belongs to his brother) superimposed atop a giant (and therefore presumably super-potent) film camera, we enter an as-yet empty movie theatre. The projectionist loads a reel (the very reel we are about to watch) onto his equipment, which, like any other machine, the director savours; the curtains are drawn back; and while vacant chairs eerily swing their seats up and down, partly in anticipation of human occupants and the coming mechanical attractions, and partly in a demonstration for us, the final viewer, of Vertov's manipulative powers of magical animation, the audience enters. Whilst one spell – the 'mesmeric' spell of Hollywood-style cinematic invisibility – is broken by Vertov's reflexivity, another – of unbridled dynamism and rhythm, and freedom from uniform temporal and spatial coherence – is cast. This, one senses, is a world quite removed from that of Flaherty or Griffith, yet all the same a world intimately and ironically connected to reality via its blatantly contrived effects: all these admissions and displays of quasi-magical artifice, Vertov repeatedly endeavours to suggest, render the world of *The Man with the Movie Camera* an essentially truer place than that of a diegesis hiding itself behind the proscenium of classical storytelling. 'The reflexivity of *Man with the Movie Camera*', notes Michael Chanan, 'fulfils the function which the Russian formalists called *ostrenanie* – estrangement or defamiliarisation – a process aimed at destabilising routine forms of perception, breaking the habit that "prevents us from really looking at things" (in Fredric Jameson's phrase), and which is in fact the recovery of perception, and therefore potentially subversive' (Chanan 2008: 84.) (Though the kino-eye, of course, is not above practising its own kind of mass hypnosis, frequently inculcating its points via pounding repetition, often in sympathy with the machines it depicts and celebrates.) The kino-eye, in its simultaneously honest and enigmatic wisdom, will hence show the workings of life, and cinema-as-life (though this may not, strictly speaking, comprise a 'cinema of fact'); moreover, it will serve, enlighten, teach and engage the Soviet society from which it sprang by offering up a view of 'the soul of the machine … '. In a phrase betraying a desire to effect change by methods arguably as psychologically underhand as any at work in Hollywood, Vertov spoke of his desire to 'train the new man' (Vertov in Feldman 1998: 42). To train, one must remember, is chiefly taken as meaning to 'instruct and discipline' – an ethos at odds with the avant-garde's professed artistic precepts apropos the rejection of deference to learned tradition, if not with Vertov's ideological leanings. Vertov's 'liberated' cinematic lesson may well be 'working in the opposite direction' from the grand illusions of the capitalist west; it may be a great deal of fun; and it may not obviously be marching to Stalin's orders: but at its heart, a lesson in conformity it most definitely remains.

As the orchestra – a group presented as a single, multi-part organism perfectly trained and in sync with both its instrumental appendages and the machines of projection – awaits its cue to begin accompanying Vertov's images, the lights dim, and Vertov holds back for a suspenseful moment, absolutely in control of timing and response. Then, after the conductor's baton has been allowed to fall, reel one begins. Not, as it happens, with a jarring or awesome display of trickery, but with an anticipatory establishing sequence that, though heavily fragmented, is reminiscent of American dramas. The camera, somewhat voyeuristically, tracks into a window, behind which – at least that is the editorial suggestion – a woman sleeps; the rest of Vertov's compound city also slumbers, its edifices, adverts, shop windows and dummies, street lamps, carriages, municipal grounds, telephones, cars, tables and trees awaiting daytime use and appreciation by the public, some of whom are apparently forced to sleep on park benches (Vertov does not hold back from showing destitution, but this is the life of the unproductive, and thus a life of unfavourable contrast with the comfortable woman in her bed rested and ready to go to work). Through these images, Vertov lends what is ultimately a heavily experimental film a relatively conventional starting point grounded in commonly experienced filmic *and* innately human narratives; moreover, the filmmaker does not right away present the spectator with coruscating or challenging material: instead of plunging us, *in media res*, into the astounding world of the kino-eye, Vertov chooses to create a kind of suspenseful, though contextually reassuring, calm before the cinematic storm. *The Man with the Movie Camera*, in its initial moments, carefully and deliberately orientates the viewer in preparation for what is to come – in this respect, Vertov defers to traditional notions regarding the power of cinema to engage psychologically on a human level, and this power's roots in narrative identification. For, despite his wish for 'total differentiation from the language of theatre and literature' (see Feldman 1998: 47), the 'supervisor' is quite aware of classical storytelling's effectiveness, astutely realising that to begin his experiment with a display of technical magic would appear both meretricious and entirely obfuscatory. In other words, Vertov wants to pull us in to his artistic world, and to achieve this, he allows us a period of recognition. Although the viewer might well infer a sense that the city, and Vertov's film, are at this moment coiled in readiness to burst into movement with the arrival of a new day (and perhaps a new dawn of post-New Economic Policy (NEP), self-sufficient Soviet socialist productivity freed from the 'disease' of capitalism represented by the NEP's sanctioning of a mixed economy), *The Man with the Movie Camera* nonetheless requires, if it is to function most effectively, a formal backdrop inherited from much earlier modes of communicative expression.

Vertov (who never seriously questions the ontology of the image, preferring to posit his compositions, and the mimetic aspect of the kino-eye, as beyond the jurisdiction of reflexivity) continues to break down urban space into its constituent parts, which 'asleep' and in close-up appear both familiar and unfamiliar; at this moment, the city's atomised components seem strange, even as they remain purposeful but as-yet unused parts of a much bigger human–mechanical machine waiting for crucial activation. Cogs lie static; wheels sit unturning; bobbins stand unspinning. Then, the eponymous Man arrives, carrying his revitalising, reanimating equipment: a camera on a tripod (the shots, of course, must at times remain steady, controlled and precise, making order out of chaos and finding discipline in *planned* execution and sympathy with the pro-filmic). It is the Man who will bring everything to life; even if in the cold light of putative reality he is undoubtedly merely another part of the new city, a functionary like everyone else – in the realm of the cinema, so Vertov implies, the city is his and his alone for description and motivation: he can even make pigeons fly backwards. In a simultaneous homage to and critique of extant silent films involving such scenes of easily constructed tension, the Man is seen preparing to film a speeding train in motion as it approaches his position of vantage on the track. Suddenly, the spectator is thrust, along with the Man, into Vertov's manifesto proper. Just as the train is about to hit the Man, his foot snags and there is a moment of (spoofed) peril before he breaks free and the train rushes past, depicted in a rapid, disorientatingly multi-angled array of different shots edited to provide a metaphorical wake-up alarm or rhythmic cockerel's crow for both the film's eventual audience and Vertov's filmic city. It is at this point that the film's metre changes, and that the city stirs into waking action. The young woman, earlier seen asleep, wakes up, fastens her stockings and washes (obviously this mildly titillating act has been staged for Vertov's benefit to give the appearance of total and privileged access to the metropolis's inner sanctums); in the first of numerous such visual equivalences, the streets too are literally and maybe symbolically cleansed – literally of the old dirt of the past, figuratively of the old policies of V. I. Lenin; the vagrants, who, unlike the young woman, are disquieted by the Man's presence, blink into the sunlight; vehicles begin to fill the streets, while the airfield readies its planes and tram lines are greased; and we again see the poster (featuring a rather un-Soviet-looking, debonair and shushing man) advertising the German film *The Awakening of a Woman* (1927), though Vertov does not yet reveal its title, preferring to use the pictorial image alone as an instructive counterpoint to his more vital form of (un-)silent cinema.

Many close-ups of the camera's lens apparatus, and the Man's cranking of its handle, are intercut with the film-within-a-film's initial observations; Vertov continually reminds us that we are watching the product of his labour, a work carried out in symbiosis with the constructs of his artistic mind, in the domain of the cinema simultaneously part of and aloof from the Soviet society it arranges and represents with often playful intent. In a montage sequence drawing a comparison between the human eye and non-organic conduits for light, the film associatively splices shots: of the young woman, who scrubs her face and repeatedly blinks; of some Venetian blinds opening and shutting; and of the camera's iris mechanism – which adjusts itself, the implication is, independently of its operator, to take in the world with an accuracy and precision unavailable to a humankind not supplemented by the fruits of industrialisation. (Frequently, the Man is relegated to second fiddle in favour of his magically animate machine; the title *The Movie Camera and the Man* might be more accurate and speak more of Vertov's beliefs: the film, observes Seth Feldman, works not so much 'from sunrise to sunset, but to the beat of an apparatus' (Feldman

1998: 49), and it is this general apparatus, on every level, which dictates the functionality of the city.) Mikhail/the Man happily hears the call of duty in order to achieve optimal productivity, as, or so Vertov claims by apposition, do the other workers in service to the Soviet idea and in harmony with their machines, here fetishised and romanticised as extensions of man. Vertov, less concerned with the softer melodies of poetic reflection than other city symphonists, depicts the city as a massive organism thrumming to *utilitarian* rhythms and rhymes: its Golem is of steam and coal, of smoke, metal, skill, divided labour and applied muscle, all of which are filmically intertwined by Vertov and Elizaveta's editing to give the impression of a giant, interconnected mesh.

Mikhail and the eye-machine, appropriately, given Vertov's aims, get everywhere amidst the bustle of a working day, filming from difficult vantages and in potentially hazardous situations (though we never, of course, see Vertov's camera: there is perhaps a natural limit on this kind of reflexivity, lest a film's textual coherence disappear into kaleidoscopic self-scrutiny). Many times availing himself of classically continuous shot-to-shot relationships, Vertov likewise does not consider it beneath him to pay respect to those spectacular or analytical aspects of Hollywood he finds useful: 'To the American adventure film with its showy dynamism … the Cine-Eyes say thanks for the rapid shot-changes and the close-up' (Vertov in Roberts 2000: 66). Climbing buildings, trains and cranes, and sitting between passing trams and high up in an open-topped car, the Man – though the Man to all intents and purposes stands in for Vertov – is at pains to demonstrate his peripatetic nimbleness and, moreover, his ability as a *worker*: he is a proletarian Harold Lloyd or Buster Keaton, toiling to entertain and educate for the Red cause. Scenes of ostensibly thrilling simplicity, in *The Man with the Movie Camera*, seldom are devoid of extra political significance. Travelling alongside some well-to-do, flapper-hatted women seated in a fast-moving carriage (these are to be taken as typical 'NEP women', remnants of a certain middle class who had benefited from Lenin's concessions, which officially ended the year prior to the film's release), the Man, standing proudly and precariously, films one of the ladies self-consciously mimicking his hand-cranking; later, she hands down to her maid a huge, heavy-looking trunk. This, Vertov seems to be saying, is the behaviour of an outmoded citizen, not only one who acts as if she is the master of slaves, but also one who is not happy or relaxed in the presence of *Kino-Pravda*, symbol of progression and revealer of truth.

A clear enough point, in the scheme of things clearly expressed. However, Vertov, sensing the need to impose a juncture, has another statement to make: mid-way through this observational sequence, in an extraordinary display of experimental chutzpah aimed at deconstructing the process of the kino-eye itself, Vertov, rather than cutting *to* the chase, cuts *the* chase; the film thus abruptly freezes a horse mid-gallop (faintly echoing Eadweard Muybridge's equine experiments), and we see some stills of faces and street scenes (and images of the labelled canisters from which they came), followed by Elizaveta at work in the edit room apparently putting together these shots. Unafraid to interrupt his rhetorical flow for the sake of a greater, *gestalt* rhetoric whose cinematic intelligence and sagacity is at such moments equal to that of any of his contemporaries, Vertov shows us, in Keith Beattie's words, how 'the combination of film-eye and film-truth vigorously inscribes a form of documentary display which relies on showing, not telling, to achieve aesthetic resolution and a perception of a revolutionary reality' (Beattie 2008: 45). Employing a series of static images that nonetheless still function together 'kinaesthetically' (according to a set of semi-mathematical principles taking into account every aspect of the shot (the *film-fact*), its relative organisation and inherent composition) and in context to create a type of 'documentary display' whose mode differs from that of the film at large, *The Man with the Movie Camera* now endeavours to revolutionise on the level of aesthetic construction. Elizaveta brings the single fragments to life, one after the other giving movement, context and meaning to expressions and scenes that previously were photographically poetic and enigmatic, yet not empowered by motion – and this is indeed in some ways a film about life as moving through time, and about Vertov's control over temporal perception (a manipulative strategy to which cinema is especially suited); when the 'chase' of the NEP women resumes, the spectator is brought back into the identificatory frame (and reminded of the film's more overt political leanings), having been jolted from this fairly conventional, Griffithesque mini-narrative of pursuit into another story of how cinema, in an age of large-scale industrial–human integration, comes to perform its wonders. '[I]t is not enough', wrote Vertov, 'to show bits of truth on the screen, separate frames of truth. These frames must be thematically organised, so that the whole is also a truth' (Aufderheide 2007: 40). As Patricia Aufderheide explains: 'Like Flaherty's "Innocent eye" of the artist and Grierson's claim to "creative treatment of actuality", Vertov's claim to the editor's right to organise the chaos of real life into a communist truth was permission for the filmmaker to do exactly as he wanted' (ibid.). Put another way: Vertov realised, with remarkable acuity and quite against the trends of the time, that his peculiar form of lesson would be more memorable for deconstructing its own didacticism.

Vertov and company, then, will take the time – and in doing so, shape the time – to demonstrate the power of film in their hands. And, as they are aware, this power is perhaps all the more effective, provocative and entertaining for allowing the viewer intellectual privy to a central reality at the core of documentary cinema's discursive quandaries: even if Vertov would postulate *Kino-Pravda* as the noblest form of truth, he is still acknowledging with some relish that this truth – a truth whose political importance to Vertov is enormous – is heavily sculpted and mediated by multifariously interactive forces and personnel. 'In *Man with the Movie Camera*', states Michael Renov, 'the flow of images is repeatedly arrested or reframed as the filmic fact is revealed to be a labour-intensive social process which engages cameramen, editors, projectionists, musicians, and audience members' (Renov 1993b: 31). Though there are limits to what Vertov can and will show in this regard (he does not make plain techniques behind the film's numerous visual effects; and he uses a proxy, Mikhail, to extend his arm into the profilmic without going as far as featuring himself – revelations that might shatter the illusion as extensively as to be the equivalent of Flaherty gleefully revealing the half-igloo), it is, for 'political' documentary, a tentative step into relativist assertion and its associated philosophical realms. *The Man with the Movie Camera* avers its *version* of reality-truth as *Our New Soviet Truth*, as something stridently conceived for the general ideological good in its 'heroic attempts to shield the proletariat from the corrupting influence of film-drama' (Vertov in Winston 2008: 166), but its representative claims are throughout (at least partially) qualified rather than blinkered by propagandistic adherence to exactly such storytelling in the name of doctrine or dogma. It is precisely, and paradoxically, Vertov's controversial (to the USSR's filmic purists), puckish dissection of his own methods, coupled with a wilful disinclination to base the film on a foundation of political hectoring, which distinguishes *The Man with the Movie Camera* from any number of contemporaneous productions – including those of Sergei Eisenstein – that more obviously seek to endorse a regime, however stylishly they may go about this.

By the film's mid-point, the city is in full swing, and the camera, which is repeatedly compared by editorial association with other machines of direction and organisation, such as traffic signals, is hard at work recording life's rituals, happy and sad, big and small. For unobtrusive outdoor shots, a prerequisite in order to realise literally ambitions of recording life unawares, Vertov constructed a sort of tent, posing as a telephone repairman so that he might capture 'life as it is', albeit usually from afar – witness, for example, the elderly woman weeping into her handkerchief at a graveside, a remarkable and poignant depiction of human misery made possible only by furtive operation. Candid indoor filming, however, was harder: Vertov's equipment was noisy, and filming nearly impossible without first diverting subjects' attention; nonetheless, the filmmaker manages an impressive level of access, and those before Vertov's lens demonstrate an equally admirable ability to carry on (almost) regardless. (And why not? After all, as Walter Benjamin remarked, 'the newsreel offers everyone the opportunity to rise from passerby to movie extra' (in Chanan 2008: 50).) A couple gets married, somewhat sheepishly; another couple gets divorced, somewhat more sheepishly (Vertov, echoing the process of matrimonial severance, then splits a shot of the street into a V shape; life's personal attachments and detachments, as Vertov makes plain, find an analogue in the methods of film editing); a funeral takes place, the coffin and corpse filmed in what could be construed as intrusively close proximity; and a baby is born into the world, the assertion is, only to die as part of the inevitable cycle of life: the pivotal moments of human existence, intercut, compared and mixed up, are thus unflinchingly represented during this segment, and in addition given fresh, condensed meaning by Vertov's playful, exceedingly cinematic reordering of time and perception. All the while, we are continually reminded, the workers keep working, the Man keeps cranking, the editor keeps cutting, and the machines keep moving on and onward, intersecting and splitting again (the maybe overly recurrent motif of the trams draws attention to the film's shifting and splicing) into a future of refined, cyclical reproduction. Death is herein nothing to be scared of, for it is natural and gives way in the blink of an eye (another motif suggestive of human vision's limitations) to the new, of which the all-seeing kino-eye, as opposed to the old, blinkered arts, is a vital organ; the past, including the old Soviet past, must be left to die; and progression in every way is the absolute key to building a utopia. Later, in the film's most celebrated and, to 1930s audiences, scandalous moment, Vertov will utilise a split-screen device to make it appear as if the Bolshoi Theatre – 'that icon of traditional Russian performance' (Feldman 1998: 41) – is falling inwards into itself: a moribund symbol of creative staleness giving way to Soviet renewal.

Praising honest, whistle-while-you-work labour as virtuous by comparison with NEP woman, the film cuts between shots of a woman being made up, unsmilingly, and a toiling woman, dowdily dressed down and merrily slapping mortar on a wall; similarly, hair is attended to, and nails are filed, alongside images of less vainly productive jobs stitching clothes and servicing machines. Different types of manufacturing and industry are juxtaposed with Elizaveta-as-editor-worker (and again, as always, the camera) examining film strips whilst her chatting comrades sew, sort newspapers and run tills with joyful dedication to the task in hand. The pace of the sequence picks up, and we see a young woman packing cigarettes into cartons, crosscut with a telephone exchange and its wall of massed sockets incessantly plugged and unplugged. In increasingly fast motion, Vertov combines techniques of filming and montage, using these together sympathetically to construct an energised, frenetic portrayal of super-efficient labour; humans, machines and the machinery of cinematic art are conjoined in total, rhythmic harmony, speeding towards a filmic climax – of film-fact melding with film-truth – during which Vertov reintroduces images of all manner of professions, sometimes for only a few frames, in a bid to dazzle with artistic and technical excellence and perhaps for a moment fuse in ecstasy, creatively speaking, with the mechanisms he has filmed. This sequence, more than any other in *The Man with the Movie Camera*, offers undeniable proof of the Kinoks' essential joy in cinematic freedom; beyond its political purpose, and a certain 'technological fetishism' (see Roberts 2000: 94), the cigarette-packing section is a simple, persuasive thrill. Never, indeed, has the Bolshoi Theatre seemed so redundant. In a documentary that has shown us death and pain, now is the time for life not caught unawares, but seized and reprocessed, appropriately, into something truly magical whose inherent character has been morphed by the *potentiated* medium of film into what remains a transcendently captivating, labour-intensive *work* of art.

Work, until this moment, has of course been a thematic watchword for Vertov – and the 'man–machine' episode, as something of a warm-down, includes Mikhail's filming of a coalmine, a steel mill and a gigantic dam, all of which are posited as emblematic of successful Soviet heavy industry. But, as a counterpoint, the film now shows us people and their (mostly young and female) bodies at leisure, on a beach, tanning, stretching and swimming. However, simple relaxation without any underlying aim of physical or social advancement is featured only fleetingly, before Vertov moves on to demonstrating, in a sequence that anticipates Leni Riefenstahl's fascistic hymn *Olympia* (1938), how the sporting body represents the person-as-organic machine, virtuously creating 'a paradise of self-improvement' (Roberts

2000: 79) through the repetitive rhythms of training. (Curiously, extreme left- and right-wing ideologies share much in terms of both general aesthetic ideals, which despite the progressiveness or otherwise of cultural trends almost always lean heavily on the classical, and a singular, concomitant distaste for corporeal neglect.) Spectators look on admiringly as, in analytically facilitative slow motion effected for the film-viewer's special and distinct benefit, a discus-thrower strives for perfection, high-jumpers leap bars, pole-vaulters push themselves into the air, various ball sports are enjoyed, and calisthenics and swimming exercises undertake to bring the whole of Soviet humanity into synchronisation, whilst in addition taming the chaos of undisciplined play by locating recreation within the sphere of the culturally useful. By contrast, chubby and apparently unsporting ladies sit idly applying lipstick, vacantly eyeing the camera, or relying on contraptions – as opposed to working with machines – to lose weight, while nubile girls put on mud-packs; Vertov's intentions here, though, may be more generally scopophilic (a pleasure in looking, especially at human bodies) than strictly political. Without doubt, his film relishes examining and gazing upon flesh, a tendency that is perhaps a creatively less-than-profound gratuity: the nude, it almost goes without saying, has since the dawn of history drawn the attention of artists of all stripes, from Hugo van der Goes to Man Ray. Ideologies, implications and purposes may shift, yet the naked body's basically human essence stays universal, even in a film such as Vertov's. Mikhail, himself wirily (virtuously) athletic, classically virile-looking and nearly naked, is also shown at the beach, but of course not without his camera, which remains propped at his side even while he bathes in the sea. The Man never, or so it seems, takes a break from duty: he is beyond censure, healthsome, and ever able to take up the call to action, wherever his urge to societal salubriousness may take him.

After a scene showing him filming (superimposed as a giant) on rooftops, alongside speeding motorcycles and with fairground riders, the Man enters another arena of 'danger' – a beer hall: not, it must be said, an environment conducive to physical wellbeing, but then this,

Vertov implies by juxtaposition, is the dark side of leisure, and herein lurk the perils of drunkenness (something with which many of Vertov's compatriots were struggling, to the detriment of all-important productivity: we have already seen images – numerous probably severely alcoholic tramps, the giant wine bottle – hinting at Vertov's distaste for public drinking). Mikhail immerses himself in both beer and intoxication, climbing magically from inside a beer glass; a lobster, in stop-frame animation, falls from its perch, also drunk; the camera sways, taking in an image of Lenin, symbol of Communist traits recently outmoded, and the Lenin Workers' Club; and a woman shoots bottles of beer – along with symbolically connected images of fascism, another hazard – at a fairground. 'Pointless' free-time activities are hence held in relief against those with an aim, literally and figuratively. Rapidly compiled and multiply overlaid shots of bar-room pursuits and grinning faces combine to give a sense of disorder and potentially explosive frippery: this is Soviet disunion, disharmony and fun for fun's sake – not something of value in Vertov's vision, which is coherent in its overarching suggestion that what the public does with its spare hours is equally as important as what it does with its working life. Nation-building, implies *The Man with the Movie Camera*, is dependent on the building of a new order predicated on focused (and the metaphor is apt) attention to the undertakings of a planned life as part of a collective civic ambition.

Before the film's final reel, which consists mostly of images already seen and represents a summation befitting Vertov's filmic manifesto, we cut back to the cinema audience, briefly. Then the camera, now autonomous and perhaps sentient, is seen to have taken on a life of its own. Given movement by stop-frame pixilation, the camera and tripod assemble and conjoin themselves, running through their sympathetic movements in a show of technical possibility to which the audience reacts with wonder. This, as it were, has been the camera's final bow, taken in gracious if presumptuous receipt of eventual applause. But the film closes with its most famous image (an image appearing on the cover of so many previous books on documentary film that its specific import has gradually been denuded): a literalisation of the kino-eye. At last, we see the camera lens and the human lens as one, flawlessly melded together and capable of showing a new (but never uncontroversial) mode of truth: the truth according to the Kinoks.

Vertov and his colleagues attracted not inconsiderable criticism, much of it from fellow Soviets dedicated to other, more obvious forms of cinematic advocacy. Eisenstein called Vertov a 'film hooligan'; Viktor Shklovsky lamented that 'Dziga Vertov cuts up newsreel', complaining that 'his work is not progressive' (both quoted by Winston 2008: 1676). Even divorced of immediate political context and considered 80 years after the fact, such accusations hold water: at times, The Man with the Movie Camera indubitably appears to be caught up in the very frivolity it undertakes to denigrate, revelling in formalistically composed vignettes whose representative nature echoes their subjects. More recently,

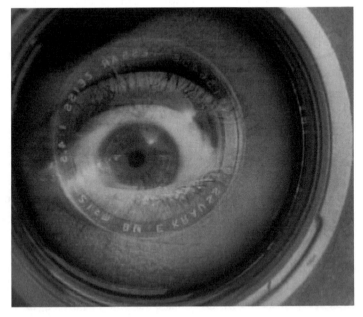

FIGURE 3.4  The kino-eye, rendered literally (The Man with the Movie Camera, 1929)

filmmaker Richard Leacock, whose own, highly sardonic observational work owes a debt to Vertov, claimed that *The Man with the Movie Camera* 'was tricks, games, and I don't see that it really has any connection with his [Vertov's] expressed desire to show life as it is' (Levin 1971: 202). There is, though, some rhetorical method in this apparently hypocritical madness: Vertov's film may not constitute an empirically unimpeachable portrait of 'life as it is', but it nonetheless evinces a palpable current of reflexive, extremely pertinent engagement with the everyday and with everybody – an engagement set up in opposition to Eisenstein's more sternly played proclamations. If Eisenstein's montage epics overtly reconstruct the Revolution's recent history with chest-beating conviction, and Shub's wily compilations bring recontextualised archive material to bear on the political dialectic, then Vertov's most well known work deals, principally at least, with poetic and formal revolutions of its own. It deconstructs factual cinema's illusions in order to interrogate the exciting methods of a relatively new art in relation to a society, post-Lenin, that might (whether safely or not) be assumed to have sufficient nous in respect of industrial developments to walk forward into the truly modern, leaving the Plato's cave of classical illusion behind for a fresh start under the Man of Steel. Vertov operates in the *now*, and that, for all misgivings, is obvious to this day. As William Rothman observes, 'For Vertov, a film like *The Man with the Movie Camera* is a simulacrum of a revolutionary new society; what matters most is the revolutionary reality being constructed' (Rothman 1997: 94). 'If Walt Whitman had heard America singing', declares Patricia Aufderheide, 'Dziga Vertov heard the Soviet singing' (Aufderheide 2007: 41).

Their work rediscovered in the west in the 1960s and celebrated by avant-garde or left-wing filmmakers such as Jean-Luc Godard (who formed the Dziga Vertov Group in homage), the Kinoks, blessed with a passion and fervour for change, helped steer the course of non-fiction film form away from what might have been a default reliance on narrative conventions. 'It is not too ridiculous', claims Graham Roberts (2007: 99), 'to state that Vertov's mixture of voyeurism and making strange has influenced everybody (directly or indirectly) from Godard to the networks of webcams such as www.camcentral.com and the rather less salubrious variations ... as well as other websites which subvert and play with voyeurism rather than simply reinforcing socialized pornography.' Yet the kino-eye, despite its wondrous visions and eventual global influence, was cursed with a significant blind spot. To err, and to end, on the side of caution, one must consider something eloquently conveyed by Seth Feldman (1998: 53):

> *The Man with the Movie Camera* is, along with everything else it is, a hymn of praise to the communist workers' paradise that was already being ridiculed in 1929 and would be a running joke inside and outside the Soviet Union for the next sixty years. The simple and horrible truth is that most of the people we see in the film would, very shortly, begin to suffer in Stalin's purges and in the artificial famine he would create in the Ukraine during the 1930s ... If what we see in *The Man with the Movie Camera* appears to be a sunny day in the life of the revolution, we must view the film now with the realisation that there remained very few days like it.

## *NIGHT MAIL* (HARRY WATT AND BASIL WRIGHT, 1936): THE POETICS AND POLITICS OF CLASS

A highly didactic salvo in John Grierson and company's hard-fought, ultimately doomed campaign to 'command, and cumulatively command, the mind of a generation' (Grierson in Winston 2008: 68), *Night Mail*, made by the General Post Office (GPO) Film Unit and concerning the London to Glasgow 'Postal Special' train, today appears suspended in very British, Depression-era amber – especially by comparison with *The Man with the Movie Camera*, or the downbeat, elegiac humanism of Grierson's American counterparts. Yet the British Documentary Movement's legacy, a heritage born of the sometimes awkward marrying of sponsored civic edification to audio-visual poetry (or 'the broad linking of socially realist depiction to public informational goals';

Corner 1996: 15), can at some level be appreciated in manifold works of cinematic and broadcast non-fiction. Most evidently, we see these traditions – which are apotheosised in *Night Mail* – recapitulated by television programming for schools, in the arts strands tending to occupy late-night slots on channels with public-service remits, and, less flatteringly, in the deadeningly strip-lit, narcotically efficient workplaces of the corporate promo-video (to which *The Office* is a 'mockumentary' antidote). But the Griersonian desire to impart messages of societal purpose via appropriate aesthetic treatments, and in particular a certain kind of 'naturalism' extruded through non-actors engaged to various degrees in the process of playing themselves at work or play, lives on also in almost every documentary that attempts to balance education, implicitly claiming of its images a semi-scientific validity as it does so, with entertainment – if not, usually, with such an austere, slightly hypocritical suspicion of the 'meretricious trappings of the studio' (Alan Lovell quoted by Thomson 2002: 359).

At heart a dyed-in-the-wool, non-revolutionary, left-wing teacher beset by the inevitability of pragmatic compromise, Grierson was distanced from his proletarian subjects by the nature of a film unit largely made up of middle-class university graduates. Driven by a Scottish Calvinist ideology lending his efforts an unshakably severe underbelly, he singularly failed to attract large audiences, or by extension to 'command the mind of a generation' more generally receptive to the equally patriotic and more vivaciously stirring exploits of music-hall leftovers such as Gracie Fields. He did, however, encourage those under his aegis, including the often conflicting Watt (who favoured realist vignettes) and Wright (who, contrapuntally, wanted more experiment), to formulate a style that, occasionally dour-seeming as it now may be, crystallised 'a point where British documentary began to throw off its early influences and develop its own distinctive character' (Anthony 2007: 41). Rather than simply reporting on a facet of British industry (as per the newsreels and 'cinemagazines', which Grierson denigrated as 'lower forms' – 'just a speedy snip-snap of some utterly unimportant ceremony' (in Winston 2000: 20)), or painting a striking but impersonal picture of generalities (as had the GPO Unit's *Coal Face* of 1935, methodologically a rehearsal for its over-ground successor), *Night Mail* realised, in part anyway, a yearning expressed by the *Observer*'s Caroline Lejeune: that the documentary 'must dramatise the lives of the men and women whom these facts involve … It must go beyond types to individuals. It must borrow something from literature, and endow the conditions of human life with something of the rich human character which Shakespeare and Dickens drew' (*ibid.*). *Night Mail*, moreover, a film that comprises the 'ultimate blend of Grierson's ethic (social purposes) and aesthetic (formal properties)', is perhaps indeed 'a paradigm of propaganda … intertwined with art' (Ellis and McLane 2007: 69). Watt and Wright's film may incorporate a superficial quantity of Dickens-style characterisation (even if 'rich human character' is stretching things), but it is there that the similarities end, all meliorative sentiments giving way to a celebration of concerted servitude. Certainly, like fellow propagandists Vertov and Victor Turin (whose railway-themed *Turksib* he admired), Grierson, though less inclined to advocate outright experimentalism, stalwartly championed a pro-labour (and basically pro-Labour) policy of 'finding beauty in industry', so that 'people would accept their industrial selves' (Grierson in Barnouw 1993: 91). However, if *Housing Problems* and *Coal Face* had contained reformist suggestions running contrary to the interests of upholders of the status quo, *Night Mail* – its affirmation of workplace happiness beyond reproach even by the Tory-led National Government – lovingly if sometimes imprecisely oiled the human cogs of industrial Britain as embodied by Sir Stephen Tallents's recently rebranded Post Office: a timely subject particularly suited to 'giving the workingman his rightful place' (*ibid.*) whilst boosting the (in this case very metonymic, or the part standing in for the industrial whole) Post Office's flagged reputation.

Grierson's love of the proletariat, along with a correlated loathing of the 'lily-fingered metropolitan actor' (in Corner 1996: 12), are emplaced immediately by the titles, which declaim – in a bold typeface redolent of the Constructivist aesthetic admired by Wright – *Night Mail*'s featuring of 'the workers of the travelling post office', and 'the workers of the L.M.S. Railway'. That we are watching largely reconstructed or prompted goings-on is obvious from the outset; the non-actors' actions, far from validating Grierson's opinion that 'spontaneous gesture has a special value on screen' (in Macdonald and Cousins 1998: 97), seem stilted – one must assume by an awareness of the film crew's presence; and location sounds and dialogue, due to technical considerations, are throughout post-dubbed with somewhat approximate fidelity to the movements on screen. Notwithstanding this feeling of awkwardness, which for twenty-first-century spectators is hugely exacerbated by the introductory Voice of God's over-enunciating received pronunciation (an accent, courtesy of Stuart Legg, bordering on royal), *Night Mail* opens with an indisputable, infectious sense of enthusiasm for its centrally symbolic postal train, carrying, so we are told, half a million letters, its embarkation seen from overhead in a tracking shot taken from a helicopter. The production is clearly keen to get its information, and a message, across: like the train itself, the film is attempting to bridge a human distance – in this case not between divides of geography, but between the divide of class – over which newsreels and entertainment cinema could not be trusted to span. *Night Mail*'s civically educational model is of a nation united through a mediated understanding of how the other half, in this case almost entirely the 'lower' half, lives: a cinema of enlightened judgement, according to Grierson, must therefore strive not for upheaval, but for an affirmation of the status quo based on a forwarding of social boundaries as necessary, useful and unchangeable.

Grierson, observes Philip Rosen, 'recalled discussions of Walter Lippmann's argument that the ideal of successful democracy requires informed, rational decision makers as subject-citizens, but that modern mass society provides insufficient generalised access to the kinds of specific knowledge necessary to produce such beings on a mass scale' (Rosen 1993: 78). As Scott Anthony notes in his accomplished pocketbook on *Night Mail*, 'The urge to address this lack of knowledge was a defining characteristic of the "Grierson school". *Night Mail* laid down an important early marker of the wartime fusion of popular anthropology and documentary cinema to come' (Anthony 2007: 25). Similarly to Watt's and Humphrey Jennings's later patriotic fillips, it is this urge that lies at the core of Night Mail's thrusting purpose and behind its perspectival flaws: a fervent need to inform of the virtues of working-class endeavour – via a lightly patronising condescension not to the noble savage, but to the immutably servile proletarian who, ironically, has little discursive input into his representation via the GPO Unit's guardian-class construction of working-class identity – is both its fuel, and, with respect to subject position, its Achilles heel.

There is a sequence featuring signalmen, and close-ups of the mechanisms they use to allow the train – 'Four million miles every year! Five hundred million letters every year!' – safe passage on its sacred journey. We then see a plate-laying gang, apparently hard at work, who step back from the tracks to let the train pass. The dialogue between them is of course overdubbed, and their accents – as are all the film's regional dialects – are a little out of place as we have, according to the film's implied logic, just left Euston; as the gang swig from bottles of beer, glance uneasily at the camera and light pipes (while silently mouthing spontaneous banter that was noted, but not used), the scripted (by Watt), post hoc words are a little implausible in their affirmation of the Post Office's efficiency: 'That'll be the postal, mate. Well on time and all, ain't she, Joe?' (There is, however, some ambiguity. Are we supposed to infer that the train is not usually on time? Are the men genuinely surprised at the train's punctuality? What ostensible inconsequentialities, truly reflective of the men's lives and personalities, might have been uttered by these workmates and not used?) Pushing further up-country, the train, and in sympathy the film, will depend increasingly on such encounters with the everyday people who facilitate, in various ways depend on and admire the Postal Special: in Night Mail a nervous impulse running up the spine of a living Britain. 'That you, Harry?' asks an elderly gentleman (presumably a station master) on the telephone; 'You'll have to shunt the local – I've got the postal on.' The locals being shunted seem quite agreeable: one, leaning from a train window, asks a guard how long they will have to wait. The

Fenland-intoned answer, 'Couple of minutes, mate', seems to placate the man, but his irritated expression suggests otherwise: there is, not for the first or last time, a hint of dissonance between the film's central current of promotion, and the realities of the daily grind as experienced by most of the non-acting participants in Watt and Wright's poetic-realist advert. To be sure, *Night Mail* is a dichotomous work, and one that merrily and continuously seconds Grierson's hatred of the 'shim-sham mechanics of the studio' (in Corner 1996: 12) whilst adhering to Hollywood continuity codes and contriving a number of little 'shams' of its own.

The middle portion of the film, replete with these kind of 'inoffensively bland' (Anthony 2007: 29), peculiarly stifled moments taken 'from the raw' and cooked according to the Grierson recipe, is devoted to many further such vignettes, all of which demonstrate a keenness by the filmmakers for aesthetic composition (Grierson, ever the pedagogue, asked of all his junior cameramen that they visit the National Gallery to 'study the lighting of the masters' (Watt in BFI 2007: 5)), and all of whose function is chiefly to educate about the precisely labour-divided, sometimes perilous and above all happily efficient nature of the postal workers' jobs in dispensing a nation's spiritual glue. An isolated farmer receives his daily paper, thrown from the train to bring news from afar (though we never see the city from which it and its deliverers came, for the metropolis is not part of *Night Mail*'s romance). Letters are sorted, connections of every kind – between control rooms, remote personnel, and passing friends and colleagues – are emphasised during *Night Mail*'s mid-way building up of editorial tempo (the film begins, appropriately, to chug like its subject, in part due to Alberto Cavalcanti's imaginative sound design), and both green and pleasant lands and darkly satanic yet vitally important industrial landscapes are taken in on the way to Glasgow. The narrator declaims, in a portentously awestruck voice: 'The mines of Wigan! The steel works of Warrington! The machine shops of Preston!': all, or so the spectator is meant to construe, must reciprocally be given the lifeblood of letters, as they and their hard-toiling men serve to give motion and body to the train.

Eventually, one step removed by the limitations of available sound and lighting equipment, we are made privy to the inner workings of the film's 'star' – the *Royal Scot* 6115 Scots Guardsman. Or, in actual fact, a Flaherty-esque, studio-assembled half carriage, upon which the players were asked to rock gently back and forth to simulate the motion of the train in lieu of any purpose-built hydraulic platform. 'We couldn't afford what they have in feature films', recalled Harry Watt, 'that is, a rocker set ... So all we could do was to move by hand, out of picture, certain things like balls of string hanging down, make them sway regularly to give the impression of the train moving, and get the chaps to sway a little bit. With the sound of the train, it gave absolute verisimilitude' (in Winston 2008: 129). ('Absolute verisimilitude' does not extend to the workers collectively swaying in the same direction, but the overall impression indeed comes over.) Relations between supervisors and juniors, within this reconstituted space striving for another kind of social believability, are gently satirised, but kept within the bounds of acceptable convention; as the filmmakers defer to normative power relations in respect of their duties to Grierson's patrons, and show that every man must know and not abuse his place in a finely organised chain of responsibility not amenable to arguments, each sorter likewise defers amiably but absolutely to his superior: the men, dignified in their labour, are given humanity, but not too much humanity.

In opposition to the tendencies of more recent 'docu-soaps', overtly political pieces or observational pieces, the letters, symbols of large-scale communication, take filmic priority over communication amongst the messengers, functionaries of Britain's all-important industrial infrastructure. A sorter, surely stultified by the job's repetitiveness even on a film set, is unable to place an unfamiliar address, and asks his stiffly suited, much older boss to clarify: 'Welsh ... makes a nice change for you.' After an unnatural pause for thought in all probability exacerbated by the demands of acting out a quotidian situation, the sorter is then seen glancing over his shoulder with a look that implies a puzzled mixture of unspoken contempt, the classically comedic double-take, and half-smiling resignation (a look with which the filmmakers, beholden to Grierson's pandering to bourgeois needs, must have sympathised). All *Night Mail*'s 'characters', as far as they can be so designated, come up against the never externalised, yet always implicit, limitations of necessity: 'In the public mind,' wrote Thomas Baird, in a 1938 eulogy to the GPO Unit, 'has been created a well-deserved respect for the Post Office, and this is reflected in good will and cooperation. Inside the service there has been evidence of a better appreciation by the workers of their separate functions in the whole great structure. There is evidence of a new pride in belonging to a service which has prestige with the public' (Baird 1938: 98). Baird never dilates regarding 'evidence'; moreover, his essay's air of middle-class, spuriously sociological wishful thinking reveals much about the contradictions inherent to the GPO Unit's mission: a call for 'film which interprets and discusses a problem' inevitably sits uneasily with the fact that *Night Mail* does neither. 'The British documentary film was not, then, the simple voice of social protest', avers William Guynn (1975: 10): 'despite its claims, it was no worker's cinema of class struggle ... it served, rather, the interests of capitalism during a period of the potentially revolutionary upsurge of the masses'. Difficulties are skirted, at the same time as – paradoxically – the labour force, held down and depoliticised, is propitiated by appeals to its vanity. (Dai Vaughan, drawing a well observed comparison between the mail workers and the film crew, additionally argues that the film undertakes a 'levelling of social ranks in the higher interests of the job's completion' (in Macdonald and Cousins 1998: 121); there is, though, little evidence for this other than the supervisor – never actually 'one of the boys' – being forced to drink a cup of milk because the train has run out of tea. Likewise, Grierson, exerting ultimate control over the GPO Unit's generation of 'good will and cooperation', remained unmovable in his elevated position of buffer betwixt sponsor and artist: the only 'levelling' to take place would have been amongst technicians and recordists.)

*Night Mail*, not without charm lent by the volleying of cheeky badinage ('Right-o, sonny boy!'; 'Take it away, 'andsome!'), does not offer any insight into the men's minds, nor does it seek to interrogate their

FIGURE 3.5 Jovial class collaboration in *Night Mail* (1936)

attitudes; a half-realised exchange between the supervisor and a (fake but fittingly nervous) 'trainee', although imparting an almost universally familiar sense of the 'new boy''s anxiety, does little to redress this, instead merely evincing a want of tighter scripting – the idealised values of spontaneity, as extolled by Grierson, by and large evade a film caught in a quandary between effaced contrivance and a desire to appear unplanned. Made, as it was, long before portable sync-sound devices allowed for much less intrusive, on-location recording (and, as we shall see, opened up new cans of worms with regard to complex issues of human 'performance'), *Night Mail* cannot reconcile an urge for documentary levels of realism – an urge harnessed to the makers' unfounded faith in non-professional performers – with the uncongenial situation in which its subjects, perpetually conscious of the camera, find themselves. Close-ups tend to reveal only a poker-faced dearth of

FIGURE 3.6 *Night Mail* (1936): moments of aesthetic modernism demonstrate a keenness to the avant-garde

sympathy with the production's requirements: above all, the postal staff appears understandably lost in a world of the over-familiar rendered alien under scrutiny. Despite sound-designer Cavalcanti's enthusiastic claim that 'Harry Watt put the sweaty sock in documentary', Watt's retrospective expressions ring with admirable honesty apropos the limitations of his efforts:

> People have often asked me how I found my 'actors' in my dramatised documentaries. I'm afraid it is a sad comment on the acting profession: you look for the extroverts, the bullshit merchants, the boring life-and-soul-of-the-party boys. They are the natural hams, but if you then wheedle and bully them down into some kind of naturalness, they're actors. I was only just realising this theory during *Night Mail*, and some of the acted scenes still make me shudder a bit.
>
> (BFI 2007: 7)

For reasons of both duty and simple incapability, Night Mail thus does not pit man against an antagonistic environment, make a case for change, or dwell on or manufacture interpersonal dramas. Rather, it seeks to downplay such matters in favour of a series of revelations often brought about by showing *and* telling (usually a no-no for most subsequent filmmakers) how the mail system ('the most important thing in the world'; Barsam 1973: 53) is working.

Night Mail does, however, during its one-and-only scene of dramatic tension – a visually accomplished climax achieved with commendable and dangerous involvedness on the part of the filmmakers – go some way towards redressing this dearth of spectatorial engagement while providing some thrillingly orchestrated cinema. The train's leather mailbags (seen earlier being tied up by the supposed trainee, who is instructed by an untypically adept, relaxed-seeming non-actor) are readied for dropping off. Nets, at the same time, are also lowered to collect mailbags from posts outside the train; here, everything must be timed with total exactitude, lest something go disastrously wrong (as indeed it had on a few occasions, resulting in one man losing his arm, and another his life: this information is, naturally enough, not provided by a work praising the Post Office's modernity). This scene, Night Mail's most consummately composed, is constructed with appropriate precision, making adept use of classically cinematic codes and a seamless unity of studio lot and on-location footage perilously obtained by reaching bodily out of a window: the filmmakers cut between close-ups of the trainee and an equally anxious-seeming instructor, who count down to the moment of release by mentally ticking off the passing of bridges, and allow the sound of the train's wheels (dubbed in Night Mail by the use of a toy train), always rhythmic and reliable, to demarcate distance. After the instructor calls out 'Now!', the pouches drop down – the process is completed, and the viewer can rest easy having genuinely learned *and* felt something. As Watt remembered of the bag-dropping section's physical obstacles:

> While there was enough light to get an exposure, Chick [Fowle, the cameraman] struggled half out of a window about ten feet behind the

apparatus. Pat [Jackson] and I hung on to his legs and prayed … The train seemed to be going faster and faster, and I could see that ugly great black bag hanging on its sinister arm and rushing inexorably at Chick's head. There was a sudden, frightening crash, as the pouch landed in the van ahead of us, and a faint 'OK' from Chick. We hauled him in, his eyes streaming with water from the rush of wind. Now it was over I think we all realised what a foolhardy thing it was to have done.

(BFI 2007: 7)

Foolhardy it may have been, but the result of Watt and his crew's commitment is that every detail of the bag-dropping sequence, from the levers that wait for action, dependent on the churning machinery below, to the totally engaged faces of men now acting with a greater commitment, has been revealed as part of a job relying on man–machine harmony and extraordinary acuity to the task in hand. The filmmakers, too, became increasingly caught up in both their subjects' lives and their own, analogous difficulties in capturing the Postal Special's functions: on screen, these functions may well be mostly artifice, yet *Night Mail*'s journey entailed discovery for all those involved, and it is just such mutual understanding, argues Scott Anthony, that begins to pull *Night Mail* into an arena of personally human, and hence much deeper and more convincing, filmic significance:

Technical limitations prevented Watt from filming actuality, thus in *Night Mail* he was forced to sympathetically reconceive the work performed by the traveling post office, in order to capture its essence on film. The instructor's rather too theatrical wink to camera was symbolic of growing trust between film-makers and postal workers, as the GPO Film Unit attempted to create a mode of representation free from Flaherty's fraudulent exoticism and *March of Time*'s reductive glibness.

(Anthony 2007: 35)

All this, a shift towards operating truly within the world depicted, would seem to represent dramatic and empirical progress; the general purpose of the film is enhanced, not reduced, by its few moments of creative connection, moments that admit to peril, difficulty, or stern-faced application devoid of scripted cheeky-chapisms. But, almost in spite of itself, at almost the last moment, *Night Mail* includes a nearly tearful-sounding voiceover from Grierson that inhabits its own, ima-gined realm of 'fraudulent' romance. For the sake of a different kind of momentum, and to give thanks for the workers' efforts, we are reminded of *Night Mail*'s central pitch, which is that of a comfortably nostalgic orator's pseudo-daydream: 'Thousands are still asleep, dream-ing of terrifying monsters … none will hear the postman's knock, without a quickening of the heart – for who can bear to hear himself forgotten … '.

Whether *Night Mail* entirely succeeds in creating a 'new mode of representation' is at best doubtful, but it is in many ways a landmark – not least due to its oddly incongruous coda, in which the didactically hammering poetry of a young W. H. Auden, combined with Benjamin Britten's onomatopoeic music, accompanies images of the Postal Special hauling its priceless cargo over rolling landscapes, a dog chasing the train as engineers feed the fire: 'This is the night mail crossing the border, bringing the cheque and the postal order … ' Certainly, this final, whimsical expression of romantic immersion in a Britain made great by its steaming industrial backbone seems parachuted in to an otherwise realist narrative; but regardless, it remains unforgettable filmmaking and one of the most iconic, revered, imitated and parodied scenes in documentary history: so much so that the rest of the film remains obscure by comparison. Artistically, perhaps its obscurity is deserved – although in terms of understanding how non-fiction cinema has frequently served as an affirmatory reflection of its ideological backcloth, *Night Mail*'s lessons are markedly salient (not, however, in the way John Grierson would have wanted).

Since the 1970s, *Night Mail*, along with the majority of the Empire Marketing Board, GPO and Crown Unit films, has been the subject of a critical backlash in response to the euphonious praise offered by enthusiasts such as Richard Barsam (1973: 52–3), who, like many other teachers over the decades (and in Barsam's case, over the Atlantic), was clearly enraptured by Grierson's educational slant, married to the 'power of sight and sound'. *Night Mail*'s original, focused, didactic usefulness in the classroom and village hall has never been in doubt, but one must be mindful both of its artistic shortcomings and its nature as a Trojan horse, within which are passively voiced, though in respect of political struggles insidious, sentiments. Brian Winston, Grierson's most high-profile debunker, has devoted hundreds of scrupulously researched pages to explaining the Scot's motives, quandaries, influence and context in a prose style amusingly far removed from Grierson's lofty hymns. In addition to arguing that Grierson stymied his crews with demands for compliance to a promotional remit, Winston remarks that: 'The perennial unattractiveness of many Griersonian documentaries, certainly unvoyeuristic ones, to audiences must be acknowledged as the obverse to their power to "show us life" in a vivid and insightful way. This is, in effect, to accept, *pace* Grierson, the negative connotations of "public education". Audiences had come to know full well that Grierson's public education purpose, however much glossed and disguised, could be a guarantee of boredom' (Winston 2008: 273). More damningly, given Grierson's ostensibly socialist extraction, William Guynn writes that:

Despite their independence from the film trade and despite their innovations in production and distribution of films, the documentarists did not succeed in liberating their art but simply made bourgeois domination more directly political by allying themselves with the state. What Marxist critics must reproach the British documentary film with is that it failed to expose the contradictions of the decadent capitalist social system. Wittingly or not, it made of itself a tool in the hands of the bourgeoisie. Succumbing to the dominant ideology, it sowed illusionism to its working class audience concerning the ultimate reformability of capitalism, and it promulgated the politics of class collaboration.

(Guynn 1975: 12)

None of this, to the hardworking filmmakers' credit as pragmatists, yet possibly to their immense discredit as artists, was unknown at the time of *Night Mail*'s production: heads bowed down, lest they roll. 'The truth is', records Harry Watt (in Chanan 2007: 40), 'that if we had indulged in real social criticism to any extent, we would immediately have been without sponsorship and our whole experiment, which was artistically a fine one, would have finished. So we compromised.' Aesthetically, the experiment was a fine one – but is not the job of the best art to say something above and beyond the exhortation of a state-endorsing advert, no matter how skilfully prepared? As outlined by Jean-Louis Comolli and Jean Narboni in their massively influential essay 'Cinema/Ideology/Criticism': 'The film is ideology presenting itself to itself, talking to itself, learning about itself. Once we realise that it is the nature of the system to turn the cinema into an instrument of ideology, we can see that the filmmaker's first task is to show up the cinema's so-called "depiction of reality". If he can do so there is a chance that we will be able to disrupt or possibly even sever the connection between the cinema and its ideological function' (Comolli and Narboni 1969: 755). On the contrary, *Night Mail* – politically speaking, a film vulnerable to the worst accusations one could level at any work of creativity aiming to provide a lesson – is, as Guynn claims, an advert subtly selling 'illusionism to its working class audience'; that it indeed 'promulgated the politics of class collaboration' is, in its own way, a disgrace hidden behind the glamour of a semi-modernist text, its traditionally cinematic magic bolstering the already heavy walls of capital. Making realist films, wrote Grierson, 'requires not only taste, but also inspiration, which is to say a very laborious, deep-seeing, deep-sympathising creative effort indeed' (in Corner 1996: 13). Vociferously inculcated, these vague ideals of 'taste' and 'effort' are to be found in *Night Mail* and its like, films freed from the pressures of the box office whilst chained to the demands of sponsors; the ideals of Grierson's professedly left-wing roots, however, are ironically and, to some, perniciously absent from his grandly wrought, innately flawed scheme of 'public information'.

## NOTE

1 As Adrian Tilley says: 'Narratives are about the survival of particular social orders rather than their transformation. They suggest that certain systems of values can transcend social unrest and instability by making a particular notion of "order out of chaos". This may be regarded as the ideological work of narrative' (in Watson 1998: 144).

# 4

## BARDS

Filmmakers soon realised that problems inherent in the Griersonian mode – tangled problems of ideological and narrative dissonance within the film text, in addition to the stultifying pitfalls of straightforward lecturing – could be overcome whilst not lessening a work's educational or historical value (though a judgement of 'value', one must remember, is conditional on one's opinion); nor, increasingly, has hammering home a preferred reading appealed to anyone other than fervent cinematic rhetoricians with contentious agendas. *Contra* Grierson, it might be argued that history and epistemology in non-fiction never need be reliant upon easily understood facsimiles of real life, propaganda, the slippery ideals of journalistic factuality, or the storytelling tropes of Hollywood. Reality, especially memory-as-reality, of course constitutes a maze of thorny issues rather than a concrete framework based on black-and-white condensations, shoehorned conclusions, or Manichean templates of Good against Bad: in every event, newsworthy or seemingly trivial, lurks contradiction, emotion, subjectivity, compromise and complication – these are the sometimes inexplicable, hazy domains of poetic contemplation, and realms within which the burden falls on art to make a little sense of our deeply flawed world on the level of the soul. In Chapter Four, we shall look at three very different films that not only approach the reconstitution of reality from such a perspective, but also, in some respects, challenge non-fiction film's supposed precepts: all three documentaries attempt to move beyond schemes of exposition and rhetoric into the arena of subjective evaluation, evincing a discernible sense of authorial ambivalence about humanity's overarching absurdity; moreover, they offer no solutions, preferring to find a peculiar solace in the invocation of questions, ghosts and mortal preoccupations.

## *NIGHT AND FOG* (ALAIN RESNAIS, 1955): ARTICULATING THE UNSPEAKABLE

*Night and Fog*, a devastating, haunting and totally essential early documentary on the death camp at Auschwitz-Berkenau and its notorious role in the Holocaust, has rightly 'become a yardstick by which other documentaries on the subject have been judged' (Grant and Hillier 2009: 161). Initially reticent about making the film (whose name is derived from the Nazis' secret *Nacht und Nebel* operation to deport all 'undesirables' – initially not just Jews – from German-occupied nations), Frenchman Alain Resnais was convinced otherwise when poet and Gusen-Mathausen survivor Jean Cayrol agreed to contribute a commentary. Rejecting the multiple-testimony, oral-history approach that would become the predominant mode adopted by non-fiction film in its coverage of the Holocaust (see, especially, Claude Lanzmann's nine-hour *Shoah*, 1985), *Night and Fog* is an affecting mix of appropriated archival footage (shot largely by camp authorities and Allied liberators) and originated material; Resnais, as William Rothman puts it, eschews the didactic in favour of taking us on 'an allegorical journey into the heart of a region in which unspeakable horrors are to be discovered' (Rothman 1997: 39). Poetic, challenging and entirely replete with pathetic evocations befitting the twentieth century's most sweepingly epochal event, the film is nonetheless perhaps devoid of most

conventional narrative pleasures: its 'journey' is not one of a protagonist, or a hero, but of a filmmaker's enquiry – an absolutely intellectual
mission into the headlands of inexorable, eternally dormant evil that
must be 'discovered' by each of us. Resnais, with France's Algerian
campaign and its contemporary horrors very much in mind, unflinchingly depicts the brutal yet all-too-human nature of the Nazi killing
machine via images so vile as to beggar belief that such atrocities could
have taken place within living memory; but he also treats his indictment with caution, constructing something more than either a cen-
otaph or a lecture. Commissioned by the Comité d'Histoire de la
Seconde Guerre Mondiale to serve as a memorial, *Night and Fog* is,
instead, film-as-cerebral-ordeal, an elegiac immersion in a collective
netherworld, beamed from a time then only ten years distant, of murderous, happily shared irrationality made sane by focused hatred. Far
from stemming ultimately from Hitler's declarations at the Wansee
Conference, the Holocaust's causes were societal and thoroughly
ingrained. '[T]he view that the crime of the extermination of the
Jews was somehow imposed by a few mad people on an unwilling
Europe', writes Laurence Rees, in his exemplary and cautionary book on
Auschwitz, 'is one of the most dangerous of all' (Rees 2005: 12).

We see a tranquil, blue sky over a field of rough grass; then the
camera cranes down, revealing a fence of rusted barbed wire leading to
a dilapidated watchtower: this is an image that may or may not be
familiar as a specific part of the Polish extermination camp at Auschwitz, but that will no doubt for most concisely signify the general,
culturally conveyed prisoner-of-war experience – monitored, held and
controlled, as *Night and Fog* now begins to do the same, visually, with the
derelict camp. While Resnais continues – through the use of evocative
tracking shots that feel ghostly in their gliding ethereality – to show
more disused buildings (in 1955 the site had not yet been turned into a
museum), the narration speaks of the surroundings' bucolic, ordinary,
everyday familiarity, for Resnais and Cayrol a dream-like suspension
within which are nonetheless held the extraordinary nightmares of
wartime destruction:

FIGURE 4.1 *Night and Fog* (1955): a strange landscape is revealed

> Even a quiet country scene, even a field harvested and crows aloft, even a road with cars and people passing, even a village fair, may lead direct to a concentration camp. Struthof, Oranienburg, Auschwitz, Belsen, Ravensbrück, Dachau – were just names like any other on the map. The blood is caked, the cries stilled, the camera now the only visitor; a strange grass grows where once the inmates trod the earth. No current passes through the wires, no step is heard but ours.
>
> (*Night and Fog*, 1955)

The spoken tone of this dulcifluously aesthetic narration, read by actor Michel Bouquet, is softly neutral, rather than angry-sounding or delivered in the Voice of God (there is no God here, vengeful or otherwise, to be put on trial). The accompanying music, by Hans Eisler, takes an equally unorthodox approach: instead of amplifying or underscoring images of great emotional power by bringing to bear the sonic force of a loudly orchestrated, ominous soundtrack, Eisler often uses whimsical pizzicato and trilling piccolo in a fashion more obviously redolent of lightly dramatic fantasy. 'In the best circumstances', according to documentarist Michael Rabiger, 'music doesn't merely illustrate, it seems to give voice to a point of view' (Rabiger 1998: 286). As Michael Renov dilates: 'In the sound era, the breach between image and its audio counterpart has rarely been acknowledged; synchronised sound, narration, or music is meant to reinforce or fuse with the image rather than question its status. Such is not the case with *Night and Fog*' (Renov 1993b: 33). Images, text and music in *Night and Fog* thus coexist with a slightly surreal tension that reflects the endlessly self-deluding, fantastical dichotomies of a humanity driven wilfully to create monstrosities and think of them as normal, useful adjuncts to progressive civilisation: nothing, after all, is more surreal, at least at a temporal distance, than the Nazis' 'Final Solution' and its structural manifestations, born not only from Hitler, but in a terrifyingly mutual 'bleak landscape of the mind' (Rees 2005: 119), where 'a strange grass grows'. 'The short-subject documentaries made about the camps in '45 and '46 did not really reach the public,' said Resnais: 'With *Night and Fog* I wanted to make a film that a great number of people would see. I thought if it was beautiful, it couldn't help but be effective' (in Flitterman-Lewis 1998: 204). As a response of sorts to the flowers placed by guards in the window boxes of Auschwitz's crematoria – the only flowers in the compound served as a monstrously cynical reassurance that what lay behind them was anodyne – 'Resnais', remarks Jay Cantor, 'makes the horrible ordinary, so we might believe it; and then he makes the ordinary horrible, so we might fear it … the tracks from our city of the living lead to the camp' (in Rothman 1997: 40). And, indeed, many of these tracks led from 'our' France, whose authorities authorised the killing of 80,000 Jews; though such specificities are reduced to fleeting mentions of place-names and glimpses of uniforms – *Night and Fog* was made in a post-war climate fearful of censorship, which Resnais resisted as much as he could – the shameful ghosts of French collaboration are present, even if one shot (of gendarmes minding a detention centre) was excised for its too-awkward depiction of Franco-German alliance.

This is not, then, a film that will hammer its fist in blaming the few; *Night and Fog* instead seeks to counter expectations around documentary as either single-minded propaganda or baldly stated instruction, and to work against 'the overriding view [that] the documentary voiceover is the filmmakers' ultimate tool for telling people what to think' (Bruzzi 2005: 50). For some, Resnais's allegorising – especially in its deliberate downplaying of anti-semitic specificities – is theoretically and politically double-edged, but it remains a rhetorical tactic whose methods of persuasion are contrapuntal to most Nazi propaganda: his film is sufficiently oblique to allow the spectator space enough for subjective thought on precisely the nature of that subjective thought, and perhaps of history (and art) in general. The Nazis did indeed 'tell people what to think', yet these people largely *wanted* to think it: they, who could so easily have been *us*, sincerely believed that the course of their actions was just and good, whilst the seeds of evil were lovingly nurtured. Rather than being, as it sometimes in hindsight appears, an anomaly external to the known universe, Auschwitz sat amongst 'regular' life, a microcosmic product of conscious design taken to extremes in the name of what was considered axiomatically beneficial. Emphasising reflection over factual elucidation, *Night and Fog*'s uncomfortable analysis hence poses many difficult questions, which penetrate to the heart of our nature as potential 'willing executioners'.

Suddenly, from the decaying, colour remains of the camp, we cut back in time to black-and-white, as 'The machine [of the Nazis] gets underway,' the Party's uniformed pomp displayed to a gleeful public whose smiles were then very real, and whose genuflection has, in many cases, long outlived the fall of Berlin. From the archives come visions of Himmler and Hitler, and of marching young men bearing potent standards: these are the proud troops who were called up – maybe from the mass-unconscious as much as from the war – to serve and protect. Men survey the land as they would for any other civic project: 'The goal is unison ... The job is begun. Building a concentration camp, like a stadium or hotel, means contractors, estimates, bids … ' There is a montage of differing styles of watchtower – an illustration of the bizarre contemplations at play behind the National Socialists' aesthetic of death – as 'architects calmly design doorways to be entered only once'. 'Meanwhile', continues the narration, in the present tense and over mute but, in this context unforgettably poignant, images of those to be deported, 'Burger, a German workman, Stern, a Jewish student in Amsterdam, Schmulski, a shopkeeper in Krakow, Annette, a schoolgirl in Bordeaux, live on unaware. Until the day only they are needed to make the camps complete.' Forlorn and bewildered, the victims, including numerous children (the enemy was their blood, for fear that they may grow into an adult, Jewish menace), are gathered and shipped like human cattle, stripped of their belongings and their nominal identity – which Cayrol, ten or more years later, has been careful to stress, seizing back from the Nazis a human denominator which was in the camps systematically numericised, or replaced with patches: the dignifying power of personal, familial naming. Resnais shows us the faces, the eyes, of the people heading for extermination (though the majority do not yet suspect this), filmed by their captors; these shots, evidence of a need to preserve the processes of destruction from within, 'may well make us wonder', notes William Rothman, 'who can be filming this, for whose eyes, for what purpose, and to what effect' (Rothman 1997: 42).

Perversely, the gas chambers were designed so that sensitive operatives – sensitive, that is, to the living image, not the deed, for most soldiers were morally convinced of their job's righteousness – would not have to look into the eyes of their targets as they shot them: it is a disturbing indictment of the Reich's notions of 'efficiency' that a large-scale 'killing machine' could be implemented to spare the feelings of executioners. Resnais, however, does not flinch from the horrific, despite a possible danger of desensitisation. It is important for the filmmaker to immerse us in a world of mountainous, politically inexplicable physical atrocity, as the guards of Auschwitz were immersed to the point of recording material, in a global context obviously incriminating, which would eventually be used against them. For most involved, once the act of murder was committed, a body became no more than rubbish, denuded of all human qualities, and only to be disposed of with the minimum of fuss. 'We exterminated nothing but enemies,' remembers Auschwitz SS member Oscar Groening (in Rees 2005: 177), whose views were typical: such goings-on were carried out in secret from the outside world, but to all concerned were quite necessary to eradicate a dehumanised internal danger. For Resnais, in order to tell a resonant story of the 'machine', these images must be recontextualised and allowed to speak of the unspeakable: from the past, to the present and future, when simply positing the Nazi Genocide as the product of hardline ideology alone is not sufficient to explain the descent of post-Enlightenment humankind to an abomination in which France, not least, was complicit: '[T]ime and again we are induced by the montage or the commentary to ask ourselves who took these images, and what it is they show. We are able to grasp neither the suffering, nor the ideology that caused it. These are the traumatic wounds of history' (Chanan 2007: 158) – wounds that remain unhealed, and that remain evidence for our endless capacity, at any time, to commit absolute wrong.

'Those caught in the act, or by error, or by ill luck,' the narration recounts, 'head for the camps', as the soundtrack parodies the German national hymn, in this instance a grotesquely comic warping of national pride. 'Acts', 'errors' and 'ill luck' are never defined, leaving us with the assumption that all deportations were the result of a mixture of these: *whose* errors, and *what* acts, exactly, could have comprised a case for killing? The spectator has little time to think (nor, of course, did those forced out of their homes, whether for Resistance activity or merely for being Jewish). On the trains, 'Hunger, thirst, suffocation, madness', are conditions not fit for animals, but humanity strives to remain human: 'a message is thrown, sometimes found: death makes its first choice ... The second is made on arrival, in the night and fog', now a metaphor for both the Holocaust and its history's nebulous, dark inexplicability. Back in the 'present' (1955) narrative strand of *Night and Fog*, the camera appears to be scanning the overgrown railway tracks, trying in some way to 'grasp the suffering', to find obvious evidence of 'traumatic wounds', yet unsure as to what it may now discover amongst the weeds that have already begun to erase, to soften and make green these metal paths to oblivion. 'Today there is sunlight on the lines. We follow them slowly, seeking what? Traces of the bodies that fell out when the cars were opened? Of survivors driven by rifle butts through the doors? Dogs barked, searchlights played, and the crematorium belched flame.' (Even in the time of the *Nacht und Nebel* operation, there was 'sunlight on the lines'; there was no literal 'dark age' during which Europe saw no sun – indeed, later the film acknowledges the 'indifferent autumnal sky': Cayrol's words refer to daylight's inability to cast light on, or to 'illuminate', the scene's true meaning, and suggest once more a figurative 'night and fog' brought down on Auschwitz.) Tilting up, the camera reveals the camp's red-brick buildings, still and unoccupied: no longer 'belching flame', these are vanquished dragons, which perhaps lie not quite dead. From this mysterious present-day scene, its evidential qualities repeatedly examined by the camera on a subjectively forensic level (its continuously probing movements imply a process of gradual discovery through constant reframing), Resnais again cuts back to archive footage of the living: a man's eyes, in close-up, stare in apparent disbelief at 'first sight of the camp, another planet' – are these aghast black circles mirroring our minds' eyes as we watch from a position of historical (but never moral) immunity?; a group of naked men are 'shaved, tattooed, numbered. Classified in ways as yet incomprehensible'; and the film illustrates the camp's hierarchy, from the lowest prisoners marked instantly for death, via the *kapos* (prisoners with duties ordained by officers, who were prone to dispose of such servants on a whim), to the SS and the *Kommandant*, 'aloofly presiding. Affecting detachment, but he *knows*.'

'The reality of these camps', continues the narration over present-day images, 'is hard for us to uncover traces of now.' Resnais moves inside the camp, scanning ranks of empty wooden bunks; we, the viewer must also *know*, despite our detachment, that these bunks were once heaving with desperate people whose feelings and status were diminished to those of vermin. 'No image, no description can capture their true dimension of constant fear': the camp, of which 'only husk and hues remain', and the film's depictions, can thus only ever serve as an inadequate index to what went on, or to the 'true dimension' of conscious, subjective terror Resnais and Cayrol seek to convey by 'engaging the viewer's associative and conceptual capacities' (Flitterman-Lewis 1998: 204). Malnourished inmates are seen being put to work digging drainage ditches, breaking rocks, or constructing their own, twisted necropolis: 'Work Liberates', reads the sign over the camp gate, originally a motivational statement aimed at the psychological shackling of Auschwitz's slaves, but becoming only a cruel joke as the compound morphed into a place of calculated mass extermination. Behind every Nazi decree is sickness, at one time logical. 'In cleanliness lies health', cautions a sign, yet cleanliness amongst prisoners was impossible, and not, for the camp's disingenuous operators, even desirable. Dysentery, rife in the cramped, unsanitary environment, was one more of death's 'choices' to purge the 'unclean'. Resnais moves his lens across the latrines, their holes echoing with inferred fragments of horror from which we must construe a more total mental picture, reconstituting for ourselves the human whole. We are to imagine not only the absolute denuding of 'civilised' dignity, the proximity of bacterial death, but also an amazing resilience. In these places, fearful of disease, was formed 'a society shaped by terror, but saner than the SS and its precepts'. Symphony orchestras and zoos, ridiculously mimicking the parent culture's distractions, exist within certain camps' walls, as do 'greenhouses where Himmler nurtured delicate plants', and 'Goethe's oak at Buchenwald, respected when the camp was built around it'. The 'real world', a culture, one must remember, which birthed Auschwitz and that nurtures plants whilst torturing humans, remains a tantalisingly close prospect; but any escape into a world that would all-too-eagerly send prisoners back is another hopeless absurdity. 'For the deportee', notes the voiceover, this real world 'was a mirage'. The world of the camp becomes clearer as it becomes more surreally detached: prisoners line up for roll call, living skeletons stripped naked and covering their genitals in a bid to maintain societal norms; SS 'gods' dispense arbitrary, lethal punishments; and a body hangs from the electrified fence, its soul long gone to an attempt not realistically to escape, but to claim back some control over death. As Rothman describes it: 'This is a privileged moment … Concentration camps are designed and built not merely to kill, but to deny their victims the possibility of "dying their own deaths".' Moreover, he continues, 'To this end, gun and camera work hand in hand' (Rothman 1997: 47). Resnais's camera, though it is in some ways arguably part of and an extension of this gaze, seeks to 'restore the reality of the world to the past' (ibid.), to give this scene its 'true dimension' via art: a humanising endeavour that the inmates, too, used as a tool for personal, psychological resistance.

'Man', speaks the narration, 'is resilient: the mind, the hands still swathed in bandages, still work.' We see 'spoons, marionettes which remain hidden … They continue to write, to take notes … They tried to help each other.' Then, drawing a comparison, the film depicts the camp hospital – a 'last resort' not for curing illness, but for creating sickness. The Nazis, of course, had their toys, too: behind 'a façade' were undertaken final degradations, 'useless operations, amputations, experimental mutilations' of starved, outwardly homogenised guinea pigs. 'Kapos would try their hand, along with the SS surgeons', whilst pharmaceutical companies, whose job is to cure disease, purchased prisoners – now reduced to the status of seemingly identical animals – for their own tests on new medicines. Phosphorus burns and castration are amongst the strange, painful imprints of the camp's authorised 'creativity'; this is the officially sanctioned 'art' of Auschwitz: the mounds of human hair for making cloth, the human soap bars, the crude, pornographic art tattooed onto removed skin. 'The fabrication of a puppet', notes Sandy Flitterman-Lewis (1998: 219), 'becomes a reverential act when seen in the context of operating rooms whose professional-looking setting masks "useless operations" … While prisoners remember recipes, imagine problems of philosophy, and write stories to exercise their minds, Nazis invent "scientific" theorems to be tested on living beings.' And it is through the artistic process, and especially through Night and Fog's own 'reverential act', that Resnais constructs an important statement, locating his film within such a scheme of expressive creativity: 'Poetry – art and craft – made the camps; poetry – art and craft – makes Resnais's response to the camps, its representation … If Resnais's art did not openly display this complicity it would distance him and us from the camp, turn us into spectators, and the camp into spectacle' (Cantor in Rothman 1997: 53). The 'spectacle' of Night and Fog admits and reflects upon the Final Solution's symptomatically manifested poetry of death, undertaken in the name of 'purification'. The film acknowledges that every part of the camp, from the pan-continentally inspired watchtowers, to the crematoria, 'pretty as a picture postcard', to the torture chamber masquerading as a hospital, to the factories put to use making sure nothing is wasted by turning people into products, involves art; similarly, the victims choose to respond with art, as does Resnais, a filmmaker concerned not with simple historical record, but with a reconstitutive mission of his own: an inversion of the Nazis' methods, whereby Night and Fog will for the viewer re-endow a broken-down mass with its essential humanness, rendering physically abstracted vestiges of history once more part of their forever perhaps incomprehensible but now intellectually accountable context. In one of Night and Fog's key shots, the camera lingers on a gas chamber's ceiling, marked by 'scrabbling fingernails, scoring even concrete'. Eisler's music, significantly, is here at its most devastatingly 'picture-postcard' pretty. There is no possible response but to imagine, and to empathise with the marks' makers – packed in too tightly to turn, driven to claw at the impossible, and hoping against hope for a deus ex machina. Through Night and Fog, we can begin to make connections between the camp ledger's endless list of names, flicked through rapidly (there are obviously many thousands of entries), between various products of artistic labour and their creators, and between frantically etched physical indices – those lasting traces of the horror of painful death – and that which created them, too.

In the film's archival strand, corpses from all over Europe, dead of disease or the gas chamber, mount up, in testimony to the Nazis' prolific art of destruction, prior to the building of larger ovens – an urge so effective that the numerous dead are pushed into pits, or left in smouldering piles having been crammed between logs on makeshift pyres. Faces stare into oblivion; emaciated limbs tangle and spread limply over each other; skin drapes itself, leathery in putrefaction; decapitated torsos lie adjacent to their severed heads, which look – and a certain psychological denial on the part of the twenty-first-century spectator might, out of understandable bewilderment, encourage this perception – like dolls' parts in a factory; and half-burned men, women and children, given overdue funereal dignity by Resnais, offer a counterpoint to the film's earlier depiction of officers and their wives, marking time in well fed, well drunk boredom while the war and the camp push on. New ovens are built, along which Resnais tracks the present-day camera, searching again for emotional echoes, forcing us to make unbearable connections; through this increased efficiency, the previously sinewy bodies become vistas of bones, stretching out to form charnel plains. Numbers become almost meaningless, as Auschwitz, its obscenity indescribable, turns human beings into undifferentiated lumps. (The Nazis, from this once-human powder, 'made fertiliser … or tried to'.) For the narrator, 'words fail' to be of any use in explaining these images: unlike the finger-marks in the gas chamber, piles of the dead speak only of a silence from the grave, in this nightmare a strangely beautiful release from a man-made hell. Bosch could not have imagined this literal and figurative inferno, realised from mankind's faith in 'reason'. Despite attempts to recycle remains, *all*, in Auschwitz, is laid waste. When the Allies arrived, though they knew the camp's purpose, they could not have been truly prepared. In *Night and Fog*'s 1945 timeline, 'The deportees watch, uncomprehending. Are they free? Will ordinary life know them?' There is no means for them (or for us, in 'ordinary life') to comprehend, as there is no option for the camp's functionaries but to pass the blame. Individuals, seen in archive footage, are held to account for war crimes. '"I'm not responsible", says the kapo. "I'm not responsible", says the officer.' No trial, though, can ever make amends, no hangings serve as just retribution, nor financial reparations make recompense. There can, perhaps, or so *Night and Fog* implies, only ever be questions.

'Who', ask Cayrol and Resnais, 'is responsible?' The film's penultimate images show yet more bodies, and living faces silently contemplating a loss; but in this context they are invoking, in addition to the tragedy of the Final Solution, something intangible whereby finality cannot be allowed to bring down a curtain of reason. There is, philosophically speaking, no definite end, and nor should there be, for an end suggests neat resolution, a closure, all matters settled, and narrative *dénouement*. Eisler's music, for the first time, sits in sympathy with the images, swelling to a dramatically mournful climax. The film closes (and close it must), whilst insistently leaving open doors: doors to the deserted camp, to the camp as it was during the war, and to memory.

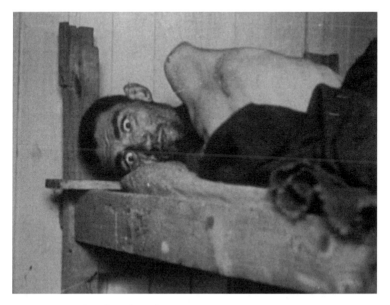

FIGURE 4.2 *Night and Fog* (1955)

Thus we must not relegate what we have seen to the status of dead-and-buried history, nor fail to make a link to the living present and the as-yet-unlived future. Scanning abstracted elements of the present-day site, the camera's images speak their own truths about encroachment and erasure by nature and time, and about cyclical decay and rebuilding. Nothing, in the world of *Night and Fog*, can safely be forever laid to rest:

> As I talk to you, cold marsh waters fill the ditches, as cold and sluggish as our memories. War has dozed off, one eye still open. Grass grows again around the blocks. An abandoned village, still full of menace. The crematorium is in disuse, Nazi wiles a thing of the past. Nine million dead haunt this scene. From this strange observatory, who watches to warn of new executioners? Do they really look so different from us? Somewhere among us remain undetected kapos, officers, informers. There are all those who didn't believe, or only sometimes. And those of us who see the monster as being buried under these ruins, finding hope in being finally rid of this totalitarian disease, pretending to believe it happened but once, in one country, not seeing what goes on around us, not heeding the unending cry.
>
> (*Night and Fog*, 1955)

The 'strange observatory' of *Night and Fog* must stay trained on all of humanity: the latent 'kapos, officers, informers' in us all. As Michael Chanan (2007: 158) observes: 'By means of this grammatical operation, "I am speaking to you about us", the film brings three different moments to coalesce in a single instant: the historic time of the depicted events, the film-time of the narration, and the present time of the viewing – whenever that is: 1956, when the film was first shown, 2004, when I write this, the future when you read it. This is one documentary that doesn't date, ever.'

*Night and Fog*, however, like most non-fiction works dealing with highly emotive subjects, has not been immune from negative criticism – chiefly for its lack of emphasis on deportees' Jewishness. For scholars of the Holocaust, this is a representationally hazardous symptom of the times in which the film was made, and a strategy that undermines its essential discursive usefulness: 'The marked absence of any discussion about the European Jews and the project of genocide', notes Andrew Hebard, 'set against a multitude of people in the archival footage wearing Jewish stars, not only reveals the extent of historical repression in the fifties along with the continual presence of anti-Semitism both then and now, but also perhaps reminds one of the most recent attempts to deny genocide through many of the revisionist histories' (Hebard 1997: 113). 'To bring the history of the film full circle', as John O'Connor writes, 'when Resnais was recently asked how he might explain this apparent bias, he explained that it had never been his central purpose to comment on the Jews and their Holocaust in the first place. He reminded the historian asking the question of him that it had been 1955, a time when France was critically embroiled in Algeria, and he explained that his main interest in making the film was to warn Frenchmen against the dangers of falling into patterns of inhumanity themselves' (O'Connor 2005: 393). *Night and Fog*, despite Resnais's declared purpose here, dodges the pertinent issue of French collaboration: notwithstanding censorial pressure, it should perhaps be more explicitly remembered – particularly by a film that after all fixates on the importance of not forgetting – that occupied France expedited a number of measures warranting 'everlasting shame': 'the complicity [in deportation] at every stage of the French authorities … And the French decision to hand over "foreign" Jews rather than their "own" Jews betrays a level of cynicism that is breathtaking even at this distance in time' (see Rees 2005: 156, 169). Never one to offer continuously cogent elucidations of his methods, whose political imperfections are in part forgivable when one considers the maybe unfathomable depth of the Holocaust's ever-contended cultural implications, Resnais, remarks David Thomson, is given to 'rather pusillanimous defenses of his own films … The contradictions are troubling' (Thomson 2002: 730–1). Indeed, by 1961, the director's statements about *Night and Fog* had gone from troubling to outright baffling: 'If one does not forget, one can neither live nor function … Forgetting ought to be constructive' (*ibid.*: 731), an opinion that in itself speaks worryingly of Europe's 'collective amnesia' regarding Jewish suffering, and sundry 'Vichy syndromes' born of a desire not to 'corrode the fragile bonds of post-war society' (Judt 2007: 808). One more irony is to be found in the fact that Night and Fog was not shown at Cannes due to German objections, even though the French government promised its exhibition was assured: West Germany, though, less afraid of painful national introspection (and more ridden with guilt) soon became the first nation to buy the film, inviting it to the Berlin festival.

Compromised yet still powerful, Night and Fog echoes unforgettably down the years. As filmmaker François Truffaut muses: 'It is almost impossible to speak about this film in the vocabulary of cinematic criticism. It is not a documentary, or an indictment, or a poem, but a meditation on the most important phenomenon of the twentieth century ... The power of this film ... is rooted in its tone, the terrible gentleness ... When we have looked at these strange, seventy-pound labourers, we understand that we're not going to "feel better" after seeing Night and Fog; quite the opposite' (in Macdonald and Cousins 1998: 217). 'The effect', writes Annette Insdorf, 'is not only opposition, but a deeper unity in which past and present blend into each other' (*ibid.*); Resnais's 'unending cry', never totally answered, never totally denied, rings out still beyond the bodies, weeds and dust.

## *MY WINNIPEG* (GUY MADDIN, 2007): A CITY OF THE MIND

A surreally stylised, multi-layered and ambivalent 'docu-fantasia', My Winnipeg presents Canadian Maddin's Manitoban hometown as a living enigma whose hypnotic, magnetic mysteries have ineradicably shaped the filmmaker's neuroses. The emphasis, accordingly, is very much on the 'My' of the title: this is a work that evokes David Lynch via Luis Buñuel in a 'zone of conversation between individual and collective memories', part of the 'struggle against documentary as prosaic, narrow, drab and ultimately pessimistic and restricting' (Laurent Roth and Raymond Bellour in Roberts 2007: 101). Far from the usual tourist-board fare, the film, often appearing to inhabit a trance-like reverie in which textbook certainty gives way to poetic free association, combines highly subjective, emotionally redolent recollections and testimony with a number of reconstructed or archivally compiled vignettes purporting to show events from Maddin's childhood, or from Winnipeg's history: many of these events, however, seem – notwithstanding a proportion of traditionally expository material – utterly implausible; we are never told which are true and which are invented, or indeed which may in some measure be a conflation of fact and imagination.

In a sense, of course, *all* are true – the film's Winnipeg is defiantly *Maddin*'s Winnipeg: this book hence makes no attempt to sort journalistic 'accountant's truth' from fiction, an adversarial act that would arguably contaminate Maddin's 'thick soup of personal memory, distorted imaginings and factoids about the city, which is probably closer to the way most people relate to their environment than the urban celebrations [of Vertov and Ruttman]' (Grant and Hillier 2009: 144). To this end, 'Mr. Maddin', notes A. O. Scott, 'is engaged less in historical inquiry than in hallucinatory autobiography, ruminating on the deep and accidental relationship between a specific place and an individual life' (Scott 2008: 1). Though sponsored by The Documentary Channel, *My Winnipeg* works mischievously against conventional documentary functions to offer something altogether more challenging – and maybe, paradoxically, a work more immersed in the 'truth' of the city and its psychological effects than any by-the-book chronicle: 'To show my Winnipeg', avers Maddin, 'I had to show myself' (in Halfyard 2007: 1). (Not that Maddin, in his search for a particular truth, is immune to the prankster's love of impishness: 'My dream', he says, 'is to show this film at the Berlin Film Festival and have hundreds of Germans watching it as a travelogue of Winnipeg' (in Gillmor 2007: 1).) This 'docu-fantasia', then, confounds as it reveals; never does it make any claim on Gospel status, but it is persuasive in its call for a suspension of logical disbelief and acquiescence to what Maddin sees as an irresistibly playful rewriting of both personal and local lore: 'Canadians, for the usual obvious reasons – being in the shadow of the greatest self-mythologisers in world history, maybe, are a bit shy about mythologising themselves and they feel the need to make their historical figures and historical events smaller than life rather than bigger than life. So I just thought, every other culture in the world, including the Inuit in Canada, are great at mythologising, so let's just give Winnipeg its fair shake [sic]' (Maddin in Halfyard 2007: 1). The myth-making metaphor of Flaherty's igloo – cut in half to illuminate with a trick – casts both light and shade over Maddin's grainy snowglobe, a microcosm arguably no more or less truthful than Nanook's, another site of romantic projection.

To begin as he means to go on, Maddin sets up his stall by blending the myths of Old Hollywood with the self-made myths of his early family life, while making an easily construable statement of authorial presence. We see a clapperboard, followed by a close-up of film noir veteran Ann Savage (whom we may or may not recognise as 'the fiercest femme fatale ever' (Maddin in Berning 2008: 1)) being fed her lines by an off-camera Maddin: clearly, this is staged dramaturgy, directed, reconstructed and controlled by a single intelligence. Savage – playing Maddin's somewhat frightening and apparently domineering mother, though he playfully insinuates throughout that this person is his real parent – will later speak these same, interrogatory lines in a newly melodramatic context, but it is Maddin's intention to create an immediate sense of artistic invention: the director, and his film, are happy to put words in people's mouths, and to give those words inflection and meaning. Savage's frame-filling countenance, from which we might normally expect to come extemporised recollection, is thus employed here by an unconventional filmmaker seeking from the off to counter non-fiction cinema's clichés, among them the talking-head device – a device, of course, which is usually interpreted as a conduit into the mind of the interviewee, not the director. One must infer that nothing, from the film's opening frames, is strictly reliable; nothing, in My Winnipeg, offers a guarantee of historical veracity.

FIGURE 4.3 The Maddin stand-in dreams of escape in *My Winnipeg* (2007)

Found and originated footage of sporting events, townscapes and day-to-day goings-on are accompanied by an archaic promotional song ('Winnipeg! Winnipeg! Wonderful Winnipeg!'), which together paint a hazily impressionistic picture of a snowbound, old-fashioned and harmlessly parochial environment singing 'one long happy song', as the lyrics extol. From this innocuousness, Maddin cuts to an actor (Darcy Fehr), presumably playing Maddin or his alter ego, fitfully drowsing on a night train bound for who-knows-where; hand-held tracking shots of passing buildings sway intoxicatedly, while Maddin and collaborator Georges Toles's ruminatory voiceover – which is more-or-less, like in *Night and Fog*, continuous for the duration – begins to tell a story of psychological imprisonment; unlike *Night and Fog*'s detached tone, the voice (Maddin's) is emotional, bitter and even angry at the narrator's tensile relationship to Winnipeg, herein a deceptively serene, difficult womb to escape: 'Winnipeg, Winnipeg, Winnipeg … My home for my entire life. My *entire* life. I must leave it … I must leave it now. How to find one's way out?' Maddin, via what will become a recurring technique, superimposes multiple shots, piling visual simile upon Freudian symbolism in a series of disconcerting graphic matches illustrating the city's curious, uncanny biology. The forks of the river, originally the main route of the trade and travel responsible for the settlement's birth, are likened to a woman's – Maddin's mother's – pubis ('the lap' of the city, pulling him maternally back to the furry, animalistic home), and arteries conveying blood cells; literal hidden depths ('the subterranean forks') are spoken of with (mock) reverence for old legends apparently secreted beneath the map; and Maddin continues to look for literal and figurative ways out through oneiric imagery and imagination, distorting the locality's nature so as better to understand, or likely undermine, its 'supernatural' gravity. Everything is intertwined, the phenomenological weirdness of extant, concrete actuality dissolving into the consequent weirdness of the filmmaker's psyche; unquestioning recollection becomes a source of scorn to be stripped away and retold. 'Thin layers of time, asphalt and snow' form a mesh of interconnected pathways, mantras, routes and meanings, a body politic and poetic to which Maddin contributes his own liberating narrative, inscribed palimpsest-like atop the official, repressive story that has rendered 'we Winnipegers' 'stupified by nostalgia': 'Our dream selves', claims Maddin, 'are our uninhibited selves' (Berning 2008: 1), for they see and unearth concealed strata.

In the first of many 'buried stories' visualised using appropriated archive footage, we learn of the Canadian Pacific Railway's annual treasure hunt, in which entrants competed to win a one-way rail ticket out of town, 'the idea being that once someone had spent a full day looking this closely at his own hometown, he'd never want to leave'. Apparently, in over 100 years not one winner ever left, so attached were they to Winnipeg – or simply, so the film implies, unable to resist its faintly sinister lure. Maddin, as we have seen, *does* (or certainly thinks he does) want to leave: to this end he will spend some time looking *very* closely at his hometown, dissecting both its superstructures and its underlying spirit with the hope of seeing and understanding this power. 'Well, I don't need a treasure hunt: I've got my own ticket,' declaims the narration, the image skipping back to the forebodingly darkened, expressionistic carriage interior containing Fehr's troubled sleep (the means of escape, frequently probed by the looming visage of a spectrally omnipresent Savage/Mrs Maddin, is portrayed as every bit as disconcerting as Winnipeg itself). 'I just have to make my way through town – through everything I've ever seen and lived, everything I've loved and forgotten … If only I could stay awake … '. Sleepwalkers – Winnipeg has 'ten times the sleepwalking rate of any other city in the world' – wander the streets, under the constantly superimposed snow, as shadowy, 1940s-styled silhouettes on aimless missions through a noir-ish prism trapping lost souls within its somnambulant evocation of filmic beguilement. A filmmaker, 'paradoxically, so avant-garde that his movies look like they were made almost a hundred years ago' (Grant and Hillier 2009: 143), Maddin evokes the codes and styles of cinema's past due not only to a genuine love of such, but also because Winnipeg seems to be acting like a movie, albeit a plotless one, upon its inhabitants: 'Because we dream of where we walk, and walk to where we dream, we are always lost.' Lost, perhaps, in the double-edged illusions of a Canadian narrative forever peripheral to the origin-point of world-sweeping North American or European film genre, as worked through in the cinema ('where we dream'), Maddin's Winnipeg is not quite expressionist, not quite film noir, but a love–hate world of shrunken, off-centre Manitoban myth that never finds solace, identity or resolution in its own marketing – a process gently ridiculed via the film's recontextualisation of quaintly asinine promotional material. Naturally, Maddin has responded by extruding from this perceived situation a playful cinematic uniqueness drawing on what he sees as Winnipeg's echoic cultural location: it is a place influenced by, but set apart from, the quintessential American image; these 'citizens of the night', contrary to their onscreen counterparts in the United States, cannot find their individualism, cannot become heroes, and so facelessly sleepwalk around town unsure of their purpose, holding bunches of keys to houses other than their own. It is this, more than anything, from which Maddin seeks artistic release: it is he who inhabits the gumshoe's role on this road to personal via geographical revelation, and he alone who will face the trials of the detective–hero by pushing at non-fiction's boundaries in an elastic archaeology of memory aimed at finding his life's, and the story of his life's, destination. As Maddin's daughter told him, 'of course it is a documentary – it's documentary about you' (in Halfyard 2007: 1).

To set a course for the future, Maddin takes us back in time, and tells us of his childhood. Home-movie frames combine with numerous family photos, which seem to speak of contented normality; there are his brothers, and the 'long, long dead chihuahua'; there is the inanely monikered Happyland, the ice-cold theme park constituting a distant echo of the unreachable Disneyland, its 'wind-chilled rollercoasters and ferris wheels enveloped in frost', but 'keeping us happy'; and there is the beauty salon run by his mother, its feminine smells and clients lingering over a resentful-sounding Maddin's development: 'At school I reeked of hair-product … lotions for the elderly … of girdles and talc, fur coats and purses … the smells of female vanity and desperation. I grew under their influences into what I am.' The voiceover describes Winnipegers' weather-beaten leisure proclivities in a sarcastically bitter manner, conveying nothing so much as professional condescension to those who might enjoy sledging, or snowshoeing, or simply falling over into cushions of snow. Yet, crucially, the tone of Maddin's narration changes, briefly, with an addendum about his home – the appearance of which Maddin laments has now been altered, and in his memories keeps altering. Slipping back into gauzy reminiscence, maybe even 'stupefied by nostalgia', like his fellow Winnipegers held by the city's umbilical cord, he daydreams: 'I will always love this shop.' Shaking himself (and us) from the reverie, however, Maddin cuts back to the train carriage and to a renewed purpose in examining his early life for the sake of getting free: 'All a dream, all a dream … I need to get out of here. What if I film my way out of here? It's time for extreme measures. I need to make my own Happyland.'

Such 'extreme measures' take the form of Maddin supposedly moving back into his childhood home, its fixtures and fittings restored to how they were during the filmmaker's youth, for a month; Maddin will then bring along 'mother' (Savage), rehearse several additional actors in portraying the rest of the Maddin family, and set about re-enacting his early life's pivotal scenes in a 'strange plunge back in time' to reset, re-evaluate and concretise the temporally distant in the present. 'Only here', says Maddin, 'can I properly recreate the archetypal episodes from my family history. Only here, can I isolate the essence of what, in this dynamic, is keeping me in Winnipeg.' Rather than waking up from the hypnotic dream-power of Winnipeg (as condensed by the historical Happyland) into a baldly factual rejection, Maddin enters an alternative dreamscape, *his own Happyland*, fighting an 'illusion' over which he has no control with another magical illusion made possible by cinema (a process over which he *does* have control, and a process allowing Madden to manipulate *his* Winnipeg according to a subjective vision). André Breton's *First Surrealist Manifesto*, of 1924, concerned itself with similarly psychoanalytic themes, stressing the blindness of logical, waking reality to influences rooted in the difficulties of youth: 'If [man] still retains a certain lucidity, all he can do is turn his back toward his childhood which, however his guides and mentors may have botched it, still strikes him as somehow charming ... now he is only interested in the fleeting, the extreme facility of everything' (in Roberts 2007: 93). As documentary filmmaker Nicolas Philibert has said, 'You have to begin to lose your memory, if only in bits and pieces, to realise that memory is what makes our lives ... Without it, we are nothing' (*ibid.*: 92). Memory, moreover, can be bent to the therapeutic purpose of a lucid dream. The essence of Maddin's memory, and its subconscious workings, henceforth becomes *My Winnipeg*'s chief concern: Maddin will attempt, repeatedly, to delve into dormant psychosexual effects at play in familial relationships, especially with his mother. (Not that this necessarily represents total honesty: one can, for fear of seeming trite, hide emotions behind exaggerated expressivity.)

After the satirical act of burying Maddin's deceased father under the living-room carpet – and thus diminishing to an awkward lump his paternal influence and existence – the family settle down to watch Winnipeg's longest-running television serial: *Ledge Man*. The show always involves the same, oversensitive man (today played by Fehr) attempting to jump from a ledge to his death; every episode, since 1956, the man's passive–aggressive, alternately soothing and berating mother, played by Savage, appears at the window and 'tells him to remember all the reasons for living': 'Don't think that they don't know that you're a coward and a baby who has to get his own way, all the time. You're looking pretty cocky now that you've given me shingles and made me lick dirt for all those reporters down there.' Savage, back in the stand-in Maddin house, watches her performance with pride. 'At the end of each episode,' says the narrator, 'the son is convinced to come into safety. But the next day, he is back up there again. Mother has never missed a day in the 50 years the show has been broadcast.' The parallels with Maddin's struggle to escape the clutches of his hometown, and his mother's apron strings, are abundant: Ledge Man's leap into the unknown world, the world outside Winnipeg, is constantly prevented by his mother's hectoring and infantilising; the Maddin surrogate (who looks like the man on train, but Brylcreemed into sartorial antiquity) is unable to get away, or to fulfil even the death drive for fear of matriarchal reprimand. (Father *has* died, but at Mother's insistence, and against Maddin's wishes, has been brought bodily back into the fold: even post-mortem, Father has not been allowed truly to pass away, instead lying tacit and still as a reminder of female dominance within the household.) 'Archetypal episodes' from the psychoanalytic id become literal episodes of a still ongoing daily drama, the struggle and ultimate failure of its protagonist acted out on television for all to see and maybe to mock, the unwelcome attention of strangers made plain by the presence of the current, old-lady tenant of the house, who refuses to leave and sits staring, blankly through fifties-style winged spectacles, at the screen (or the screen-within-a-screen) onto which are projected the director's deepest anxieties.

Once again including the clapperboard, Maddin features his verbal direction and Savage's (one supposes genuinely) fluffed lines, which he reflexively jokes is Mother 'doing it to be difficult … we fight on the set, and a refusal to acknowledge the real past becomes scientifically significant'. *My Winnipeg*, of course, centrally engages in just such a refutation of historical reality; its wonderfully spurious stories of civic eccentricity, its folklorically embellished legends, and its interconnected vignettes concerning domestic incidents are relayed as they emanate from the filmmaker's subjectively therapeutic, emotionally amplified version of the past, here more *personally* useful and productive than Winnipeg's or the Maddin family's properly 'true' history. As Maddin has explained of this creative licence, 'I love my mother to bits … [but] She can read our sexual histories as we etch them in body fluids on the walls. She can read exactly what happens … I think mothers can read consciences, and if you have a guilty conscience that's calling you out, it's going to call you out in the voice of your mother. Let's face it' (in Berning 2008: 1). Continuing to 'face it' and to 'vivisect his own childhood' via 'scientific' reconstruction, Maddin sets about replaying a dramatic confrontation between Mother and Maddin's teenage sister, who has come home with a bestially symbolic, bloodied deer pelt on the car bonnet, the vestige of a collision, and an encounter with a boy, Mother sees as reprehensible. The accusatory lines from the film's introduction reappear, as Maddin creates an ultra-melodramatic, exaggeratedly generic exchange meant to look like a long-lost 'woman's weepie' picture, complete with a soundtrack of swelling strings, exhumed from an imaginary archive somewhere in Maddin's mind. 'I wasn't born yesterday, dearie,' says Mother, now reaching back into the performance tropes of mid-century Hollywood genre to embody the archetypal, bordering on stereotypical, strident voice of oppressive motherhood set in cruel opposition to teenage lust. 'Where did it happen? On the back seat? Did he pin you down? Or did you lie down and let nature take its course? No innocent girl stays out past ten with blood on her fender!' (Maddin, as if wishing affectionately to go beyond a critique of his mother's 'deliberate' messing-up of lines to annoy him, in addition highlights the film's artifice by incorporating many fleeting gestures of the kind usually rejected in the cutting room: Savage's recitals are peppered with nervous-looking glances to camera, and to the director, suggesting a lack of confidence befitting an actress just emergent from a 51-year retirement, and more at home in cinema's golden age.) Melodrama, and its over-endowed conventions, are here utilised, according to the filmmaker, not solely to lampoon, but also to get at fresh understanding by using generically specific, theatrically unsubtle performance as an ironic mode of release:

> Good melodrama presents uninhibited versions of ourselves. So melodramatic plotlines are related to dream plotlines in that one way; they're just as uninhibited as the plotlines of our dreams. And good melodrama does it well, and bad melodrama does it poorly. Almost every film is melodramatic. You don't want to see something that's completely natural, otherwise you'd just watch security camera tapes of people buying chewing gum at gas stations and things like that … my favorite emotional filmmakers, the ones who work on me in the most powerful ways, quite often work on me on a second or third viewing only. And they're extremely stylised. I like Joseph von Sternberg, who helmed those Marlene Dietrich pictures … I also like Ernst Lubitsch, who stylises everything in comedy, but who can still destroy you with genuine agony, romantic agony, while you're laughing.
>
> (Maddin in Berning 2008: 1)

'Maddin', notes David Church, 'makes the sort of pictures that he wishes (or literally dreams) had been made by directors both great and forgotten, but in doing so, he creates something distinctly his own – and paradoxically, something strikingly original and new in modern cinema … hand-crafting something fresh (and, he hopes, emotionally eviscerating) from so such artifice and potential camp' (Church 2006: 1). Never 'completely natural', nor self-effacing, My Winnipeg is close to the diametric opposite of observationally purist non-fiction, whose fly-on-the-wall ambitions yield herein to something more ubiquitously watchful. Maddin's perspective, so far as it can be called, knows no such bounds as a wall. As Mother, part of the townscape and of the mysterious buried landscape – indeed part of the city's very supernatural substance – can apparently see all, and read minds, so the film responds in kind, stripping down the numerous psychological operations at work on Maddin's psyche into emotively constituent allegories, as if in a cinematic theme park (Maddin's 'own Happyland') wherein emotional rollercoasters replace their literal counterparts. Openly going through a process of pretending in order to examine what, precisely, is the memory-truth of a given situation – in this instance Maddin's childhood – the film argues, obliquely, for a liberating, penetrating removal of non-fiction's strictures, even going so far as comparing its spiritually revelatory methods to those of Winnipeg's celebrated self-proclaimed psychics and mediums, depicted in the subsequent sequence (replete with silent-movie-style iris effects and intertitles) producing ectoplasm and conducting séances, who 'have always been skilled at reading past the surface and into the hidden depths of their city'. Winnipeg, however, is too peculiar even to hold a conventional séance: a ritual contacting of the dead morphs into a ballet recital, the rites of spiritualism equated with the rites of art.

Maddin, on the lookout also for hidden depths in Winnipeg's benign-looking superstructures, recounts the story of an earth-covered hill made entirely of refuse, on which sledgers accidentally impale themselves on protuberant shards of rusted metal: another metaphor representing Winnipeg's sometimes poisonous soul, 'dreaming its filthy dreams of garbage' beneath a slumbering exterior. Even the barbed unpleasantness of Garbage Hill, however, is preferable to the city's harshly bemoaned recent architectural additions – chiefly because they are not yet the cherished sites of individual, or collective, memory. Complaining bitterly about the building of Winnipeg's 'sterile new thrift rink' (this contemporarily set material is shown in comparatively 'sterile', low-contrast, modern-looking colour), and yet more bitterly about the demolition of the old, the film posits the latter as mythically significant in Maddin's life; it is a living place of birth and of masculine nurture acting, in loco parentis, for his now dead father, a local stalwart who worked in the hockey arena and, 'with nothing left to do' upon the national team's 1970 disbanding, gave up on life. 'The real tragedy', stemming from civic heartlessness and a lack of poetic sympathy, would seem to be that Winnipeg is now erasing all trace of an edifice whose testosterone-filled chambers were to Maddin both an almost literal father and the locus of numerous rites of passage. Shots of wrecker-balls smashing the 'ice hockey cathedral [that] fit Winnipeg and its sport like a skull fits its brain' precede the story, read with increasing fervour, of Maddin's entrance into the world – an entrance of religious-like centrality to the city's narrative – from one of the rink's changing rooms, deep in the very body, the very brain, of Winnipeg. Springing forth as a baby born apparently not from Mother but from the spirit and symbols of male endeavour, we see the infant Maddin, superimposed and hovering helplessly between pucks and skates moving on the ice. Hockey, and its importance to the director's personality, becomes another dream; superannuated, elderly veterans, once legends in their city, return from the past to play one last game in the half-standing old venue, vital and strong again as a reminder of historical glories, their potent nicknames etched forever on Maddin's life. Unlike the majority of Winnipeg's citizens, who sleepwalk to nowhere, these are perhaps the film's only true heroes, men who have powered their way to celebrity, albeit transient. They never, though, managed to fulfil Maddin's longing for total escape, and remain physically and mythologically bound down to parochial folklore by shared addresses, loves and business interests unable to counter the National Hockey League (NHL)'s deleterious effect on the city's professional players. With touchingly romantic serendipity, for Maddin's film, the rink's carcass, upon its supposedly final pulling down by explosives, is only partially destroyed: 'Kind of a strange victory. Only the part of the arena added in 1979 to accommodate the arrival of the NHL in town falls off the arena ... This, I interpret as a sign: a sign that we should never have joined that league.'

There are many, polysemic signs in this city of auguries: that Winnipegers are forbidden by law to dispose of old signage is not unconnected to such symbols' nature as parts of the bigger, deeper map that Maddin wishes to scrutinise. Re-emphasising the theme of supernatural entrapment, in what constitutes the film's most astonishingly surreal sequence pertaining to signs or omens, Maddin tells of the horses that once fled a stable fire into the river. Depicted in shadow-puppet-style animation, the animals rear up in fright and swim for their lives; but, 'everything clogs' with cold, and the horses are frozen to death, heads protruding like chess pieces from an all-white board (*My Winnipeg*'s imagery at this point brings to mind Surrealist antecedents such as Buñuel and Salvador Dali's *Un Chien Andalou* (1928), and Georges Franju's 1949 *Blood of the Beasts*). The bodies, like so much else in Winnipeg, stay buried by the cold, hidden under mystery and legend, indices to something mad and yet beautiful. Needless to say, the locals – unafraid of Winnipeg's magnetism, for unlike Maddin they do not have the gift of artistic vision needed to see a way out under the tip of the iceberg – sense neither a portent nor foreboding, and blithely use the horse heads as morbidly kitsch props for society parties and picnics. Invoking the converse of these people, Maddin imagines a final 'What if?', inventing Citizen Girl, a proletarian superheroine to right all perceived wrongs and remake Winnipeg as a just and fair, alternate-universe self in accordance with the director's wishes. 'Then, I would know it's finally ok to leave.' The film ends with Mother, hugging Maddin's brother, dead but brought back to life, prostrate in the snow; the pair has found intimacy again – an intimacy and love perversely denied, in this land of esoteric secrets and mystical possession, to the living.

Evincing just the sort of 'dangerous' tendencies against which the sober-minded teacher John Grierson warned – namely those of art cinema and of the experimental avant-garde – *My Winnipeg* revels in alternative strategies, or what Elizabeth Cowie, in a study of non-fiction and modes of display, called 'the more disreputable features of cinema usually associated with the entertainment film, namely, the pleasures and fascination of film as spectacle' (in Beattie 2008: 23). 'This line of argument', comments Keith Beattie (*ibid.*), 'is extended in the

FIGURE 4.4 Surrealistic images of beautiful futility abound in Maddin's 'docu-
fantasia' (*My Winnipeg*, 2007)

recognition that such "disreputable" features are productively inscribed
within documentary representation through forms of display understood as the vehicle for a form of spectacle capable of producing
knowledge.' Maddin's 'docu-fantasia', in keeping with Cowie's analysis,
posits its spectators as 'desiring, as well as knowing' (*ibid*.), a link
between spectacle, subjectivity and knowledge-truth that has been elu-
cidated by, among others, Frankfurt scholar Theodor Adorno: '[T]he
value of thought is measured by its distance from the continuity of the
familiar ... knowledge comes to us through a network of prejudices,
opinions, innervations, self-corrections, presuppositions and exaggera-
tions, in short through the dense, firmly-founded but by no means
uniformly transparent medium of experience' (in Renov 2008: 46). *My
Winnipeg* is thus documentary as oblique autobiography, a lucid daydream
taking us into the mind of its creator as he seeks to unravel the titular
city's mystical bindings, which have crept inexorably around him since

infancy: only in this way can he hope to 'film his way out', and only in this way can he join the ranks of those documentary mavericks 'who have celebrated the nature of, and attempted to capture, the uncapturable of live as it is lived' (Roberts 2007: 101). But has Maddin managed to escape? At the time of writing, he wants to set up a base in Toronto (whose International Film Festival awarded *My Winnipeg* Best Canadian Feature), though he is also still committed to teaching at the University of Manitoba. 'I don't know if you can get out of Winnipeg. The trains don't go out. They just loop around the perimeter and come back' (in Gillmor 2007: 1).

## *WALTZ WITH BASHIR* (ARI FOLMAN, 2008): CONFLICT AND MEMORY

Pounding, electronic music beats like an urgent jackhammer; under a jaundiced sky, a pack of enraged, lupine dogs, with equally yellow eyes, tears through washed-out city streets towards its target: a man in a high window, looking down as the angrily barking animals wait for him … A harrowing dream sequence befitting the most nightmarish of fictions, and the unconventional opening of Ari Folman's *Waltz with Bashir*: Israel's first animated feature in four decades, and maybe the first ever full-length animated documentary. Perhaps surprisingly, there *is* a long-standing tradition of animated non-fiction, albeit a less-than-abundant one: see, for example, Windsor McKay's *The Sinking of the Lusitania* (1918), depicting an event of which no directly indexical, filmed material exists; the 1970s work of the Leeds Animation Workshop; Folman's own series *The Material that Love is Made Of* (2004); and Aardman Animations' *Creature Comforts* series of the late 1980s to early 1990s, which use stop-motion, clay models of comical animals to give bizarre, new visual life to vox pops on mundane, very British concerns, in the process satirising the performative, sometimes emotionally evasive nature of interviewees' responses. Michael Moore, Barbara Caspar (in her *Who's Afraid of Kathy Acker?*, 2007) and, as we have seen, Guy Maddin, are amongst those filmmakers of recent years to use brief, very stylised cartoon episodes within long-format documentaries – often as a parodic, succinct means of deploying ironic humour, or of conveying subjective thought via an obviously 'creative' treatment highlighting a film's shift into a discursive zone outside the normative bounds of 'actuality'. The relative paucity of cartoon material – material of an obviously 'unreal', humanly mediated basis – employed in non-fiction cinema is, given the form's historical tendency towards reliance on directly mimetic (and thus inherently 'trustworthy') photographic images, to be expected; nevertheless, as a rhetorical and artistic practice, such an approach remains underexploited. As Paul Ward explains: 'Animation represents one of the clearest challenges to simplistic models of what documentary is and can be, quite simply because you cannot have an animated film that is anything less than completely "created" … [Animation] can perfectly trace the contours of [the] thought process in a way that is out of reach for live action. Animation is the perfect way in which to communicate that there is more to our collective experience of things than meets the eye' (Ward 2005: 85, 91).

It is just this communication of inner experience that concerns *Waltz with Bashir*, an account of the 1982 invasion by Israel of Lebanon and its lasting impact on Folman, an Israel Defense Forces (IDF) veteran, and his colleagues. Mystified by blackouts in his memory from his tenure in the army, Folman, after attending many fruitless counselling sessions, decided to consult several also-serving friends, whilst advertising on the Internet for stories and recollections of the war, which began pouring in. One event in particular, during the IDF's merciless siege of Beirut, seemed to have had a devastating psychological effect on those soldiers (including the amnesia-troubled Folman) who found themselves on the periphery: the Sabra and Shatila refugee camp massacre, committed by Israel-allied Christian Phalangists in revenge for the bomb-blast assassination, days before he was due to be sworn in as Lebanon's new president, of charismatic leader Bashir Gemayel (from whose name comes Folman's title) – an atrocity in which around 3,000 civilians were killed. Then-defence minister Ariel Sharon, following his prolongation of what was meant to be a limited campaign aimed at expelling Palestine Liberation Organization (PLO) troops from southern Lebanon, was forced to step down (though he would reappear years later as prime minister) – the killing spree, undertaken as the IDF lit flares to facilitate night-time shooting, having 'changed the face of Israel and debased its cherished rectitude to the point where the government and army were implicated in the commission of atrocities. Sabra and Shatila had become synonymous with infamy' (Schiff and Ya'ari 1985: 280).

Gradually, Folman's collection of individual testimonies coalesced into a bigger, if still complex, picture of human comprehension distorted under the weight of trauma; now passed into the domain of contested memory, the war, with its ghastly nadir capping off a national embarrassment born of belligerence, is for its middle-aged Israeli ground fighters – men whom the film (which has been accused of the typically Israeli practice of 'shooting and crying') absolves of ultimate guilt – a fragmentary 'bad acid trip' of surreal nightmares and hallucinatory flashbacks. Still, Folman, his basic methodology a multi-point broadening of Maddin's reconstructive therapy in *My Winnipeg*, seeks an elusive, bullet-riddled resolution behind all this subjective invocation – of which the subjective invocation, for the heavy-hearted veterans, is of course a vitally revealing part. Combining interviews (dialogues between Folman and cohorts that were shot on video and then drawn by animators using the video as a reference) with reconstructions based on both imagination and received history, *Waltz with Bashir* comes across far less like the productions of Pixar or DreamWorks than as a starkly beautiful, if at times overpoweringly masculine, blend of Jeremy Isaacs's 1973 documentary series *The World at War*, the computer game *Grand Theft Auto* and Coppola's *Apocalypse Now* (1979), aesthetically a locus of admitted reference for Folman. At once real and unreal, the film, largely via its linearly animated distancing from live-action cinema's photo-processed (or digitally captured) verism, straddles the representational boundary usually dividing what are perceived in documentary film to be absolutes: what *did*, and what did *not*, happen. Associated at worst with *Boys' Own*-type comic-book immaturity, and at best with the more intelligent, relatively perspicacious hipness of the adult-oriented 'graphic novel', this is a stylistic removal whose novelty, for one thing, could be interpreted as an easy way out of fully addressing controversial issues: along with the use of cartoon renderings comes an implied semi-dismissal of live action's dubious yet familiar obligations. (It will, I hope, be clear to any reader of this book that the camera *can* and *does* lie; the cartoonist's or animator's pen, conversely, has never been the subject of a specious maxim regarding unmovable honesty, and hence carries lighter baggage in the way of expectation. In terms of filmic persuasion, animation and related methods are a rhetorical double-edged sword for documentarists who wish to be especially creative with actuality: with cartoons, there is greater 'poetic licence', but less *automatic* authority.) A move away from live action is not, perhaps, a serious artistic compromise within the autobiographically precise story of Marjane Satrapi's Middle Eastern-themed *Persepolis* (2007), for instance: it might, however, be considered problematic for an earnest work reassessing and reconstituting the tragic, shameful events of a half-forgotten campaign fought by apparently literally misguided, blind-firing troops. *Waltz with Bashir* is critical of Israel's government, but offers no politically concrete conclusions, preferring to navigate its electrifying way through a maze of experience towards a middle-point of barbaric pointlessness made possible by basically innocent, confused, frightened youths. It *is* a war film, nominally about a *specific* war, yet it also uses the general trope of war, filtered through shock-and-awe visuals, as a vivid backdrop for its creator's driving preoccupations – which, together with the artwork's heady brew, arguably fail to contribute to the historical record, whilst ironically serving to diffuse the savageness of the revenge killings: 'What comfort is it to the relatives of the Sabra and Shatila victims', writes Anthony Lane, 'that a few conscripts who stood by and did nothing are now free to articulate, and even to lyricise, their internal pain?' (in Hudson 2008: 1).

Centrally, Folman circumvents accusations of turning the IDF into the tragedy's victim–poets by a self-proclaimed attempt to interrogate the 'trustworthiness of memory itself' (Nathan 2008: 110), while piecing together a quilt of *internal* truth from mental patches formed at 'an age when you don't think at all' (Folman in *ibid.*). 'For me,' says Folman, 'the film is about memory – where do our memories go when we suppress them? – the question of whether memories still live inside us or have their own way of living' (in Jaafar 2008: 30). As for the decision to use classical cell, 'cut-out', Flash and 3-D animation (and certainly *not* rotoscoping of the type seen in Richard Linklater's 2006 *A Scanner Darkly*), Folman told journalist Andrew O'Hehir it was an easy one: '[T]he scenes in my mind were always drawn, always animated. So there was not another option. I would never do it any other way. And, honestly, I think I wouldn't be sitting here with you today if this was not an animated film. You wouldn't care about what happened to a guy like me 25 years ago, when I was just a common soldier in Lebanon, if you weren't told, "Oh, it's a very cool animated film. You have to see this film." As a filmmaker it gave me total freedom to do whatever I liked. To go from one dimension to another. To go from real stories to the subconscious to dreams to hallucinations to drugs to fear of death to anxiety, everything. I had the liberty to play with everything in one story line' (in O'Hehir 2009: 1). 'There is no real or unreal', seconds *Waltz with Bashir*'s art director David Polonsky: 'It allowed such freedom of expression' (in Nathan 2008: 112). Out of conflict, then, comes forth for Folman liberty, in the plastic shape of animation, and a resultant, heavy dose of undeniable coolness.

The rock-video-like introduction's ominous, attention-grabbing dogs, it turns out, come from the recurring dream of Boaz Rein-Buskila, one of Folman's co-conscripts. After what Folman likens to 'the opening of a chess game', or a 'deliberate strategy ... to stun [the audience] within those first two minutes' (in O'Hehir 2009: 1), the film cuts to the first of its reanimated interviews, set inside a darkened bar on a rainy night – generically perfect conditions, in fact, for the setting up of an otherwordly narrative, as Boaz and Ari begin the film's selective descent into a cloudy past. Immediately, it becomes clear that animation, essentially, has allowed a propitious manipulation of scenery and figures that suits Folman's dramatic purposes: if his talking heads were *not* recontextualised within such an astute, noir-infused synthesis of 'the cool of Japan, a sci-fi mood, the zaniness of M*A*S*H' (Nathan 2008: 113), then talking heads − a perhaps overused testimonial device freighted with those, at least to heavily narrative filmmakers, old-fashioned documentary yokes of cliché and triteness − they would remain. Rendered, graphically, with a linear, low-key, high-contrast realism that evokes the New Hollywood's takes on war, but moving with a strange, eerie mix of marionette-like buoyancy and leaden weariness, *Waltz with Bashir*'s figures float, burdened-seeming, through a parallel domain of captivatingly expressed semi-reality whose dominant hues are the vintage browns, greys and yellows of Coppola's *Godfather* trilogy (a palette itself learned from prior examples, chiefly the paintings of old masters). We are definitely watching a cartoon; there are indeed traceable elements of the manga template; yet this has been filtered through a very cinematographic sensibility predicated not only on Folman's patchily recollected army experience, but also on a definitely *not* forgotten understanding of film art as aesthetic practice. Crucially, the director is more than aware of that practice's relationship to audience perception, knowing full well the commercial power of association within the 'marketplace of ideas'. Things appear distanced, refracted, but belong to a recognisable tradition of cultural submersion, in which the key to gaining the spectator's trust − and Folman, a concise, chess-playing storyteller wishing to 'stun' as much as to intrigue, assumes of us a relatively short attention span − lies in the shorthand communication of pop-cultural savvyness. *Waltz with Bashir*, though addressing a little-discussed war, thus occupies a fairly 'safe' zone in terms of its cinematic art, familiar use of 'war film' iconography and narrative grammar, which is mostly appropriated from extant, tried-and-tested sources. The film's stylistic innovations are considerable, if superficial, but rather than invent a new game, Folman sticks fundamentally to what he knows, rethinking only his strategy, rather than redrawing the board. Absolute innovation, in its literal sense extremely uncommon, is herein secondary to a thrilling *fusion* of learned ideas deployed with élan.

FIGURE 4.5 Scenes of conventional realism anchor *Waltz with Bashir* (2008) in a familiar aesthetic

The 'present' time frame – of the interviews conducted by the 45-year-old Folman – repeatedly gives way to subjective flashbacks, of course a filmic staple, and one whose nature permits ambiguity. 'We tried to do a *Rashomon*', says Folman, again citing his film amongst a tradition of almost unanimously accepted 'cool', 'to tell the events through the fantasies and hallucinations of each character. They remember the scenes, but the details shift' (*ibid.*). (Errol Morris's 1988 film *The Thin Blue Line* is an earlier, famous documentary utilising different flashbacks on the same event.) Deemed too emotionally fragile to kill a man, Boaz recounts the tale of how his superiors asked him, during a night-time raid on a Lebanese village, to 'liquidate' exactly 26 dogs, lest they warn of the IDF's approach: it is these ghost dogs of war, all 26 of them, who come snarling back from the past into Boaz's conscience, a haunting metaphor, perhaps, for the Phalangist troops on their rampage, or for the revenging spirits of the dead refugees. Folman, at least at the film's outset, has no similar recollections – his (ever-so-slightly handsomer) cartoon self appears contrite, lamenting things 'not stored in my system' – but agrees with Boaz that filmmaking might be therapy: 'I'll think of something', he says, the pair going their separate ways over the

neon-lit, glossy-wet streets. 'That night', says Folman's narration, 'I had
a flashback.' With his comrades-in-arms, a young, naked Folman emerges onto a beach from the maternal waters of a flare-illuminated sea, its
womb-evoking symbolism (a trope used many times in the cinema of
war) heavy with indications of birthing and above all innocence thrust
into a worldly chaos existing in all-too-close proximity to the comforts
of motherly nature. Almost literally, these men–infants are born pur-
blind into bewilderment and conflict, something the aesthetically
minded director was keen to emphasise, throughout both the film and
its attendant publicity, via this condensatory image:

> We call this the 'super scene' because it's the establishing shot of the
> whole film. You see it three times. We put this image on everything
> from the posters to the logos. It should be hallucinatory but also rea-
> listic. There is something about the combination of the sea and the
> city … in cities like Beirut and Haifa, where I grew up, the beach is like
> the city itself. You put up the night flares, which for anyone who has
> ever been in battle are something you'll never forget, on top. It colours
> everything, bathes everything in deep orange. We wanted to make a
> realistic scene in a very dreamy way, so that you would be confused
> until the very end about whether it happened or not.
>
> (In Jaafar 2008: 29)

The 'super scene''s hallucinatory feeling fits perfectly with Paul Wells's
description, after Stanley Cavell, of animation as 'a mode of expression
which both re-defines the material world and captures the oscillation
between interior and exterior states, thus engaging with matters both of
(aesthetic, spiritual and intellectual) consciousness and the reception of
a pragmatic (socio-cultural) "reality"' (Wells 2002: 7). Indeed, it is
likely that if these scenes, moving 'between interior and exterior states',
were not animated cartoons but live-action reconstructions, we would
perceive them as somehow fanciful or absurd; within a film whose
interview/recall/confessional narrative is essentially driven (as opposed
to My Winnipeg) by the testimonial language of traditional documentary

exposition, however, the representational codes of animation (its setting up of an alternative, flexible space wherein processes of blatant depiction interact with signified 'reality') permit entirely greater licence, on the part of the filmmaker, to give visual expression to dream states. Folman's decision to animate the interviews, also, makes for a seamless and more cogent whole, serving to conjoin the worlds of subjective flashback, oral history and more-or-less absolute factuality. *Waltz with Bashir* – notwithstanding its historically marginalised subject matter (and controversial perspective) – in formal terms possesses neither the instant authority of dryly composed, would-be definitive films such as *The World at War* or *Shoah*, nor the impact of *Night and Fog*'s differently organised delving into a horrific past. Yet it has other, distinct virtues: those of a marked willingness to examine memory as inexact, and to consolidate and thus give (dis-)concerted voice to fragmented inner truths previously floating in isolation, the presumed products of unique trauma.

Folman's flashback culminates in a close-up of his sorrowful face, as dozens of ghostly, wailing women and children pass him by on a street; from this, we cut to the middle-aged Folman, on the search for elucidation, ringing the doorbell of another friend: film director, actor and therapist Ori Sivan, now living with his family in a remote settlement. Folman explains his puzzlement that Boaz's dog-dream should have triggered the beach episode. 'Memory is fascinating,' says Ori, explaining a 'psychological experiment' whereby adults were shown real images from their childhood, along with a faked composite: 'Their portrait was pasted into a fairground they'd never visited. 80 percent recognised themselves. They recognised the fake photo as real! … They remembered a completely fabricated experience. Memory is dynamic. It's alive.' Illustrated with depictions of clowns, balloons and ferris wheels – that exhibit a magic–realist tendency to intrude, slightly disorientatingly, on the 'real-life' setting of Ori's house – the experiment, by implication, sounds a cautionary note against the discredited techniques of 'recovered memory therapy' (and its dangerous implications: false memories, 'recovered' by zealous psychoanalysts from patients seeking to locate the genesis of their troubles, and consequently a resolution, have led on a number of occasions to criminal prosecution for abuse). So Folman is eager not to create, via this documentary, outright invention that might lay unfair blame: he must acknowledge the subjective plasticity of memory, whether memories appear 'realistic' or bizarre, and emplace the notion of memory within his film not as the basis for factual assertion so much as a psychologically originated, often warped mirror held to a distant time that encroaches, like the ferris wheel, sometimes strangely on the present. To quote filmmaker Nicolas Philibert once more, 'Our memory is our coherence, our reason, our feeling, even our action' (in Roberts 2007: 92); but memory, itself 'alive', can at times be an unreliable, unreasonable, incoherent witness. This is what *Waltz with Bashir*, in its examination of a war now fought in the head's 'dark places', is about, and this is what it tries to address. 'Memory takes us', says Ori, 'where we want to go.'

Sharing a joint (a risky instrument of perception-altering potency that may take us places we *don't* want to go), Folman and Carmi Can'an, these days a successful businessman in the falafel trade, discuss the latter's experiences. (Folman wants to make sketches: Carmi says it's 'fine as long as you draw but don't film', an incisive comment on the film's representational freedom from directly mimetic recording and its impositions.) To the eighties, retro-chic sound of OMD's 'Enola Gay', we see the boat that took Carmi to Lebanon: actually an old commando ship disguised as a pleasure cruiser to mislead the enemy. Most of the soldiers are partying, but Carmi, a self-described 'nerd' who was anxious to prove his masculinity as 'the best fighter and some big hero', is vomiting over the side. Falling asleep ('I sleep when I'm scared'), the young soldier begins to dream – of a giant, sexily beautiful sea-nymph who climbs onto the deck and takes him away, cradled on her stomach, across the motherly water and back to the safety of the feminine. From this supernaturally calm vantage, Carmi sees the ship explode into flames, but does not flinch. When he wakes, however, he and the other nervous soldiers arrive on a beach, and indiscriminately open fire on a car containing a civilian family. They survey the carnage, but do not comprehend this 'dark place', any more than Carmi really comprehends the dream.

Here, despite the narrative's relatively seamless continuity between supposed states of factually faithful recall and of imaginings, which we in all likelihood understand to be dreams simply because of their physical impossibility, the film seems earnestly to be portraying history as it happened: there is, of course, no magical 'guarantee' of any scene's historical veracity (nobody says, 'Now I promise this really happened'), but the post-*Saving Private Ryan* codes of the generic war film – on-the-ground, 'hand-held' camera, desaturated colours and unflinching bloodiness – are reproduced as if, paradoxically, to suggest authenticity. Folman's animated documentary thus on occasion mimics the 'realist' fiction film's methods of copying the portable-camera-filmed documentary aesthetic (though the omniscient camera, in all reconstructed war zones, usually has impossible privy, proximity and safety, something acknowledged by Folman in the later scene featuring a cameraman cowering under fire). *Waltz with Bashir* does this, even if it is often not literally stated, because it sometimes needs to differentiate between total subjectivity and grammatically encoded actuality for the purpose of

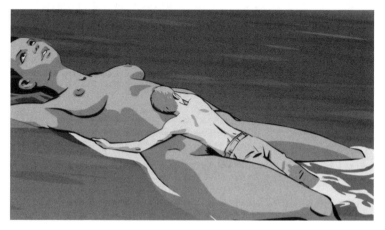

FIGURE 4.6 *Waltz with Bashir* (2008): a soldier dreams

*locating trauma in deed.* Simply put, it cannot function, cinematically, as a representation *purely* of dreams: there must be construed some basis in fact, whereby testimony comes over as trustworthy – in this particular case via the documentary 'contract', with the viewer, written both in the interview's conventionally testimonial function, and in generic terms borrowed from Hollywood. Although Folman has at this juncture lost his memories of the war, apart from brief flashbacks whose nature appears largely oneiric, he (and by extension his film) requires more than just the dreams of others to set him on the path to discovery; he needs to know – *we* need to know – about the dead family in the car, without which the sea-nymph episode loses its context of phantasmagoric, youthful escape from guilt or murderous association. Folman, questioning his friend but unable to ascertain whether the naked sea-emergence (which features Carmi also) might actually have taken place, attempts to recontextualise his own dream; rather than a means of immediate escape, he seeks a farther-sighted comprehension, which may lead to absolution, based on using *Waltz with Bashir* to immerse his psyche in the conflict's effects. If Maddin, finding freedom in deliberate falsehood, composed the playfully ambiguous *My Winnipeg* to portray the relationship of his hometown to his mind, Folman's film, even if its methods are analogous, extends (limited) roots into shared history and the human desire to gather knowledge; however this knowledge crosses into the realm of mental construction, *Waltz with Bashir* nonetheless looks ultimately not to mystify, but to reveal: 'If I had to sum it up', says Folman, 'it's me getting connected to who I used to be when I was 17' (in McClanahan 2009: 1). (As we have seen, the documentary form is partly about 'epistephilia', a 'pleasure in knowing that marks out a distinctive form of social engagement' (Nichols 1991: 178). In order that Folman fully share his quest for connection, he allows us to indulge in a 'social engagement' with not just the men's minds, but also their minds' relationship to implicitly 'knowable' events.)

During a cab ride, the 45-year-old Folman has a moment of revelation as the veil of repression falls away. 'Suddenly', he narrates, to the sound of Max Richter's taut score (around which, unusually for a documentary, much of the film was cut), 'all the memories came back. Not a hallucination, nor my subconscious.' As if to stress the documentary importance of 'knowability' via historical fidelity, Folman emphasises a distinction, at this point asking of us a degree of trust in the director's ability – a capacity that the whole piece, by and large, calls into question – to sort precise recall from psychologically concocted imagery. Folman and his colleagues sit atop a fast-rolling tank, sheltered on one side by thick palms: the men shoot machine-guns constantly and aimlessly across the landscape, knowing not who or what they might destroy. Afterwards, Folman is asked to 'dump' IDF bodies at a helicopter base, a task that filled the young man, who had never seen such gruesome sights before, with dread. These are, in a sense, Folman's own wounds opening up in order to heal; this is the reality of war, a reality much more disturbing than anything brought forth from 'hallucinations' or the 'subconscious'. The apparent reliability of these memories serves as a narrative springboard into another interview with another friend, Ronnie Dayag, who describes a nearly miraculous, lone escape from a beach fire-fight into the darkened sea – always the site of motherly protection, and editorially equated in *Waltz with Bashir* to Dayag's mother, with whom he was close. Nothing, though, is without painful consequences: Ronnie, it transpires, is ridden with guilt for not being there to help rescue his friends, 'as if I had fled the battlefield just to save my own skin'. Standing at his fallen comrades' gravesides, Ronnie felt ashamed, so stopped going, and tried to forget what had happened: of course, Ronnie now becomes emblematically part of Folman's ground-level revisiting of the war and its effects on lost youth – he is offered a kind of absolution via the film's sensitive interrogation of his feelings as a 'simple soldier', whereas defence minister Sharon, seen far removed from the carnage and eating a huge plate of fried eggs whilst giving telephoned orders to attack, is most definitely not. All, though, is vague: wider motives are never discussed, and Sharon, who remains a silently looming presence, escapes total indictment.

In this respect, *Waltz with Bashir* evinces an affinity with the 1980s cycle of Hollywood Vietnam films seeking to repaint GIs as bewildered and callow *naïfs* sent to waste their innocence in pursuit of obscure ends. Arguably a politically diffusive tactic aimed at the absolute shifting of ultimate blame onto a nation's ideological fundament (the young, within such tropes, are always innocent, misguided or corrupted by the *immediate situation*'s barbarity), it nevertheless demonstrates Folman's admitted purpose: 'I was a soldier; we were clueless. We didn't know what was happening ... I couldn't care less about Ariel Sharon and his government. I have nothing to do with them, not then and most of all not now' (in O'Hehir 2009: 1). Ronnie, speaking after the film's release and of its impact on his life, declares that he 'feels good' about the numerous phone calls he has received from old friends; they see his place in the microcosm of war more clearly and with a fresh understanding of his emotions (see Freedland 2008). This is a film that remedially psychologises the troops, but that deliberately does not afford those on high that privilege; neither does it explicate the war's complex background details and legacy, nor attempt to provide much specific context or meaning beyond the battlefield-as-trauma device. As its nature as a cartoon distances it from what Susan Sontag (2002: 154) called the 'death mask' of photographic indexicality, so its limited, sketch-like methodology colours it in another way: 'A truly social documentary', notes Allan Sekula, 'will frame the crime, the trial, the system of justice and its official myths' (in Haughey 2007: 58); to which Anthony Haughey adds, in fairness, 'No easy task given the messiness of most conflicts, the intractable nature of "evidence" and the politics of silence that emerges in the aftermath of conflict' (*ibid.*). Folman is acutely aware of the two critical flanks lined up against his work: that it suffers from its unwillingness to express the perspectives of both sides (maybe we should hear not just from IDF soldiers, but from the families of those killed); and that, whilst claiming to be deeply concerned with the soldiers' functions as unwitting agents of territorial aggression, it nevertheless sees no need to tie this aggression down to a rhetorical mast of Israeli policy. It is probable, however, that if *Waltz with Bashir*, not a 'truly social documentary' *per se*, but a personal mediation, were to have turned its attention to the cultural and social mechanisms behind the slaughter, then it would have cast its net too wide. 'That young people can die for politics or religion', said Folman, with an idealism suggesting a lack of suitability to penetrative commentary (and its 'dry', uncool conventions), 'is something I cannot understand' (Nathan 2008: 114). Despite seeing the war as a 'breaking point' in Israeli history and the first time that that nation had prosecuted an unjust campaign, Folman and his co-filmmakers prefer to observe things from the emotionally shell-shocked perspective of men trying to revisit their 17-year-old, 'clueless' selves: looking not upward at the awkward, fathomlessly receding 'chain-reaction of negligence' (Schiff and Ya'ari 1985: 285), but inward at the eternally dynamic psychology of suspended boyhood. Herein, adult men – now all settled and relatively adjusted – set about redrawing the war comic from the (to some) indulgent vantage of the analyst's couch, even including analysts into the bargain.

Visiting a psychology professor, Zahava Solomon, Folman stays focused on his main theme of compiling a mental tapestry. 'We call them disassociative events', explains the professor. 'It's when a person is in a situation but feels outside it.' (A phrase obliquely reflective of

FIGURE 4.7  Folman reinvents the interview in *Waltz with Bashir* (2008)

*Waltz with Bashir*'s socio-political stance, and alienating aesthetic, in general.) She tells the story of how a young man, an amateur photographer, coped with being at war by pretending to view everything as if through the lens of an imaginary camera: 'He said to himself, "Wow! What great scenes!"' Day to day, confronted with misery and death, his defence worked fine, until suddenly, as he chanced upon the bodies of numerous dead and dying, slaughtered Arabian horses lying around the Beirut Hippodrome, his 'camera broke' and his coping strategy collapsed. Dead horses, curiously, are one of the most affecting and thus most used images in cinematic history (see *My Winnipeg* for a recent example) – it seems appropriate, then, that such a vision tore the photographer from his shell: 'Horror surrounded him, and he freaked out', unable to reconcile this cinematically disturbing vista with his mental schema for the 'real' world. All this can constructively be read, primarily, as a means of helping Folman reach his 17-year-old self; it can also, however, be seen to comment, pivotally, on *Waltz with Bashir*'s spellbinding character: how is Folman, a man looking for psychological insight, going to break his own illusion? Ought he even to try?

Something of a calm before the storm, the film's middle section deals, quite beautifully via its putting together of 'great scenes', with what the director *does* remember from his youth: his many visits home on leave to find that all is going on as normal without him, his pretty lover Yaeli dumping him just before he left for action, and his wandering around an abandoned airport, whose surreal emptiness, looted shops and bombed-out planes made a lasting impression; there is even a hard-core pornography scene, made censorially permissible by the animation medium, which is viewed on wobbly VHS by a portly officer as he nonchalantly gives the order to blow up every red Mercedes in town (a report has come in about possible car bombs: 'A real blast', jokes Folman, with a sense of humour bordering on Schwarzeneggerian). Then, while posted to a lookout and hallucinating that his ex-girlfriend is watching over him, the hitherto dreamily arranged, meandering narrative takes a sharp turn towards what Folman calls 'hard-core' documentary: essentially the cinema of 'reliable', factual exposition, no matter how *Waltz with Bashir* holds back from analysis. His younger self gets a call, over the field radio, from the pornography-watching officer (who is still slouched in the same armchair, watching nothing but static), telling him that Bashir Gemayel has been killed. It is the equivalent of the photographer's dead horses, snapping the film into a deathly trajectory (we presumably already know about the massacre, so it was a matter of when, and how, Folman decided to introduce it). 'You'll be in Beirut in two hours', says the superior soldier; Folman fantasises about his own death, and how Yaeli will be overcome with guilt. 'I am afraid', he narrates portentously, 'of what will happen next.' Again, the film avails itself of generic grammar. Studio-based talking heads, against a neutral backdrop and now without Folman's interviewer to distract from the final act's thrust, introduce the action with journalistic authority (an authority peculiarly bolstered by the extremely unusual experience of watching spontaneous, accidental gestures – coughs, pauses and mumblings – transposed onto cartoon figures). We see soldiers in an explosive-wracked street come under heavy fire and fall dead, unable to escape – one, on his own and terrified, dances the title's waltz, firing randomly into buildings adorned with giant portraits of the just-assassinated leader. Although this macabre, poetically acute exhibition never happened, it is a poignant, perhaps necessary illustration of Folman's assertion that these young men are being led a merry dance into oblivion for the sake of remote, distantly iconic, supernaturally machinating politicians: Bashir, says Carmi, was 'like David Bowie', a cult figure of power exercising dominion over pop-cultural realms also. Someone, Carmi points out, was bound to take revenge.

When it happens – and the film is at pains to make sure we are under no illusion as to what group commits this act – the massacre, as described by witnesses, recalls images from the Warsaw Ghetto (a controversial equivalence, but one Folman insists is justified: 'The Holocaust is in our DNA ... When [people] saw the footage, it matched the memory. They freaked out because they saw the disgrace' (in Nathan 2008: 114). Coming full circle around both the film and Folman's newly intact memory, the wailing women in chadors reappear, making fresh sense of their first appearance. To the sound of lamentation, the film centres finally upon Folman's young countenance, coming face to face, as it were, with the return of the repressed. But this is not quite the end. As if to acknowledge, but perhaps not quite deal with, the difficulties of representation encountered when putting together animated depictions of atrocities, Folman includes several minutes of live-action, archival footage of the massacre's aftermath. Though undoubtedly affecting, these images seem like an afterthought designed to wrench the viewer back into an empathetic engagement with mimetic reality; the power of photography's indexical 'death mask' is rammed home in a sequence underlining, by contrast, animation's distancing effects. Can animation not truly represent such things, or possess sufficient rhetorical gravity? Has Folman's film, for the most part, occupied a zone of poetically charged, but not realistically potent, signification? In the end, it is a tough call. 'I didn't want anyone leaving the theatre thinking it was a cool animated movie', says Folman, slightly confusingly (ibid.). It would seem, on reflection, that the director is trying to have things both ways, and ending up with a compromise that serves mostly to bring into harsh relief the problematic flip-side of using a 'cool' aesthetic. The ending is, in its own way, a devastating coda, which nonetheless reflects uneasily over the preceding 80 minutes' explorations; simultaneously, the film has throughout disavowed the importance of contextual detail, and asked for emotionally based spectatorial alignment, a plea most obvious and maybe effective in its last, photographed frames – frames that 'break' Folman's special, paradoxical camera, his way of dealing with representation and of ensuring public interest.

One way of avoiding framing a situation is to concentrate on basically human universals, on the heart-breaking sensations evoked by images of the dead, and of functionaries killing and being killed for remote geopolitical ends: Folman's obligations to edify are debatable (a film does not, after all, have to be all things to all people), but that he 'couldn't care less' about government might offer a hostage to fortune. A definitive, personal yet explicatory study of the First Lebanon War would indeed be 'no easy task', but *Waltz with Bashir*'s eschewal of all such material lends it at times the appearance of a rough draft, rather than a fulsomely engaged project. What the film does do, however, is bring to light the pleasures, potentials and pitfalls of animation as a documentary device. As Walter Benjamin once said, arguing for a more artificially mediated version of photographic reality, 'less than ever does a simple *reproduction of reality* express something about reality' (in Haughey 2007: 55); Sontag, likewise, decried how overexposure to graphically horrific images within our obsessively visual 'scopic regime' may, like extreme sexual pornography, 'corrupt' and 'anesthetise' (*ibid.*). Possibly, there are reflexive solutions to these problems, somewhere, to be found in the animation medium – a medium that 'may be viewed as a fundamental questioning and interrogation of the representational apparatus upon which the dissemination of ideas rests' (Wells 2002: 12). *Waltz with Bashir* elegantly picks up, beguilingly dances with, but ultimately fails to run with all these issues, and those summed up by Paul Ward when he describes the creative possibilities of animated documentary as being rooted not solely in the creative interpretation of the spoken word, but in a *fundamental rupture* with the 'apparent "naturalness" of the link between image and sound' (Ward 2005: 99) constituting the formal bedrock of traditional documentary since the coming of synchronised audio. Folman, undoubtedly the author of a significant work that will inspire many others to probe more deeply than the surface of non-fiction animation's potential, has lit a torch for his successors to carry. As for the historian's view of the massacre: '[W]hen it was all over and the terrible truth had come out, almost everyone scrambled to pass the blame as far as it would go rather than ask themselves what went wrong. If there is a moral to the painful episode of Sabra and Shatila, it has yet to be acknowledged' (Schiff and Ya'ari 1985: 285). That the Second Lebanon War was unfolding during *Waltz with Bashir*'s production suggests, sadly, that little has since been learned.

# 5

## PERFORMERS

Many of the discussions in Part II have been partly about non-fiction's longstanding tendency to incorporate (and elicit) aspects of performance, and the implications this holds for documentary realism, narrative, observation, 'authenticity' and reconstruction. In Chapter Five, however, the last of our case studies looks at recent films that in methodologically differing ways *centralise* and *depend on* traditionally performative strategies; demonstrate how these are adopted by particular filmmakers and/or their subjects as a practised way of life; or highlight non-fiction's usually inexorable (yet as often concealed) reliance on enactment: Jonathan Caouette's *Tarnation* (a performance of a filmmaker's uneasy youth); Michael Moore's *Sicko* (which posits the larger-than-life director as political and presentational 'star'); Sacha Gervasi's tale of fraternal crises *Anvil: The Story of Anvil* (2009); and Nirit Peled's *Say My Name*, a rare female take on the usually hyper-masculine 'rockumentary', which focuses on not one or two artists, but many and various struggling rappers on both sides of the Atlantic.

## *TARNATION* (JONATHAN CAOUETTE, 2003): PERFORMANCE AND AUTOBIOGRAPHY

Stylistically assimilating numerous cinematic traditions – which range fully from the puckish avant-gardisms of Kenneth Anger and Stan

Brakhage to the observational naturalism of fly-on-the-wall direct cinema – *Tarnation* is a hectically composed chimera: a kaleidoscopic 'self-inscription' (literally, a writing of the self) based on stream-of-consciousness reconstitution (of old amateur movies, photographs, found footage and answering machine messages; cf. Jarecki's *Capturing the Friedmans*, 2003), overt performance, interviews and an underlying foundation of highly confessional identity politics. All of which come clashing together, and at times jarringly diverge, to comprise a sympathetically vigorous, semi-linear portrait of Caouette's exuberant, if dysfunctional, personal life. Made on an extremely low budget, using Apple's entry-level iMovie video-editing software, *Tarnation*, though it feels resolutely home-made, nonetheless represents an extravagant culmination of Caouette's long-gestating artistic desires, which were bound from an early age to find release via film. As he says of his obsession for recording and archiving for the purposes of self-documentation: 'Filming things had a critical life-and-death purpose. It was always a defense mechanism and a way to have a sense of control over my life. Filming was also a way to control and defend myself against my environment and disassociate myself from the horrors around me' (in Anon. 2005: 3). *Tarnation*, a film really *all* about 'Me', is thus undeniably self-indulgent, yet it mostly succeeds in making a virtue of unflinching auto-analysis and painful honesty; sharing with *Waltz with Bashir* and *My Winnipeg* its therapeutic properties designed to come to terms with 'horrors', it asserts its maker's sense of dislocation (a sense conveyed, ironically, in pursuit of a new kind of belonging) as both defining and personally challenging. It is avowedly authorial in nature, though concerned with a sort of 'domestic ethnography' citing the family as 'the most fundamental crucible of psychosexual identity' (Renov 2008: 45; see also Russell 1999: 275–314);[1] and it belongs, very loosely, to a sub-group of documentary definable as the 'first-person diary' film, a means of usually introspective or relatively parochial expression favoured by filmmakers such as Judith Helfland (see *A Healthy Baby Girl*, 1997), Deborah Hoffman (see, especially, *Complaints of a Dutiful Daughter*, 1995), Ross McElwee and the prolific Lithuanian film-diarist Jonas

Mekas, who in 2001 released a five-hour film entitled *As I Was Moving Ahead, Occasionally I Saw Brief Glimpses of Beauty*, put together from half a century's worth of archive material chronicling his life. In addition, *Tarnation* engages in a semi-underground discourse first emergent in the post-sixties climate of cultural empowerment for minorities of colour, ideology or sexuality: 'voices proclaiming and celebrating their own "freakishness", articulating their most intimate fears and secrets' (Jon Dovey in Chanan 2007: 248); in this respect, its ancestors are those sexually and politically emotive works by Marlon Riggs in the United States, and Briton Isaac Julien (see Chapter Two), as well as the numerous instillations by conceptual video artists in the 1970s to deal frankly with the artist's own body via the new medium's capability to 'write *through* the body, to write *as* the body' (Renov 2008: 43).

Diaristic filmmaking, 'a genre somewhere between the essay, reportage and the well-told tale' (Chanan 2007: 246), in its most popular contemporary forms stems largely from the increased availability of technological facilities: critically, the 1980s boom in cheap camcorders, and the more recent digital mini-revolutions of the Internet, the multifunctional, super-compact camera-phone, and the desktop PC- or Mac-run edit suite. (Much has rightly been made of this 'democratisation', yet it is only partial. Informational and financial access to the knowledge bases needed to make effective films is still limited to those with discursive privilege, wherever such 'cultural capital' may originate. Along with the thrilling potential for everybody to become an autodidact, self-chronicling, inventive filmmaker has arrived a tidal wave of pointless, binary-encoded vanity projects as deep as Web servers can hold. As Richard Leacock once remarked, 'Anyone can use a pen, but how many people can write great novels?'; in Saunders 2007: 191.) Over the past three decades, a concomitant proliferation of broadcast media, seen in the diversification and growth of cable and satellite channels, has given rise to a generation of artists – with new-found access to relevant technological aids – shaped and versed by saturation in the post-modern codes of advertising and MTV, and in the recycling of pop-cultural motifs to present an eminently consumable version of the world broken down into bite-sized chunks of familiar-but-strange iconography. It is a confusing vista, but one in which Caouette and his like, from feature documentarists all the way down to the numerous video-bloggers today making use of YouTube as an outlet for auto-biographical creativity (and, as often, vapid exhibitionism), have immersed themselves perhaps as a 'response to the challenge of social location in postmodern society' (Patricia Aufderheide in ibid.: 246). Autobiography and documentary, however, as we have seen in previous chapters, are not always easy bedfellows, at least philosophically speak-ing. Michael Renov has postulated that 'autobiography, even when con-structed of indexical parts, remains an agnostic in the house of certainty … the "truths" that autobiography offers are often those of the interior rather than the exterior' (Renov 2008: 41). Jean-Michel Frodon, of *Cahiers de Cinema*, has applied to *Tarnation* the slippery label 'autofiction', although its maker takes issue with this neologism, deny-ing that the film presents anything other than a deeply truthful, cultu-rally acute explication of temporal, social and psychological contexts, and those contexts' formative bearing on his life: 'Autofiction? … I don't really like the notion of fiction in that word, I think. Of course there have been some reenactments, but those reenacted parts in *Tarnation* that I did during the editing process are not fictional to me. I just needed them to tell the story of my life, and as I didn't have a camera in every important moment, I would just capture them later' (in Von Boehm 2008: 1). Caouette is happy to see himself as fundamen-tally, intrinsically a performer, and his debut film as a consolidation of a life's work acting out a quest for the unique meaning of Jonathan: which, naturally, is most appropriately sought by throwing off the shackles of generic, 'old' storytelling – the clichés of which media-lit-erate post-modernists like Caouette would identify as somewhat passé – in favour of confetti-like vignettes dropped strategically but scatteredly into place to offer the spectator a view of a *habitus* (roughly, one's acquired beliefs, tastes and thought patterns) tangled not only in total media absorption/refraction, but also in the rich tapestries of a broken family.

*Tarnation* begins with a sequence (treated digitally, like much of the film's video-originated material, with overlaid scratches and artificial degradation effects) featuring Renee, Jonathan's faded beauty of a mother, in a kitchen singing a jaunty, 'happy-clappy' song of Christian worship extolling uninhibited yet humble individuality: 'This little light of mine, I'm gonna let it shine! Let it shine, let it shine, let it shine!' At this point, we know almost nothing of this person, who dances cheerfully around for the camera, other than that she is a rosary-wearing, probably blue-collar Catholic who is fond of stage musicals (she sports a *Les Miserables* T-shirt). Even with no foreknowledge, however, it is hard not to construe that Renee's general situation has gone a little awry, and to ask oneself why Caouette chose to open his film this way. It certainly seems like a 'family' moment, the proxemic codes (the codes of interpersonal distance) between cameraman and subject suggesting relaxed intimacy: would Renee 'shine' like this for anyone other than kin? Here is a 'self-portraiture', notes Michael Renov, 'refracted through a familial Other … Due to kinship ties, subject and object are bound up in one another' (Renov 2008: 44). This brief introduction, then, is a summary of *Tarnation*'s stall: the film will let Jonathan and his nearest cast a light of autobiographical examination – from within, and onto those around them. Soon, after a quasi-candid, naturalistic but obviously enacted (given the various camera placements) scene establishing the director's contented, New York-based love life with his partner David, it is revealed that Jonathan's mother, back home in Texas, has been suffering from mental illness and has taken an overdose of the anti-depressant lithium: Jonathan, preoccupied and concerned, performs – in every sense – an Internet search and makes an emotional phone call to the hospital. In an extreme close-up (a device whose figuratively penetrative nature might in other forms of documentary elicit accusations of voyeurism, but whose use here appears inversely *self*-exploitative), we see tearful anguish etched deeply into the face of a sensitively good-looking, photogenic young man unafraid of the camera and perhaps born to become a star by cathartic means: he wretches into the toilet bowl, having set up an appropriate framing before so doing, and says he has a fever 'from all the stress'. Again, *Tarnation* emphasises the highly dramatic, pivotal significance of Renee to Jonathan's life, mental and physical: it is his mother who will set in motion a process of 'taboo-busting': 'Mental illness has been whitewashed by Hollywood', he says; 'I wanted to show what it's really like. I often think about what my mother could have been' (in McLean 2005: 1). A black-and-white, slow-motion image of Renee, half-smiling to the camera, appears, dissolving to a dreamily soft-focus shot of the woman embracing her son: this, maybe, is the alternative-universe, idealised Renee of Jonathan's imagination, a woman untroubled by psychiatric intrusions or depressive angst. The shot does not last long, soon giving way to a pensive-looking Jonathan on a train to Texas. (There are a multitude of train shots throughout the film, a motif described by Caouette as indicative of existential transience: 'I think life is a train. It is sort of gazing out of the window and seeing terrain go by very quickly to great music'; in Von Boehm 2008: 1.)

Film, however, is not bound by life's absolutes: it has the 'power to stop and reverse time's inexorable passage, providing a powerful tool for the obsessive investigation of the past, autobiography's stock-in-trade' (Renov 2008: 43). A rapidly edited montage of grainy old images – of factories, graveyards, country roads and dilapidated housing – flashes past, in a dreamy rush of ghostly reverie invoking conventional filmic representations of hypnotically elicited recollection. We are falling through a landscape of incidental memories, literally back in time towards something formative: *Tarnation* here plunges us down the rabbit hole of Caouette's abundant archive, to the accompaniment of an archaic self-help tape (the use of which seems at once ironic and sincere) that detachedly advises one to 'keep interested in your own career, however humble: it is a real possession in the changing fortunes of time'. *Tarnation*, of course, is just such a 'real possession' – a way to exert a degree of discursive, contextual control over the past (and the future) by gathering up the knotted cords of memory and evidence, parsing them into freshly meaningful structures, and endowing them, by their incorporation into this very personal story, with cinematic poignancy.

Whilst Jonathan makes the train ride home, gazing contemplatively out of the window, the film takes us on a turbulent ride across thematically quite familiar terrain: a human landscape commonly traversed, as we have seen, by the multitude of documentarists to have used non-fiction film, autobiographically or not, as a vital tool for 're/calling the past into the present, and preserving something of the past or present for future contemplation' – the never-ending search for 'the "then" in the "now"' (Austin 2008: 51). Doing away with any pretence of plotting a chartable, evidentially verifiable route across objective history, *Tarnation* whisks us back, in a feverish flurry, to the outset of Caouette's vividly illuminated narrative.

Having been seized by this temporal whirlwind and vigorously spun around, the spectator is given some traditionally orientating backstory, via a series of titles over a slide show: 'Once upon a time in a small Texas town ... ' What at least begins as a happily-ever-after-type fairy tale unfolds, and eventually entirely unwinds, to the sound of Iron and Wine's wistful 'Naked as We Came', and Glen Campbell's 'Wichita Lineman', a curiously timeless, eternally resonant song about loneliness and desolation, its narrator existing painfully outside of humanity, hearing his loved one 'singing in the wire'. We are told of how Jonathan's grandparents, Adolph and Rosemary, met, fell in love and got married; they had a daughter, Renee. 'Everything in their lives', attest the titles and family-album photographs, 'was bright, happy and promising'. Renee was spotted by a talent scout and became a child model, appearing in magazines and on television; but, one day, she suffered a debilitating fall from a tree, which paralysed her for six months: thinking that this was 'all in her head', Renee's parents submitted her for a course of electro-convulsive therapy, a devastating ordeal from which she never totally recovered. Nonetheless, Renee went on to meet Steve, from New Hampshire, with whom she had Jonathan; Steve, though, not a family man, soon left town. From 1965 to 1999, Renee entered numerous psychiatric hospitals. Despite their eagerness to apply ECT, none of the professionals therein were able to apply a clinical diagnosis. Moving to Chicago, with no money or home, the young mother and son experienced another trauma: Renee was raped, in front of Jonathan, by a stranger who had taken them in from the street. After an especially alarming episode of his mother's increasingly strange behaviour, during which she 'disturbed' fellow travellers on a Greyhound bus, Jonathan spent six weeks in a foster home, while Renee was put in prison. Jonathan then went back to Texas, to stay with Adolph and Rosemary, but was quickly removed by welfare officials, who put him in several foster families over the course of the next two years. In these homes, at only four years old, he was beaten and tied up, all the while his memory of Renee – her original personality apparently now erased – fading. Eventually, Jonathan was again adopted by his grandparents.

The story's implications for Jonathan are naturally immense, its convoluted tortuousness amounting to a boyhood consistently upended. Caouette, though, stayed strong: shaped by his ordeals and experiences, the young man worked to carve out a psychological place in the world

FIGURE 5.1 *Tarnation*'s (2003) most arresting performance, as the 11-year-old Caouette brings to life 'Hilary Laura Lou'

by observing, recording and performing a version of life as he saw it, acutely assimilated and reworked to restore emotional order. His resilience, exhibitionism and intelligence come together, especially during the early phases of the as-yet-unnamed *Tarnation*'s production, to form a defence mechanism predicated on searching for the meaning of 'I' in channelling and mediating the performative actions of others. A captivating sequence follows in which we see the director's 11-year-old, to-camera performance of another, fictitious life: that of a tearful southern woman abused by her husband. It is in some ways a disturbing monologue, coming as it does from a young boy with a clearly super-precociously developed sense of theatricality. It is realistically nuanced, if at the same time melodramatically hammy, brimming over with an eerily inhabited, possessed-seeming keenness to invest everything he has in this one, great gush of dramaturgy. Equally, it is darkly satirical, and simply extremely camp – but most importantly, perhaps, it is a purposeful filtering of Caouette's voracious media consumption: 'That night I had watched an episode of *The Bionic Woman* where Lindsay Wagner was going through this *Stepford Wives*-type situation. And on PBS I had seen *For Colored Girls Who've Considered Suicide When the Rainbow was Enuf* with Alfre Woodard and that moved me a great deal. So I just sort of set the camera up, meshed those two characters with something to do with my mother, and out popped Hilary Laura Lou. I remember definitely feeling committed to the character and her pain, but I also was having great fun with it. At age 11, I certainly didn't have a developed sense of camp, but I did have a sense of humour. I guess I just always liked operating on many different levels of understanding all at the same time' (in Soden 2006: 3).

All this, coupled with *Tarnation*'s 'different levels of understanding', stems from something Caouette, keen to work outside the boundaries of formal expectation, describes as 'instinctual': the film often skips between such performances (there are dozens of much shorter, silent ones, too, which split into fractions of the frame like a personality breaking up) and vaguely hallucinogenic, fleeting depictions of clouds, abstracted bits of civic or industrial architecture, faces, bodies and sundry other articles pertaining to the director's preternaturally sensual, 'cafeteria Catholic' grasp of the world and of the cinema. *Tarnation*, existing proudly in its own, discombobulating sphere, revels in repeatedly summoning a disorientating visual tornado that evinces distinct shades of *The Wizard of Oz*, a cautionary fantasy of domestic escapism by which the young Jonathan was beguiled ('I really wanted Dorothy to get home, but I also wanted her to stay in Oz. I would get so excited watching that movie, I'd just about burst' (in Soden 2006: 4)). Often, *Tarnation*'s 'tornado' passages comprise images frantically sped up, mirrored, overlaid multiply atop one another, or otherwise distorted: back home, in Caouette's reconstituted past life, now perhaps both fantasy *and* reality, the family itself is by implication a warped microcosm refracted through a psychic Oz from which there is no permanent return. Grandmother Rosemary, clearly for some years 'not herself', yet in some ways an amplified, performative version of herself extruded through a life of hardship and world-weary resilience, appears to have rubbed off on her charge also. In 'Texas 1984' – the titles offer *some* orientation for Jonathan's story to make concrete sense when he needs it to – we see, rendered in ethereally lo-fi VHS (a dead format spookily brought back to life), snatches of the relationship of Rosemary, who is introduced as a kindly if somewhat eccentric presence, with her grandson. Markedly childlike, and maybe heavily intoxicated (though by exactly what is not made plain), she is happy to be filmed gigglingly repeating the phrase, 'I'm Charlie from the Chocolate Factory', wandering around the house, applying make-up and woozily contemplating her next hairstyle. (One is invited to ask whether this not entirely composed woman is 'fit' to adjudge her daughter suitable for ECT: or, for that matter, to bring up children. Where, if she is not, *should* Jonathan be?) Jonathan responds, in the film, by including another of his melodramatic, female characters: a neurotically disturbed girl, fiddling with her hair and suddenly erupting into a psychotic shriek, whose similarities to Rosemary are clear. A picture of fragments emerges wherein history eerily repeats itself: *Tarnation*, simultaneously an acknowledgement of, a part of and a break with this process, effects, by its totally assimilative comprehension of a given situation, what could be the *only* way for Jonathan eventually to come to terms with (and use) this repetition. Only by hypnagocically grasping the past and making it his own might he creatively heave himself away from the vicious cycle.

Indeed, much of Caouette's development, as dealt with in *Tarnation*'s not-so-secret diary, is connected via this mesh of influence, projection and continual imprinting: his experiences and interpersonal influences are complexly but definitely entwined. In 1986, Jonathan – understandably looking for emotional palliation in the dangerous act of juvenile emulation – fell in with enthusiastic dopers (as had his mother) and was given a joint spiked with the much stronger psychotropic agent PCP: the drug set in motion a disturbing illness, manifesting itself in feelings of disassociation and depersonalisation. (The film sincerely offers a medical description of 'Depersonalisation Disorder: Persistent or recurrent episodes of feeling detached from, and as if one is and

FIGURE 5.2 Images from numerous sources multiply and fragment (*Tarnation*, 2003)

outside observer of, one's mental processes.' Strangely, Caouette here uses a clinical definition as back-up, as if he cannot choose better words, even though the institutions from which such verbal pathologising comes had ostensibly ruined his mother's life.) Sent to hospital, Jonathan thereafter 'felt like he were living in a dream', a state that, together with the rare stance lent by being an 'outside observer of one's mental processes', can only have impacted heavily on the semi-ethnographic nature of his autobiographising. As he says: 'Living with depersonalisation is like constantly adjusting a pair of glasses with the wrong prescription ... The flip side of this is that because I am so hyper-aware of mortality and reality, I really appreciate and admire everything I experience and the people in my life ... I really want audience members to feel like they are peeking in on something different and intense and glorious and real. Life is just too beautiful to live in any other way' (in Anon. 2005: 6).

Around the same time, at age 13, he discovered a new outlet for expression: going to gay new-wave clubs (sometimes, using his aptitude for acting, dressed as a female goth – a ploy to cheat age restrictions). Participation in a 'scene', most notably that of 'queercore', allowed him both the reassurances of tribal identity and, crucially to *Tarnation*'s aesthetic, access to movies of the cult underground, whose luridly outré visions he found inspirational. At this point, moreover, forever posing and confident, he begins to look like nothing so much as a 'too beautiful' throwback to the days of Andy Warhol's Factory-era 'superstars': variously a young Paul America, a wannabe Chelsea Girl, a white-wigged socialite, or any star straight out of Paul Morrissey's gleefully sardonic riffs on the ultra-cool avant-garde of 1960s and 1970s New York City (an obvious destination for Caouette later on). But *Tarnation* could not, for the most part, be said to operate in the same way as Warhol's films, even as Caouette personally adopts a deferential, urban surface aesthetic. Warhol's 'I just turned on the camera and walked away' approach, a quasi-disengaged attitude that works to oppose the traditions of experimental film's earnest 'pursuit of authenticity and selfhood' (see Rees 1999: 69), is quite at odds with *Tarnation*'s rapid-fire, 57-varieties mish-mash – which, though it *does* draw on different types of 'structural film' for its Brackhage-like ticks (the artificial scratches and degradation), and incorporates Warhol-style repetition, is ultimately altogether less jaundiced, its vignettes instead comprising genuinely hopeful outpourings concerning the 'glorious and real' paradoxes encountered on this quest for identity. Caouette's iMac, after all, is no Factory, nor does it constitute (for him) a means of production whereby authenticity, or the authorial 'aura', is in any way interrogated; his self-inscribing signature runs through the film like the embedded writing in a stick of rock, even if every frame owes its existence to previous works, and every persona therein harks back to the quests of others. In this way, the lazy-seeming use of iMovie's title, effect and transition templates can be understood as literally fitting: Caouette, throughout his life, and *Tarnation* (the two might to all intents and purposes be as one), is trying on a series of literal and metaphorical uniforms, all adopted and evaluated in capriciously transient succession, to see which ones fit. Some will return; some will be discarded; all are part of the febrile rush to expression. Fighting back via group affiliation, countering the difficulties of a home life in turmoil, Jonathan is having *fun*, hurriedly feeding what he sees and loves back into his life, much of which will likewise feed back into *Tarnation*: the culmination of film-infused fantasies 'of being in rock musicals like *Hair*', and of meeting the producer Robert Stigwood, with whom Jonathan (as always referred to in the favoured third person of the historically august *biographical* chronicler) 'could collaborate on a rock opera about Jonathan's life'. (Gus Van Sant, *Tarnation*'s champion, would take the Stigwood role.)

We witness scenes from Caouette's first effort at narrative filmmaking: a gleefully ridiculous Super-8 horror spoof called *The Ankle Slasher*. Another movie (entitled *The Goddamn Whore*) sees Jonathan, as ever unafraid to co-opt family into his long-running media scheme, direct a foul-mouthed Rosemary, while *Spit and Blood Boys*, from 1988, is a self-conscious, pretentious attempt to assert punk and homosexual credentials by fusing the fearless artistic tropes of coastal gayness with gore-centred body-shocks (two men, one made-up as starkly white, the other black, embrace and kiss, drooling fake blood over one another). If this footage – and the sheer quantity alone is impressive – constitutes by and large the fun but embarrassing (for the spectator, at least) product of an inchoate teenager simmering with hardly unique 'issues', it is nonetheless not without allure: Caouette, laying himself bare as a shamelessly fixated copyist/parodist, meticulously catalogues his own methods of derivation and introspective exploitation, possibly sensing the need to balance out *Tarnation*'s less straightforward moments. (Any filmmaker who will admit to once making *Blue Velvet*, the musical, *with the songs of Marianne Faithfull*, deserves some kind of praise for going beyond simple camp into an arena of meta-brazenness. Where were the makers of *Jerry Springer The Opera* when this was going on?) For, when the film shifts into its last third, which is concerned with the adult Jonathan's reunion with and study of his still mentally disturbed mother, the methodology of this indubitably unique 'autofiction' – as it strives for such uniqueness on both formal *and* directly evidential levels – becomes increasingly fraught with ethical difficulties.

Though undoubtedly Jonathan is happy in every way to expose *himself* to macro-examinations, and moreover ideally to make a career out of warts-and-all candour extending to the comprehensive coverage of his own peccadilloes, the familial 'Others' are seen to be ambivalent, vulnerable and uncomfortable with such behaviour. If the introduction asserted Renee's infant-like happiness to 'shine', then that quality is not always apparent. Despite what Caouette says regarding critics who accuse him of 'whoring out my mother for my own fame' ('I think that's a crock of shit') (in McLean 2005: 1), *Tarnation*'s inexorable juggernaut indeed rubs abrasively up against its peripheral subjects and their dutiful, familial inability to decline involvement – in the case of Rosemary, who suffers a debilitating stroke, later to die, this representational quandary is immediately apparent ('Do your Bette Davis imitation, Grandma', implores Jonathan, but Rosemary can't find the words); in the case of Renee, it is more subtle. Caouette, as we have seen, claims the film is about Renee, but it is really about him, *via* her. Renee is, for *Tarnation*, an ethnographically justificatory way in to its self-examination: if Renee doesn't at least partly cooperate, then the film is effectively high and dry, its heart drowned out by the overbearing 'look-at-me'-isms of a solipsistic neophyte merely proclaiming, not explaining, his own specialness. The 11-year-old Jonathan's performances are unforgettably extraordinary; the grown-up, failing actor's stereotypically bohemian inculcations of popularity and theatrical extroversion rather less so. Desperately enacted cries for help, which in turn became staged suicide attempts, give way to the endless dry-run auditions and mini-screen tests of a semi-professional gadfly basically undistinguished from his peers and their surely all-too-similar stories: dreams of Broadway, for all such people, inevitably leak into the waking hours to render every social action over-enunciatedly performative. By the end of the second act, although the film still possesses an aesthetic vibrancy that pulses with a sense of its own adventure, the narrative's trajectory is looking decidedly bereft of a target: Adolph, who must for many years have been the most continuously present, senior male influence on the director's life, is relegated to the status of a well meaning old buffoon (with enough gumption to threaten to call the police to stop his grandson filming: naturally, Caouette's ethos of brash reflexivity means that this, like several other angry protestations aimed at reducing the complainant's exposure, ironically makes the final edit in the name of 'reality'); Rosemary, a previous source of fascination, has passed away; Jonathan has moved east to seek fame and fortune, whilst unable to transcend his wage-earner as a doorman; and life, as a stage, goes on: sideways into the everyday struggles faced by any one of the thousands of day-jobbing hopefuls come to the Big Apple.

But, in 2000, Renee arrives in New York like an avatar of dysfunction bestowing on *Tarnation* much-needed evidence of Philip Larkin's naughtily phrased truism. Obviously, Jonathan dearly loves his mother; yet the film at times borders on what Elbert Ventura, in a highly damning and articulate critique for the online magazine *Reverse Shot*, called 'Exploitation masquerading as tribute ... Nothing is out of bounds; everything is material' (Ventura 2005: 1). Jonathan interviews a nervously trembling, probably medicated Renee at his and boyfriend David's compact-and-bijou Brooklyn apartment, pressing a little too hard for details of the 'psychotic' Rosemary's abusive episodes, Renee's time in mental institutions and the accident that led to these treatments. Several times, harangued, Renee walks away from the interrogation: 'Tell me! Tell me!' says Jonathan, 'It's not your fault. Will you please just help me with my stupid film?' Sometimes, the director gives away more than intended about his motivations. Almost certainly never considering the film truly 'stupid', Caouette most likely includes these ostensibly flattering snippets to bolster, disingenuously, a methodology (a methodology of uncompromising, attention-seeking soul-baring) pregnant not only with personal reflexivity's admirable qualities, but with its dark flipside based on forcing those around him, of differing inclination and fragile equability, into *Tarnation*'s post-modern confession booth under the pretext that the project is a 'stupid' and therefore benign work of adolescent folly. She is not falling for it. 'Talk to me! Mommy, this is the kind of shit that you talk to me about all day', implores Caouette: Renee, goes the spurious logic, should be willing to put her 'shit' on record for the sake of defining *Tarnation*'s Me: *your* child, *your* family, *your* little light. *Sight and Sound*'s B. Ruby Rich (2006: 1) praises these moments as 'necessary reminder[s] of the power relations that lurk behind the surface of most documentaries and contribute to their shape and direction', but Jonathan simply does not let up, or hold back from showing his exasperation in facial close-ups detailing what can only be construed as affected sulking. (Such shots recur, towards the film's close, with a frequency giving the impression of a man suspended in a state of arrested, mirror-phase obsession – perhaps, on the evidence of *Tarnation*, quite willingly. As Dylan Evans notes, after Jacques Lacan, '[T]he moment after the subject has jubilantly assumed his image as his own, he turns his head round toward this adult who represents the big Other, as if to call on him to ratify this image ... It is the mother who first occupies the position of the big Other for the child, because it is she who receives the child's primitive cries and retroactively sanctions them as a particular message' (in Evans 1996: 119, 136). For Caouette, a Wiki-age Narcissus in love with his own, multi-mediated reflection, the identificatory, self-image-making artistic act depends on *total* acceptance of the film-as-mirror, and the film/mirror-as-self.) Walking away again, Renee will not play ball. 'I have enough problems, honey, without bringing up the past. Ok?' 'You know', complains Jonathan, in another revelation loaded with accidental subtexts and emotional blackmail, 'I'd like to find out a few things about *myself*, too.' Attempting to elicit further self-knowledge (all the more to 'ratify his image') Caouette, remarkably, manages to feature his father, Steve, who is in town on business. Bringing his mum and dad together, Jonathan succeeds in creating some genuinely touching, if fleeting, moments of interpersonal poignancy, as the three sit talking for the first time in three decades, relaxed-seeming with the camera, if not totally with each other. There is tension, not to mention some sexually odd banter indicating, predictably, an utterly shattered love that Jonathan cannot repair; yet his now less intrusive filmmaking is here sympathetic to the older subjects' understandable sensitivities. It is enough, for Jonathan, to observe: though he remarks that the situation is 'surreal', he does not feel the need to psychoanalyse, possibly because he is aware of the intrinsic, autobiographical value of this material to his cause, wherever it may end up in the cut.

The trio's reunion turns out to be the calm before the traumatic storm of Renee's lithium overdose, to which *Tarnation* returns via a series of flashbacks to the film's introductory images. After a five-year absence, Jonathan comes back to Texas to find Renee 'brain-damaged' by drugs and living in squalor: it is in this condition that we first saw her, without the alarming situational context. In maybe *Tarnation*'s most disturbing sequence, Renee sings, swoons, laughs and rants nonsensically, whilst dancing with a pumpkin and finally offering her sarcastic resignation: 'I swear to God this is a pumpkin! Woo-hooo! Smile, you're on Candid Camera todaaaaay!' Renee can barely hold it together, but this uncharacteristically long take looks like the culmination of Caouette's study: undoubtedly fascinating, somewhat in the manner of a car crash, the scene *does* fulfil the filmmaker's stated need to show us what mental illness is really like, on an intimate level if not a deeply psychological one. Yet its revelations come at a moral and ethical cost, most evidently to Renee's dignity – an anthropologically slippery concept, admittedly, the crux of which, one could argue, is nevertheless definably contingent more heavily on the general impression given by *Tarnation* than Renee's feelings apropos the 'candid camera': her hardly informed 'consent'. Jonathan is at pains to stress his mother's eventually warm response to the film; the issues at stake, however, go beyond his subjects' *post hoc* assent. Where Frederick Wiseman had invoked similar problems in his *Titicut Follies* (see Chapter One) to the ultimately honourable end of cleaning up a despicable institution, for example, here the fact that Jonathan is family perhaps does not give him *carte blanche* to train his kino-eye on one grossly damaged woman in the throes of mental collapse. During this display – a performance not of calculated, youthful identity-seeking but of long-gone disrepair – Caouette says nothing, as if to emphasise his engrossment and encourage the spectator's. The once very interactive author has become, depending on one's opinion, either a detachedly unsympathetic observer or merely a showman of the grotesque, although in fairness, he could add nothing other than platitudes, having already decided to show us *everything*. *Tarnation* benefits, narratively and spectacularly, from Renee's misfortune, without which it would at times seem shallow – but the upshot is worrying. As it plumbs the depths of 'acceptable' candour, to a point where it arguably becomes a freak show hiding behind a fig leaf of genuine but abused mutual affection, it takes the grave risk of taking our acceptance for granted. Caouette confronts Adolph about the supposed childhood molestations of Renee by himself and Rosemary (now no longer here to answer for herself): 'You're trying to scheme something on me!' replies the elderly man, 'Tend to your own business!' Adolph, obviously, admits to nothing: no matter, Caouette's own business, as we have seen, is *making* his whirlwind of a movie, rather than eliciting absolute fact.

Following another tornado of images gleaned from photo albums, Super-8 and camcorder footage, Jonathan returns, with his mother, to the Brave New World of New York. Things certainly seem happier in this Tirnanog, and it is here the film concludes. Renee frolics and laughs with the bright young things, accepted but maybe also a novelty and accessory. Adding a last note of auto-ethnographic validation, Jonathan, in a tearful soliloquy, says that Renee is 'in my hair, she's behind my eyes, she's under my skin ... She's downstairs'. *Tarnation*'s last image is of mother and son, cuddled up on the sofa together, 'fucked up' but getting along, hopeful for the future. (How superficially similar, yet how perversely different this is from Guy Maddin's ending to *My Winnipeg*, an also contrived but more honestly representative depiction of mother–son dysfunction.) Of course, it is all another performance, another set-up for the camera, but one that fits perfectly the film's controversial, overarching assertion that all human life is just an ongoing process of acting out what it means to say 'I'.

Attracting near-universal acclaim on the festival circuit for its undoubtedly dazzling visual flair, heralding of a new direction in documentary production, and low-budget, late-night embrace of the

FIGURE 5.3 Jonathan and Renee in *Tarnation* (2003)

creative freedoms afforded by such an approach, *Tarnation* is not without its share of fervent critics. 'A damning avatar of American narcissism', wrote Elbert Ventura, summing up the case for the prosecution, Caouette's film 'is a quintessential artifact of this home-movie-obsessed generation – the unquestioning belief in the infinite interestingness of his life qualifies him as just another citizen of our reality-TV nation. By itself, this solipsism would be merely annoying. But in implicating his family in his own drama-queen dreams, Caouette crosses the line ... Has he no sense of decency?' (Ventura 2005: 1). Since *Tarnation*, a number of similarly minded films, almost always of lesser ambition, have come and gone. Doug Block's 51 *Birch Street* (2006), Alexander Olch's *The Windmill Movie* (2008) and above all Jarecki's Oscar-nominated *Capturing the Friedmans* (2003) have transcended the template's 'narcissistic' tendencies and found unique relevance in their exhumation of the archival past and re-endowing of such footage with fresh meaning. *Tarnation*, however, remains an often beautiful, often infuriatingly flawed exemplar of a genus's first blossoming, holding forth shamelessly as the inevitable emissary of its maker's milieu: 'The media', notes Ursula Frohne, 'have become the last authority for self-perception, the "reality test" of the social persona: I am seen, therefore I am' (Frohne 2002: 262). Moreover, Caouette has ventured into what Michael Renov imperatively argues is a much-needed, typically twenty-first-century arena wherein autobiography intersects with the political:

> The assertion of 'who we are', particularly for a citizenry massively separated from the engines of representation – the advertising, news, and entertainment industries – is a vital expression of agency. We are not only what we do in a world of images; we are also what we show ourselves to be. I would therefore argue that Jonathan Caouette's struggles for self-definition, his sorting through of identities that include southern, queer, child prodigy, abuse survivor, foster child, and mama's boy, is an act of survival rather than an aesthetic choice. *Tarnation*, like so many works of its ilk, enacts a politics of the body

(the guts, the bowels, the balls) rather than of the mind. But it is a vital politics nonetheless.

(Renov 2008: 48)

'The time has certainly arrived', concludes Renov, 'for a reassessment, for the open acknowledgement that the subject in documentary has, to a surprising degree, become the subject of documentary' (2004: xxiv). As *Tarnation*'s tagline puts it, 'Your greatest creation is the life you lead' – a manifesto for both gross indulgence and abundant joy, two voices competing incessantly throughout Caouette's groundbreaking public-access diary.

## *SICKO* (MICHAEL MOORE, 2007): MICHAEL MOORE, DOCUMENTARY SUPERSTAR

Compared with the polemics that made his name – *Roger and Me* (1989), *Bowling for Columbine* (2002) and *Fahrenheit 9/11* (2004) – Michael Moore's *Sicko*, about the numerous deficiencies of for-profit healthcare, looks likely to receive relatively little scholarly attention. Yet, though the brasher *Capitalism: A Love Story* (2009) is imminent as I write, it represents an adaptive mutation for the usually unsubtle master of reformist hullabaloo. Moving away from the perhaps necessarily heavy-handed, obviously rhetorical tactics of his establishing works towards a considered, cogent and powerful style that gains as much from its tempered maturity as its passionate posturing, ironic humour and tragicomic stunts (all of which are present, if reined in), *Sicko*, a film dependent on our foreknowledge and perception of Moore as much as any pre-existing sensitivity to problems inherent to the American healthcare system, nonetheless hits home with aplomb. Moore's great genius, centrally, is his ability nearly always to make us *care* – at least for the duration of whatever film by which we're being persuaded – and *Sicko*, its toning-down largely facilitated by Moore's established fame, notoriety and newly grown-up ease with the cinematic medium, manages this quite acutely.

As we have seen in Chapter One, Moore is not a journalist; he is not bound, despite what his detractors might say, to the professional reporter's ideals of 'fairness'; nor does he in any way share that occupation's usual tendency towards 'zealously, if surreptitiously, serving the status quo'. 'Without the loyalty of these professionals on The New York Times and other august (mostly liberal) media institutions "of record"', continues filmmaker John Pilger (2007: 30), 'the criminal invasion of Iraq might not have happened and a million people would be alive today. Deployed in Hollywood's sanctum – the cinema – Moore's Fahrenheit 9/11 shone a light in their eyes, reached into the memory hole, and told the truth. That is why audiences all over the world stood and cheered.' Pilger, finding Moore's opinions in tune with his own, implies that Moore's truth and the truth are basically one and the same – they are not. Moreover, the fact is that if Moore's films endeavoured to convey the whole, objective truth (a conceptual red herring for nearly all those unfamiliar with the history of non-fiction film), then that would render his work both functionally impotent and 'about as compelling as network television' (Sharrett and Luhr 2005: 254). As Brian Winston notes, 'Moore liberates documentary from this spurious tradition [of objectivity] and admits it is a species of editorialising in its essence. Complaints that he is partial, biased, unfair and simple-minded (while all true) are completely irrelevant to the basic documentary value of his work' (Winston 2008: 274). Already immovably in the limelight, thanks to a startling, vividly controversial style astutely constructed in acknowledgement that 'subtlety in American politics has as much chance of being noticed as a sleeping man in a room full of the newly dead' (see Schultz 2006: 194), the 'gonzo demagogue' has of late stepped analytically back from this received public image, using his perception (of the public's perception) as a means to channel arguments via an increasedly egalitarian methodology. In Sicko, his light shines not in people's eyes, but is instead diffused over the broader impulses of corporate government power-sharing: a relationship, Moore asserts, run ethically amok in the spurious name of Freedom.

This is not to say that *Sicko* is not 'flawed'. As with any and all of Michael Moore's films, there are at times lapses of judgement and undeniable weaknesses to its arguments (arguments that are by and large strong and, yes, *fair*). But its 'basic documentary value' remains intact, helped and not hindered by the now less overbearing presence of the big man himself, here performing a sort of restrained, mark II version of the filmic persona he has worked hard to perfect. 'The material speaks for itself', said Moore of *Sicko*. 'I hardly had to do a thing to it. I made this film in the hopes of reaching across the great divide in this country, so I made it in a nonpartisan way. I started with the premise that illness knows no political stripe. And, of course, ultimately, *Sicko* may end up being a more dangerous film because it's less controversial, because it does reach out and will appeal to all kinds of people and not just the Democrats. And because of that, if it reaches more people, it has a better chance of having some impact' (in McCreadie 2008: 70). Moore, it would appear, has tempered his approach, and accordingly his pro-filmic personality, to suit his subject. The 'satirical apparatus' (*ibid.*) has been taken down a gear; there are few of the expected harassments (and fewer cartoons); rather, *Sicko* holds everything it critiques in perspective against a *shared*, systemic illness endemic to American capitalism and state-sanctioned drives to promote corporate freedoms at the cost of all others. 'Moore', says Pilger, 'shames the supine American media' (2007: 30), and it is to Moore's credit that *Sicko* achieves this without setting up a straw man (in *Bowling for Columbine*, the doddering and victimised National Rifle Association figurehead Charlton Heston, on whom Moore in retrospect landed an easy sucker punch), or looking for grand conspiracy (as was the case with Moore's slightly egotistical, overlong, overstated and sadly over-optimistic attempt to oust George W. Bush). Indeed, *Sicko* sees Moore make his case with deftness and an attractive air of sympathy, while not diluting the important essence of 'Mike'; though the act, as always, is maybe contrived, it is nonetheless an act that appears less like personal compromise than a precisely engineered attack whose effectiveness rests equally on perspicacious self-possession, careful deployment of the Moore trademarks and *controlled* anger.

The film opens with a familiar, easy target – George W. Bush, making an asinine public remark about gynaecologists 'showing their love for women' – but swiftly moves on to a series of tales, narrated by a conspicuously offscreen Moore, of amiable folk whose lack of health insurance has led to them taking extreme measures: Adam was forced to perform self-surgery (which he recorded for posterity on a camcorder) to suture a grisly wound; Rick had to decide which finger to reattach following an accident with a saw. This is darkly comic stuff, set up by the general absurdity of Bush-as-idiot-chief; and these people, his poorer constituents, are as usual well selected for their brightly sympathetic characters. However, just as one might sense a thread, Moore pauses, cutting to a montage of chirpy, fifties-era clips (including a home movie of a very young Moore that functions to posit the filmmaker, concisely, within the Middle American mainstream) avowing the white, suburban ideals of middle-class aspiration: 'This movie isn't about them. It's about the 250 million of you who *have* health insurance. Those of you who are living The American Dream.' Altogether more tragic, the stories that follow – which are mostly shot in a direct cinema-type, observational style lending them the ostensibly unmotivated, unprompted rhetorical gravity of a traditionally naturalistic study – are replete with pathos. Former hardworking professionals Larry and Donna Smith, between them stricken with cancer and heart disease, have no option but to give up their home and move into their put-upon daughter's storage room. The costs, despite their insurance, soon amounted to a greater burden than they could bear. As Moore says, indicting the unfairness of the system to those who have contributed all their lives, 'It wasn't supposed to end up like this.' Donna cries, in a close-up that speaks of her alignment with the filmmaker championing her cause; the moment does not seem like exploitation, rather an open and important (both for the film and for Donna) admission of painful struggle, reluctant dependence (the converse of the American Dream of individualism and self-reliance) and near-defeat. It is, remarks Larry, 'a weird situation'. Frank, a sprightly 79, has to work as a janitor to buy the drugs he and his wife need: 'If there are golden years,' he laments with a brave face, 'I can't find 'em.' Numerous examples are given of insurers' unwillingness to pay out, to all generations, with varying degrees of consequence: teenagers are denied insurance for being marginally under- or overweight; deaf children are given only single, not double, cochlear implants, because of their nature as a 'luxury' (without Moore's consent, the parent alerts the implant provider of Moore's interest and they relent: here the filmmaker, in typical fashion, editorially flaunts his power to make real differences to the real lives of ordinary Americans: something he incontrovertibly *has* done, and of which he is openly proud, although such iterations of power have always been a double-edged sword); Diane, interviewed about what her insurance company deemed a 'non-life-threatening tumour', later died from it; Laurel, a youngster suffering with cancer, is now battling to stay alive after failing to get adequate care; Tracy and his wife Julie (a hospital employee) are unable to find approval for the 'experimental' treatment of Tracy's terminal kidney disease; and Maria, wrongly told by Blue Shield that she did not in fact have a tumour, gets appropriate attention only upon visiting her native Japan. Dense with information at every level, *Sicko* gradually builds its case, gathering emotional testimony from many and variously affected individuals, who are always named and always apparently treated – whether pragmatically or otherwise – as dignified friends and allies in a difficult and just fight. Statistics form a part of Moore's argument, but only a part: numbers and charts come and go in a continual demonstration of filthy lucre's role in all this, yet humanity, to Moore, is what really counts – what really adds up. Julie, choking back tears while recalling her husband's death, offers a summation: 'You [the health maintenance organisations, HMOs] preach these visions and values, that we care for the sick, the dying, the poor, that we're a healthcare that leaves no-one behind. You left him [Tracy] behind. You didn't even give him a start. I was as if he was nothing.' 'Moore', writes Saira Khan, using appropriately monetary language, 'makes people see both sides of the coin' (in Beckman 2007: 34).

The human facet of health insurance is illustrated, too, and a certain contriteness and reluctance amongst its paid functionaries, people on the inside who've 'seen everything' as regards the HMOs' often cruel methods, become clearly evidential of the business's sweepingly amoral disregard. An avuncular walrus of a man, Lee Einer regrets his days spent as a (surely improbable) HMO 'hitman', whose job it was to save the company money by scanning applications for mistakes and disqualifying factors. 'You're not slipping through the cracks', expounds Einer, his easygoing, sardonic wit chiming exactly with Moore's: 'somebody made that crack and swept you towards it … I am glad I'm out of it.' Becky Malke, a charming and personable young telephone salesperson 'in charge of keeping sick people away from one of America's top insurance companies', is upset and maybe ashamed to declare the huge litany of conditions her employers flatly will not cover: many of which, it must be said, are surprisingly exclusive. (Moore, in *Sicko*'s first example of a 'goofball wrapper encasing social critique' (Sharrett and Luhr 2005: 253), here spoofs the portentous introduction to *Star Wars*, scrolling the massively long list in yellow text across a star field, only cutting when it becomes apparent that it will take too long fully to reveal.) Becky, unlike the other interviewees, weeps not for herself or her family, but for the people she must reject on these grounds; the camera zooms in, better to emphasise her sorrow and her dilemma, wringing maximum rhetorical force from a remarkable sequence: she is just another victim, beholden to a horribly real Dark Side.

Moore, looking for some sort of root to this evil, seeks out a Darth Vader figure, and more or less finds one in the recognisably demonic shape of Richard M. Nixon – a literally criminal president who has so far escaped Moore's ire (though nobody else's). Stopping just short of unequivocally blaming Nixon – Moore realises the malaise runs ideologically far deeper than one man (this will be no *Nixon and Me*) – he nonetheless features damning tapes, made by a President foolishly obsessive about putting everything on record, which trace the White House's blithe pursuit of profiteering in cahoots with private medical providers. 'I'm not too keen on any of these damn medical programs', complains Nixon, when discussing Edgar Kaiser's Permanente HMO: his worries are soon put to rest. 'This is a private enterprise one … All the incentives are toward less medical care', advises aide John Ehrlichman. 'Because the less care they give them, the more money they make.' 'Fine', responds Nixon, who is then seen giving a television broadcast announcing a 'new national health strategy', the result of which, Moore points out, is that 'in the ensuing years, patients were given less and less care'. The ill and desperate crowd hospital corridors, in a demonstration of 'the plan hatched between Nixon and Edgar Kaiser' and its less-than-caring motivation. 'The system', notes Moore, was broken. As he stated in an interview to promote *Sicko*, '[W]hat's even more broken is the fact that our Congress and White House are bought and paid for by these two industries, which rival the oil industry in terms of money and influence. They have a vested interest in maintaining their control. But they're not dumb. They know which way the wind is blowing and that this is the No. 1 domestic issue with Americans. Their job now is to try to control it so that universal health care is run through them, so that they can still skim the money, make the obscene profits and keep their investors happy ... The right wing and the G.O.P. have done a wonderful job brainwashing people that government doesn't work, and then, as Al Franken says, they get elected and proceed to prove the point. [Laughs]' (in Kluger 2007: 1). Despite the Kennedy–Johnson years' (limited) progress in terms of instituting Medicare and Medicaid – two very expensive packages (both of which Nixon kept) aimed at helping, respectively, the old and the poor – mainstream liberals do not come off well either. Siding with the leftist consensus that, by the close of the sixties, '"liberal" had become almost synonymous with "sellout"' (Kurlansky 2005: 166), Moore features a scathing depiction of Hillary Clinton and her pusillanimous backing down from the championing of extensive healthcare reform via the President's Task Force, chaired by his wife. In a sequence the film's backer, Harvey Weinstein, wanted removed due to his friendship with Clinton, Moore presents the 'sassy, smart, sexy' First Lady as ultimately a coward driven by self-interest: what was once her 'top priority' is quietly buried under a well funded drive by Republicans chanting a mantra based on accusations of sneaking socialism. The spectre of communism, as always, strikes fear into the hearts of the flag-bearers of Freedom – something Moore takes especial glee in emphasising and lampooning: ever since the most affable of cold warriors, Ronald Reagan (featured in an audio track from the 1950s warning of the 'evils' of socialised medicine), and his ilk's insidious scaremongering, suggests the film, America has been unduly terrified of anything close to 'medicine for everyone'.

But can such programmes, funded in capitalist regimes by taxation, not be beneficial? Moore certainly thinks so, and thus begins an epic, globetrotting examination of other countries' unbroken systems. Starting in Canada (a favoured locus of nearby comparison for Moore: see *Bowling for Columbine*), the director extols the relative ease with which people can apparently gain access to treatment. We follow a young woman, suffering from cervical cancer and deemed by American insurers 'too young' at 22, who has decided to drive across the border every time she requires treatment – using the ploy of getting her male, Canada-residing friend Kyle to pose as her common-law husband. 'It's little white lies', she says (implicitly underscoring Moore's methods), but it works. 'You don't have to bring your cheque book when you go to hospital here', replies Kyle, more than happy to assist. The American media, though, given voice by a highly selective montage of news clips showing alarmist, right-wing commentators pontificating like tele-vangelists, seem wholly critical of Canada's health provision: to see for himself, and to give the viewer their expected response, Moore visits some comfortably well-off northern relatives, Bob and Estelle. Finally, his timing applied with judicious sensitivity to cries that he, too, often imposes himself bodily on his subjects' most personal moments, Moore appears on camera. This time, though, the 'calculated performance of working-class rage' (Aufderheide 2007: 7) is cooled in favour of a quiet, almost priestly responsiveness; the 'Kmart-meets-farmers-market persona' (Schultz 2006: 6) has mostly given way to a black T-shirted, clean-shaven, subdued and maturely considered 'Mike', who stands back, reposed with thoughtfulness. The 'Man from Flint', his own socially evangelical agenda repositioned to take in not just 'Joe Six-Pack' but also the white-collar sector, has semiotically assimilated himself into the bourgeoisie – all, of course, in the name of performative persuasion. Bob and Estelle, who 'have nothing against America', will not even cross the border without buying medical insurance, such is their wariness of the United States' pricey healthcare: 'What middle-class Canadian could absorb that?' At the local golf course, Larry, a well-to-do Conservative-voter, explains that he, too, is dismayed at American policy; treating an arm injury while in Florida would have cost $24,000, so he simply came back home and got it seen to for nothing. 'It's just the way it's always been', says Larry, in a golf cart driven adeptly by Moore; 'The powers that be [in America] don't share our beliefs that healthcare ought to be universal.' A Canadian doctor effuses over the general quality of his service (and the fact that nobody in Canada would have to choose between fingers); and Moore interviews several people in a doctors' waiting room – all speak of the doctors doing an 'amazing job', and of the wonderfully short waiting times. 'We know in America people, like, pay for their healthcare', says one young woman, 'but we just don't really understand that concept.' Indeed, it all *seems* absurdly unfair.

FIGURE 5.4 Michael Moore tones down his act in *Sicko* (2007)

When Moore starts drawing such wilfully black-and-white comparisons, however, he gives his mass of critics such obvious hostages to fortune that it is tempting to speculate on a deliberate policy. (One might recall, as a stark example, *Fahrenheit 9/11*'s passionately stated, but in hindsight ill-advised, portrayal of Saddam's Iraq, in which 'Moore brushed aside the millions forced into exile and the mass graves and torture chambers and decided instead to present life in one of the worst tyrannies of the late twentieth century as sweet' (Cohen 2007: 321). Bush Jnr's war may have been wrong, and Moore's film overall a healthy expression of freedom of speech, but Iraq, pre-occupation, was not in any respect 'right' according to received Western standards of civil liberty (certainly, no dissent was allowed *there*). At incoherent, contradictory moments like these, Moore's remedial propaganda – usually a cogent force for intelligent re-evaluation – becomes arguably deleterious 'counter-knowledge'.) The more vociferous amongst the Moore-naysayers, like respected political journalist Peter Oborne, will typically complain of a methodology that is 'flip, vacant and intellectually dishonest', whilst deriding Moore's 'cheap stunts and emotional manipulation' (in Beckman 2007: 34). Still more, notably David Hardy and Jason Clarke (founder of the now apparently defunct website www. moorelies.com), who have co-written a book called *Michael Moore is a Big Fat Stupid White Man* (ironically itself riddled with errors), take issue with 'Moorewellian spin' (Hardy and Clarke 2004: 83). Yet, in response to *Sicko*'s painting of Canada's medical system as virtually utopian in contrast to the USA's, even those of a more mild-mannered, conventionally liberal and usually pro-Moore bent could be heard raising serious concerns about his otherwise very valid case. As Karin Luisa Badt notes, 'Canadian journalists protested in the press conferences that he was wrong, there are long waits for doctors in Canada. It is not as painless a process as Moore shows, in his one filmic foray into a Toronto waiting room. With love, one Canadian noted: "But *why why why*, Michael, did you exaggerate? There is no need to make our system look 100 percent perfect. This makes you vulnerable to attack! Protect yourself. I have been telling you this for years!"' (Badt 2007: 1). 'His romanticised take on Canada's single-payer health-care system', seconds Jeffrey Kluger (2007: 1), 'is a few data points shy of a controlled study.'

Along similar lines, Moore jets off to England and then France, there to examine these places' attitudes in relation to America's. Arriving in the UK, and affecting a BBC News baseball cap, presumably to reflect Anglophile pride, Moore is (quasi-)astounded to discover that prescriptions are universally priced (at £6.65), and that under-16s, recipients of welfare and the elderly get them for free. Still, the goofball persona is turned down as he talks, on-camera so as best to display his rather evidently feigned incredulity, to the grateful denizens of 'Great Britain', who appear aghast at the United States' lack of compassion. After lampooning (and thereby dismissing) the 'Red Menace' with a clip from an old Soviet propaganda film, he also speaks to a well paid, pleasantly countenanced young doctor – who lives in a luxurious, half-million-dollar London townhouse and drives an Audi – and to Tony Benn, a stolidly Old Left figure equally venerated and ridiculed by British residents (or at least those of a certain age), who praises the free-at-point-of-service potential of the tax-funded National Health Service, set up by his Labour Party forebears, as a fundamental bastion not of the dreaded communism, but of *democracy*. It is the ballot box, avers Benn, which holds the key to change. Surrounded by busts of Keir Hardie and the quaintly kitsch knick-knacks of a life spent in conscientious, latterly hard-fought devotion to British socialism, Benn cuts a charmingly archaic figure harking back to the heyday of the ideals he espouses. All very well, and indeed in the UK we (mostly, notwithstanding creeping privatisation) value the NHS, at least in principle. Yet Moore, in his keenness to champion a nation able to rebuild itself after the crushing Blitz of the Second World War (which he somewhat patronisingly likens to the 9/11 attacks for the benefit of American viewers unable to comprehend European events without a frame of Stateside comparison), simply 'ignores a two-tier system that neglects the elderly and the mentally ill' (Pilger 2007: 32). Not to mention the thousands of badly paid porters, nurses, cleaners and administrators run into the ground through overwork and poor resources – a situation leading to 'superbugs', equipment rationing, drug shortages and the all-round air of a geographically unequal institution that has never really operated at full tilt. (Compare any British inner-city emergency ward with one in an outlying province, and one will find huge discrepancies.) 'Ordinary' working people, usually the human crux of Moore's demographic focus, are not, in *Sicko*, given a central voice, because its argument seeks to demonstrate, to the relatively rich, the absolute *democratic* feasibility – or, rather, essential nature – of medicine for all, bought by public funds and supported by political guardians who must 'stuff [doctors'] mouths with gold', in NHS-founder Aneurin Bevan's words, if need be. Where there is a middle-class will, Moore insists, there is a way: and biased selectivity, for the cause of what he undeniably sees as the greater good, is the abiding way of 'Mike', who is, as ever, acting out a self-designated role as the world's most high-profile rhetorical pragmatist. The NHS is not perfect, that much any Briton will know; yet almost by the same token, it turns nobody away and its core strives for total social inclusivity, however ultimately difficult. 'If you have power', says Benn, 'you *use* it, to meet the needs of you and your community.' Perhaps Moore's brand of propaganda, turned in *Sicko* to the true service of the people, as opposed to heartfelt if vituperative political hectoring or a vague critique of American 'fear', is a 'good' exercise of this power; perhaps, the film continually suggests, this *civilising* force is the best thing a committed documentary can be. Moore's treatment of actuality – and endorsement of nationally owned British services, which seem implausibly to run like clockwork – is here every bit as creative as Grierson's (a methodology, as we have seen, frequently compromised by a duty to sponsors whose idea of public education was corrupted by a desire to reinforce class strata); but *Sicko* tactically sidesteps any face-to-face involvement in grass-roots proletarian expression (although its ideological stance is basically of the left), wanting not to alienate or rabble-rouse, but rather to mobilise middle-American countryfolk with a paean to what the promises of civic inspiration hold for *them*.

In Paris (after a token chat with a former resident of … Flint, Michigan!), Moore finds some attractive young intellectuals – a deliberate casting decision pandering to American stereotypes of French café society – who offer their experiences, all of which are fairly sanguine. In the comfortable apartment of two professionals, again chosen for their enviable lifestyle, Moore presents a story of good living, reasonable taxation and domestic tranquillity: here are emblems of twenty-first-century achievement, the upwardly mobile middle classes living without fear or the worry that illness will push them into poverty. Astonished at the level of overall contentment, quality of childcare, and the generosity of French maternity and sickness leave, the director provides a simple, biological fact that must, for most, cut through any qualms: 'They enjoy their wine, their cigarettes and their fatty foods, yet, just like the Canadians and the Brits, they live much longer than we do. Something about that seems grossly unfair.' And Moore's rationale, as ever, is provocative: 'The story line is: France, bad; France, cowards. What crime did France commit? We wouldn't have had this country without their support in the Revolution. They gave us that statue that sits out in New York Harbor. They responded immediately after 9/11. And they remain eternally grateful for what we did during World War II' (in Kluger 2007: 1). Whatever the USA's political relationship to France, what Moore finds, he says, is 'enough to make me want to put away my freedom fries'. To hammer the point home, Moore returns to America, and to an elderly, broke and confused woman turned back out onto the street after a Los Angeles hospital – in accordance with Nixon's favoured Kaiser Permanente insurers – refuses to take her in. Seen in CCTV footage, she wanders destitute, to a soundtrack of elegiac strings, as passers-by ignore her. Rhetorically, the juxtaposition is affecting on a human level: Moore expertly tugs on our heartstrings with an undeniably pathetic tale of 'modern' humanity gone tragically inhumane for the sake of the dollar. If this is the wealthiest nation in the world, implies *Sicko*, then something is deeply wrong on an ideological level; if this is America, the Land of the Free, then what of the supposed converse, the lands of the hated Communists?

In a gloriously conceived act of incendiary chutzpah, Moore enacts the film's big stunt, a now expected device and one of Moore's

FIGURE 5.5 *Sicko* (2007): the mostly restrained film nonetheless incorporates one of Moore's 'stunts': taking a boatload of 9/11 rescue workers to Cuba

signature, heavy-hitting moves aimed at generating a heated response. Gathering up several chronically ill rescue workers rendered sick (and financially crippled) by the job of looking for survivors in the toxic aftermath of the 2001 World Trade Center attack, Moore loads them onto a boat and takes them to Cuba, in the hope he will procure there the services they need. (Moore is not allowed, though, to show us how they got there; one presumes they did not in actual fact go the 90 miles by sea.) Turned away from the United States' compound at Guantanamo Bay (where, we learn, terrorist-suspect inmates receive treatment superior to non-'evildoers'), Moore and his cadre of illegal hopefuls head for Castro's heartland; tearfully grateful, the 9/11 veterans surprisingly get affordable medicines, therapy and abundant sympathy in a place demonised for five decades as a frighteningly close bastion of Stalinist corruption, or, since the overthrow of Batista's US-friendly brand of despotism, 'the worst place on earth'. In this sequence there lies stirring hope, in the mould of the Biblical Good Samaritan helping his supposed enemy; but, similarly to that story's parable of virtue, there are undertones of expected reciprocity, the Golden Rule being loaded with political implications about the giving and subsequent *receiving* of help: the truth of the wider situation, and of any moral assertion, is as always a complicated matter. Interviewing Che Guevara's paediatrician daughter Aleida – for some on the right, tantamount to interviewing a child of Satan – Moore gives a pleasing, reassuringly motherly voice to Cuban aristocracy; yet in so doing he purposely presents a skewed view of a regime presiding over a permanently aggrieved, universally poor populace living in constant fear of spies and statist reprimands. Whilst Cubans, according to Moore's piously intoned narration, 'believe in preventative medicine, and it seems that there's a doctor on every block', they nevertheless are burdened in numerous other ways quite intolerable to most American – or, for that matter, French or British – passport-holders. Doctors on the island, paid as little as $15 a month, are accompanied by minders and subjected to curfew for fear of their defection; patients have no rights to refusal, privacy or protest. A question at the crux of the issue is that if the well known, publicly left-liberal sympathiser Moore were *not* there with his cameras, how many of his American friends would be welcomed so warmly in Cuba without any apparent billing for the foreign currency the country so desperately needs? Moreover, could they *ever* be welcomed as regularly visiting medical tourists, or always given the precise equivalent of the best American care? The official literature says yes, in theory, but it would be informative to know, roughly, the costs and feasibility for average Americans having to dodge US authorities without the powerful totem of Michael Moore to aid their passage. (As it would be nice to hear an explanation as to why Cuban citizens are not always given the same level of care afforded dollar-paying visitors.) *Sicko*, continuing on its single-minded mission of persuasion, skirts these obvious queries, in the process just about pulling off what Karin Luisa Badt calls the 'brilliant wildness of this surprise ending – where the rescue workers get amazing treatment not from Guantanamo (where they are refused), but in a public Cuban hospital.' This, continues Badt, 'is what makes this film an emotional masterpiece. It is also what makes Moore open once again to attack. Why push Americans' buttons *so* much? By flagging Cuba as a Mecca, he's bound to be booed as a sell-out Commie, and this about a country that not even Communists would uphold as an ideal' (Badt 2007: 1). As usual, Moore's defence is both a little glib, and utterly plain: 'I am making a movie. I am not writing a book. I have a 108 time frame. What you call oversimplification, I call a whopping good way to tell a story, which leaves no one bored' (ibid.).

A 'whopping good story' has certainly been told, and one Moore cannot resist topping off with his own, highly mediatised version of the Good Samaritan. Hearing that Jim Kenefick, the man who runs the world's biggest anti-Michael Moore website, has had to shut it down due to the spiralling costs of his wife's healthcare, Moore 'anonymously' donates the necessary $12,000 in order that the site might continue to exercise free speech and 'continue to run me into the ground'. Again, of course, the gesture is not all about selfless kindness, but a play for power based on proving Moore's credentials as a truly *American* voice of reason, a man who not only says and does what he feels is required to effect a change, but in addition encourages others to do so, even if they are in contradiction. In giving Kenefick the money, it is true that Moore generously sustains an outlet for one of his harshest opponents, and allows Kenefick's wife to get better; at the same time, the celebrity purports to trump him morally as, in effect, a superior citizen – a move possible only due to Moore's superior wealth (a fortune, it has been repeatedly pointed out, which was accrued in the free-speech-allowing, fittingly paradoxical heartland of 'Stupid White Men' Moore simultaneously deplores and embraces). To counter any such analysis, Moore, seen contemplatingly gazing into the Seine's mirror-like muse as if to declare tacitly his total philosophical maturation (and righteous narcissism), declares that, 'In the end, it was hard for me to acknowledge that we truly are all in the same boat, and that we sink or swim together.' Naturally, the Kenefick donation made the final cut, and naturally, it ends the film on a resolutely Moore-ish note of performance, contradiction, complexity and outright entertainment.

'*Sicko*', concludes Pilger, 'is so good you forgive its flaws' (2007: 32), a view shared by reviewer Roger Ebert, who endorsed the film wholeheartedly whilst declaring his personal experiences with health insurers to have been positive, and nurse Jan Rodolfo, who declared that it 'demonstrates the potential for a true national movement because it's obviously inspiring so many people in so many places' (ibid.). Always the provocateur, Moore by his very nature will endlessly attract passionate criticism from numerous perspectives; these responses, often considered and as often openly hateful, testify to his twin abilities to engage and to enrage, in the name of doing subjective, biased, selective and controversial *good*. (To his credit, Moore includes less-than-positive reviews and comments on his website, www.michaelmoore.com, and usually seeks to answer these in detail.) The media, and especially the Internet, are alive with a 'blizzard of detailed accusation and counter-accusation' (Cathcart 2007: 33) apropos *Sicko*'s relationship to quantifiable facts, yet, as Brian Cathcart opines, 'the idea that people must always get their facts right, like almost everything that is labeled common sense, is incomplete and unsatisfactory. Life is more complicated than that, so, perhaps surprisingly, there are grey areas between right and wrong' (ibid.). The most pronouncedly divisive of *Les Nouvelles Égotistes*, and hence the most famous, Moore will continue to inspire and irritate on a grander scale than his arguably more cerebral analogues Jon Ronson, Mark Thomas and Nick Broomfield, all of whom lack Moore's sensational ability to drum up global interest. As for anybody seeking to fill his Hush Puppies: 'There are twenty thousand people out there who want to be the next Michael Moore', observes Professor Robert Thompson, 'on both sides of the fence. Many are called. A few will be chosen' (in McCreadie 2008: 72). Already, the affable Morgan Spurlock – at one time a clear successor – appears to have run out of steam, following up his laudably effective, health-related hit *Super Size Me* with the unfunny and pointless *Where in the World is Osama bin Laden?* (2007): a 'stunt' film as redundant as any ever produced. Moore's three-point 'Prescription for Change', posted on his website, is straightforward, if optimistic: 'Every resident of the United Sates must have free, universal health care for life; All health insurance companies must be abolished; and Pharmaceutical companies must be strictly regulated like a public utility.' Although *Sicko* doubtless will not prompt a healthcare revolution, it deserves attention for constituting Moore's most sagacious and devastating argument yet against the pitfalls of uncaring capitalism – the ideological principles of which he was once more dissecting in 2009.

## *SAY MY NAME* (NIRIT PELED, 2009); *ANVIL: THE STORY OF ANVIL* (SACHA GERVASI, 2009): ROCKUMENTARY REVIVALS

Part of a rockumentary or 'rock-doc' tradition stretching back to the Maysles brothers' *What's Happening!* (1964), Donn Pennebaker's *Dont Look Back* (1967), and on through Scorsese's *The Last Waltz* (1978) plus numerous others since, *Say My Name* and *Anvil: The Story of Anvil* are in many ways conceived similarly to their illustrious antecedents. Both are examples of films that feature musicians; both operate, at least partly, as promotional vehicles for these musicians' talents; both, as has become quite usual for the rockumentary – a type of film Keith Beattie credits, notwithstanding the churned-out borrowings of reality TV, with turning 'direct cinema into a commercially and widely available form' (Beattie 2008: 81) – mix the 'reactive observationalism' of pure direct cinema with interviews and prompted discussions; and both by-and-large seek to give a sympathetic outlet to their subjects' mindsets via a mutually conducive approach favouring congeniality over antagonism, in the process hoping to educe moments of intimacy, emotional honesty and revelation from people quite amenable and used to the camera's presence. Crucially, the non-fiction musical has proven neatly to facilitate an abnegation of early direct cinema's fanciful claims to absolute privy and 'candid' naturalism, via its emphasis on subjects whose very personae, on-stage and off, are built around 'performing the self', to appropriate sociologist Erving Goffman (this much the rock-doc has in common with reality TV, a vehicle for 'wannabes' of all stripes essentially acting out characters they think the viewing public will find memorable or likeable); *Anvil* and *Say My Name*, typically, purport to offer access to a world of entertainers by definition in admittance of its own, perpetually PR-conscious nature as 'showbiz', and to most spectators readily interpretable as such.

It is in their shared desire to breathe new life into the rockumentary format, though, that these two exactly contemporaneous works diverge drastically, perspectively speaking, even as they aesthetically and thematically intertwine. *Say My Name*, a film (a *rapumentary*?) 'Dedicated to all women out there demanding respect for themselves', comes from a broadly feminist vantage aimed at redressing the hip-hop scene's dominant, entrenchedly chauvinistic values – attitudes summed up by Duke University's Mark Anthony Neal: 'Say "women in hip-hop" and the conversation is quickly reduced to what is widely known as the genre's "women problem" … the monolithic and repetitious representation of hip-hop as simply a sexist male rapper surrounded by an entourage of nameless and faceless gyrating bodies in video after video' (Neal 2009: 1). Made by a woman, *about* women, *Say My Name* addresses these issues of representation, giving us an egalitarian view of a sisterhood finding expression in singing out harmoniously against the oppressively male-dominated, masculinist sphere of the rap music industry: doubly, the film acts as a response to the heavily macho tradition of the observation-/performance-based musical documentary, eschewing the formally timeless narrative crises of direct, interpersonal competition or will-they-won't-they barrier-hurdling favoured by most of its phallocentric predecessors. (During *Dont Look Back*, for instance, Pennebaker finds all-important crises – a trope beloved of direct cinema – in Dylan's sparring with a student, romantic rejection of Joan Baez, and meeting with rival Donovan; in *Hail Hail Rock and Roll* (Taylor Hackford, 1987), we see alpha male Chuck Berry's attempts to subjugate his celebrity backing band, including Keith Richards and Eric Clapton; in *Dig!* (Ondi Timoner, 2004), The Dandy Warhols' fracturing friendship with The Brian Jonestown Massacre forms the core of the film's thrust; and in *Metallica: Some Kind of Monster* (Joe Berlinger and Bruce Sinofsky, 2004), the group members' epic fight to get on for long enough to produce a record sustains an unusually long rock-doc. By contrast, Scot McFadyen's recent *Iron Maiden: Flight 666* (2009) is a worshipful fan's perspective on a touring machine so well oiled its only tinge of drama comes from whether or not drummer Nicko McBrain will recover from a minor golfing injury. He does.) *Say My Name*, in the most obvious indication that Peled (who describes herself as a 'community-based cultural artist and filmmaker') is savvy to her work's singular purpose, entirely relegates the instant gratifications of person-on-person cinematic melodrama to its many subjects' greater fight to be heard, first and foremost in *union*, as 'all women demanding respect'. Mostly shot from low angles, as if to pay sympathetic homage, Peled's subjects, against a backdrop of densely urbanised community and its simultaneous dangers and comforts (of drug abuse, teenage pregnancy, HIV and violence offset by the benefits of inspirational mutuality), all speak of looking for *respect* as lyricists, not as sex symbols – a desire seconded by the director's conveyed approach, which is to offer herself as simply another sister, quietly watching, tacitly absorbing and paying respect to a multitude from a subject position of deference.

Conversely, *Anvil: The Story of Anvil* anchors itself deeply in a central relationship (between vocalist/guitarist Steve 'Lips' Kudlow and drummer Robb Reiner), and that relationship's troubles, which are played out over the course of the Canadian band's umpteenth make-or-break tour: so far, Gervasi sticks to a standard rock-doc template drawn up around a frame of off-stage dramas juxtaposed with on-stage performances. What distinguishes this film from others that have gone before, however, is that the band is, by most measures of creative and financial attainment, an utter failure, and that the crisis at *Anvil*'s centre is around whether the band will manage to organise itself into anything like a functioning unit; contrary to the young female rappers featured by Peled, who likewise may ultimately encounter commercial defeat, Anvil, countless self-released records into their meagre career and 50 years of age, are unable accurately to comprehend themselves – in *Anvil*'s case as largely forgotten also-rans peddling lyrics that are offensive in their sexism sung over turgid music that makes Spinal Tap's grandiosely spoofed riffs look remarkably inventive. (Which they are: but then director Rob Reiner, unlike his unrelated nearly-namesake, understands the metal genre's basic absurdities and its practitioners' mindsets.) In his autobiography, co-written with Lips, Robb unwittingly and wonderfully echoes the line from *This is Spinal Tap* about the band's appeal becoming 'more selective': 'I suppose you could say our market fragmented and our music became more exclusive' (in Lips and Reiner 2009: 16). As noted by MC Lyte, in *Say My Name*, 'female MCs' names have always been larger than their record sales', a view that, rather than blaming other musicians for stealing acts (as does Reiner's jealous assessment), accurately cites corporate focus on sellable glamour as the reason behind skill being devalued in favour of marketability.

Though filmmaker Gervasi is a long-time friend of the band (and roadied for them and partied with them as a teenager), he nonetheless occupies an ambivalent stance: *Anvil* asks us to sympathise with these puppyish losers and find abundant humanity in their arrestedly teenage, boys'-club squabbles, but also to laugh at middle-aged men blind to the limits of their own, passé mediocrity. Here, the *consciously* performative – an enacted illusion perfected by the rock-doc's usual stars – appears to yield to moments of oblivious, accidentally revelatory ingenuousness:

FIGURE 5.6 Lips rocks out (*Anvil: The Story of Anvil*, 2009)

Gervasi, in his revisiting of boy–men via a position of upper-middle-class, educated discursive elevation (and via a trust earned due to impressive bohemian connections in London), has struck the direct-cinema mother lode. Lips plays his guitar with a dildo, to scanty, drunk audiences in European clubs, and wonders why he's being 'shit on' for doing 'everything right'; they compose songs (with titles like 'Show Me Your Tits') whose juvenile idiocy (or tongue-in-cheek charm, depending on one's interpretation of the composers' intentions) is matched only by a disregard for melody, then muse disbelievingly over the reasons A&R men turn them down; and they bicker like chagrined boys left out of the big-hitting team they improbably influenced: the greater talents of Metallica, Anthrax, Slayer and Megadeth, all of whom apparently took Anvil's speed-metal blueprint and applied an extra measure of intelligent musicality, something Anvil, whose music is fun but undeveloped, do not and never will possess. Robb is a skilled drummer, as he never tires of saying, tied down to a bitter psychological dependence on his childhood 'brother''s unstoppable enthusiasm and nostalgia for a long-gone era when things were looking up. In an indication of his general state of development, he several times petulantly threatens to walk out, but never quite does, presumably because he is unable to think of somewhere else to take his drums. Reiner also paints crude pictures of monolithic, venerated anvils, figureless townscapes (in an emotionally stunted tribute to Edward Hopper, who in contradistinction comprehended the modern human condition and the place of humanity), and grotesquely textured turds in toilet bowls, all of which he proudly displays to Gervasi, who does not need to offer any comment. Metallica drummer Lars Ulrich (who pops up in *Anvil* to give a brief endorsement), a wealthy, art-collecting subscriber to the tenets of expensive psychotherapy, regarded the camera, during the making of *Some Kind of Monster*, as a 'truth instigator' (in Beattie 2008: 80); Gervasi, though, is dealing with people apparently not perceptive enough to envisage the final product, or to sense that participation in this film is potentially a life-changing experience – and therein lies *Anvil*'s gruesome fascination. These pro-filmic actions, by Robb and Lips, do not *seem* like the plays to the gallery of egotists. Above and beyond Metallica's indulgences, which are revealing in their own way as the time-marking follies of musically bankrupt millionaires looking for a new direction, Gervasi has found their psychically repressed counterparts, isolated to the Great White North and with a grindingly, hilariously repetitive back catalogue unaffected by record company pressure to mature away from hormonal attention-seeking.

Lips and Robb are, inescapably, figures of both hope (especially for anybody clinging to the hedonistic, basely tempting desires of the old rock-and-roll dream) and ridicule: where Peled offers insightfully performative, necessarily self-aware intellectual green shoots, some of which will naturally wither, Gervasi offers a picture of deluded men who have long been drinking in the Last-Chance Saloon, stuck in menial day jobs they loathe, blaming mismanagement and bad production for their misfortunes and dependent on kindly families resigned to thwarted ambitions. That many thought *Anvil* was faked says much about the band's entertainingly preposterous nature, and of Gervasi's motivations in calling on his old friends: Anvil – sometimes unattractive, sometimes juvenile, intensely optimistic and over the hill – in many ways stretch belief; yet, despite all this, they speak (to men of a certain age) of a chance, however slight, for masculine rebirth and hopes for immortal potency via brutal guitars. There is a land, somewhere over the film's rainbow, of endless beer, groupies and parties for those who will keep carrying the torch, and sporting the same old T-shirts of obstinate allegiance. Outright arrogance, within Anvil, is thankfully diffused into a comedic lack of introspection and a conviction that lyrics such as, 'Can't get to sleep 'cause I hear you squealin'/Like a stuck little pig you love the feelin'' are acceptable if delivered wearing spandex and a goofy smile: quite possibly, this air of the playground is the only thing that has facilitated Anvil's doggedness and validated its fans' veneration. (To be fair, the same has sustained the likes of AC/DC, who, whilst writing analogous material, marry this tendency to a sardonic grasp of hard rock's inherent immaturity, which they communicate using vaudeville-esque *double entendres*.) In *Say My Name*, arrogance mostly becomes confidence that the 'bitch-and-ho-paradigm' (Pierce 2009: 1), upheld equally by the overt cruelties of male rappers and the farcical drivel of Anvil (they may be parodic, but this is *not Spinal Tap*), can eventually, notwithstanding the difficulties of a commercial environment given to prioritising 'booty', be overturned. The rappers Peled features, from the sassy newcomer Chocolate Thai to the cerebral and world-famous Monie Love, are streetwise, gorgeous and tough, but sufficiently serious and sensible not attitudinally to emulate their male counterparts' thuggery. To be sure, *Anvil* is the bigger cinematic draw, and the more instantly accessible due to its easily construed, guileless characters and dramatically mapped-out situation (all in all, these amount to what Gervasi must have realised was a box-office gift); with predictable and fitting poignancy, *Say My Name* resides in comparative, undeserved obscurity, winning admirers on the festival circuit if not creating the kind of revenue attracted by *Anvil*, a work that, against the warning of Pennebaker and his muse Bob Dylan, looks mostly backwards. It may be, in fact, that Peled's film's own fight for public respect mirrors that of its subjects: the in-production sequel, *Say My Name in Africa*, is unlikely to make bigger waves. Analysing *Anvil*'s success, Gervasi explicates the economic context: 'People want stories of hope right now. People don't want to hear about how awful America is or how terrible life is. They want to hear that it's possible to make it through these times' (in Abaius 2009: 1). Conservative times, as is often the case, call out for and celebrate conservative narratives. For all its heroes' never-give-up, ostensibly anti-establishment eccentricities, *Anvil* basically endorses the gospel of patriarchy, tireless individual enterprise ('If at first you don't succeed, try, try again!') and classically masculine assertion; how different would the public's reception have been if Lips and Robb were seen to be claiming welfare, rather than begging from family (or George Bush Snr's 'thousand points of light')? We root for these men, whose uncomplicated minds hark back to imaginary better days, whilst we ourselves seek vicarious distractions from workaday hassles. And the simpler the story, perhaps, the more easily its encouragements will imprint themselves on the 'wide popular mindset' (*ibid*.), just when they are needed.

FIGURE 5.7 Chocolate Thai represents in *Say My Name* (2009)

*Anvil* and *Say My Name* represent two sides of the same rock-and-roll coin, a mythically invested token for 'getting out', for personal revival and for 'making it': the regressive last gasp of white, fraternal bigotry, wrapped in the studs and leather of a four-decades-old, 'cock-rock' status quo (no pun intended), and the progressive, genuine upthrust of black community art undertaken in the service of social change, its markedly worthy methods uncannily constituting a positive, unambiguous answer to Gervasi's parading of anachronisms. The lesser-known, less talented artists in *Say My Name* might well, for the most part, in time suffer the indignities of not forging a career in music, and fade back into the harsh realities of the poor, urban mass; they, too, may in some ways be naive, even if this naivety does not extend to letting their on-camera guard down (as opposed to *Anvil's*, *Say My Name's* subjects occasionally come across as a little *too* archly keen to use the film as an audition: there are shades of the Kids from *Fame* keepin' it real with homegirls); yet their voices, one senses, are never raised in vain or merely for a thrill, even if, as the film suggests, for every Queen Latifah and Missy Elliot there are a hundred who never break through. The irony inherent to *Anvil's* 'hymn to the human spirit' is that the band has finally thus found a large measure of fame – though it is a celebrity perhaps most strongly felt amongst champions of a 'harmless' chauvinism veiled by the admittedly beguiling charms of stereotypical, cartoon-like personalities whose redemption comes not through talent, but through unapprised persistence, faith in the power of painfully dated clichés and, above all, Gervasi's commercial astuteness. Talking ostensibly of his heavy-rocking subjects, but probably more acutely of the filmic golden ticket without which Anvil would be almost literally unknown, Gervasi, availed of the privileges of a Juilliard education, speaks volumes: 'Don't do what other people tell you to do. Only do what you believe in. If you're coming from the heart, whatever you're doing, you can't really fail' (in Tallerico 2009: 1). *Anvil*, as much as *Say My Name* (and as much as any other documentary featured in this book), comes truly from self-belief and from the heart: it is perhaps up to the spectator to assess whether this heart beats more with joy, or with burden. Anvil, it transpires, are 'big in Japan' – this is where the film finds its satisfyingly uplifting ending, as, at last, crowds call out for more; yet this adoration (on one level a genuine expression of endearment offering the timeless dramatic device of the hero/heroes' return) is pregnant with undertones of mockery, a sound Anvil themselves, their particular turning of adversity into art forever retrograde and their fame as randomly bestowed as the most imbecilic of reality TV stars, seem unable to hear.

## NOTES

1 'Anthroplogist Jay Ruby', notes Patricia Aufderheide, 'argues that only if a film is produced by a trained ethnographer, using ethnographic field methods, and with the intention of making a peer-reviewed ethnography should it be called an ethnographic film' (Aufderheide 2007: 106).

# CONCLUSION

## New Challenges, Territories and Directions

'In the various scenarios which are now evolving for video, including its migration to the internet which is just beginning, the old canons of the institutional documentary are once again being thrown into question, and new methodologies and ways of working are emerging, there in the interstices, where they are always born'

Michael Chanan (2007: 19)

'The Web has become a rupture in the wall between the private and the public sphere'

Bjørn Sørenssen (2008: 53)

Until there is seismic shift in the basic nature of film and video – a technological shift, in other words, in the fundamental way these means of expression are consumed – we are still at the mercy, despite formal mutations and increasingly ingenious storage methods, of the ocularly apprehended image (and its accompanying sound waves). Watching and listening remain for now the only ways to appreciate movies, whether they are projected in the cinema or viewed on a television or computer monitor. Various changes *are*, of course, taking place that affect the way such moving images are distributed, promoted and created; these changes are mostly related to the Internet, and all the double-edged possibilites this potentially revolutionary 'web' entails.

Bjørn Sørenssen, accentuating the positive, succinctly maps out a three-point summary of 'new media' effects on non-fiction film:

1:  New technology provides new means of expression. As a result of this the film medium (i.e. forms of audio-visual expression) develops from being exclusive and privileged to a common and publicly available form of expression.
2:  This, in turn, opens space for a more democratic use of the medium.
3:  It also opens up new possibilities for modern (contemporary) and different forms and usages (avant-garde).

(2008: 49)

So, according to this analysis, the new media (in the shape, largely, of what is called 'Web 2.0') offer true democratisation and increased participation, giving everybody the chance to transcend cultural boundaries and share in expression. Where once only Developed Worlders with access to training and expensive facilites could create films, now it is in theory possible for all to find an outlet, and viewers. As Sørenssen's third point makes clear, this might in addition lead to a greater diversity of formal experimentation, by artists freed from the shackles of generic expectation or the needs of mass marketing. Optimists of this new epoch, notes Alexander Galloway, praise what they see as '[h]eightened interpersonal communication, ease from the burden of representation, new perspectives on the problem of the body, greater choice in consumer society, unprecedented opportunites for free expression, and, above all, speed' (in Juhasz 2008: 301). Certainly, many have made use of these new channels to find a voice that would otherwise be denied; many have even found sizeable audiences – notably video bloggers (or 'vloggers') like 'Geriatric1927', whose regular musings, posted to the Internet video-hosting site YouTube, draw not only numerous views, but comments on how better to produce these vlogs. This suggests some potential for genuine democratisation and a faster interactivity going beyond the production-consumption dialectic usually at play between producers and audiences, as Geriatric1927 (alias Peter Oakley, his online name a deliberate highlighting of demographic extremity) often takes this advice, its suggestions feeding back into his work. The 'rupture in the wall' becomes clearly apparent, as does a need for extra vigilence in parsing this vast amount of material into something comprehensible. Just because we can all engage in the process of 'making', does this mean we are all artists?

Many say resoundingly No. Access has increased, yet so, consequently, has excess. 'The banality of this revolution is far more notable than its populism', notes Alexandra Juhasz. 'Its failures utterly profound given its radical promise' (2008: 300). Less the ultimate, man-machine realisation of Vertov's *Kino-Pravda*, or the irrigator of a radical valley once kept barren by the dams of elitism, the Internet might be more a mountain of audio-visual trash in which are buried a few diamonds (including *The Man with the Movie Camera* – now freely available, as are many other works, via www.archive.org). 'The main problem with

FIGURE 6.1  Geriatric1927's YouTube channel

YouTube as a distribution channel', writes Sørenssen, 'is the signal/ noise ratio: every item has to contend for space with an avalanche of homebrew video snippets of laughing babies, stupid dogs, [and] an unending number of popular film and TV show emulations' (2008: 55). Nothing, according to this view, has essentially altered the dominance of traditionally hegemonic forms of expression – on YouTube, the avant-garde struggles for breath not only against millions of pointlessly published home movies, but also under the weight of music videos, advertising, spliced-up broadcast television formats and mainstream film trailers. The biggest 'old canons', as must be expected, are perpetually firing back. The more YouTube becomes a commercially massive project, the more, inevitably, it toes commercial lines: this is for now the way of the world, and no amount of uploading will absolutely alter this. Minorites are speaking out, at a greater volume, and globally; in response, the majority ups its game, assimilating and commodifying the stylistic traits of the underground whilst keeping real expressions of anger safely suppressed.

There is promise, though, somewhere hidden behind the laughing babies, stupid dogs, alien autopsies, freak shows, MTV promos and paranoid conspiracy films. All one has to do is search – indeed, intellectually active consumption may be something crucial to getting the most out of YouTube or Google Video. A search for 'experimental documentary' (currently bringing 9,700 results) turns up some artistically interesting shorts, including Fernando Barrientos's *Once Upon a Tram Ride*, about a protester in The Hague, which would otherwise not have found an outlet. YouTube is international and more or less an informal free-for-all (and at the moment a largely unpoliced minefield of fakery and counter-knowledge), but for those in the UK, the BBC's Film Network Documentary site, for instance, gives tutorials and feedback opportunities of a more seriously intended nature (there is also less likelihood of viewers' comments descending into expletive-ridden invectives); Channel 4's 4Docs, a revamped version of the torch-bearing FourDocs, operates in a similar vein, working alongside the Channel 4 BRITDOC Foundation to train, promote and generally facilitate the work of promising newcomers. The greater industry, moreover, is having to listen and respond to fundamental changes that may affect its capacity for profit (always a strong motivation): 'The rapid growth of social media', asserts Liz Rosenthal, 'has created a new audience which is no longer made up of passive viewers of media – they are active creators, collaborators, distributors and even financiers. As audiences access stories through different media platforms and devices, we're beginning to see new possibilities for storytelling as films are no longer bound to 90-minute formats. Film as we know it is beginning to transform' (2009: 1).

Though Rosenthal refers mostly to mainstream fiction film and its attached marketing strategies, there are nonetheless implications for documentary, whose enthusiasts might turn evermore not into whole-sale producers of their own, singularly authored works, but into part-authors of larger projects taking into account digital-age interactivity. 'In 2003', continues Rosenthal, 'director Peter Greenaway prophesied: "If the cinema intends to survive, it has to make a pact and a relationship with concepts of interactivity and it has to see itself as only part of a multimedia cultural adventure"' (ibid.). In other words, the producer-audience relationship, always in effect but not always too evidently, may become more intimate, more entwined and more direct. A part of this 'adventure' – an adventure moving ever further from the arguably reductive certainties of orthodox heroes and villains – will entail the architectures of narrative and characterisation changing to fit the needs of cross-platform production: as documentaries increasingly look to simultaneous exhibition over the Internet, attached portable devices and on the television, stories must adapt beyond the conventional, hour-and-a-half, three-act structure into something else. But into what?

Spike Jonze and Suroosh Alvi's online television network VBS.tv, spun off from the youth-cultural organ *Vice* magazine, sees itself as at the vanguard of a formal shift. Its slogan declares an intention of 'rescuing you from television's deathlike grip', and its content offers mostly short, always highly subjective material coming over like a super-hip hybrid of MTV-style brashness and on-the-street, 'immersionist' activist-journalism:

this is documentary film as curated by the techno-savvy, neo-gonzo descendents of Hunter S. Thompson and Tom Wolfe, taking the publisher's dollars, of course, yet reaching out both massively and on their own terms. (Although the site is – quietly – backed by Viacom, via MTV Networks, which also screens VBS's videos, the mainstream parent organisations tend to view VBS as something of a petri dish in which to experiment with online media – with the result that much of their 'deathlike grip' remains unapparent, at least while they watch and learn.) Elsewhere, the Active Ingredient team's ongoing *Dark Forest Project* describes itself thus: '*The Dark Forest* and BR163 Expedition is an interactive documentary in two parts. *The Dark Forest* senses and documents an expedition along a road that is being built through the heart of the Amazon and connects the tropical forest to Sherwood Forest in the UK – through a new interactive artwork and schools exchange ... The project brings together a team of film makers, artists and technologists utilising mobile, location and sensing technologies – to create a documentary film, website, and a new artwork.' The regularly blogging team asks, 'How can mobile technology contribute to democracy, culture, art, ecology, peace, education, health and the third sector?' (see www.thedarkforest.tv). Certainly, one hopes that they will find answers – though as they themselves admit, it is going to take time (something, despite the instantaneous point-to-point speed of digital communications, that the new interactivity, especially if used as part of a large-scale study, must factor into its methods). Inspired by her own experiences, Victoria Mapplebeck's InBox (in pre-production for British television's Channel 4) examines the phenomenon of SMS texting and its import regarding modern relationships: the project will comprise a short, animated film (using only text) about Mapplebeck's text-only dialogue with her ex-partner – the father of her child, about whose gestation he was informed by text – much linguistic data collected from various teenage participants' mobile phones, and the gradual presentation of these data on a multi-contributor website. 'The once private peer-to-peer dialogues of our collaborators will be presented for public scrutiny and translation', writes Mapplebeck, in her proposal. 'How will they feel about making public the private spaces of their phone memories?' (Once again, the private becomes public, and the slippage between the two forms the basis of a documentary. Mapplebeck and her ex, however, in order to maintain nominal privacy, will along with the other subjects be known only as 'X' and 'Y', hence drawing a fuzzy-ish ethical line between 'acceptable' personal openness and the 'unnaceptable' publicising of privately intended messages, a line to which Mapplebeck points by the very act of enforcing anonymity.) While 'convergent' projects like these must paradoxically fragment, narratively and scopically, the challenge will be to keep them from dissipating into incoherence: should one aspect of a nebulous, multi-media production be able to stand on its own for a whole, if there is no guarantee of general and full spectatorial (as opposed to participatory) commitment to the entire project?

All this is not, obviously, to suggest that the 'old' ways of projection and reception are dead (for they are far from it), or that there will be no more cinematically standard, feature-length 'super-docs' of the like seen in recent years. We are not, yet, in a post-documentary age, and this conclusion's questions, for the moment, do not pertain to super-session, but to supplementation: the long work of the 'documentary project' – the enormous, growing, troublesomely hard-to-define body of work dedicated to helping us understand ourselves and the world – is never done and dusted, never set in stone, or celluloid, or binary code. Just as life on Earth rarely yields up in an instant a biologically divergent entity, our art seldomly transmogrifies overnight, instead borrowing, referencing and adapting – tendencies not always effecting the quick exclusion of that which has gone before. As Patrica Aufderheide opines:

> The problem of how to represent reality will continue to be worth wrestling with, because the documentary says, 'This really happened, and it was important enough to show you. Watch it.' The importance of documentary may be in public affairs or celebrity-driven entertainment. It may be important for fourteen-year-old skateboarders or residents of one apartment building; it may be important until the end of the

semester or the end of time. Documentary makes connections, grounded in real life experience that is undeniable because you can see and hear it.

(2007: 128)

We, as humans, can both adapt to *and* change our environment on a profoundly deep level; the fundamental web of connections that constitutes 'real life experience' is open to transformation. One day, the abovementioned seismic shift will come, possibly in the shape of brain-computer interfaces or cybernetic advances, after which film guide-books such as this will themselves be seen as cryptic documents of a bygone age when folks had to emplace themselves in front of a screen and look. To 'see' and 'hear' – to 'watch it' – will, at some maybe far-flung stage, mean something else, and the documentary, however the term's import might have mutated, will then reflect this amongst its truth-telling discourses. We are still, essentially, in sensorial thrall to the Lumières' train, Flaherty's igloo, the camera's little window, the symbolic media-as-message and the 'creative treament of actuality'. 'Documentary' is indeed a clumsy word: but, even after nearly a century, stand it must.

# A SELECT CHRONOLOGICAL FILMOGRAPHY

Here is a short, annotated list of films this author considers interesting, entertaining and/or significant. In the best documentary tradition, it is subjective, selective, biased and arbitrary. (I have omitted those works discussed at length in this book.)

*In the Land of the Headhunters* (1914, Edward S. Curtis)
A sensationalised, dated and fascinating look at Native Americans, made pre-*Nanook*.
*Grass* (1925, Merian C. Cooper *et al.*)
Silent, ethnographic film about Persian tribespeople making a hazardous journey.
*Berlin: Symphony of a City* (1927, Walter Ruttman)
Masterpiece of the 'city symphony' sub-genre.
*The Fall of the Romanov Dynasty* (1927, Esfir Shub)
Fervent compilation film, of Communist thrust and of clever editing.
*Rain* (1929, Joris Ivens)
Gorgeous depiction of the titular subject.
*Land Without Bread* (1932, Luis Buñuel)
Parodic take on rural Spanish poverty, by a master surrealist who may have been the first to send up non-fiction's usual attitudes.

*Man of Aran* (1934, Robert Flaherty)

Flaherty visits the islands, turning back the clock to the pre-modern.

*Triumph of the Will* (1934, Leni Riefenstahl)

Nazi puff-piece, dazzlingly constructed and orchestrated.

*Olympia* (1938, Leni Riefenstahl)

As above, with added athletics.

*Battle of San Pietro* (1945, John Huston)

Anti-war coverage from the Second World War.

*Louisiana Story* (1948, Robert Flaherty)

Flaherty's last film is elegiac and beautiful.

*Blood of the Beasts* (1949, Georges Franju)

Horrific look at a Paris slaughterhouse, aesthetically accomplished.

*Kon-Tiki* (1950, Thor Heyerdahl)

Norwegians set sail for Polynesia.

*Chronicle of a Summer* (1963, Jean Rouch and Edgar Morin)

Meditation on the possibilities of 'cinema truth'.

*Primary* (1963, Robert Drew)

Groundbreaking, flawed first stab for the direct-cinema pioneers.

*Happy Mother's Day* (1963, Richard Leacock)

Quintuplets are delivered in the eye of a media storm: direct cinema discovers satire.

*Dont Look Back* (1967, D. A. Pennebaker)

Pennebaker discovers Bob Dylan, and does away with the apostrophe; Dylan remains a mystery wrapped in an enigma wrapped in the best songs of his career.

*Titicut Follies* (1967, Frederick Wiseman)

Former lawyer Wiseman makes his first film; the results, set in an archaic mental asylum, keep many other lawyers busy.

*High School* (1968, Frederick Wiseman)

Wiseman enters a middle-class school and dissects its insidious methods: everything the students learn, it seems, is aimed at feeding the needs of the military–industrial complex.

*In the Year of the Pig* (1968, Emile de Antonio)

Brilliant attack on the American rationale for war in Vietnam.

*The Sorrow and the Pity* (1969, Marcel Ophüls)

Very long, very thorough investigation into French resistance – and collaboration – during the Vichy government.

*Salesman* (1969, Albert and David Maysles)

The Maysles brothers follow a group of Arthur Miller-esque Bible salesmen, after which they ...

*Gimme Shelter* (1970, Albert and David Maysles and Charlotte Zwerin)

... go on the road with the Rolling Stones, who ill-advisedly get the Hells Angels to police a gig.

*Woodstock* (1970, Michael Wadleigh)

The ultimate concert movie, epically realised.

*Grey Gardens* (1975, Albert and David Maysles)

Cult classic of voyeuristic appeal, set in the eponymous, tumbledown mansion of two Kennedy nieces.

*The Last Waltz* (1978, Martin Scorsese)

The final, supremely musicianly concert of The Band (and guests), documented by the co-editor of *Woodstock*.

*This is Spinal Tap* (1984, Rob Reiner)

A washed-up rock band goes on the road. Or does it? 'Marti DiBergi' – a character based on Scorsese – presents a 'mock-umentary' whose devastating accuracy and humour offer much insight into 'proper' documentaries, also. So well acted, many thought it was real.

*The Times of Harvey Milk* (1984, Rob Epstein)

Sympathetic profile of the late activist.

*Shoah* (1985, Claude Lanzmann)

Vast and affecting oral history of the Holocaust.

*Sherman's March* (1986, Ross McElwee)

The filmmaker examines his relationships with various women.

*Cane Toads* (1988, Mark Lewis)

Humorous, 'unnatural history' of the out-of-control Australian pest.

*The Thin Blue Line* (1988, Errol Morris)

Noir-like, extremely original film that saved a man's life.

*Roger and Me* (1989, Michael Moore)

Michael Moore's first polemic, which sets the unmissable and controversial tone for everything to come.

*The Leader, his Driver, and the Driver's Wife* (1990, Nick Broomfield)

Glorious, mischievous portrait of a South African racist political leader losing his grip – while British filmmaker Broomfield gently prods.

*Paris is Burning* (1990, Jennie Livingston)

A documentary about drag artists, Livingston's film has inspired a great deal of debate around gender, performance and subject positioning.

*Baraka* (1992, Ron Fricke)

Beautiful, 70 mm-shot depiction of our world.

*Crumb* (1994, Terry Zwigoff)

A portrait of the counter-cultural cartoonist, his sexual psyche and his even less conventional family.

*Geri* (1999, Molly Dineen)

Recently out of the Spice Girls, the young Ms Halliwell searches for herself, accompanied by Dineen's camera and middle-class discourse.

*Secret Rulers of the World* (2001, Jon Ronson)

Mildly paranoid, hugely entertaining glimpse into the hidden world of global power elites, made in five parts for British television's Channel 4.

*To Be and to Have* (2002, Nicolas Philibert)

An acclaimed, mostly observationally filmed visit to a French classroom, in which a dedicated teacher shows respect and patience (compare with Wiseman's *High School*).

*Capturing the Friedmans* (2003, Andrew Jarecki)

Troubling examination of a family's abusive past.

*Aileen: The Life and Death of a Serial Killer* (2003, Nick Broomfield)

Broomfield revisits the tragic Aileen Wuornos, days before her execution, and elicits more than expected.

*The Fog of War* (2003, Errol Morris)

An attempt at absolution by former US Secretary of Defense Robert McNamara, declaration of 'war crimes' included.

*Metallica: Some Kind of Monster* (2004, Joe Berlinger and Bruce Sinofsky)

Absorbing heavy-metal rockumentary, shot over many years as the ageing band sinks into squabbling, unnecessary therapy and noticeable hair-loss.

*Super Size Me* (2004, Morgan Spurlock)

Morgan Spurlock takes McDonald's to task and gets ill: much to our interest and the fast-food giant's chagrin.

*An Inconvenient Truth* (2006, Davis Guggenheim)

Terrifying anti-global-warming presentation. Though the figures have been disputed, Gore makes an engrossing case.

*Man on Wire* (2007, James Marsh)

Heist documentary, featuring interviews, archival footage and recon-structions, about a wire-walk stunt.

*My Kid Could Paint That* (2007, Amir Bar-Lev)

Intriguing story of an improbably talented child artist – and the artist's maybe too-vicarious parents.

*Encounters at the End of the World* (2008)

Werner Herzog offers a glimpse into the bizarre daily lives of research scientists in Antarctica. Features a discussion on gay penguins.

# BIBLIOGRAPHY

Abaius, Cole (2009) 'Exclusive Interview: The Director of *Anvil* Docs Our Faces Off', online at www.filmschoolrejects.com/features/anvil-director-sacha-gervasi-interview.php.

Allen, Robert C. and Douglas Gomery (1985) 'Case Study: The Beginnings of American Cinema Verité', in Robert C. Allen and Douglas Gomery, *Film History: Theory and Practice*. New York: Knopf, 213–41.

Amigoni, David (2000) *The English Novel and Prose Narrative*. Edinburgh: Edinburgh University Press.

Anderson, Carolyn and Thomas W. Benson (1991) *Documentary Dilemmas: Frederick Wiseman's* Titicut Follies. Carbondale and Edwardsville: Southern Illinois University Press.

Anon. (2005) 'An Interview with Jonathan Caouette' (DVD sleeve booklet). London: Optimum Home Entertainment.

——(2006) 'Housing Problems', online at www.bfi.org.uk/nftva/catalogues/film/4/609/1046.

——(2009) 'Iranian Documentary Filmmakers Boycott Cinema Verite Documentary Film Festival', online at www.payvand.com/news/09/aug/1179.html.

Anthony, Scott (2007) *BFI Film Classics: Night Mail*. London: British Film Institute.

Arthur, Paul (1993) 'Jargons of Authenticity: Three American Moments', in Michael Renov (ed.) *Theorizing Documentary*. New York: Routledge, 108–34.

——(2005) 'Extreme Makeover: The Changing Face of Documentary', *Cineaste*, 30, 3, 18–23.

Atkins, Thomas R. (ed.) (1976) *Frederick Wiseman*. New York: Simon & Schuster.

Aufderheide, Patricia (2007) *Documentary Film: A Very Short Introduction*. Oxford: Oxford University Press.

Austin, Thomas (2007) *Watching the World: Screen Documentary and Audiences*. Manchester: Manchester University Press.

——(2008) ' … To Leave the Confinements of His Humanness', in Thomas Austin and Wilma de Jong (eds) *Rethinking Documentary: New Perspectives, New Practices*. Maidenhead: Open University Press, 51–66.

Austin, Thomas and Wilma de Jong (eds) (2008) *Rethinking Documentary: New Perspectives, New Practices*. Maidenhead: Open University Press.

Bachman, Gideon (1961) 'The Frontiers of Realist Cinema: The Work of Ricky Leacock', *Film Culture*, 22, Summer, 12–33.

Badt, Karin Luisa (2007) 'Stay Well, or Else', online at www.brightlightsfilm.com/57/mooreiv.html.

Baird, Thomas (1938) 'Films and the Public Services in Great Britain', *The Public Opinion Quarterly*, 2, 2, 96–9.

Barnouw, Erik (1964) 'Films of Social Comment', *Film Comment*, 2, 1, 16–17.

——(1990) *Tube of Plenty: The Evolution of American Television* (2nd revised edn). New York: Oxford University Press.

——(1993) *Documentary: A History of the Non-Fiction Film* (2nd revised edn). New York: Oxford University Press.

Barsam, Richard M. (1973) *Non-Fiction Film: A Critical History*. Bloomington: Indiana University Press.

——(1986) 'American Direct Cinema: The Re-Presentation of Reality', *Persistence of Vision*, 3, 4, 131–57.

Bazin, André (1971) *What is Cinema?* (transl. Hugh Gray). Berkeley: University of California Press.

Beattie, Keith (2008) *Documentary Display: Re-Viewing Nonfiction Film and Video*. London: Wallflower Press.

Beckman, Jonathan (2007) 'Michael Moore: Hero or Villain?', *The New Statesman*, October, 34.

Beevor, Anthony (2009) 'The Indoctrination Game', *The Sunday Times Magazine*, January 18, 11.

Benson, Thomas W. and Carolyn Anderson (1989) *Reality Fictions: The Films of Frederick Wiseman*. Carbondale and Edwardsville: Southern Illinois University Press.

Berger, John (1972) *Ways of Seeing*. London: Penguin.

Berning, Beverly (2008) 'A Conversation with *My Winnipeg* Director Guy Maddin', online at www.culturevulture.net/Movies/mywinnipeginterview_7-08.htm.

Beyerle, Monika (1997) *Authentisierungsstrategien im Documentarfilm: Das americanische Direct Cinema der 60er Jahre*. Frankfurt am Main: WVT Wissenchaftlicher Verlag Trier.

BFI (2007) *Night Mail*. London: BFI Publishing.

Biressi, Anita and Heather Nunn (2005) *Reality TV: Realism and Revelation*. London: Wallflower Press.

Biskind, Peter (1977) 'Harlan County, USA', Jump Cut, 14, 3–4.

——(1998) *Easy Riders, Raging Bulls: How the Sex 'n' Drugs 'n' Rock 'n' Roll Generation Saved Hollywood*. London: Bloomsbury.

Bordwell, David and Kristin Thompson (2000) *Film Art: An Introduction* (6th edn). New York: McGraw-Hill.

——(2002) *Film History: An Introduction*. New York: McGraw-Hill.

Bottomore, Stephen (2001) 'Rediscovering Early Non-Fiction Film', Film History, 13, 2, 160–73.

Braudy, Leo and Marshall Cohen (eds) (1999) *Film Theory and Criticism: Introductory Readings* (5th edn). New York: Oxford University Press.

Bruzzi, Stella (2000) *New Documentary: A Critical Introduction*. London: Routledge.

——(2005) *New Documentary: A Critical Introduction* (2nd edn). London: Routledge.

Cameron, Ian and Mark Shivas (1963) 'New Methods, New Approach', *Movie*, 8, April, 12–15.

Campbell, Russell (1978) *Cinema Strikes Back: Radical Filmmaking in the United States 1930–1942*. Ann Arbor, MI: UMI Research Press.

Carter, Dan T. (1995) *The Politics of Rage*. New York: Simon & Schuster.

Cathcart, Brian (2007) 'Truth, Lies and Fools', *The New Statesman*, October, 33.

Chanan, Michael (2007) *The Politics of Documentary*. London: BFI Publishing.

——(2008) 'Filming the "Invisible"', in Thomas Austin and Wilma de Jong (eds) *Rethinking Documentary: New Perspectives, New Practices*. Maidenhead: Open University Press, 121–32.

Church, David (2006) 'An Interview with Guy Maddin', online at www.offscreen. com/biblio/phile/essays/branded_brain.

Cohen, Nick (2007) *What's Left? How Liberals Lost Their Way*. London: Fourth Estate.

Comolli, Jean-Louis and Jean Narboni (1969) 'Cinema/Ideology/Criticism', in Leo Braudy and Marshall Cohen (eds) (1999) *Film Theory and Citicism: Introductory Readings* (5th edn). New York: Oxford University Press, 752–759.

Cook, Pam (ed.) (2007) *The Cinema Book* (3rd edn). London: British Film Institute.

Corner, John (1996) *The Art of Record: A Critical Introduction to Documentary*. Manchester: Manchester University Press.

Dovey, Jon (2008) 'Simulating the Public Sphere', in Thomas Austin and Wilma de Jong (eds) *Rethinking Documentary: New Perspectives, New Practices*. Maidenhead: Open University Press, 246–57.

Eisenstein, Sergei (1929) 'Beyond the Shot', in Leo Braudy and Marshall Cohen (eds) (1999) *Film Theory and Criticism: Introductory Readings* (5th edn). New York: Oxford University Press, 15–42.

Ellis, Jack C. (1989) *The Documentary Idea: A Critical History of English-Language Documentary and Video*. Englewood Cliffs, NJ: Prentice-Hall.

Ellis, Jack C. and Betsy McLane (2007) *A New History of Documentary Film*. New York: Continuum.

Evans, Dylan (1996) *An Introductory Dictionary of Lacanian Psychoanalysis*. London: Routledge.

Evans, Harold (1997) *Pictures on a Page: Photo-Journalism, Graphics and Picture Editing*. London: Pimlico.

Feldman, Seth (1998) 'Peace Between Man and Machine', in Barry Keith Grant and Jeannette Sloniowski (eds) *Documenting the Documentary: Close Readings of Documentary Film and Video*. Detroit: Wayne State University Press, 40–54.

Flaherty, Frances Hubbard (1972) *The Odyssey of a Film Maker*. Urbana: Beta Phi Mui.

Flinn, Carol (1998) 'Containing Fire: Performance in *Paris is Burning*', in Barry Keith Grant and Jeannette Sloniowski (eds) *Documenting the Documentary: Close*

*Readings of Documentary Film and Video*. Detroit: Wayne State University Press, 429–45.

Flitterman-Lewis, Sandy (1998) 'Documenting the Ineffable', in Barry Keith Grant and Jeannette Sloniowski (eds) *Documenting the Documentary: Close Readings of Documentary Film and Video*. Detroit: Wayne State University Press, 204–22.

Fraser, Nick (2009) 'Don't Give Me the Facts, Give Me a Film', *The Guardian*, November 1, 27.

Freedland, Jonathan (2008) 'Lest We Forget', online at www.guardian.co.uk/film/2008/oct/25/waltz-with-bashir-ari-folman.

Frohne, Ursula (2002) '"Screen Tests": Media Narcissism, Theatricality, and the Internalised Observer', in Thomas Levin, Ursula Frohne and Peter Weibel (eds) *CNTRL [SPACE]: Rhetorics of Surveillance from Bentham to Big Brother*. Karlsruhe: ZKM/MIT, 252–77.

Gardiner, Juliet (2008) 'Working-Class Heroes', *Sight and Sound*, 18, 4, 92.

Gillmor, Alison (2007) 'Home Truths: Guy Maddin Takes a Dream-like Tour of Winnipeg', online at www.cbc.ca/arts/tiff/features/tiffmaddin.html.

Goldsmith, David A. (2003) *The Documentary Makers*. Hove: RotoVision.

Graham, Peter (1964) 'Cinéma-Vérité in France', *Film Quarterly*, 17, 4, 30–6.

Grant, Barry Keith (1992) *Voyages of Discovery: The Cinema of Frederick Wiseman*. Chicago: University of Illinois Press.

——(1998) 'Ethnography in the First Person: Frederick Wiseman's *Titicut Follies*', in Barry Keith Grant and Jeannette Sloniowski (eds) *Documenting the Documentary: Close Readings of Documentary Film and Video*. Detroit: Wayne State University Press, 238–53.

Grant, Barry Keith and Jim Hillier (2009) *100 Documentary Films*. London: BFI/Palgrave.

Grant, Barry Keith and Jeannette Sloniowski (eds) (1998) *Documenting the Documentary: Close Readings of Documentary Film and Video*. Detroit: Wayne State University Press.

Gray, Hugh (1950) 'Robert Flaherty and the Naturalistic Documentary', *Hollywood Quarterly*, 5, 1, 41–8.

Grierson, John (1954) 'The BBC and All That', *The Quarterly of Film, Radio and Television*, 9, 1, 46–59.

Grierson, John (1966) *Grierson on Documentary* (ed. Forsyth Hardy). London: Faber & Faber.

Gritten, David (2003) 'Why Truth is Stronger than Fiction', in *The Telegraph*, June 28, third editorial, online at www.telegraph.co.uk/culture/film/3597489/ Why-truth-is-stronger-than-fiction.html.

Grossman, Alan and Aine O'Brien (eds) (2007) *Projecting Migration: Transcultural Documentary Practice*. London: Wallflower Press.

Guynn, William (1975) 'Paul Rotha's Documentary Diary: Politics of the British Documentary', *Jump Cut*, 6, 10–12.

Halfyard, Kurt (2007) 'Guy Maddin Talks *My Winnipeg*, Self-Mythologizing, Psychological Honesty, and even The Host', online at http://twitchfilm.net/ interviews/2007/10/guy-maddin-talks-up-my-winnipeg-self-mythologizing-pyschological-honesty-an.php.

Hall, Jeanne (1991) 'Realism as a Style in Cinema Verite: A Critical Analysis of *Primary*', *Cinema Journal*, 30, 4, 24–50.

——(1998) 'Don't You Ever Just Watch? American Cinema Verité and *Don't Look Back*', in Barry Keith Grant and Jeannette Sloniowski (eds) *Documenting the Documentary: Close Readings of Documentary Film and Video*. Detroit: Wayne State University Press, 223–37.

Hardy, David T. and Jason Clarke (2004) *Michael Moore is a Big Fat Stupid White Man*. New York: Regan.

Hardy, Forsyth (ed.) (1979) *John Grierson: A Documentary Biography*. London: Faber & Faber.

Harper, Graeme and Rob Stone (eds) (2007) *The Unsilvered Screen: Surrealism on Film*. London: Wallflower Press.

Haughey, Anthony (2007) 'Imagining the Unimaginable: Disputed Territory', in Alan Grossman and Aine O'Brien (eds) *Projecting Migration: Transcultural Documentary Practice*. London: Wallflower Press, 53–70.

Hebard, Andrew (1997) 'Disruptive Histories: Toward a Radical Politics of Remembrance in Alain Resnais's *Night and Fog*', *New German Critique*, 71, Summer, 87–113.

Holland, Patricia (1997) *The Television Handbook*. London: Routledge.

Hood, Stuart (1983) 'John Grierson and the Documentary Film Movement', in James Curran and Vincent Porter (eds) *British Cinema History*. London: Weidenfeld & Nicholson, 99–112.

Hudson, D. W. (2008) 'Interview. Ari Folman', online at http://daily.greencine. com/archives/007250.html.

Issari, M. Ali (1971) *Cinema-Verite*. East Lansing: Michigan State University Press.

Jaafar, Ali (2008) 'A Soldier's Tale', *Sight and Sound*, 18, 12, 28–31.

Jacobs, Lewis (ed.) (1979) *The Documentary Tradition* (2nd edn). New York: W. W. Norton.

Jeffries, John W. (1978) 'The "Quest for National Purpose" of 1960', *American Quarterly*, 30, 4, 451–70.

Jolin, Dan (2008) 'Review: *Waltz with Bashir*', *Empire*, 234, December, 76.

de Jong, Wilma (2008) 'An Interview with Ralph Lee', in Thomas Austin and Wilma de Jong (eds) *Rethinking Documentary: New Perspectives, New Practices*. Maidenhead: Open University Press, 167–71.

Judt, Tony (2007) *Post-War: A History of Europe Since 1945*. London: Pimlico.

Juhasz, Alexandra (2008) 'Documentary on YouTube', in Thomas Austin and Wilma de Jong (eds) *Rethinking Documentary: New Perspectives, New Practices*. Maidenhead: Open University Press, 299–312.

Kilborn, Richard and John Izod (1997) *Confronting Reality: An Introduction to Television Documentary*. Manchester: Manchester University Press.

Kluger, Jeffrey (2007) 'Michael Moore's New Diagnosis', online at www.time.com/time/health/article/0,8599,1622178,00.html.

Kurlanksy, Mark (2005) *1968: The Year that Rocked the World*. London: Vantage.

Latham, James (2007) '"Your Life is Not a Very Good Script": David Holzman's Diary and Documentary Expression in Late-1960s America and Beyond', online at http://findarticles.com/p/articles/mi_go1931/is_3_26/ai_n29394587.

Leach, Jim (1998) 'The Poetics of Propaganda', in Barry Keith Grant and Jeannette Sloniowski (eds) *Documenting the Documentary: Close Readings of Documentary Film and Video*. Detroit: Wayne State University Press, 154–70.

Levin, G. Roy (1971) *Documentary Explorations: 15 Interviews with Film-Makers*. New York: Doubleday.

Lips and Robb Reiner (2009) *Anvil: The Story of Anvil*. London: Bantam.

McClanahan, Erik (2009) 'Waltz with Bashir: Interview with Ari Folman', online at www.secretsofthecity.com/magazine/blogs/talk-about-talkies/2009/01/waltz-with-bashir-interview-with-ari-folman.

McCreadie, Marsha (2008) *Documentary Superstars: How Today's Filmmakers are Re-Inventing the Form*. New York: Allworth.

Macdonald, Kevin and Mark Cousins (1998) *Imagining Reality: The Faber Book of Documentary*. London: Faber & Faber.

MacDougall, David (2006) *The Corporeal Image: Film, Ethnography, and the Senses*. Princeton: Princeton University Press.

McLean, Gareth (2005) 'My Life, the Horror Movie', online at www.guardian.co.uk/film/2005/apr/16/features.weekend.

Mamber, Stephen (1974) *Cinema Verite in America: Studies in Uncontrolled Documentary*. Cambridge, MA: MIT Press.

Marcorelles, Louis (1973) *Living Cinema: New Directions in Contemporary Film-Making*. London: George Allen & Unwin.

Nathan, Ian (2008) 'Art of Darkness', *Empire*, 234, December, 110–14.

Neal, Mark Anthony (2009) 'Say My Name: Women in Hip-Hop', online at http://newblackman.blogspot.com/2009/08/say-my-name-women-in-hip-hop.html.

Nichols, Bill (1981) *Ideology and the Image*. Bloomington: Indiana University Press.

——(1983) 'The Voice of Documentary', *Film Quarterly*, 36, 3, 17–30.

——(ed.) (1985) *Movies and Methods Volume 2*. Berkeley: University of California Press.

——(1987) 'History, Myth, and Narrative in Documentary', *Film Quarterly*, 41, 1, 9–20.

——(1991) *Representing Reality*. Bloomington: Indiana University Press.

——(1994) *Blurred Boundaries*. Bloomington: Indiana University Press.

——(2001a) *Introduction to Documentary*. Bloomington and Indianapolis: Indiana University Press.

——(2001b) 'Documentary Film and the Modernist Avant-Garde', *Critical Inquiry*, 27, 4, 580–610.

——(2007) 'Documentary', in Pam Cook (ed.) *The Cinema Book* (3d edn). London: British Film Institute.

O'Connell, P. J. (1992) *Robert Drew and the Development of Cinema Verite in America*. Carbondale and Edwardsville: Southern Illinois University Press.

O'Connor, John (2005) 'Historical Analysis, Stage One: Content, Production, and Reception', in Alan Rosenthal and John Corner (eds) *New Challenges for Documentary* (2nd edn). Manchester: Manchester University Press, 382–96.

O'Hehir, Andrew (2009) 'War as a "Bad Acid Trip"', online at http://archive.salon.com/ent/movies/btm/feature/2008/12/26/folman/print.html.

Orvell, Miles (1994) 'Documentary Film and the Power of Interrogation', *Film Quarterly*, 48, 2, 10–18.

Osmond, Andres (2008) 'Review: *Waltz with Bashir*', *Sight and Sound*, 18, 12, 79–80.

Paget, Derek (1998) *No Other Way to Tell It: Dramadoc/Docudrama on Television*. Manchester: Manchester University Press.

Petric, Vlada (1984) 'Esther Shub: Film as a Historical Discourse', in Thomas Waugh (ed.) *Show Us Life: Toward a History and Aesthetic of a Committed Documentary*. Metuchen, NJ: Scarecrow Press, 21–46.

Pierce, Leonard (2009) 'Day Four, Or, From Remy to Rogen', online at www. avclub.com/articles/film-day-four-or-from-remy-to-rogen,25257.

Pilger, John (2007) 'Who's Afraid of Michael Moore?', *The New Statesman*, October, 30–4.

Rabiger, Michael (1998) *Directing the Documentary* (3rd edn). Woburn, MA: Focal Press.

Rees, A. L. (1999) *A History of Experimental Film and Video*. London: British Film Institute.

Rees, Laurence (2005) *Auschwitz: The Nazis and the 'Final Solution'*. London: BBC Books.

Renov, Michael (1986) 'Rethinking Documentary: Towards a Taxonomy of Mediation', *Wide Angle*, 8, 3, 71–7.

——(ed.) (1993a) *Theorizing Documentary*. New York: Routledge.

——(1993b) 'Toward a Poetics of Documentary', in Michael Renov (ed.) *Theorizing Documentary*. New York: Routledge, 12–36.

——(2004) *The Subject of Documentary*. Minneapolis: University of Minnesota Press.

——(2008) 'First-Person Films: Some Theses on Self-Inscription', in Thomas Austin and Wilma de Jong (eds) *Rethinking Documentary: New Perspectives, New Practices*. Maidenhead: Open University Press, 39–50.

Rich, B. Ruby (2006) 'Documentary Disciplines: An Introduction', *Cinema Journal* 46, 1, 108–15.

Roberts, Graham (2000) *The Man with the Movie Camera*. London: I. B. Tauris.

——(2007) 'Soluble Fish: How Surrealism Saved Documentary from John Grierson', in Graeme Harper and Rob Stone (eds) *The Unsilvered Screen: Surrealism on Film*. London: Wallflower Press, 90–101.

Ronson, Jon (2002) 'The Egos Have Landed', online at www.bfi.org.uk/ sightandsound/feature/37.

Rosen, Philip (1993) 'Document and Documentary', in Michael Renov (ed.) *Theorizing Documentary*. New York: Routledge, 58–89.

Rosenthal, Alan (1971) *The New Documentary in Action: A Casebook in Film Making*. New York and Berkeley: University of California Press.

——(ed.) (1988) *New Challenges for Documentary*. Berkeley and Los Angeles: University of California Press.

——(2002) *Writing, Directing and Producing Documentary Films and Videos*. Carbondale and Edwardsville: Southern Illinois University Press.

Rosenthal, Alan and John Corner (eds) (2005) *New Challenges for Documentary* (2nd edn). Manchester: Manchester University Press.

Rosenthal, Liz (2009) 'The Future for Film Has Already Been Written', online at www.screendaily.com/5004727.article.

Rothman, William (1997) *Documentary Film Classics*. New York: Cambridge University Press.

Rothwell, Jerry (2008) 'Filmmakers and their Subjects', in Thomas Austin and Wilma de Jong (eds) *Rethinking Documentary: New Perspectives, New Practices*. Maidenhead: Open University Press, 152–6.

Russell, Catherine (1999) *Experimental Ethnography: The Work of Film in the Age of Video*. Durham, NC: Duke University Press.

Saunders, Dave (2007) *Direct Cinema: Observational Documentary and the Politics of the Sixties*. London: Wallflower Press.

Scheibler, Susan (1993) 'Constantly Performing the Documentary', in Michael Renov (ed.) *Theorizing Documentary*. New York: Routledge, 135–50.

Schiff, Ze'ev and Ehud Ya'ari (1985) *Israel's Lebanon War*. London: Unwin.

Schultz, Emily (2006) *Michael Moore: A Biography*. London: Vision.

Scott, A. O. (2008) 'Movie Review: *My Winnipeg* (2007)', online at http://movies.nytimes.com/2008/06/13/movies/13winn.html.

Sharrett, Christopher and William Luhr (2005) '*Bowling for Columbine*: A Review', in Alan Rosenthal and John Corner (eds) *New Challenges for Documentary* (2nd edn). Manchester: Manchester University Press, 253–9.

Shohat, Ella and Robert Stam (1994) *Unthinking Eurocentrism*. London: Routledge.

Soden, Christopher (2006) 'Interview with Jonathan Caouette, Director of *Tarnation*', online at http://blogcritics.org/video/article/interview-with-jonathan-caouette-director-of/page-3.

Sontag, Susan (1975) 'Fascinating Fascism', in *Under the Sign of Saturn*. New York: Farrar, Straus and Giroux, 73–105.

——(2001) *Against Interpretation*. London: Vintage.

——(2002) *On Photography*. London: Penguin Classics.

——(2003) *Regarding the Pain of Others*. London: Penguin.

Sørenssen, Bjørn (2008) 'Digital Video', *Studies in Documentary Film*, 2, 1, 47–59.

Stewart, Jez (2008) '*Target for Tonight* (1941)', online at www.screenonline.org. uk/film/id/577991/index.html.

Stollery, Martin (2002) 'Eisenstein, Shub and the Gender of the Author as Producer', *Film History*, 14, 1, 87–99.

Stubbs, Liz (2002) *Documentary Filmmakers Speak*. New York: Allworth Press.

Sussex, Elizabeth (1975) *The Rise and Fall of British Documentary*. Berkeley: University of California Press.

Tallerico, Brian (2009) 'Interview: Sacha Gervasi Rocks Out With Massively Successful "Anvil! The Story of Anvil"', online at www.hollywoodchicago. com/news/7658/interview-sacha-gervasi-rocks-out-with-massively-successful-anvil-the-story-of-anvil.

Thomson, David (2002) *The New Biographical Dictionary of Film*. London: Little, Brown.

Tobias, Michael (ed.) (1998) *The Search For Reality: The Art of Documentary Filmmaking*. Studio City, CA: Michael Wiese Productions.

Vaughan, Dai (1999) *For Documentary: Twelve Essays*. Berkeley: University of California Press.

Ventura, Elbert (2005) 'Elbert Ventura on *Tarnation*', online at www.reverseshot. com/legacy/spring05/tarnation.html.

Von Boehm, Felix (2008) 'Man with a Movie Camera: Visiting Jonathan Caouette', online at www.brightlightsfilm.com/60/60caouetteiv.html.

Ward, Paul (2005) *Documentary: The Margins of Reality*. London: Wallflower Press.

Warren, Charles (ed.) (1996) *Beyond Document: Essays on Nonfiction Film*. Hanover, NH: Wesleyan University Press.

Watson, James (1998) *Media Communication*. London: Palgrave Macmillan.

Waugh, Thomas (1985) 'Beyond Vérité: Emile de Antonio and the New Documentary of the Seventies', in Bill Nichols (ed.) *Movies and Methods Volume* 2. Berkeley: University of California Press.

Wayne, Mike (2008) 'Documentary as Critical and Creative Research', in Thomas Austin and Wilma de Jong (eds) *Rethinking Documentary: New Perspectives, New Practices*. Maidenhead: Open University Press, 82–94.

Wells, Paul (2002) *Animation and America*. New Brunswick, NJ: Rutgers.

Williams, Linda (1993) 'Mirrors Without Memories: Truth, History, and the New Documentary', *Film Quarterly*, 46, 3, 9–21.

Winston, Brian (1993) 'Documentary Film as Scientific Inscription', in Michael Renov (ed.) *Theorizing Documentary*. New York: Routledge, 37–57.

——(1995) *Claiming the Real: Documentary Film Revisited*. London: British Film Institute.

——(2000) *Lies, Damn Lies and Documentaries*. London: British Film Institute.

——(2008) *Claiming the Real: Documentary – Grierson and Beyond*. London: British Film Institute/Palgrave.

Wollheim, Peter (1980) 'Robert Flaherty's Inuit Photographs', *Canada Forum*, 13, 12–14.

Wood, Jason (2005) *Nick Broomfield: Documenting Icons*. London: Faber & Faber.

Zheutlin, Barbara (1981) 'The Politics of Documentary: A Symposium', in Alan Rosenthal and John Corner (eds) (2005) *New Challenges for Documentary* (2nd edn). Manchester: Manchester University Press, 150–66.

# INDEX